PAUL BURSTON

THE
BLACK
PATH

How far would you go to face the truth?

Published by Accent Press Ltd 2016

ISBN 9781786150455

Copyright © Paul Burston 2016

For Jacqui Niven, with love.

PROLOGUE

Police search for killers of
'loving husband and devoted father'
by *Gazette* reporter

Tributes have been paid to a local man who died at the weekend. Richard Thomas, 35, of St Nicholas Road, Bridgend, confronted a gang of teenagers who were causing a disturbance outside his house on Sunday afternoon. He suffered several stab wounds to the stomach and died in hospital as a result of his injuries. He leaves behind a wife and young daughter.

Detective Sergeant Rhys Williams told the *Gazette*: 'This is a shocking crime and a tragic waste of life. Investigations are ongoing and we are appealing for any witnesses who may have information regarding the attack to come forward.'

Mr Thomas was described as a loving husband and devoted father who died a hero. One neighbour, who did not wish to be named, said: 'It's a terrible loss for the family. They had their share of problems like everyone else, but nobody expects something like this to happen right on their own doorstep.'

Anyone with any information should contact the incident room at Bridgend CID.

The day it happened, Helen didn't make a sound.

She knows that doesn't seem right – there must have been tears, surely? But whenever she casts her mind back to that day, what she remembers is the stillness.

She'd spent the morning with her face buried in a book. That was the phrase her mother used, although in the weeks that followed she chose her words more carefully. Some days she didn't say anything at all, and her eyes would meet Helen's and turn away as if even the sight of her only child made her angry. But that was afterwards. She'd always had plenty to say for herself before then.

Helen still remembers the way her mother kicked off over the rabbit. Two weeks earlier, her father came home from the pub carrying a cardboard box with holes in the sides.

'It's for you, sweetheart.'

Helen didn't know how to react. It wasn't even her birthday.

But her father smiled and said he didn't need a reason to give his special girl a present. The rabbit was soft and white with pink frightened eyes and a fat belly. When Helen held it to her face she felt its little heart thumping and was terrified that her own heart might burst in sympathy.

Her mother hit the roof, turning on her father with that angry face of hers. 'Have you completely lost your mind? A pet is a big commitment. There's no prizes for guessing who'll be the one who ends up looking after it.'

She refused to have the rabbit in the house, so it lived in the back garden in a hutch her father assembled the next day in the shed he liked to call his office. Helen welcomed any opportunity to see inside her father's shed. It had a small workbench, a filing cabinet, and shelves full of old coins and glass bottles. Her father said the bottles and coins were valuable, which was why he kept his office door locked even when he was inside. He had another office he went to every day, except on the weekends or those days when his stomach was playing up or he had one of his headaches. Helen had never seen that office, but she'd always imagined that it was quite different from the shed.

The garden backed onto scrubland. Beyond that was the river and running beside the river was the Black Path. Helen wasn't allowed to play by the river and she certainly wasn't allowed anywhere near the Black Path. Up the Black Path there were older boys who smoked cigarettes and built bonfires. There was a place called the Witches' Den, where real witches gathered at night. And right at the top was a hospital where people went when they were sad or kept hearing strange voices. Her parents both agreed that the Black Path was no place for a young girl, and since they never usually agreed on anything, Helen had thought about it and decided that they were right.

So mostly she played in the back garden. And it was there that she spent the last few hours before her world was torn apart – lying on a blanket on the warm grass, her face buried in a book while her father pottered around inside his shed. Shortly before tea time she heard his key in the lock and he reappeared blinking into the sunshine, promising to mow the front lawn while his wife put her feet up and his daughter gave that poor rabbit some exercise.

'Run, rabbit, run!' he laughed, lifting it out of the hutch and bundling it into Helen's arms before heading off in search of his mower. She'd wanted to go after him. Her mother always said that she was never far behind her father, that she was like his shadow. Helen has often wondered how different things might have been had she followed him that day, whether she might have been able to prevent what happened.

The rabbit refused to run. It sat on the grass, nose twitching, staring up at her with its bulging pink eyes. She pushed it gently with her hand, but it wouldn't move. She nudged it again. It waddled forward a few steps and then stopped. It wasn't until a few weeks later that she discovered that the reason the rabbit was so fat was because its belly was full of babies. Cleaning out the hutch she found a lifeless lump of them buried beneath the straw, pale and hairless and squashed together like sardines. She remembers crying then – great, uncontrollable sobs that shook her whole body and made her face wet with tears.

She didn't see what happened to her father. She didn't see the fight or the flash of the knife. She didn't hear the boys shouting or her mother's screams. The first sound she was aware of was the wailing of sirens. Then her mother was grabbing her by the arm and dragging her into the kitchen.

'Stay here,' she said, and went back outside. But Helen didn't stay in the kitchen. She ran into the front room and pressed her nose against the window. They were taking her father away in an ambulance. She saw the flashing blue lights and told herself that the doctors would fix him, the way they fixed people on television. Then her mother's friend Jackie arrived and whisked her off to her house and gave her Coke and biscuits.

Helen remembers thinking that she shouldn't have been playing with the rabbit in the garden. She shouldn't have been at Jackie's house drinking Coke and eating biscuits when her father was lying in the hospital. She remembers wondering if the boys who hurt her father had come from the Black Path.

And that's all she can remember. She was ten years old and it was summertime and it was a Sunday.

PART ONE

CHAPTER ONE

'Helen?'

She hears her mother's voice calling from far away.

Not now, she thinks, and reaches under the table for her handbag. A knot of anxiety tightens in her stomach as she fishes inside for the list she prepared earlier. Her fingers close around the folded piece of paper and she relaxes a little. If the phone rings, she'll be prepared. It's better to write things down, so she doesn't forget. She never knows when Owen will call or how much time they'll have.

'Alright, love?' her mother asks, and now there's a familiar image to go with the disembodied voice. She's up to her elbows in a washing-up bowl brimming with suds. The remains of the Sunday roast are congealing on a large serving plate on the hob next to her.

'I'm fine.'

'Only you looked like you were miles away.'

Helen forces a smile. She'd give anything to be miles away. Anywhere would be better than spending another dreary afternoon with her mother and Frank. She can't wait for her husband to come home and for everything to be back to normal.

Her mother must have read her mind. 'Any word from Owen?'

Helen bows her head so that her hair shields her face.

1

Strawberry blonde, her father called it – though not everyone was as kind.

'Not for a few days.'

'Well, no news is good news,' her mother chirps. 'Isn't that right, Frank?'

Frank looks up from his newspaper. 'Have you seen this?' he says, stabbing his finger at the offending article. 'Some lowlifes have only gone and desecrated the cenotaph in town!'

'I don't think "desecrated" is the right word,' her mother says. 'It's not the same as a grave.' She colours slightly and glances at Helen.

Frank reaches for his can of lager. 'Call it what you want. The bastards want stringing up!'

'Don't swear at the table, Frank!' Her mother turns to Helen and rolls her eyes. 'What's he like, eh?'

Helen looks away. She has no intention of answering that question. Not now. Not ever. To answer honestly would only upset the peace – and it's a fragile kind of peace even at the best of times. Frank is the man her mother took up with shortly after her father died. To say that Helen has never really warmed to him would be putting it mildly. The first time her mother brought Frank home, Helen had just turned eleven.

'Someone told me it was your birthday,' the strange man said, filling the room with his unfamiliar smell and big bulky body. 'So I brought you a present.' He handed her a parcel wrapped in shiny pink paper.

Helen knew from the moment he opened his mouth that he wasn't really giving her a present for her birthday. He was trying to buy her affection.

'Thanks,' she said, placing the parcel on the table.

'Well, aren't you going to open it?' her mother asked. 'Honestly, Frank, I don't know what's got into her lately.'

Of course you don't, Helen wanted to shout. Because you never ask!

She refused to open the present in front of Frank. It sat on the table for over an hour, until her mother finally lost her temper and sent her upstairs to her room. Listening from the landing, Helen heard them talking in muted voices. Then her mother laughed. It was an unfamiliar sound – high-pitched and girlish. Helen couldn't remember the last time she'd heard her laugh like that. A few weeks later, her mother announced that the house was being sold and that they were moving in with Frank. 'It'll be good for us,' she said. 'A fresh start.'

Right from the outset, Helen hated these new living arrangements with an intensity that was almost physical. She hated the new house with its strange furniture and rooms her father had never set foot in. She resented Frank's presence the same way she resented seeing other girls' fathers collecting them from school. Why did it have to be her dad who died, and not theirs? For months afterwards, she couldn't walk past the local petrol station without wanting to tear up the bunches of flowers in their cellophane wrapping. Everything reminded her of him.

Fifteen years have passed since then, but Helen still misses her father with a dull ache that never goes away. She still has the cutting from the local newspaper, the one where he's described as a hero – a far cry from the forgotten man whose grave her mother stopped visiting years ago. Frank has never said a word against her father – at least not in her presence. But it's clear that he's the reason her mother refuses to keep her father's memory alive. It wasn't only her surname that changed when she married Frank. Her first husband had called her Mandy. Now she prefers to be known as Amanda. It's as if she wilfully severed every link with her old life – every link except the daughter who bears such a strong physical resemblance to the man she seems determined to forget.

Helen dreads these Sunday lunches with Amanda and Frank. She hates the forced sense of family occasion and the air of quiet desperation that hangs over the dining table, prompting her mother to fill every pause with inane observations, subtle reproaches and nervous vocal tics. But with her own husband thousands of miles away in Afghanistan, they're the closest family Helen has – physically at any rate. It's only a few miles from the house her mother calls home to the terrace she and Owen bought the year after they were married.

'It's a bit small,' was her mother's verdict, the day they showed her and Frank around. 'Especially for a young couple planning on starting a family.'

Helen had never expressed any such intentions to her mother. Six years on, there's nothing to suggest that her plans have changed. But since Owen was sent to Iraq and now Afghanistan, there's been less talk of babies and more talk about what a wonderful job our boys are doing, out there where wars are fought and heroes are made. Patriotism is a great silencer, Helen has found. It can even silence her mother. Some of the time.

'You'll never guess who I was talking to the other day,' Amanda says, rinsing off the last of the dishes and reaching for a tea towel. 'Iona Gregory. You remember Iona. She used to live behind us at the other house.'

The other house, Helen thinks. The house where her father lived, where she was happy.

'Her daughter Rhian was in the year below you at school,' her mother continues.

'I didn't really know her.' Helen pushes back her chair. 'Here, let me give you a hand with those.'

'You stay there,' Amanda replies, tightening her grip on the tea towel as if she expects it to be torn from her. 'I'm quite capable of drying a few dishes.' She lifts a dinner plate from the draining board and goes at it with a furious circular motion, polishing until it squeaks.

'Anyway, she's got a baby now,' she continues. 'Rhian, I mean. Her mother showed me a photo. A lovely little girl. I say little – she must be almost eighteen months by now.'

Helen sinks back in her chair. 'That's nice.' There are many things she could say, many lies she could tell to account for the fact that she doesn't have a baby of her own. The one thing she can never tell her mother is the truth, which she can barely admit to herself. She doesn't want a child that might one day lose its father, the way she lost hers.

Her mother stares at her. She looks as if she's about to say something, then her face stiffens and she looks away.

It's better this way, Helen thinks. Better than all the times she blurted out the wrong thing – and there've been plenty of those. She remembers the night they watched a film starring Nicole Kidman. Frank had gone to the pub. It was one of those rare occasions when Helen had actually been looking forward to spending some time alone with her mother. She'd even brought popcorn. Then halfway through the film her mother turned to her and said, 'I don't know why people think she's beautiful, do you?'

'But she's lovely, Mum.'

Her mother sniffed. 'I can't see it, myself. There's something so washed-out and ghostly about redheads.'

It seemed to have escaped her notice that her own daughter had red hair – just like her father.

After he died, Helen felt like a ghost. The feeling lasted for a few weeks, or possibly even a few months. All she remembers is the unbearable pain of missing him and the urge to lose herself in books and the strange comfort of maths homework. Everything else is a blur. There were no after-school activities and few friends. She kept everyone at a distance. Even her mother. Especially her mother.

She looks up at the woman standing a few feet away and wonders if she is any happier now as Amanda than she was back then as Mandy? It's hard to tell. But they seem to be drifting further apart all the time. Suddenly everything – the best tablecloth, the radio burbling away in the background, Frank sprawled in the chair where her father ought to be – everything feels like a sham.

'I should go soon,' Helen says.

'But you haven't let your dinner go down yet.'

'I know, but I've got things to do. Y'know, stuff for work.'

Sundays are when she irons her work clothes, plans what she's going to wear for the week, and arranges the outfits on rows of hangers in the wardrobe. She knows it isn't everyone's idea of fun, but she finds it comforting. It gives her a sense of order.

Her mother begins stacking the plates. 'I don't know why you took that job in the first place. It's not as if you need the money.'

The job is a recent development, fresh enough in everyone's minds for her mother to still find some novelty in voicing her disapproval. And the annoying part is, she has a point. Helen doesn't need the money, not really. She'd always managed perfectly well on Owen's salary. A lance corporal in the British army doesn't earn a fortune, but their outgoings are minimal. And thanks to the life insurance payment she received from her father's estate, she doesn't have a large mortgage to worry about.

She isn't well off, but she isn't struggling either – at least not financially.

But when Owen was first stationed in Iraq, and the realities of being married to a serving soldier sank in, she found she needed something to occupy her mind. The job at the training company only provides a modest income, but it gets her out of the house and gives her a sense of purpose and something resembling a social life.

'It's not about the money,' Helen says. 'It's about me doing something for myself.'

Her mother, who hasn't worked a day in Helen's lifetime, clears her throat and gives a wounded look. Her mother has a vast arsenal of looks, and she isn't shy with any of them. This particular look seems to say, 'So what if I didn't go out to work? I had you, didn't I? That was work enough!'

Helen smiles and adds quickly, 'Besides, I'd go mad cooped up in that house all day on my own.'

She makes it sound like she's joking, but she isn't. She needs that job and all that comes with it. She needs to lead as normal a life as possible because how else is she supposed to cope? War isn't normal. Not knowing if your husband will come home alive isn't normal. Why can't her mother of all people see that?

'You wouldn't be on your own if you'd gone to live in St Athan,' Frank says. 'You could have had a lovely home over at the camp with all the other army wives.'

'But I didn't want to be an army wife,' Helen replies.

Frank grins. 'You married the wrong man then, didn't you?'

Helen glares at him. 'You know what I mean. I didn't want to live in service accommodation. And neither did Owen.'

This isn't strictly true. Owen would have been

perfectly happy in St Athan. It was her decision to buy the house. It was enough that the army decided when and where to send her husband. She didn't want them telling her where to live, what furniture to have, or what she could or couldn't hang on her walls. But she has no intention of explaining herself to Frank.

She holds his gaze for a moment, wonders if she should just leave it there, then hears herself say, 'We wanted a place of our own.'

'Well, it's lucky you could afford it,' Frank replies.

'I'd hardly call it lucky,' Helen snaps. 'That was the money from my dad, remember?'

Suddenly it feels as if all the air has been sucked from the room. Her mother stops stacking the plates and stares off into space. She looks lost, like someone who's wandered into a room and forgotten what they came in for.

Helen feels her anger subside and a rush of sympathy take its place. 'I love that house,' she says in a calmer voice. 'We both do. But it can get a bit lonely stuck at home all by myself.'

Frank takes a swill of lager and stifles a belch. 'You should get yourself a cat. A dog's too much trouble. Anyway, men are better with dogs. They're pack animals. They need to be shown who's boss.'

And a woman couldn't possibly be boss, Helen thinks. Her father would never have come out with a sexist comment like that. He always encouraged her to aim high. She was his special girl and one day she would do something truly wonderful with her life. Or at least that was the plan. What would he make of her small house and her little life, married to a man stationed halfway across the world and spending Sunday with her mother and a man who drinks lager straight from the can at the dinner table?

'Well?' she hears her mother say.

'Sorry?'

'I was just asking if you had anything nice planned this week.'

'Not really,' Helen says. 'I might go out for a few drinks with the girls from work on Friday.'

Angela and Kath have been pestering her to join them on a night out for weeks. But she never does. She never goes anywhere. And she's beginning to think that maybe she should.

'You want to watch yourself, going out in town,' Frank says. 'It's not long since that poor lad was kicked to death, up by the railway bridge.'

'For heaven's sake, Frank!' Amanda snaps.

'They should string them up,' Frank mutters. 'Or bring back national service. That would teach them a thing or two.'

Like how to kill someone more efficiently, Helen thinks, then forces the idea from her head. Her stepfather has a long list of people he believes would benefit from national service. To the best of her knowledge, the nearest he's ever come to serving his country is hanging out with his drinking buddies from the Territorial Army base across the road.

Right, she decides. That's it. If Frank thinks that going out with the girls is such a bad idea, then she's left with no other choice. She'll have to go.

'I'm off,' she says, rising from her chair.

Frank tries to catch her eye but she ignores him and gathers up her jacket and bag.

Her mother insists on walking her to the door. 'I know it's not easy,' she says in a hushed voice as Helen steps outside into the soft summer air.

Helen turns to look at her. 'You mean Frank?'

Her mother frowns. 'I mean with Owen being away. But it won't be for ever. You've still got your whole lives ahead of you. And just think – he'll be able to retire at forty.'

An ugly thought lodges itself in Helen's brain. She tries to ignore it but the thought turns into words and a familiar voice whispers inside her head.

If he lives that long.

CHAPTER TWO

'Alright, McGrath?'

Owen looks up from his makeshift sunlounger and squints at the man standing over him. Gradually the face comes into focus and he sees that it's Jackson. There was a time when they were friends – of sorts. They come from the same area of South Wales, joined the army at the same time, trained together, even made it from private to lance corporal together. That all changed when Jackson was involved in a fight back home, broke some lad's jaw and was demoted. These days there's a certain degree of tension between them. There's also an over-familiarity on Jackson's part that wouldn't normally be tolerated but is a reflection of the time they've known each other. Not that this makes Owen dislike him any less.

'Fine, thanks,' he says. 'Just catching some rays.'

The desert sky is the palest blue, so pale it's practically white. Feeling the hot sun on his face, he can almost convince himself that he's on holiday and not snatching a quick half hour behind the tent when, technically speaking, he's still on duty. He resents Jackson for the intrusion, and for bringing him back to the reality of Camp Bastion where you can never really relax and you're never entirely alone. A few feet away, a fresh-faced young soldier lies basking in his boxer shorts, listening to his iPod. Private Collins only arrived a few days ago. All Owen really knows about him is his name and rank. They may be escaping the boredom together, but they've exchanged no more than a few words.

'Shame about Armstrong,' Jackson says. 'Fucking ragheads!'

Collins looks up, then settles back with his iPod.

Earlier this afternoon, a soldier from another platoon was killed by a roadside bomb while out on patrol. Details are still emerging, but the word is that he radioed in to say there was a funny smell in the air moments before an improvised explosive device ripped apart his Viking personnel carrier. Three others survived by leaping from the vehicle. The body of the dead man was found forty metres away from the scene of the blast.

What everyone thinks, but no-one dares say, is that he'll be the first of many. There are far fewer casualties during the spring months, when the insurgents have their energies focussed on the poppy harvest. Just one reason why the arrival of summer here isn't greeted with quite the same enthusiasm it receives back home.

The entire battalion is supposed to be one big happy family and the loss of a soldier – any soldier – is felt by everyone. Still Owen is relieved that it wasn't a member of his own platoon. It's far easier to become attached to thirty men than to six hundred. Even when those thirty men include someone like Jackson. Contrary to popular belief, the army isn't populated entirely by heroes. There are some right tossers too.

'He was a good man,' Owen says, though he can't really put a face to the name. Was Armstrong the lad who was always playing video games at the internet café? Or the one who was usually at the gym? Did he have a wife? Kids?

'Some of the infantry lads thought he was a bit queer,' Jackson smirks. 'The way he was always hanging around the gym. What do you reckon?'

'I don't think it matters', Owen says. 'And neither does the army. So if you've got a problem, I suggest you take it up with the MoD.' Attitudes like Jackson's aren't uncommon in the forces. The law may have changed, but some of the people signing up haven't. There are still 'no queers in the infantry', though of course that doesn't really mean anything. Especially here. Especially now.

'I was just saying,' Jackson replies. 'You know how word gets around.'

'You're talking about a man who died serving his country,' Owen says. 'So show some fucking respect. Now if you don't mind, you're blocking my sunlight.'

Jackson looks as if he's about to say something, then thinks better of it. 'Catch you later,' he says. 'And don't worry. Your secret's safe with me.'

Owen glares at him. 'Meaning?'

'Your little tanning shop, of course,' Jackson winks and slopes off, casting a shadow over Collins as he goes. The young private raises his head, turns towards Owen, and shrugs.

Owen closes his eyes and stretches out, enjoying the warmth of the sun on his skin. He can picture Armstrong now – stocky build, blond hair. He can't have been more than twenty-three. Soon he'll be just another news item, another statistic – except to the friends and family he leaves behind. At some point in the next few hours an army messenger will arrive at someone's door and inform them that their son or husband is dead. Those are the words they'll use – 'he's dead'. There'll be no pussy-footing around, no attempt to soften the blow. The message will be delivered bluntly, in words that aren't open to misinterpretation. And somebody's heart will be broken.

Owen's thoughts turn to Helen. He hasn't spoken to her in almost a week. He can think of a million excuses – his phone card expired, the welfare phone wasn't working, he was out in the field – but the truth is that sometimes it's simply easier not to talk to her. Sometimes he doesn't want reminders of home to distract him from the job or expose the chinks in his emotional armour, which is as necessary for his survival as the protective clothing lying next to the sun lounger. He loves his wife. But he's a world away from her now. Here, movie nights mean war films, never romantic comedies. Here, men psych themselves up for battle by listening to 'Smack My Bitch Up' on their iPods. Here, you're never far away from your helmet and your body armour and your rifle, because the civilian driving the creaky old bus around the camp or selling pirated DVDs at the local market might not be as friendly as he seems. Here, the normal rules don't apply, and when you're not busy killing time the stark reality is that at some point you'll either kill or be killed. And with every person you kill, the more removed you become from those you left behind.

Owen has killed three men, including the sniper who shot at them when they were out on patrol yesterday. The first kill was the worst. It was in Iraq, long after the war was over, when British troops were supposed to keep the peace. The boy couldn't have been more than fifteen. Owen remembers every detail. His finger was on the trigger, there was a short, sharp crack and then a puff of red spray shot out of the boy's head. He was dead before he hit the ground.

At least yesterday's hit was a grown man. Not that it made a hell of a lot of difference. It was still a life, and the loss of life isn't something he likes to think about. Thinking is dangerous. It's better not to think. And better not to talk. Soldiers don't discuss how many people they've killed. Everyone knows that, even the likes of Jackson. Death is ever present. You can feel it, smell it, touch it. But you never talk about it. This is part of the unspoken bond between men who serve together.

He thinks of Armstrong. He must have seen him a hundred times: eaten in the same cookhouse, sat to check emails in the same internet café, worked out at the same gym. Yet he didn't even know his first name. He doesn't know the first names of half the men in his own platoon. This is what the army does to you. This is what war does to you. 'Tour of duty' is such a misleading term for what goes on here – especially now, when withdrawal is on the cards and compounds that were once filled with tents or military vehicles lie empty. If the endless hours of boredom and monotony don't get you, the anxiety will. The camp is becoming a ghost town. At one of the shops yesterday Owen saw a set of drinking glasses emblazoned with the words 'Been there, done that' and a mug that read 'Happiness is Helmand in the rear-view mirror.' But he's not out yet – and neither are the four thousand other British military personnel still serving here. There's still the distinct possibility that they won't all make it home alive.

He wonders if Armstrong has a wife, and if she'll be the one receiving the news today. Maybe she's spared herself the agony and they've already parted. Many of the soldiers Owen knows were married at eighteen and divorced by twenty-five. For them, active service is a million times better than the petty bullshit of training. Basic training is designed to weed out the weaklings, and there isn't a soldier he knows who isn't pleased and proud to have left all that behind. But for the wives it's a different story. If the threat of infidelity and lads' weekends away didn't destroy a marriage, the strain of wondering if your husband was coming back in one piece often did.

His thoughts return to Helen. There's no point in taking the bus over to the internet café today. With Armstrong dead, communications will be shut down until midnight at least. But tomorrow, yes, tomorrow he'll send an email to his wife.

'Bitch!' Collins lifts his head angrily. He catches Owen looking at him and grins. 'Fucking iPod!' he says. 'Battery's dead. I don't suppose you've got your monkey handy?'

Owen smiles. A monkey is the name soldiers give to a solar cell worn as part of the uniform and used to convert the sun's energy into enough power to recharge an iPod or a laptop. The lad may be new but he already knows the lingo. He shakes his head. 'Sorry, mate.'

Collins looks at his watch. 'Ah, well. Time I was off anyway.' He leaps up, pulls on his uniform and body armour and adjusts his helmet. He tilts his head and raises a hand in a mock salute. 'See you around, soldier.'

Owen laughs. 'Yeah. See you around.'

CHAPTER THREE

Helen pulls the car door closed and feels the weight of tension lift from her shoulders. Tossing her handbag onto the passenger seat, she glances back at her mother's front window. The blue light is flickering from the flat screen television. Frank had probably been waiting for her to leave. She pictures him sprawled in his armchair watching the rugby, lager can in hand. If his team wins, he'll celebrate with a few more cans. If they lose, he'll console himself with a lot more.

Reaching to adjust the rear-view mirror, her fingers brush against the worry beads Owen brought back from Iraq. He didn't tell her exactly how he came by them, and she never asked. Sometimes it's better not to know. She sighs deeply and breathes in the warm smell of leather and the faint, comforting tang of air freshener.

It's only a small car, a second-hand silver Matiz, but Helen loves it in a way nobody can understand – not even Owen, and he understands her better than anyone. She imagines him seated beside her, urging her to check her mirror before pulling out. 'Bloody women drivers!' But they'd both know that he was only joking. Owen was the one who encouraged her to drive.

She'd been reluctant at first. The thought of being in control of a fast-moving vehicle filled her with dread. It was only through Owen's gentle persistence that she'd plucked up the courage to enrol at the local driving school and apply for her test.

'So what if you fail?' Owen had said. 'Most people fail their first time. Try again. Fail again. Just try not to fail so badly the second time.'

It was a silly thing for a man in his position to say. Soldiers were trained not to fail. For them, failure could mean the difference between life and death. But then Owen wasn't like most soldiers. There was no doubting his ability or his courage. She'd feared for him when he fought in Iraq, and admired his conviction when he returned home to find that public opinion was rapidly turning against the war – even in a town like this, where patriotism ran high and the local cemetery was filled with generations of dead soldiers.

But there was a gentler side to him too. He cried at soppy films. It was a running joke between them. He was her big soft soldier boy, her sweet and tender fighting man.

He was there the day she took her driving test and passed with flying colours. Helen couldn't have been more surprised, but Owen had acted as if it was a foregone conclusion.

'See,' he said when they tore off the 'L' plates and climbed into the car. 'I knew you wouldn't let me down.'

'But you said it would be okay if I failed.'

He turned to her and winked. 'I lied.'

The roads are clear and soon she's driving through the sprawl of prefabs known as Wildmill and then up past The Saints where she spent the first eleven years of her life. Wildmill is where the town's drug dealers do most of their trade. Sometimes the local paper would report that an addict had overdosed or hanged themselves, at which point her mother and Frank would exchange a knowing look as if to say 'serves them right'.

After The Saints, the road veers up Litchard Hill where Helen used to walk to primary school. She'd loved school before her father died, before she was forced to face the terrifying anonymity of the comprehensive with its noisy classrooms ruled by hard-faced girls with purple nylon uniforms and their boyfriends' names scratched into their forearms.

Soon the landscape changes and the main road gives way to narrow streets and rows of small shops, terraces with stone cladding and pebbledash fronts and modern semis with Welsh names and mock Tudor extensions. The valleys were once a symbol of industry in South Wales, but those days are long gone. There are no coal mines anymore, and few opportunities. Teenage pregnancies are common. Jobs are not.

It's mainly from the valleys that the men come at the weekends, descending on Bridgend in packs, looking for a few pints and someone to vent their frustrations on and leaving the streets stained with blood and covered in broken glass. Every week the police riot vans line up next to the taxi rank in the centre of town, waiting for the first sign of trouble. And every week the trouble would arrive in the shape of the valley boys with their thick necks and bullet heads.

Helen remembers Owen telling her about the time he went on a training exercise in the Brecon Beacons and saw a sign that read: 'Warning. This is a military zone. Do not touch anything as it may explode and kill you!' Sometimes she wonders if they should erect a similar sign in the centre of Bridgend, one that reads: 'Warning. This is a danger zone. Do not look at anyone as they may explode and kill you!' She tries not to dwell on the violence. She doesn't want to give Frank the satisfaction. But she'd heard about that lad who was kicked to death up by the railway bridge. He wasn't the first, either. It wasn't that long ago that a young woman had her face slashed in one of the pubs. Helen remembers the picture in the *Gazette*.

She's approaching a T-junction when a sudden movement catches her eye. A figure appears from nowhere and runs out into the road. She slams on the brakes and the car screeches to a halt. The late afternoon sun glares off the windscreen, making it hard for her to tell if the figure is male or female. The figure turns to face her, slapping both hands hard on the bonnet.

'Stupid cow!'

It's a girl, probably no older than sixteen. Her face is pale and pinched, her eyes glazed. As she moves towards the driver's door, Helen resists the urge to wind down the window and ask if she's okay. Girls like this are never okay. She's probably drunk, or on drugs – or both.

Instinctively, Helen locks the car doors.

The girl raps her bony knuckles on the driver's window. 'You could have killed me then. Stupid bitch!'

'Sorry,' Helen mouths.

The girl smirks, revealing discoloured teeth. 'Call it twenty quid and we're quits.'

Helen shrugs apologetically. She has no intention of opening the door to this girl or helping to feed her habit. But she can't just sit here. What if the girl tries to break the window?

She glances in the rear-view mirror. Further along the pavement, two teenage boys ride their mountain bikes in wide, lazy circles. Apart from that, the streets are empty. Not even a passing car.

'C'mon!' the girl says, her voice rising dangerously.

20

'Twenty quid. Or I'll report you. My friends saw you. They've got your registration number.'

She points at the boys, who duck their heads and laugh.

'Leave it!' one of them shouts. 'We're late enough as it is.'

'But she could have killed me.' The girl raps on the driver's window again. 'Cough up, bitch!'

Helen puts her foot down on the accelerator and speeds off.

She's still shaking when she arrives home. The house is in a row of small terraces arranged in an L-shape on a steep incline off the main road. In front of them is a large patch of grass where people come to walk their dogs during the day and teenagers congregate at night. She parks and pauses to catch her breath before getting out of the car and hurrying inside.

She shuts the front door behind her and looks around the familiar hall. On the wall facing the staircase is a framed photo of Owen at his passing-out parade, alongside a picture of them both together on their wedding day. That was the day plain old Helen Thomas became Helen McGrath, wife of Lance Corporal Owen McGrath. She'd worn her hair in a French pleat, and the make-up artist had given her a face she barely recognized. Her mother had sent a copy of the wedding photo to the local paper, where it appeared with a short article reminding readers of her father's death. The headline read, 'Tragic local girl finds happiness at last.'

The living room is dominated by a brown leather sofa so big they'd had to winch it in through the front window. She sees the light on the ansaphone blinking and thinks for a moment that Owen has called the landline instead of her mobile. But it's just someone trying to sell her car insurance. Disappointed, she turns on the laptop and checks her emails. Nothing.

Sundays are the hardest. Sundays were always the hardest, even when she was still at school. Back then it was the empty space left by her father that made the day stretch on forever. Now it's the empty space left by her husband. At least tomorrow another working week will begin. She takes pride in her work and comfort in the small administrative tasks she performs with such efficiency. The attention to detail helps take her mind off the bigger picture.

She closes the laptop and walks briskly into the kitchen. There are no dirty dishes in the sink. Everything has been washed, dried and put back in its place. She takes out the ironing board and plugs in the steam iron before unloading the clothes from the tumble dryer and arranging them in a neat pile on the table.

Why hasn't he written?

When Owen was first stationed in Iraq, he used to write to her all the time. She'd arrive home to find the familiar blue envelopes on the doormat and her heart would skip. The separation still hurt, but at least she knew he was missing her as much as she missed him. More importantly, she knew he was safe. Is he safe now? Is he missing her? Or has something happened to him?

She unplugs the iron and goes upstairs. The letters are in a shoe box under the bed, the envelopes tied together in bundles. She takes out one of the older letters, written shortly after he arrived in Basra.

'*Remember that holiday in Snowdonia?*' she reads. '*Well, it's a bit like that, only with less rain. In fact, it's hot as hell. I can't work out if I'm tanned or just toasted!*

But mostly I'm bored. Every day is the same out here. You lose track of time. I've been thinking of things to do when I get home. We should get away more, go to Amsterdam or maybe Paris. Somewhere they serve cold beer! Miss you loads. Better sign off now. This pen is drying up. See, I told you it was hot!'

His earlier letters were always so thoughtful. Sometimes he'd illustrate them with stick figures and cartoon faces. '*Me today,*' he'd written in one, next to a stick figure of a man lounging in a chair with a rifle by his side, staring up at a clock. Then '*me tomorrow*' with a similar man in the same position. A good joke would be followed by a smiley face, a bad one with a figure clasping their hands to their head, mouth wide open, like the man in *The Scream*. '*Excuse me while I explode with laughter,*' he'd write. Then, '*PS: this letter will self-destruct in three seconds.*'

It wasn't the jokes that brought a smile to her face. It was the way he made light of his situation. But it didn't last. Two months after he'd arrived in Iraq, the letters became less frequent. Days would pass, and there'd be no word from him. Then one would arrive, apologizing for the lack of correspondence and assuring her that everything was fine. But she knew him better than that. The tone had changed. There were fewer jokes and no silly cartoons. The letters were shorter, some no longer than postcards. '*Not much to report,*' he'd written in one. '*Days hot. Nights cold. Missing you. Love, Owen.*' After that, there'd been nothing for a whole week. She'd feared the worst until another letter arrived, informing her that he was coming home.

She'd been so excited at the prospect of seeing him again. But the thrill of being reunited and the pleasure they took in each other's bodies couldn't hide the fact there was something different about him. It had taken five days before he finally opened up and told her what had happened. He'd shot and killed a young boy. 'It's part of what I was trained to do,' he said. 'But that doesn't mean I have to feel good about it.' She'd suggested that he talk to someone, but he'd refused.

'And tell them what? That I feel bad about doing my job? I'm sure they'd love that!'

Still, it hadn't prevented him from going to Afghanistan.

'But why do you have to go?' she'd asked when he told her the news.

'You know why,' was his reply.

'You could leave the army, get a job here.'

'Doing what?' He looked almost angry with her. 'This is what I do, Helen. This is who I am.'

Was this latest silence an omen? Of the fifty or so letters in the bundle, there are only a few from Afghanistan, written in the weeks after he arrived. The most recent is dated June 3 – almost three weeks ago. There have been a couple of emails since then, and one short phone call. She could tell by the tone of his voice that something was troubling him, that the distance between them wasn't just physical.

She takes a deep breath and places the letters to one side. Also in the box are mementos of the only other man she's ever loved.

Helen grew up with so few physical reminders of her father. Her mother had seen to that. A week after his funeral, Helen arrived home from school to find a white builders' van parked outside the house. A workman came up the driveway carrying a broken doorframe above his head. She recognized it instantly. Running round to the back garden, she found her mother watching silently as another man took a sledgehammer to the remains of her father's shed.

'You're early,' her mother said. Her voice was distant, as if the destruction of the shed meant nothing to her.

'How could you?' Helen screamed.

'It's for the best,' her mother replied.

The man took another swing with the sledgehammer. There was a terrible groaning sound and what remained of the shed scattered across the lawn. Helen fell to her knees and scrambled through the debris, searching frantically for anything she could find of her father's – broken hinges, bottle tops and a handful of his old coins. When she looked up again, her mother had gone. All these years later, Helen still hasn't quite forgiven her.

She stares down at the contents of the shoe box. Not much, really – just a handful of faded photographs, a yellowing newspaper cutting, a couple of leather bookmarks and a blue pocket dictionary inscribed with his spidery handwriting – *'To my darling daughter, hoping you find it useful for many years to come.'* And there, glinting in the half-light, are some of his old coins. They aren't worth anything, or so her mother says. She had them valued shortly after he died and seemed pleased to report that these things he'd treasured weren't worth keeping. But to Helen they're more precious than gold. Her father once held these coins.

She takes one out and places it in the palm of her hand. The surface is tarnished and the edges are worn. On one side there's a profile of a young-looking Elizabeth II, and on the other a picture of Britannia and the date – 1970. She remembers her father telling her that this was the year before these old pennies became obsolete, and for some strange reason the thought saddens her. She replaces the coin, slides the box back under the bed and heads downstairs.

Later, when the clothes are all ironed and a feeling of order has been restored, she allows herself a large glass of wine. She's never been much of a drinker. She fears the loss of control, worries that she might make a fool of herself. But tonight, in the safety of her own home, with nobody to bear witness to her drinking, she sits on the sofa and lets the wine do its work, soothing her anxieties away. It doesn't take much. Owen always said she was a cheap date and sometimes teases her about the fact that her tolerance for alcohol is no greater now than when they first met. She tries not to think about him, tries to focus her mind on the week ahead.

Finally, when the first glass has given way to a second, and her head is cloudy with wine, she climbs the stairs and prepares herself for bed.

Things will look better in the morning, she tells herself. They always do.

CHAPTER FOUR

The dream always begins in the same way. It's dark, and she's walking up the Black Path. Hiding among the twisted trees are the boys her parents warned her about. She sees the glow of their cigarettes and hears the murmur of their voices, punctuated with bursts of vicious laughter. In the distance, there's the crackle of a bonfire and the crying of animals. Horrified, she realizes that the path is littered with the bodies of baby rabbits, pink and hairless, like the ones she found mashed together under the straw when she was ten.

Then her father appears at her shoulder. He's walking beside her, telling her not to be afraid. She's not a child anymore and if she just keeps moving forward then everything will be alright. The Black Path isn't so scary after all. The ground is black because of the coal and iron ore deposits in the soil. The trees are just trees, and the boys with bonfires are just kids messing about. The rabbits aren't real and those cries are the sound of foxes. It's just a path, and if she can make it to the top, she'll see that it's perfectly safe.

Soon the path opens into a clearing. There's a large tree covered in scars where people have carved their names into the bark. In the middle of the clearing is a gravestone, bleached white against the black soil.

Nervously, she turns to her father. 'I can't go on.'

'You must,' he replies.

'But there's a grave. Somebody died.'

Her father smiles. 'Everyone dies. It's nothing to be afraid of.'

There's a rattle of laughter like gunfire from behind the trees. She stares into the darkness and sees something moving in the shadows.

'Look!' But her father has gone. She's alone, barefoot in the middle of the Black Path.

Sometimes the dream ends there. Sometimes it ends with her turning to find a boy with black hair and dark, glittering eyes holding a white rabbit by the neck and twisting its head until its body goes limp.

Tonight the dream ends differently, with her staring at the gravestone. At the base of the stone she notices a small wooden cross, faded with age. Next to it, someone has placed a wreath of red paper poppies. Etched in the granite are the words, 'Lance Corporal Owen McGrath.'

She wakes up gasping for breath, her chest heaving, damp hair plastered across her face.

It's not real, she tells herself. It doesn't mean anything.

But another voice answers back.

What if it does? What if it's a premonition?

Her hand trembles as she reaches for the bedside lamp, almost knocking it over before her fingers finally find the switch. Light spills onto the bed, illuminating the cream duvet cover and chasing the dark thoughts away.

Everything is fine. It was just a dream.

She stares up at the ceiling, breathing deeply until her heart rate slows and the Black Path recedes back into her subconscious. She turns onto her side, her hand curled against Owen's pillow. He'll be home soon. All she has to do is wait. Stay strong.

The clock on the nightstand says the time is just past

1 a.m. But she knows there's no point in trying to get back to sleep now. She needs to distract herself, to avoid thinking. Climbing out of bed, she pulls on her dressing gown and pads into the landing. The loose floorboard creaks as she heads downstairs.

The house is dark and strange at this time of night. The orange glow of a streetlight glimmers through the living room curtains. Settling on the sofa, tucking her feet under her, she reaches for the remote and turns on the TV. A woman with blonde hair and pink lips is encouraging viewers to dial the number at the bottom of the screen and meet other single people in their area. Helen channel hops to another station where two men are discussing sports results, then on to a film she's already seen, starring Tom Cruise. Then the picture changes and suddenly a news reporter is talking to a woman while, behind them, firefighters struggle to control the flames leaping through the windows of a small terraced house that looks remarkably similar to her own.

But what really strikes Helen is the look on the woman's face. It's the same stunned expression she's seen at military funerals, on women whose loved ones have been killed in action.

CHAPTER FIVE

It's still early but the cookhouse is already filling up. Men drift in with their rifles slung over their shoulders and gather in groups around the brew kit, helping themselves to foam cups of tea and coffee. The air is thick with the smell of fried bacon.

Normally this is enough to give Owen an appetite. But he can't face a fry-up today. He grabs a coffee, fills a bowl with porridge, some dried fruit mix and a few pieces of pineapple and finds an empty place at a table.

He's barely begun to eat when Jackson appears, his plate piled high with a full English breakfast – eggs, bacon, sausage, beans and toast.

'Mind if I sit?' He doesn't wait for a reply. His feet are already under the table.

'It's a free country.' Owen smiles grimly at his own joke. This is anything but a free country.

'Two weeks and I'm out of here,' Jackson says. 'Can't fucking wait. I'm sick of this shit hole!'

Owen glares at him. 'Do you mind? I'm trying to eat.'

'So I see.' Jackson points his knife at Owen's bowl. 'Call that breakfast?'

'It's porridge. I'm sure you've seen it before.'

'Seen it, yeah. Not eaten it, though. I prefer proper scoff.' Jackson grins and shovels a forkful of bacon and egg into his mouth. 'Fighting food,' he says. 'An army marches on its stomach.'

'I haven't seen a lot of marching around here,' Owen replies.

'You can say that again.' Jackson thumps a fist against his chest and belches. 'Give me Iraq over this any day. At least there we saw some action.'

At the mention of Iraq, Owen feels the food in his mouth turn to ash. He sees the face of the boy he shot. It was his first kill, and it's still the one that troubles him the most. It was so close range, so intimate, and the boy was so very young. Was he even shaving? Had he kissed a girl yet?

Owen swallows. 'So you're off home then?'

'I've been here eight weeks. I'm due some R&R.'

'And there was I thinking you were a fighting man.'

Jackson's expression changes. 'We both know that tosser had it coming,' he growls. 'Nobody messes around with my missus.'

Owen takes a sip of his coffee. It's no better than usual but at least it washes the taste of ashes from his mouth. He studies the man opposite. The fight that led to Jackson being demoted had occurred four months ago, in a bar back home. Jackson claimed that the 'tosser' concerned was making a play for his wife, Leanne, and that he simply told him to shove off. It was the other guy who threw the first punch – Jackson was merely acting in self-defence. The security staff at the bar said differently and the CCTV footage, though inconclusive, seemed to back them up. What nobody could dispute was that Jackson came away with barely a bruise, while the other man's jaw was broken in two places. When he threatened to press charges, Jackson was hauled in and reprimanded.

Looking at him now, it's hard for Owen to picture Jackson as anything other than the aggressor. Thick-set, with a bullet head and a menacing glint in his eye, he radiates violence the way certain breeds of dog give off warning signals. There are even rumours that he beats his wife. As far as Owen knows, Leanne has never phoned the police or filed a complaint with the authorities. But he can imagine the fear her husband instils in her.

Owen never saw his own father hit his mother. But he remembers him seething on the sofa or pacing the room and grinding his teeth like a boxer, the anger coming off him in waves. Like many soldiers, Owen comes from what people used to call a broken home – though whenever he hears those words now, he pictures a building with its roof blown off and crouching families running for cover. A young boy can survive many things. He's proof of that. Children here aren't always so lucky.

He looks at Jackson shovelling food into his face. Maybe he's not a wife beater. And maybe his own father never raised a hand to his mother. It's possible that her clinical depression had nothing to do with the way he treated her. But Owen remembers the whimpers behind closed doors, the unexplained bruises, his mother crying in the kitchen. From what he's seen of her, Leanne is a meek, mousey woman, as frail in her own way as his mother had been. And men who boast about keeping their wives in line are often the kind of men who treat them as punch bags.

'I was on the phone to the missus last night,' Jackson says, folding a slice of toast in one meaty hand and cramming it into his mouth. 'She said your Helen was looking well.'

Owen frowns. Helen and Leanne barely know each other. They've met a couple of times at most. And since Jackson and his wife live twenty miles away in service accommodation in St Athan, he can't see any reason why

33

their paths would ever cross.

Jackson must have read his mind. 'She was driving up by the wives' estate,' he adds, spitting crumbs across the table. 'Leanne saw her at the traffic lights. Said she was all dolled up, like she had somewhere special to go – or someone special to see.' He raises his eyebrows and grins unpleasantly.

'Yeah, right!' says Owen. Helen would never cheat on him. He's sure of it.

'Leanne waved at her,' Jackson says. 'But she just drove off. It was like she didn't want to be spotted.'

'Leanne's mistaken,' Owen replies. 'There's no reason for Helen to go near the estate. There's nothing there that interests her.'

Jackson's lip curls. 'Leanne wondered whether she was thinking of moving into the quarter.'

'Why would we?' Owen asks. 'We have a house of our own.'

'That's what I said,' Jackson smirks. 'I said to her, "Leanne, why would Lance Corporal McGrath and his lovely wife want to move to St Athan? They're far too grand for the likes of us!" But she swore it was her.'

'It can't have been,' Owen says. 'Helen's very happy where we are.'

'She drives a silver Matiz, doesn't she?' asks Jackson.

How the hell does Jackson know what car Helen drives? Owen thinks. The Matiz is a fairly recent purchase.

Jackson looks pleased with himself. 'Well, doesn't she?'

'So?'

'So there you go. It was her. Leanne's not stupid. She knows what she saw.' He loads the last of the baked beans onto his fork and gulps them down.

Owen considers this for a moment, then remembers. 'When did you say you spoke to Leanne?'

'Last night,' Jackson replies, wiping his plate with his remaining slice of toast.

Owen smiles. 'That's not possible. We were on an Op Minimize last night. Armstrong was killed, remember? No communications.'

Jackson shrugs and glances away. 'Then it must have been the night before.'

'Come off it, Jackson,' Owen says. 'You don't even know what day it is.'

'At least I know where my wife is and what she's up to. When did you last speak to your missus, anyway?'

'That's none of your business.'

'Well, the next time you talk to her, tell her Leanne said to say hello.'

'Fuck off, Jackson.'

Jackson grins and rises to his feet. 'No need to get shirty with me, mate! I'm just the messenger!'

CHAPTER SIX

'I'm the backbone of the team,' Natalie says. 'Those aren't my words. That's Simon talking.'

Natalie is second in the chain of command at Greenwood Training and likes to demonstrate her authority by marching briskly through the open-plan office with a long flowing cardigan flapping behind her, arms folded tightly across her chest, clutching a portfolio.

'He only says that because you're so bossy,' one of the other women pipes up.

It's Angela, who handles the accounts. Sometimes Helen wonders what Angela is doing in a place like this, and how she's survived so long without being fired. Few people ever dare stand up to Natalie.

'I'm also dangerous when provoked,' Natalie says, and swipes at Angela with the portfolio, narrowly missing her head. She laughs unconvincingly and gives a final flip of her cardigan before disappearing into the conference room for her Monday morning briefing with Simon – the head of the company.

'You're mad, you are!' Angela's friend Kath says in a hushed voice. 'She'll have you for that, she will!'

Kath has a habit of stating the obvious, and then repeating herself in case nobody understood her the first time. In anyone else, Helen might find this irritating. But there's something so sweet and guileless about Kath that to find fault with her would be like kicking a kitten.

'Well, she gets on my bloody nerves,' Angela says. 'She's like one of them Russian dolls.' She pauses, relishing the bewildered look on Kath's face. Then she breaks into a grin. 'They're full of themselves too!'

Kath gasps and giggles. Helen smiles gamely, pretending she's hearing the joke for the first time. She's fond of Angela, and more than a little dazzled by her. Growing up an only child, Helen often wondered what it would be like to have a sister – someone to act as an emotional buffer between her and her mother. She knows that Angela is the eldest of three children, and that she practically raised her younger siblings: 'It was either that or see them taken into care.' She wonders what it was like, having a big sister like Angela to look up to, wonders if it made up for the lack of parenting.

'So where are we off to this Friday then, girls?' Angela asks. 'Paris? New York? Or shall we settle for a night out in Cardiff?'

'I'm game,' says Kath.

'Don't tempt me!' Angela rolls her eyes. 'What about you, Helen? It's pay day this week. We might even stretch to a bit of tapas.'

Helen shuffles some papers and tries to look distracted. She feels exhausted. The nightmare was still with her when she woke this morning, the white gravestone glowing bright behind her eyes. Suddenly, the thought of going out just to spite Frank doesn't seem like such a good idea after all.

'I might just have a quiet night in.'

'You can have a quiet night in anytime,' Angela says.

'Yeah,' says Kath. 'Don't be such a kill joy!' She blushes and blinks nervously. 'I didn't mean –'

'It's alright,' Helen says quickly.

'No, what I meant was –'

'I said it's fine!' Helen snaps.

'Honestly, Kath!' says Angela. 'Sometimes you've got as much sensitivity as God gave lettuce!'

She hurries over to Helen's desk and slips a comforting arm around her shoulder. 'Do you want to pop off to the loo for a bit? Me and Kath will cover for you.'

Helen shakes her head.

'Do you need a tissue, then?'

Angela produces one before Helen can respond. She takes it and dabs her eyes. 'Sorry, I had a rough night.'

'Don't be daft.' Angela gives her shoulder a little squeeze.

Helen forces a smile. 'It's just been a bit hard lately. I haven't heard from Owen in over a week.'

Angela nods knowingly. 'No wonder you're upset.'

'Especially with all those stories on the news,' Kath chips in. 'I don't know how –'

Angela glares at her.

'Sorry', says Kath.

'No, she's right,' Helen says. 'I mean, I try not to think about it. I turn the TV over whenever it comes on. I try not to read the papers. But it's always there. And then I feel guilty for feeling sorry for myself.'

'Well, I think you're very brave, Helen,' Angela says. 'Sometimes I think it must be harder for the wives than the soldiers they're married to.'

'What makes you say that?'

'Well, he's the one who chose to join the army, isn't he? It wasn't something you had any say in.'

'But I chose him,' Helen replies.

She remembers the first time she ever laid eyes on Owen. It was at someone's eighteenth, the daughter of a man Frank's car-repair firm did business with. Her mother had insisted on dragging her along, despite her protests that she wouldn't know anyone and wasn't looking her best.

'Don't be silly,' her mother had chided. 'Who's going to be looking at you?'

But someone had looked at her, and he liked what he saw. Owen had arrived with a friend, a fellow soldier, and made a beeline for her the moment he entered the room, offering to fetch her a drink and keeping her entertained for hours. She'd never felt so at ease with a boy before. Soon they were on their first date, then their second, and before she knew it they were sitting on the beach at Southerndown and he was asking her to marry him and she was saying yes.

Did she choose him? She remembers thinking how handsome he looked in his uniform, and how charming he was. But there was more to it than that. He made her feel safe, as if nothing bad would ever happen to her. What would she give to rekindle that feeling now?

'You know what I think?' Angela says.

Helen shakes her head.

'I think you should come out with us on Friday night. And I promise you we'll have a bloody good time and make it a night to remember.'

Helen smiles tentatively.

'C'mon! It's what Owen would want. He wouldn't want you sat at home on your own worrying. He'd want you out having a good time.'

Helen has heard people employ this kind of reasoning before. It's the same argument her mother gave after settling down with Frank. 'It's what your father would have wanted. He wouldn't want me spending the rest of my life on my own.'

'So what'll it be?' asks Angela. 'A night in front of the

telly with a ready meal for one? Or a night out on the razz with two of the hottest girls this side of the Severn Tunnel?'

Helen manages a laugh. 'Well, if you put it like that…'

It hadn't taken more than a week or two for Helen to realize that work could be a great solace. Convincing her husband had taken a little longer. She'd lied when she told her mother that Owen fully supported her decision to get a job. His support had been conditional at best. It wasn't that he was against the idea of her working. It was more about the timing. As far as he knew, they were still trying for a baby. And he thought all her energy should be focussed on that.

'Are you sure about this?' he'd asked, the first time she broached the subject. 'I'm quite capable of supporting my family.'

They'd just been to the supermarket and were unloading the bags from the boot of the car.

'I know you are, love,' she said. She knew better than to pick him up on the word 'family', with all that implied. 'But it wouldn't hurt for me to get out of the house more. Especially when you're away.'

He looked wounded. 'I thought you understood, Helen. Being in the army isn't like a regular job.'

'I know.'

'Well, it doesn't sound like it.'

Grabbing another bag, he lost his grip and a carrier containing a bottle of wine and two cartons of orange juice slipped through his fingers and smashed on the road. 'Great!'

Helen reached for a shard of glass.

'Leave it!' he said. 'I'll clear it up when we've got this lot indoors.'

Later, over dinner, he apologized for his outburst, blaming the strain of knowing that soon he'd be packed off to Afghanistan. 'I hate being away from you. But I have to go. You know that.'

'I know,' she said. 'I just think that if I had a job too, maybe it would help take my mind off things when you were away. And the extra money would come in handy.'

After dinner, Owen had popped out to the local shop and returned with a bottle of champagne.

'But we can't afford this,' Helen said, laughing as he danced around the kitchen, finally locating two champagne flutes which hadn't been used since their wedding anniversary.

'Don't spoil the moment,' he replied, cracking open the bottle. 'Let's just enjoy it. If you really want a job, that's fine with me. I just want you to be happy.'

If only all their disagreements had been so easy to resolve.

'How many kids do you want?' he'd asked her, the night before he left for Afghanistan. 'Boys or girls? Or one of both?'

Like her, Owen had been an only child. Unlike her, he was determined that any child of his would grow up with a brother or sister.

'Why stop at two?' he laughed. 'Let's have lots of kids. Let's have an army!'

She should have said something. Instead she'd changed the subject, the way she did whenever he joked about 'making babies'. Her husband didn't know that she took the pill. That night, the deception had played on her conscience. If he'd asked her what was wrong, she'd have been tempted to tell him, 'I don't find the idea of making babies much of a turn-on.'

But he didn't ask. He simply lay there, his body barely

touching hers until, finally, he drifted off to sleep. She lay awake for hours, feeling his warm breath on the nape of her neck. Was he dreaming of her? Or was he already lost to the world of war waiting for him thousands of miles away?

The following morning over the breakfast table, she saw the difference in him. He seemed so remote. The second tour of duty was harder than the first – that's what people said. Little did she know then how true this would prove to be. But when his lift arrived, and he kissed her chastely on the cheek, she knew she'd made the right decision. She had no intention of getting pregnant. But she would let him go on thinking that one day he would have a couple, a bunch, even an army of children to call his own.

Helen glances guiltily at the framed photo on her desk. The man smiling back at her from the photo is oblivious to the fact that his wife is deceiving him. She wonders what he'd think of her if he knew and why she hasn't heard from him. Is it possible that he suspects something? Is that why he hasn't called? Or is the truth more terrible than she dares to imagine?

A shiver washes over her. She rises quickly from her desk and hurries to the ladies.

Inside, she locks the cubicle door and sits on the toilet with the lid down. She balls both her hands into little fists and presses them against the sides of her head.

I must not cry at work, she tells herself. *I must not cry at work*. She may have passed her three-month trial period, but she's still barely six months into the job. If she makes a scene like this they might start to regret the decision to keep her on.

There've been days like this before. When Owen was

stationed in Iraq for seven months, she worried herself sick about him. Missiles were landing on the base on a regular basis, so communication was often impossible. Then he'd be off on an operation and she wouldn't hear from him for days or sometimes weeks. He came home safe and sound in the end. And he'll make it back this time too, she tells herself. She just has to hold on to that thought and everything will be alright.

An idea comes to her. Tonight, after work, she'll drive over to the shopping centre and put together a parcel for him – magazines, sweets, factor 50 sun lotion and E45 cream, all the things she knows he'll be missing. She'll write him a letter, telling him how well she's doing. Maybe if she can convince him, she can convince herself too.

She stands up and flushes the toilet. Dabbing her eyes with a tissue, she takes a deep breath and opens the door.

Natalie is standing at the wash basin, reapplying her make-up. She looks over her shoulder as Helen approaches.

'Everything alright, Helen?'

'Yes, thanks.'

Natalie looks doubtful. 'Only you seem a bit upset.'

Helen forces a smile. 'No, I'm okay.'

'Good. Because you know how much I value your work here. But if Simon was to get the impression that you weren't up to the job –'

'I'm fine,' Helen says quickly. 'Totally fine. I had a bit of a headache, but it's gone now.'

Natalie narrows her eyes. 'I'm glad to hear it. I'll see you in the conference room in ten minutes.' She moves towards the door. 'And Helen?'

'Yes?'

'Don't bring your personal problems into work.'

CHAPTER SEVEN

Owen and some other members of the battalion are watching *Jarhead* for what feels like the hundredth time. Still, it makes a change from *Apocalypse Now*, *Band of Brothers* and *The Hurt Locker*. They're gathered around a flat-screen TV and DVD player, the origins of which are unknown, though rumour has it they were liberated from some Afghan's house.

The tent is large enough for forty beds. Away from the screen, the blue glow of laptops and games consoles can be seen under the mosquito nets as soldiers make their own entertainment. The beds are separated by concrete blocks which are supposed to provide extra cover in the event of a mortar attack. In Owen's experience, all they really did was add to the debris. Back when he served in Iraq, they used to joke that the beds were readymade concrete tombs. That was until the tent next along was hit and he saw for the first time the grim reality of war as men came crawling out from the wreckage with limbs missing. One had lost a leg. Another's hand was dangling by a piece of skin. Nothing prepared a man for the horror of seeing his fellow soldiers blown to pieces. Owen remembers the shock at seeing illegal drugs administered to the injured before they made it to the field hospital.

There hasn't been a single mortar attack on the base

since he arrived in Afghanistan, which isn't to say that he and his little film club can afford to let their guard down. No soldier's body armour is more than a few feet away. Helmets are at arm's length. It's a strange kind of escapism, watching a film about the boredom of war while a part of you is conscious of the possibility of an attack. The enemy change tactics all the time. Right now they tend to rely on IEDs. But who's to say that they aren't planning a new surprise? The compound is huge – four miles long and two miles wide – and the walls are heavily fortified. But the possibility of a strike, however, remote, is ever present. The feeling of anxiety combined with adrenaline is one Owen has never been able to put into words. It's something only a soldier would understand.

There are around a dozen men in all, some reclining on the edges of the beds, others sitting on plastic chairs. Jackson is here, and Collins, the young private who likes to sunbathe and eats muesli for breakfast.

Nobody is paying close attention to the film. They've all seen it before. It's more about the ritual of watching and waiting for a favourite scene or piece of dialogue, a bit like going to see a band and waiting for a favourite song, the one everyone knows and sings along to. People talk and joke and shout things at the screen. Owen passes round the bags of mints and hard gums that arrived this morning. The letter is folded in his pocket, unopened.

'Where'd you get these, McGrath?' someone asks.

'The wife sent them,' he replies and feels a pang of guilt. 'The wife'. Not even 'my wife', which at least suggests some sense of responsibility, some emotional connection. He still hasn't written to Helen, or phoned. He can't find the words. He hasn't been sleeping well. He's been having dreams, nightmares about some of the things he'd witnessed, but mostly about the kid he shot in Iraq. Owen keeps seeing him falling, like a puppet with its strings cut. He wakes up each morning feeling disoriented and has to remind himself of where he is and why he's here.

Jake Gyllenhaal is dancing in his G-string and Santa hat when the shouting begins.

'Hey, Brokeback!' someone yells. It's Jackson, of course. At first, Owen thinks he's shouting at the screen. Then he realizes that the comment is directed at Collins.

If the boy is intimidated, he doesn't let it show. 'Wrong movie,' Collins says. 'That was a film with actors playing at being cowboys. This is a film with actors playing at being soldiers.'

Someone laughs, which provokes Jackson even further.

'Don't get funny with me, Collins. Why did you join the army anyway?'

'Same reason as you. To serve my country.'

'Queen and country more like,' Jackson sneers. 'It must be great for you here, with all us men. I bet you really get off on it.'

'No more than you, mate,' Collins replies.

'Are you calling me queer?' Jackson is angry now. Owen can see the vein throbbing in his left temple.

'I'm not calling you anything,' Collins says. 'We're here for the same reason. We have a job to do. But nobody forced us to join the army. We're here because we like it.'

'And what about him?', Jackson asks, gesturing at the screen. 'Jake whatshisname. Do you like him too?'

'I've never met him.'

'You know what I mean,' Jackson says.

There are jeers, followed by more laughter. Nobody is

paying attention to the film anymore. All eyes are on Collins. Nothing has happened for days. The possibility of a fight offers a welcome respite from the boredom.

'Well?' Jackson says. He looks around at the others and grins. 'Do you want to fuck him or not?'

Collins doesn't respond.

Jackson grabs himself by the genitals and steps forward, thrusting out his groin. 'Or maybe you'd prefer a bit of this?'

Collins reddens. More laughter.

Watching Collins, Owen feels a sudden welling in his stomach – a mixture of revulsion, identification and pity. He thinks back to his first day at the army cadets. He was fourteen, and an older boy was smoking a cigarette.

'Press your hand against my chest,' he told Owen. 'And I bet you I can make the smoke come out of my ears.'

The boy inhaled and held his breath. Owen placed his right hand against the boy's chest and the next thing he knew the cigarette was burning into the back of his hand. He went home and cried, but instead of comforting him, his father gave him a good hiding.

'Come home crying again,' he said, 'and I'll give you something to cry about.'

So yes, Owen knows a thing or two about bullies.

'That's enough, Jackson,' he snaps.

'What's it to you, McGrath? Jackson snarls back. He's really stepping out of line now. He may be a senior private, and one many of the younger privates look up to, but he's still only that – a private. And whatever their personal history, a private doesn't speak to a lance corporal the way Jackson is speaking to Owen. Especially not in front of an audience.

'I could ask you the same question,' Owen says.

Jackson looks confused. 'What's that supposed to mean?'

'Why are you so bothered about who's gay and who isn't? First Armstrong and now Collins. It's becoming quite an obsession.'

At the mention of the dead soldier, the mood changes. The men shift about, their eyes shining solemnly.

Jackson looks around for support but finds none. He stands up, looks at Owen as if he's about to say something and then thinks better of it. He grabs his body armour and storms off. Slowly the others drift away. The film is still playing, the soundtrack barely drowning out the sound of someone snoring a few feet away.

Owen waits until they're out of earshot before turning to Collins. 'Don't ever do that again!'

Collins blinks at him in surprise. 'I thought you were on my side.'

'There are no sides. Just stay out of Jackson's way. I don't want any trouble.'

'But he started it.'

'And I'm ending it. Understood?'

Collins catches his eye for a moment. Then he nods. 'Whatever you say, Corporal.'

CHAPTER EIGHT

Friday comes around too soon and there's still no word from Owen. 'No news is good news,' Helen tells herself as she showers and brushes her teeth. It's the sort of thing her mother would say, but sometimes there's comfort in repeating a mantra, however unconvincing it sounds.

There was another report on the news last night – another soldier killed, another political row about boots on the ground in Afghanistan and the rights and wrongs of withdrawing troops from a country ravaged by decades of war. She'd tried to ignore it, but there was something hypnotic and infuriating about the way the politicians spoke about 'our boys' as if they were personally related. How many of *their* sons were out there? How many of them lived in fear of someone they loved not coming home?

She pictures her husband reading her letter, lying on his bed, a pillow propped behind his head, her parcel from home open beside him. The sweets are a mixture of extra strong mints, butterscotch and hard gums – his favourites, though knowing him, they'll be shared. The magazines he'll read once and pass around. The E45 cream and sunscreen he'll keep for himself. His biggest complaint about Afghanistan isn't the boredom or the danger of insurgents – it's the severity of the weather. The creams will help protect his skin against the elements. It's comforting to think that she's taking care of him in some small way.

She dresses for work in a black skirt and pale grey blouse and digs out a pair of jeans and a silver halterneck top for the evening. Pubs and clubs have never been her idea of fun but it's too late to back out now. Angela and Kath seem genuinely delighted that she's agreed to go out with them, and anything is better than another night alone in front of the TV.

She folds the jeans into a carrier bag. Standing in front of the full length mirror, she holds up the halterneck. Owen had been with her when she bought it.

'What do you think?' she'd asked him.

She must have tried on half a dozen tops by then, and he'd liked them all. 'Babes, you look beautiful in anything.' He grinned. 'Or nothing.'

Helen remembers the way the shop assistant had raised an eyebrow at her, as if to say, 'Good catch!'

He was a good catch, wasn't he? Still is. Despite their differences, and the fact that his job took him away from her for months at a time. He's still her Owen.

She drops the halterneck into the carrier bag, sits down at the dressing table and studies her face in the mirror. Maybe her mother had been right. Maybe there is 'something ghostly about redheads'. Right now, she looks as pale as a corpse. She didn't sleep well, but that's nothing new. She can't recall the last time she had a decent night's sleep. All she remembers is waking up in the early hours of the morning with her heart pounding, gasping for air.

Hastily, she applies her make-up and runs downstairs. She grabs her house keys but leaves the car keys in the wooden bowl by the front door. She'll take the train today. The journey into Bridgend only takes ten minutes, then she can jump on a bus or walk up through town if the rain holds off. Of course, it'll mean taking a taxi home tonight. She finds the card for a local cab firm and drops it into her bag.

Outside the sky is heavy and grey like wet sheep's wool. The air seems to cling to her face, adding to the feeling of claustrophobia she often experiences when walking these streets. She picks up her pace and makes it to the station with plenty of time to spare. The departure board shows that the train is running seven minutes late. When it finally pulls in, there isn't a spare seat left. She has to stand next to the toilet, which she hates. But at least the journey won't take long.

Next to her is a woman in her forties with a teenage girl who is clearly her daughter. The older woman is dressed in various shades of blue, with a turquoise necklace and matching ear-rings. The daughter is a riot of clashing colours – a green skirt over blue jeans, an orange vest over a purple shirt, and dyed scarlet hair which hangs heavily around her pale, sullen face.

As the train pulls out of the station, the mother turns to the girl. 'Do you like my outfit?' she asks, clearly proud of the choices she's made.

'Do you want my honest opinion?' the girl replies.

Something in her tone reminds Helen of herself when she was a teenager. Her mother had often described her as defiant, especially where Frank was concerned.

The older woman nods.

'You look weird. You're too colour-coordinated.'

The mother holds out a foot encased in a bright pink running shoe. 'My shoes don't match.'

'They're ugly,' the girl says flatly.

The older woman's smile fades. Then her face hardens. 'Maybe I like ugly,' she snaps. 'Remember your father.'

The day before he died, Richard Thomas stopped in for a pint at The Jolly Brewer pub in Park Street. The barmaid, Jane Morgan, remembered it well because he didn't seem his usual self. He barely spoke to her, simply asking for 'a pint of the usual'. When she tried to engage him in conversation, asking about his wife and daughter, he smiled weakly but said nothing. After paying for his pint of bitter and telling her to 'have one for yourself', he sat in the corner, barely acknowledging the nods and greetings from people he'd been happily chatting with only days before.

A few nights earlier, she'd watched him laughing and joking with some of the regulars. 'He was friends with everyone,' she said. 'There was that time he won money on the horses and insisted on buying a round for the entire pub. And his daughter – Helen – he never stopped talking about her. One night he came in with a pet rabbit he'd bought for her on the way home from work. You should have seen him. He was like a big kid.'

Miss Morgan confirmed that Mr Thomas was a regular at the pub. 'He came in most days. But that afternoon there was something different about him. He must have sat there for almost an hour, nursing his pint and staring into space. When he left, I remember thinking, *There goes a man who looks like he could use a hug*. He wasn't himself at all.'

When Mr Thomas failed to show up the following night, or the night after that, she assumed that he'd had a row with his wife and she'd put a stop to him coming to the pub. According to her niece Lisa Johns, who lived next door to the Thomases, Richard and his wife Mandy often argued. 'That Mandy Thomas is a right miserable cow,' Jane recalled Lisa saying a few weeks earlier. 'I pity that poor man, being married to her. She'd try the patience of a saint.'

What did Jane make of Mandy Thomas? 'I bumped into her a few times at Tesco's. She always seemed perfectly pleasant to me. A bit quiet, perhaps. But you never really know what goes on behind closed doors, do you? People aren't always who you think they are.'

According to Ms Morgan, Richard Thomas was a popular man – 'the life and soul of the party'. She was first informed of his death by Lisa Johns, who phoned her in tears that same afternoon. 'She ran to the bathroom and was physically sick,' Ms Morgan said.

Why was her niece so upset? 'Why wouldn't she be? It's a terrible thing to have happened. And teenage girls are easily upset. They take these things to heart.'

Asked if she could think of anyone who might hold a grudge against Mr Thomas, Ms Morgan shook her head vigorously. 'No. No one.'

***

Fridays at the office are always busy. Today is busier than most. With the monthly reports due and Natalie being even more demanding than usual, Helen doesn't even have time for lunch. Before she knows it, she's filing the last of the week's spreadsheets and shutting down her computer for the weekend.

If only she could shut her brain down as easily. She wishes she was going straight home. Maybe there'll be a letter from Owen waiting for her on the doormat. She pulls out her iPhone and checks her emails. Nothing.

Looking up, she sees Simon striding towards her, a serious look on his face. 'Everything okay, Helen?' he asks.

She slides her phone into her pocket. 'Yes, Mr Greenwood.'

'Good.' He hovers at her desk. 'And please, call me Simon.' He pauses. 'Natalie not around?'

'She left half an hour ago. Dentist.'

'Oh yes, of course. Right. Well, I wonder if we could have a quick word in my office?'

'Is there a problem?' Helen asks.

'She can't work late tonight, Simon,' Angela chips in. 'We've got a train to catch.'

'No, of course not,' he replies hastily. 'Monday morning, then?'

Helen nods meekly, quietly wondering what the boss could possibly want with her and fearing the worst.

He turns to Angela. 'So where are you ladies heading off to? Anywhere nice?'

'Cardiff', Angela replies. 'You can tag along with us if you like.' She grins mischievously.

'That's very kind of you. But the wife and I have plans. You know, Friday night and all that.'

'Does she keep you on a short leash, then?' Angela winks.

'I wouldn't put it quite like that!' He blushes and clears his throat. 'Well, you girls go ahead and get ready. I still have a few things to attend to.'

'Whatever you say, boss,' Angela replies. She turns to Helen and Kath. 'C'mon, girls! You heard the man. Let's get our warpaint on!'

They troop off to the ladies, where they change out of their work clothes and Angela helps Helen to touch up her make-up.

'You've got lovely skin,' she says, smoothing on a little blusher. 'I'd kill for a complexion like yours.'

'Do you think Mr Greenwood's going to fire me?' Helen asks.

'What?' Angela snorts. 'Is he hell! What gives you that idea?'

'Natalie caught me crying in here the other day. Maybe she told him.'

Angela raises an eyebrow. 'I wouldn't put it past her. But so what? You're a good worker and she's a lazy cow who barely lifts a finger. I swear she passes off half of your work as her own. Simon's not stupid. If anyone should watch their back around here, it's Natalie. So stop fretting.' She smiles. 'There. You're done! Now, how about a little something to get us in the mood?'

Reaching into her handbag, she produces a hip flask.

'You're terrible, Ange!' Kath giggles, grabbing the flask and taking a swig. 'I thought your body was a temple?'

Earlier, Angela had been extolling the virtues of her latest detox diet, which seemed to consist of juice, smoothies, raw vegetables and not a lot else.

'My body is a temple during the week,' Angela grins. 'At the weekend, it's a distillery on legs.' She snatches the flask from Kath and offers it to Helen.

'No, thanks.'

'C'mon,' Angela says. 'You won't catch anything.' She holds the flask up to Helen's nose. 'Go on. Try some.'

Cautiously, Helen sniffs the liquid inside. 'What is it?'

Angela laughs. 'It's a delicate blend of port and Blue WKD – otherwise known as Cheeky Vimto. It tastes like Vimto, but it gives you a nice buzz.'

Helen hesitates.

'Live a little,' Angela says. 'It's Friday night. Time to unwind. Take your mind off things.'

Helen feels a sudden flutter in her stomach.

Pull yourself together! she thinks. *You're going out with the girls. You're doing what normal people do. Where's the harm in that?*

She raises the flask to her lips and takes a sip. It tastes disgusting.

'Well?' says Angela.

Helen forces a smile. 'You're right. It's just like Vimto.'

CHAPTER NINE

'Look out, girls!' Angela announces. 'The entertainment has arrived.'

They're seated outside Las Iguanas, where she and Kath are making the most of the two-for-one cocktail offer. The table is covered in cocktail glasses – most of them empty.

Helen turns to look as a gaggle of girls in basques, fishnet stockings and feather boas come tottering into view. One wears a pink cowboy hat and has arms like sides of ham. The girl in the centre sports a bridal veil festooned with condoms.

'If you ever see me dressed like that, please shoot me,' Angela says.

'What was your hen night like, Helen?' Kath asks.

Helen forces a smile and reaches for her mojito. 'Nothing like that.'

'No, you've got a bit more class,' Angela says.

And far fewer friends, Helen thinks. Her hen night had been just her, her mother and a couple of soldiers' wives and girlfriends she barely knew then and hasn't seen since. At least this lot seem to be enjoying themselves.

'Right, where to next?' Angela asks.

'Let's go to Pulse!' Kath says.

Angela looks at her. 'What part of "I'm on the pull tonight" don't you understand, Kath? We are not going to a gay bar.'

'But I love the gays!' Kath wails. She's beginning to slur her words, and her tendency towards girlish overstatement is becoming more pronounced.

'I love them too, Kath,' Angela says. 'Just not in that way. Tonight I want a man who'll love me back. And me front!' She snorts with laughter at her own joke. 'Any other ideas? Helen?'

Helen struggles to find something sensible to say but her head is fuzzy from the alcohol. There are still four brightly coloured drinks left on the table, two of which are hers.

'Hang on!' Kath says. She rises unsteadily to her feet and turns to move, catching Angela's glass with the back of her hand. It rolls off the table and smashes to the ground.

'Oi! Watch my fucking bag!'

From the corner of her eye, Helen sees a flash of red leather as a woman at the next table snatches her bag from the floor and begins wiping at it furiously with a serviette. Nervously, she turns away, avoiding further eye contact.

'Sorry, love,' Kath calls over her shoulder. She points at Angela. 'Mind my drink. I'm off to wet my lettuce.'

'She's a daft cow,' Angela smiles as Kath disappears inside. 'But I love her to bits. She's okay, really.' She pauses. 'How about you? Are you okay?'

'I'm fine.'

'Only you can talk about it, y'know.'

Helen laughs nervously. 'Can I?'

'Of course you can,' Angela says. 'We're mates, aren't we?' She reaches across the table and squeezes Helen's hand.

'Thanks,' Helen says. She's never really thought of Angela as a mate before. She's always felt like a bit of a gooseberry where Angela and Kath are concerned. Two's company, three's a crowd. She's grateful to Angela for the gesture, and for making her feel included.

'I'm sure it can't be easy,' Angela says. 'But Owen will be home before you know it.'

Helen swallows hard. 'I still haven't heard from him.'

'But you'd know if something had happened to him, wouldn't you? Someone would have told you.'

Helen nods.

'Well, there you are, then,' Angela says. 'He'll be fine. I'm sure of it. Now, let's get these drinks down us before Kath comes back and knocks the whole bloody lot over.'

Time flies. Helen has lost count of the number of bars they've visited and the number of drinks she's had. She's feeling happy and light-headed. The train journey back to Bridgend passes in a blur of chatter and laughter. The next thing she knows, they're in a bar called The Phoenix and Kath is complaining that she feels nauseous. Angela brings her a glass of water before leading them over to a corner banquet where they sit staring up at the video screens above the bar.

'Send your texts to this number!' the screens read, followed by an offer to 'spice things up with a £5 curry special.'

Helen watches as the text messages start to appear.

'Holly and Carol out on the prowl,' says one.

'Kyle is the birthday boy tonight. Show him some love!' says another.

Someone goes past in a white T-shirt with a familiar green logo that should read 'Paramedic' but instead says 'Paralytic'. Another boy's T-shirt reads: 'You Look Like I Need A Drink'.

'Get him!' says Angela. 'He's got a jaw you could dig

roads with. Never mind a drink. What he needs is a plastic surgeon!'

Helen laughs. She can't remember the last time she felt so relaxed.

A familiar song comes on – 'I Gotta Feeling' by The Black Eyed Peas. The crowd roars its approval and she grins and throws out her arms, swept up in the optimism of the lyrics. Then Angela and Kath are hauling her onto the dance floor and everyone is singing along, assuring her that tonight will be a good, good night.

A blue light flashes outside the window. The first of the police riot vans has arrived.

By the time the crowd at The Phoenix starts to thin out and Angela suggests that they move on to The Railway Inn, Helen has forgotten all about work and Owen, and everything seems hysterically funny.

Angela's text on the video screen above the bar is funny. 'Kath and Ange on the lash,' it reads. 'Up for fun and looking lush!'

The riot vans lined up outside are funny, but not as funny as the community drugs van parked outside the chip shop.

'Quick, Kath!' Angela says. 'Go and ask if they've got any coke!'

The glass crunching underfoot is also funny. 'I feel like I'm walking on broken glass,' Kath warbles. She turns and frowns. 'Who sang that?'

'You did,' Angela replies, and they both fall about laughing.

People lurch by, voices raised, faces looming into view. But Helen isn't focussed on them. She's being pulled along in the wake of Angela and Kath, like something floating out to sea. She pictures herself buoyed up over deep dark water and realises that she isn't afraid.

The Railway is heaving. Gangs of drunken rugby boys throw themselves around the dance floor. Helen watches as a group of middle-aged women circle the men like vultures, flapping their arms and making strange pecking motions with their necks in an approximation of dancing.

'C'mon!' says Angela. 'Let's show them how it's done!'

She grabs Helen's hand and leads her onto the dance floor, bumping and grinding like a girl in an R&B video. At one point, she stumbles backwards and collides with one of the older women.

'Sorry!' Angela says, and pulls a face.

Helen giggles.

The woman scowls. 'What are you laughing at?'

But Helen isn't paying attention. Someone else has caught Angela's eye – a cute blond boy in a tight T-shirt. He has a broad smile and a tan, and one arm is supporting his friend, who can barely stand up and is swaying out of time with the music. Angela dances over towards them and boldly runs her fingers down the side of the blond boy's face and onto his chest. He says something in her ear and pushes her hand away. She shrugs, yawns dramatically and dances her way back towards Helen.

'Blondie said not tonight,' Angela says. 'His mate has just joined the army. It's their last big night out together, apparently.' She sees the look on Helen's face and changes the subject. 'C'mon, let's go to the bar.'

No sooner has Angela ordered a round than Kath groans. 'I think I'm going to be sick.'

'Perfect timing!' Angela says. 'Helen, stay and watch the drinks. I'll take her outside for some fresh air. We won't be long.'

Helen nods, though she's starting to feel a little

nauseous herself. She leans against the bar and tries to focus.

'Are you alright, love?' the barman asks when he returns with Angela's change. As he places the coins in her hand, Helen notices the tattoo on his forearm – a coat of arms, with a grinning skull and the words 'Death Before Dishonour'.

'I'm fine,' she mumbles. But she's not fine. Her limbs are heavy, and she seems to have lost control of her legs.

'Only you don't look too clever,' the barman says. 'Where's your friends? Don't tell me they've buggered off and left you.'

'No,' Helen replies. 'They'll be back in a minute.'

Five minutes pass. Then another five minutes, and another. There's still no sign of Angela and Kath.

The barman reappears. 'Looks like they've forgotten you,' he says.

A familiar fear of abandonment stirs in Helen's stomach. Where are they?

'Tell me to mind my own business,' the barman says. 'Only we get some right dickheads in here. And you don't look like you're on the pull.'

Helen's fingers clench around her wedding ring. 'I'm married.'

The barman grins. 'Husband let you off the leash for the night, has he?'

'He's away,' Helen says. She glances at the barman's tattoo. 'In Afghan.'

The barman's smile fades. 'Oh. I see.'

Their eyes lock for a moment.

'Well, you take care, love.'

Helen's throat tightens. She wishes Owen was here. He would never have left her alone in a strange bar.

'I'm sorry,' she says, and turns away. She reaches for

her handbag, trips and bumps into someone. A glass falls and shatters at her feet.

'Silly cow!' a woman's voice snaps. 'Watch where you're going!'

She doesn't look back. Frantically, she scans the room, pushing past crowds of people until finally – yes, there it is! – the door.

She stumbles outside, feels the crunch of broken glass underfoot and the cool air on her face. Her head spins. She takes a few deep breaths and tries to focus. A girl in a pink dress staggers past with her hand clasped to her mouth, vomit spilling through her fingers. A siren screams as an ambulance speeds by, blue lights flashing. Helen watches it disappear. Where the hell are Angela and Kath?

An older woman lurches towards her. She looks vaguely familiar. Her hair is blonde on top and black at the sides and has been pulled up into a huge, teased explosion. She holds a cigarette in one hand and a fast food carton in the other. Behind her, two other women are sucking furiously on their cigarettes. Struggling to focus, Helen stares at them. All three are dressed in outfits designed for girls half their age – short skirts, plunging necklines, bare shoulders.

'What are you looking at?' the woman with the exploding hair shouts as they approach.

'What?' Helen asks, confused. 'Nothing.'

'Oh, so you're saying I'm nothing, are you?'

'She was laughing at us before,' another voice says. 'On the dance floor'.

An image of Angela dancing flashes before Helen's eyes. 'I wasn't,' she says. 'I didn't mean –'

'Well, that's funny,' the blonde woman says. 'Cos you had a smirk on your face just now. Are you trying to start something? Cos if you are, just say.'

Helen shakes her head. She looks around for Angela and Kath, but they're nowhere to be seen. It's just her. Alone. Terrified.

The blonde woman comes closer, so close that Helen can smell the smoke on her breath and feel the heat from the carton she holds in her hand. She takes a long drag on her cigarette, leans forward and blows a thick cloud of smoke into Helen's face.

Helen coughs and retches.

'What's the matter?' the woman asks, stepping back and turning to her friends. 'Can't hold your drink?'

The other women cackle and draw closer. Their eyes are shining, mouths puckered in looks of barely contained glee. They can sense the violence in the air. Helen feels it too. Her heart hammers inside her chest.

The blonde woman takes another step forward. Helen sees the glowing tip of the cigarette edging towards her. Fear turns to panic and she closes her eyes, tries to pretend this isn't happening. Suddenly she's back at the school gates. Girls in purple nylon uniforms are crowding around her as someone empties the contents of her school bag over her head and a packet of tampons falls to the floor. 'She's on the rag!' someone screams. 'Helen's on the rag!' A burning sensation brings her back to the present with a jolt. Her face is on fire. She flinches, puts her hand to her cheek and opens her eyes.

'There you go, luv,' the woman sneers. 'That'll teach you!'

Helen feels something hot and sticky running down her face. Is she bleeding? She stares at her hand and sees a steaming mess of ... something. She feels the contents of her stomach rise up her throat and clasps her hand to her mouth.

'Get away from her, you bitch!'

No time to adjust her sights as a small woman with gold hoop earrings and a mane of black hair appears from nowhere and throws herself between them. The woman's body seems to rise up and leave the ground as her hand lashes out and the smoking woman's cigarette flies through the air.

'I'd do one if I was you!' she shouts.

The older woman holds her ground. 'This is none of your fucking business! This is between me and this stuck-up cunt!' She jabs a polished red fingernail inches from Helen's face.

'Yeah, well I'm making it my business. Now, get away from her or I'll rip your fucking face off!'

The older woman smirks. 'I'd like to see you try.'

'No, you wouldn't!' The younger woman thrusts her jaw out menacingly. 'Trust me. You don't want to mess with me.'

There's a moment's hesitation.

'Leave it, Linda,' one of the other women says. 'She's not worth it.'

The blonde woman backs down. Turning to her friend, she shrugs. 'Lucky for her I just had my nails done, or she'd be dead meat!'

The group clatter off down the street, leaving Helen and her knight in shining armour alone.

'Are you okay?' the strange woman asks.

Helen's whole body shakes.

'Christ, you're really freaked out, aren't you?'

Helen nods, blinking back tears.

'Let's have a look at your face.' She produces a tissue and begins wiping Helen's cheek.

'Am I bleeding?' Helen asks.

The woman frowns, then laughs. 'Bleeding? No, that old cow shoved curry sauce in your face. Your cheek looks a bit red, but that's all.'

She continues wiping and, when she's done, she cups Helen's face in her hands and stares into her eyes.

'You're going to be okay,' she says. 'Are you pissed? You are pissed, aren't you. Where do you live? Do you remember where you live?'

Helen mumbles, 'Brynmenyn.'

'I'm from Sarn,' the woman says. 'So we're practically neighbours. I'm Siân by the way. And before you say anything, I've heard it all before.'

Helen looks at her blankly.

'Siân from Sarn!' The woman flashes a grin. 'Like it's some bloody big joke! C'mon, there's a taxi over there. Let's get you home.'

CHAPTER TEN

'Morning, Corporal!'

The voice comes from behind a large punch bag. Owen is surprised to find someone else in the gym this early in the morning. Surprised, and a little disappointed. One of the few compensations for the insomnia he's suffered these past few weeks is spending these early hours alone with his thoughts.

The fact that the voice belongs to Collins only adds to his irritation. He doesn't have anything against the lad, but since the run-in with Jackson a few nights ago, he's been conscious of the tension between them and annoyed at feeling drawn into someone else's dispute. As much as he dislikes Jackson, Owen resents Collins for putting him in such a difficult position. He warned the lad to stay out of Jackson's way. If Collins chooses to ignore his advice, that's his look-out.

'What's up?' he says. 'Couldn't sleep?'

Collins takes a jab at the bag. 'A soldier never sleeps, Corporal. Sleep is for sissies.'

Owen smiles. 'You'd better not let Jackson hear you talking like that! You might give him ideas.'

The lad continues punching. 'I don't care what Jackson thinks of me. I'm as much of a man as him. Or you.' He lifts his head and swipes the sweat with the back of his hand.

Owen meets his gaze. 'I don't doubt it'.

'Prove it, then.'

'What?'

'Go a few rounds with me.'

'No, you're alright, thanks.'

Collins grins. He has a soft, youthful face. But his jaw is strong and there's a determined look in his eyes. 'What's the matter?' he asks. 'Afraid I'll beat you?'

'I didn't come here to spar with anyone,' Owen says. And yet here he is, already sparring – verbally, at least. Jackson may be trouble, but Collins certainly knows how to wind a man up.

The gym is housed in a huge tent and is open around the clock, though it's rare to find anyone here quite this early. It was dark when Owen left his bed and walked the short distance in his sweatpants and T-shirt. Now the sun is starting to rise, but the air is still cool. The air conditioners are on full blast, but they won't be needed for another hour or two.

For a battlefield gym, the place is surprisingly well equipped – more so than the one back in Iraq. Soldiers there were used to training without any equipment whatsoever, using their own body weight to maintain the level of fitness required for the job. Owen has seen men perform squats with fellow soldiers on their backs, or improvise with a small ledge for tricep dips. A gym like this is something of a luxury. There are free weights and some multi-gym equipment, mats, punch bags and even a few treadmills.

There's one big difference between this and a regular gym, and it's this Owen thinks of as he watches Collins take another jab at the punch bag. Here, a shower means a ship shower, rather like a portaloo. You step in, run a small amount of water, soap yourself up, and rinse off. Water in the camp is strictly rationed. There's no time to enjoy the sensation of hot water on tired muscles. But at least these showers are private. Try as he might, Owen isn't entirely comfortable with the idea of showering next to a man who might be gay.

Over by the treadmills is a wooden shelf where Collins has placed his helmet and body armour. Owen has left his own body armour in his tent. It's only a short distance away, and he'd rather leg it back than lug it around with him. The last thing he wants after a heavy workout is to be weighed down with his kit.

He walks over to the treadmill and punches in a few numbers. The machine starts up and he steps on, pacing himself slowly at first, then gradually building up speed. Soon he can feel beads of sweat breaking out on his forehead. He wipes it with his forearm and increases the resistance. The pounding of his footsteps becomes louder and his breath shorter. His legs and lungs begin to ache. He's in good physical shape, but he likes to push himself to the limits of his endurance. It's a hangover from his boot camp days. But working his body like this feels a lot better than climbing ropes or crawling through the mud on his hands and knees.

He settles into a pace and lets his mind wander. So much has changed since he first swapped his unhappy childhood for the rigours of basic training. He's made a life for himself. He has a wife and a house. Helen is his family now, not the mother who started drifting away when he was small or the father he regarded with a detachment far colder and more final than hatred. One day soon they'll have a baby, and the transition from troubled child to happy family man will be complete. But for now there's the army – the men he serves with and on whose courage he depends. Men like Collins. Even men like Jackson.

The young private is still jabbing away at the punch bag. Owen wonders who he's picturing as he delivers those punches. Jackson, perhaps? Or is he just trying to prove a point, to demonstrate that he's every bit the man he claims to be? Owen has met lads like Collins before – new to the army, never having shot a man or been in the line of fire, always acting like they had something to prove, always wanting to 'get some'. They calmed down eventually. The lucky ones, anyway.

Abruptly, the boy stops punching and walks towards him.

'Well, that's me done,' he says. His face is flushed, his short dark hair soaked with sweat.

Owen nods, saving his breath.

'So what's on the menu today?' Collins asks. 'Another day of sitting on our arses doing fuck all?'

Owen smiles despite himself. 'Welcome to the world of war.'

The boy grins. 'See you later in the tanning shop then?'

'Yeah, maybe.'

As Collins heads off in the direction of the shower, Owen turns off the treadmill and makes his way over to the shoulder press. Upper body and back strength is vital when you spend so much of your time weighed down with body armour, weapon, ammo and a rucksack. He's straining under the weight of his third set when the siren sounds. It's like a car alarm, loud and insistent. But this isn't someone breaking into next door's Volvo. The base is under attack.

Seconds later, there's the tell-tale whistle and warbling sound of an incoming rocket. Muscle memory kicks in and he throws himself face down on the floor, covering his head with his hands. Rockets are designed to hit the ground at a low angle, sending red hot shards of metal casing through the air, ripping through everything in their path. Without his body armour he has no means of protection. His heart races as he pictures himself after the blast – squirming around in a crimson, sticky mess, chunks of flesh missing, bones hanging out, body fluids soaking into the Afghan soil.

But the impact never comes. From outside the tent, he hears half a dozen voices shouting simultaneously. He pictures the trucks peppered with holes, their windows blown in. Dawn raids had been a regular method of attack in Iraq, but it's the first time he's experienced one here. No wonder the voices sound panicked.

He raises his head and sees Collins half dressed, running towards his body armour. There's another whistling sound, closer this time. Owen looks up over his shoulder. Horrified, he sees a second rocket come tearing through the roof of the tent. It lands at the far end of the gym.

'Stay down!' Collins shouts.

Their eyes meet.

There's a moment's delay as Collins finishes kitting up, then the younger soldier runs towards him.

Owen ducks his head. Moments later, he feels the full weight of the younger man's body as he throws himself on top of him, forming a human shield. They lie in this position for what seems like an eternity but is probably no more than a minute. Owen waits for the explosion, but none comes. There's no deafening bang, no blinding flash, no red hot metal tearing through flesh. The rocket doesn't detonate.

Finally, he feels Collins exhale. With his warm breath on Owen's ear, he whispers, 'I think we're okay.'

CHAPTER ELEVEN

As she regains consciousness, Helen hears the sound of someone moving about downstairs. Her first thought is that Owen is in the kitchen preparing one of his famous fry-ups. Then she remembers. Owen is in Afghanistan. She went out drinking with the girls from work. Some women attacked her in the street, and another woman came to her rescue.

Footsteps sound on the stairs. The floorboard on the landing creaks, there's a knock on the bedroom door and there the woman is, grinning. 'You're alive, then!'

Her skin is tanned, her hair thick and black. She's dressed in a simple white vest top and jeans. Though physically small, she seems larger than life, like someone famous. Her eyes are dark and seem to glitter as she speaks. When she smiles, her teeth are startlingly white.

Helen tries to smile back, but it's too much of an effort. She's been hungover before, but never like this. Her head is pounding. There's a terrible taste in her mouth. And there's something unnerving about this strange woman standing in the doorway to her bedroom. She doesn't know her. She can't even remember her name.

'I'm Siân,' the woman says. 'Remember? I was there when that cow shoved her chips and curry sauce in your face.'

Helen puts her hand to her cheek.

'You're alright,' Siân says, stepping into the room. 'It looks a bit red, but it'll soon fade. I brought you home in a taxi last night. You weren't looking too clever so I stayed over to make sure you were okay. I crashed on the sofa. I hope you don't mind.'

Helen tries to take it all in, but all she can feel is the pain in her head and a flush of embarrassment. She can't remember getting home. But at least she is home. She's in her own bed. She's safe. And it's all thanks to the woman standing a few feet away.

'Thank you,' she says. 'I'm Helen.'

'I know. I couldn't get much sense out of you last night, but at least you knew your name and address.' Siân shrugs. 'Now, I'm not one for outstaying my welcome. So if you want me to clear off, just say. I won't be offended.'

Helen hesitates for a moment. Then her manners get the better of her. 'No,' she says. 'Stay for a bit.'

'Okay. But tell me when you want me to sling my hook. You've probably got things to do.'

Helen smiles despite herself.

'Not really. Just as well. I don't think I'm in any fit state.'

'You'll be fine in a few hours. It's just a hangover. And the shock. You did seem pretty freaked out.'

'Weren't you scared?'

Siân shakes her head. 'Nah. It takes a lot to scare me. I'm from Sarn, remember?' She holds her fists up like a boxer. 'I've dealt with a lot worse than them before.'

Helen laughs.

'So how come you were out on your own? Where's your husband?'

She must sense Helen's discomfort because she adds quickly, 'I saw the wedding photo downstairs. Tell me to mind my own business if you like. I'm just a naturally curious person.'

'He's away,' Helen says. 'On business.'

'Army business?' Siân smiles. 'Sorry. I saw that photo too.'

'He's on tour,' Helen says, then quickly changes the subject. 'My head's killing me. I think I've got some paracetamol somewhere.' She starts to haul herself out of bed, then suddenly feels self-conscious about exposing her bare thighs in front of a stranger. Silly really, after the show she's already made of herself.

'Stay there,' says Siân. 'I'll bring you something better.'

She turns and disappears. Minutes later she's back with a glass of water. She drops two large white tablets into the glass.

Helen props herself up and watches as the water fizzes. 'What's that?'

'Solpadeine. It's a mixture of paracetamol and codeine. The codeine works like endorphins.'

Helen looks at her blankly.

'Endorphins. Y'know, like the buzz you get at the gym?'

Helen doesn't know. She hasn't been near a gym in years. 'And you carry these with you?'

'Only when I'm planning on getting completely wasted.'

'But you weren't, were you? Wasted?'

'The night was still young.'

Helen looks at her. 'Sorry I spoilt your night.'

'Don't be daft. Now are you going to get that down you, or not?'

Helen raises the glass to her lips and takes a sip of the cloudy liquid. 'It tastes bitter.'

Siân smiles. 'Mind if I sit down?'

Without waiting for an answer, she perches herself on the foot of the bed. 'Do you know the best cure for a hangover? Porridge. Warm milk, a bit of honey. Works wonders. I can make some for you if you like.'

Helen pictures the sorry state of her kitchen cupboards. She hasn't been to the supermarket in over a week. The only cereal she has is cornflakes. She's even out of milk.

Siân must have read her mind. 'I'll just pop out and get a few things,' she says, leaping to her feet. 'It's no trouble. The keys are downstairs. I'll be back before you know it.'

Before Helen can put up any kind of protest, she's gone.

The sunlight burns through the blinds, illuminating the room and the tiny dust motes that swirl and eddy in the air. Helen hears the front door slam and lies back on the pillow. She closes her eyes and tries to gather her thoughts. Frank was right. She should never have gone out. It isn't safe. Anything could have happened to her last night. She could have been robbed, or raped, or ended up in the local paper with her face slashed open, like that woman a few weeks ago. Thank God Siân came along when she did.

But you don't even know who this woman is! And she just walked off with your house keys!

Helen opens her eyes.

Her handbag! She can't remember where it is. Everything is inside that bag. Her purse. Her phone. Her credit cards. She scans the room. Nothing. She throws back the duvet, pulls on her dressing gown and runs downstairs. The bag isn't where she usually leaves it, hanging at the bottom of the stairs. For a split second she has the awful sinking feeling that her fears have been confirmed. Then she spots the bag lying on the kitchen table. Opening it, she's hit with a mixture of relief and shame. Her purse and phone are still safely inside. The phone is switched on. There isn't a single missed call or text message.

So much for Angela and Kath looking out for her. And to think she was even starting to consider Angela a friend.

The last time Helen had brought a friend home she was twelve. It was the year she'd changed schools, not long after they'd moved house and her mother had taken up with Frank. She'd had friendships before then. There'd been birthday parties, sleepovers, invitations to tea. But everything changed when her father died. She still remembers the headteacher making the announcement during morning assembly – and the way everyone turned to look at her and then looked away. It was as if she'd committed some awful crime or caught some dreadful disease.

Rebecca Green was a loner like her, but tougher and more glamorous than the rest of the girls in year seven. Her black hair was always backcombed and her purple nylon uniform had been taken in at the sides and shortened to reveal a few extra inches of thigh. She talked back to the teachers and wore a knowing smirk that came from being a few months older and having a boyfriend who was rumoured to ride a motorbike.

The day she sat next to her in the school canteen, Helen could hardly believe it. She remembers the looks she'd got from the other girls that day, the way they'd stared at her as if they were seeing her for the first time. In a matter of days, she'd gone from being the least interesting girl in her class to the one everyone was suddenly eager to make friends with. Of course she'd known all along that it wasn't really her they were interested in. But it was a good feeling – while it lasted.

A few weeks later, she'd invited Rebecca back to her house for tea. Frank had arrived home early from work and was sitting at the kitchen table with a can of lager. Helen had tried to hurry Rebecca upstairs to her room.

'Not so fast,' Frank said. 'It's not often you bring friends home. What's your name then, love?'

Rebecca tossed her hair and pouted her lips. 'Rebecca. But you can call me Becky.'

Frank slapped his thigh. 'What do you think, Amanda? Can we call this young lady Becky?'

Helen's mother was standing at the kitchen sink, noisily filling the kettle. 'I'll make us some tea. Or perhaps Rebecca would prefer squash?'

Rebecca wound a lock of hair around her finger. 'I'd rather have a can of lager.'

Frank chuckled. 'You're a bit young for that.'

'Then just a sip of yours?'

Another chuckle. 'How about a shandy? What do you say, Amanda? A glass of shandy for the girls?'

Her mother looked flustered, twisting a tea towel in her hands. 'I'm not having children drinking in my house.'

'C'mon, Amanda. A glass of shandy won't hurt.'

Rebecca giggled. 'Your dad's a right laugh!'

'He's not my father!' Helen shouted, before running upstairs to her room and slamming the door. She sat on her bed fighting back tears. Why did her father have to die? Why did Frank have to be here? By the time her mother had coaxed her back down, her new friend had gone.

Helen hasn't thought about Rebecca Green in years. Picturing her now, it suddenly strikes her that Rebecca bore a striking resemblance to Siân.

She's stepping out of the shower when she hears the key in the door and Siân's voice call up the stairs.

'It's only me. Sorry I was a bit longer than I thought. Give me ten minutes and we'll have you on the mend.'

Helen wraps herself in her dressing gown and wipes the condensation from the bathroom mirror. A ghost face stares back at her.

Great, she thinks. *If my mother could see me now*.

But Siân had been telling the truth. There's no blistering, no serious burn marks, just a redness to her cheek. It could have been a lot worse. It scares her to think what might have happened had Siân not appeared when she did. But she had, and that's all that matters. Think positive. Put on a brave face.

There are dark circles under her eyes. She applies some moisturizer and concealer. It seems pointless to bother with make-up, but suddenly she finds herself reaching for some foundation and then pencilling in her eyebrows. Some mascara goes on next, and a hint of blusher. Then, when she's satisfied that she no longer resembles the living dead, she pulls on a pair of jeans and a black top and heads downstairs.

Siân is standing at the hob, stirring a pan of milk. She turns as Helen approaches. 'Wow! What a transformation! You look stunning!'

'Don't be silly,' Helen says. She's never been very good at taking compliments. And there's something disconcerting about seeing another woman cooking in her kitchen. She feels like a guest in her own home.

'Seriously,' Siân insists. 'You look great. What was her name? Helen something. They made a film about her – with Brad Pitt.'

Helen looks at her blankly.

'That's it!' Siân says. 'Helen of Troy. The face that launched a thousand ships!'

Helen blushes. 'More like the face that launched a thousand chips!'

Their eyes meet. Then Helen starts laughing, gently at first, then louder as she finds confidence in that fact that she just cracked a joke – and not just any joke, but a joke about something so traumatic, she really shouldn't be laughing at all. This isn't her usual way of coping with things. This isn't her. Yet she finds it strangely liberating.

Siân looks startled, then she starts laughing too. Soon they're both doubled over in fits of giggles. They laugh until their faces are flushed and tears roll down their cheeks.

Siân holds up her hands in mock surrender. 'Enough!' she says. 'Stop!'

Helen wipes her eyes and grips the back of a chair to steady herself. She can't remember the last time she laughed like this, so hard that she can barely catch her breath.

'We shouldn't laugh,' Siân says. 'That old cow could have really hurt you.'

'I know,' Helen replies, remembering the women closing in on her and the absolute terror she felt.

Siân stares at her solemnly. 'But you're okay?'

Helen nods. 'I am.'

'You never told me what you were doing out on your own. Wouldn't your husband mind?'

'I was with friends. But they disappeared.'

Siân raises an eyebrow. 'Some friends.'

'Well, they're more work colleagues really.'

Helen thinks of Angela. She seemed so sincere when they had that talk in Cardiff. How could she have just abandoned her like that?

'I don't really have friends,' she hears herself say.

Siân grins. 'You do now.'

Helen smiles, looks up at the window, sees that it's just starting to rain.

CHAPTER TWELVE

'Hey, Corporal! Wait up!'

Owen is just leaving the cookhouse. He doesn't need to look round to know who the voice belongs to.

'Are you alright?' Collins asks as he falls in beside him.

'Of course. Why shouldn't I be?'

'I meant after what happened earlier, at the gym.'

'What are you getting at, Collins?'

'That rocket attack. It was pretty hairy.'

'I've lived through worse.'

'Exciting, though.'

There's that cocky grin again. Part of Owen wants to wipe the smile off the lad's face, but part of him feels obliged to smile back. What Collins did had taken guts. Owen owes him, if not his life, then certainly his respect. He stops in his tracks. 'Can I ask you something?'

'Sure. Shoot away.'

'Is it true?'

'Is what true?'

'What Jackson said. About you being, y'know…?'

Collins holds his gaze. 'Would it make any difference to you if it was?'

'Your personal life's your own business. But I wouldn't go round making a big deal about it if I were you. Some of the other lads aren't so open-minded.'

Owen wonders how open-minded he is himself, really. He can't deny that he's intrigued by Collins, even flattered by the attention. But the fact that he's flattered also makes him uneasy. What does it say about him? Any fool can see that Collins is good-looking – broad shoulders, strong jawline, piercing blue eyes. But is that the same as finding him attractive? Owen has never looked at another man in that way before, so he has no way of knowing. He wants to end the conversation there, but Collins won't let it rest.

'Why are you asking me this now?' he demands.

'I'm just trying to warn you to exercise a little caution.'

'You want me to pretend that I'm not gay?'

Embarrassed, Owen looks around.

'It's okay,' Collins whispers. 'Nobody heard.' He smiles. 'You can say the word, you know. It's not catching.'

'Very funny. You're not the first gay person I've ever met.'

'So why be so coy about it? You could have said something when it all kicked off. Why didn't you ask me then?'

'I didn't think it was any of my business.'

'And now it is? Why? Because of what happened at the gym?'

Owen recalls the weight of the young man on his back and feels himself colouring. 'Nothing happened at the gym.'

Collins raises an eyebrow. 'Seriously? You call that nothing?'

'The rocket didn't explode.'

'You had a narrow escape, you mean.' Another knowing smile.

Owen bristles. What's the lad's problem? He seems determined to make an issue of this when, really, there's nothing else to be said. He'd shown courage. There'd been a certain level of physical intimacy between them. But it was no more than one would expect under the circumstances. It doesn't mean anything.

'Listen, Collins,' Owen says. 'What you did back there – it was brave, and I'm grateful. But that's all it was.'

The lad nods. 'If you say so, Corporal.'

They walk in silence for a few minutes. Around them, men are filing in and out of the cookhouse. Owen is relieved to see that Jackson isn't among them. The last thing he needs now is an audience. Still, it's better to have this conversation out here in the open than be caught with Collins somewhere more private. He knows how quickly rumours can spread, especially where someone like Jackson is concerned. Already there are murmurs about Armstrong being gay, despite several men testifying to the fact that he'd left behind a grieving widow and child.

'I'd stay out of Jackson's way if I were you.' Owen lowers his voice. 'I know him. He's trouble.'

'He doesn't scare me.'

'He should. He could make life very difficult for you.'

Collins opens his mouth to say something but Owen cuts him off. 'I know what it says on paper. I know what the official line is. But that doesn't mean shit out here. If someone like Jackson wants to stir up trouble, there's not a lot I can do to protect you.'

'I wasn't asking you to,' Collins replies. 'But it's good to know you care.'

'Don't push it,' Owen says. Christ, the lad's annoying. It's a wonder he made it through basic training in one piece. Owen can only begin to imagine what someone like

Collins must have gone through to get where he was today.

'Why the army?' he asks.

'It wasn't so I could throw myself at guys like you, if that's what you're thinking.'

Owen feels himself flushing again. 'I wasn't,' he says. Or was he? He swallows. 'So why then?'

'Same as everyone else. It's a job. And I needed to get away.'

'From your family?'

'From my boyfriend.'

'Oh.' Owen lowers his eyes. 'Right.'

'Aren't you going to ask me why?'

'Not if it's personal.'

'It's no more personal than you talking about your wife,' Collins says. 'You do talk about her, don't you? Only the other lads go on about their wives and girlfriends all the time. I've hardly heard you mention yours.'

'I'm not like those other lads.'

'I didn't think you were.' Again, that knowing smile.

'You know what I mean,' Owen snaps. He pauses. 'So what about this friend of yours?'

'Boyfriend, you mean. What about him?'

'What's he like?'

'Nothing like you. Though there is a certain physical resemblance.'

'Very funny. You said you needed to get away from him. Why?'

Collins shrugs. 'He was too clingy. I need my own space. But you'd know all about that.'

'Would I?'

'Why else did you join the army?'

Owen glares at him. 'To serve my country. Or didn't they teach you that in training?'

'Relax!' Collins grins and punches his arm. 'I'm just messing with you.'

'Yeah, well, leave it out!' Owen looks around. There are still a few soldiers milling about, but nobody is paying any attention to him and Collins. They're too preoccupied. This morning's mortar attack is still fresh in everyone's minds. There were no casualties, but nerves are on edge. There's a heightened sense of awareness as men who've been bored out of their skulls for weeks await orders. Already there's talk of stepping up desert patrols.

Collins must have read his mind. 'Looks like we'll finally see some action.'

'Looks like.'

'I'll leave you to it, then.' He gives a sharp nod and turns to walk away, then stops. 'And Corporal?'

Owen sighs. 'What?'

'About that boyfriend. He's history.'

CHAPTER THIRTEEN

'The weather's clearing,' Siân says.

Helen looks up.

They're seated on opposite sides of the kitchen table. Outside the clouds have lifted and sunlight sparkles on the tiny beads of rain still clinging to the window.

'How are you feeling?'

'Much better, thanks.'

'I told you that porridge would do the trick. It's good you threw up last night. At least the worst of it was out of your system.'

Helen's scalp prickles. 'I vomited?'

'Don't worry. It wasn't in the taxi. It was when we got home. I held your hair for you as you chucked your guts down the loo.'

Shame burns Helen's cheeks and she buries her head in her hands. 'I don't remember that.'

'We've all been there,' Siân says. 'The important thing is that you're feeling better. Now, do you fancy doing something?'

Helen shrugs. 'I suppose I should get some food in.'

'No need. I saw your cupboards were empty so I picked up a few extras for you at Sainsbury's. There's some chicken breasts in the fridge, and a few bags of mixed salad.'

'But you shouldn't have.'

'It's no bother.'

Helen reaches for her handbag. 'How much do I owe you?'

'You don't. It's a gift.'

'But that's not right,' Helen protests.

'Rubbish,' Siân says, pushing her chair back. 'I'll tell you what's not right. It's not right that your so-called friends dumped you last night. It's not right that those old slappers attacked you. There's plenty of things in life that are not right. This is just someone doing something nice for you. Accept it for what it is.'

'But you've already done more than enough for me,' Helen says. 'I feel awkward accepting things from –' She nearly says 'a stranger' but catches herself just in time. 'From someone I've only just met.'

Siân grabs her jacket, which is hanging on the back of a chair. It's made of soft black leather and looks expensive. From one of the inside pockets, she produces a wallet and opens it to reveal a thick wedge of notes.

'I don't need you to pay me back,' she says. 'I'm flush, see?'

Helen's first instinct is to ask why anyone would carry so much cash around. Then she remembers her mother asking her father the same thing. 'What do you need all that money for, Richard? What about these bills? Richard! I'm talking to you!'

Siân smiles. 'If it makes you feel better I can always come back later and help you eat it.'

'Why? Where are you going?'

'I'm not. We are. We should get you out of the house for a bit. Go for a walk. Get some fresh air in your lungs.'

Helen hesitates. 'Don't you want a shower first? And some clean underwear?'

'I showered earlier, while you were sleeping. And I

always carry a clean pair of knickers with me.' Siân winks. 'You know, just in case I get lucky.'

She reaches under the table and holds up a worn red leatherette rucksack. It's roughly the size of an overnight bag, with half a dozen external pockets fastened with zips and buckles. The material has lost its sheen and is scratched in places, revealing the lining. The condition of the bag seems so at odds with Siân's groomed appearance, Helen finds herself wondering if it has some sentimental value, like the scarf her father had given her shortly before he died and she'd refused to take off for months afterwards.

'I don't remember you having a bag last night,' she says. Though even as she speaks, she has a vague recollection of seeing a red bag somewhere.

'I'm surprised you can remember anything from last night,' Siân replies. 'You were totally wasted.'

Helen blushes and reaches to clear the empty bowls.

But Siân is already on her feet. 'Leave that to me,' she says, gathering them up and carrying them over to the sink. She turns on the tap and looks over her shoulder. 'You go and put some shoes on. I'll be done in two ticks.'

Statement from Jackie Evans
Aged 37
Friend of Richard and Mandy Thomas

There are conflicting accounts of Mr Thomas's movements between the hours of 5pm and 7pm on the night before he died. According to barmaid Jane Morgan, he left The Jolly Brewer no later than 5 p.m. We know from Jane's niece Lisa Johns that he arrived home shortly after 7 p.m. [see following statement].

93

Another witness, a Mrs Jackie Evans, recalled seeing Mr Thomas heading towards the Black Path – the historical footpath which runs close to the house where Mr Thomas lived with his wife and daughter. Mrs Evans described herself as a close friend of the Thomases. 'I sometimes babysit for their daughter, Helen,' she said. 'She calls me Auntie Jackie.'

At around 6.20 p.m., Mrs Evans was out walking her dog and saw Mr Thomas approaching the path, a known hangout for local teenagers. 'He had a carrier bag with him,' Mrs Evans said. 'He looked as if he'd just been shopping and was heading home. Which is why I thought it seemed a bit odd.'

Asked if she had spoken to Mr Thomas, Mrs Evans explained that he was some distance away. Did she have any idea what might be in the carrier bag? Did it look heavy? 'I really couldn't say.' When questioned further, Mrs Evans retracted her previous statement, saying she couldn't be certain that it was Mr Thomas she saw. 'I had my back to him most of the time. I was more concerned about the dog. He's a rescue dog. He needs a lot of attention.' Could she think of any reason why Mr Thomas would be headed towards the Black Path? 'I really don't know.'

What we do know is that when Mr Thomas arrived home shortly after 7 p.m., he didn't have a carrier bag with him and he was in an extremely agitated state.

***

As she steps outside, Helen has a flashback to the night before. She's searching for her house keys, and Siân is talking to the taxi driver. Helen can't picture the driver, but she remembers opening her handbag and stumbling as she climbed out of the car, and the sound of metal on stone as the keys hit the pavement. What a mess she must have been. What an embarrassing drunken mess.

'Okay?' Siân asks brightly.

'Fine,' Helen replies. She looks at the red rucksack slung over Siân's arm. 'Are you sure you want to carry that bag? You can always leave it here and pick it up later.'

'You're alright,' Siân says, hoisting the bag onto her back. 'I'd rather hold onto it.'

Helen double locks the front door and slides the keys into her front pocket. 'Right. Which way?'

'We can walk over to Sarn and admire the architectural wonders of South Wales.' Siân's face suggests that she's being ironic. 'Or we can head towards Blackmill. That way there's a chance we might see something that's not made out of concrete.'

'It's a bit far,' Helen says. Blackmill is two miles away.

'We can always take your car.'

Helen glances at the car parked outside her house. How does Siân know she drives?

'Only joking,' Siân adds quickly. 'We don't have to walk all the way. We can just follow the river for a bit.' She directs Helen attention down the street, to the corner where two rows of houses are divided by a grass track which leads to an old railway line. 'If we cut through there and follow the railway line, there's a cycle path that runs by the river. We can walk up as far as the ford.'

Helen looks at her blankly.

Siân frowns. 'You must have been to the ford. Up by the farm.'

Helen shakes her head. 'No.'

'And how long have you lived here?'

'A few years.'

Siân's eyes widen in mock amazement. 'You need to get out more,' she says, and flashes a grin. 'C'mon. It won't take us long. Twenty minutes tops.'

They head down the street, cut between the buildings and begin walking along the disused railway line. The tracks are red with rust. Grass grows between the concrete sleepers.

Siân skips ahead and jumps up onto the track, placing one foot in front of the other like a tightrope walker. 'I used to love playing dare on the railway line when I was little,' she calls over her shoulder. 'No-one could beat me. Not even the boys.'

'Not this one?' Helen asks. By the looks of it, this line hasn't been used in decades.

'Nah. The main one. Through town. Up by the Black Path.'

'You played there?'

'Yeah. Why not?'

'I wasn't allowed to play there. My parents said it was dangerous.'

Siân steps off the track. 'Maybe they were right. A woman was raped there a few months ago.' She pauses, then shrugs. 'Good job nobody tried any of that shit with me. I'd have had their balls for earrings.'

The cycle path is busier than Helen was expecting. It's not just the cyclists, though there are plenty of them – men speeding past in their lycra, women pedalling by with friendly nods and baskets full of shopping. There are also joggers and people out walking their dogs.

The sun is bright and the sound of the river soothes away the remains of Helen's hangover. Siân was right, she thinks. The fresh air is doing her good. She wonders why she and Owen never take walks like this. Maybe when he returns home they should make a point of getting out more and enjoying the countryside, instead of spending so much time holed up indoors.

'Penny for your thoughts?' says Siân.

'I was just thinking how nice it is.'

'Nice?' Siân scoffs. 'Is that the worst word in the English language or what? A *nice* walk. A *nice* cup of tea. A *nice* family. *Nice*!'

Helen feels herself colouring.

'I'm just pulling your leg.' Siân smiles. 'So what about me? Am I *nice*? Think very carefully before you answer.'

Helen laughs warily. 'You seem okay.'

'Well, that's good to know. You seem rather *nice* too. So that's us sorted.'

They walk in silence for a while. Soon they come to a farm gate. Behind the gate lies a field, with a view of the river crossing and an old farmhouse. As they approach, a large brown horse comes galloping over and sticks its head over the fence, greeting them with a loud snort.

Siân reaches up and pets the horse's nose. 'Who's a good boy?' she says in a soft, girly voice. 'I bet you want an apple, don't you? Maybe next time we'll bring you one.' She turns to Helen. 'Isn't he gorgeous?'

Helen smiles but keeps her distance. Large animals make her nervous. 'So tell me a bit about yourself.'

Siân begins stroking the horse's neck. 'Well, as you can see, I love horses. I had one when I was a kid. He was called Rocky, like the boxer. Then one day he broke his leg and we had to have him put down.'

'I'm sorry.'

'Don't be. It's all part of growing up, isn't it? So what else do you want to know?'

'Anything. What do you do?'

Siân snorts. 'Is that how you define people? By what they do for a living?'

Helen blushes. 'No.'

'Good. Because I like to think there's a bit more to me than that'. Siân pats the horse's head and steps away from the gate. 'C'mon. It's not far now.'

Helen pictures the thick wodge of notes in Siân's wallet. 'But you must have a job?'

'I'm what you call a member of the leisured classes. And before you ask, I'm not on benefits.'

'Sorry. I didn't mean –'

'It's okay.' Siân grins. 'There's nothing else to say, really. Trust me. It's boring. So what about your job? Do you like it?'

'I do,' Helen replies. 'I'm not some high powered executive or anything. I work for a training company. It's mostly admin. But I enjoy it.'

'I bet you were good at school. Which one did you go to?'

'Brynteg. You?'

'I didn't. Not much anyway. It was okay until I was about fourteen, but after that I couldn't really see the point. My dad said I had a problem with authority.'

'What did you do?'

Siân shrugs. 'Nothing much. I just bunked off. I wasn't expelled or anything. Every now and then they'd haul my dad in and threaten to have me thrown out, but he always talked them round. He was really cool, my dad. I learned more from him than I did from any of those fuckwit teachers.'

Helen notices that Siân refers to her father in the past

tense. She remembers her own father collecting her at the school gate, the walks home via the sweetshop, the promises not to tell her mother or let the sweets ruin her appetite.

'What about you?' asks Siân.

'Sorry?'

'What were you like at school? Were you a swot? I bet you were! You've got that look about you.'

Helen doesn't know whether to take this as an insult or an opportunity to impress. 'I did okay at maths. And I liked business studies. But I wasn't top of the class or anything.'

Siân stops walking. 'Why do you do that?'

'Do what?'

'Put yourself down all the time. I bet you did a lot better at school than you're letting on.'

Helen struggles to find the right words. 'I just didn't want you thinking –'

'What? That you're cleverer than me?' Siân laughs. 'That wouldn't bother me. There's different ways of being clever. Me, I was crap at school. Couldn't wait to get out. Failed every exam they put in front of me. But I'm clever in other ways.'

She taps her forefinger against the side of her head. 'I'm sharp, I am. I know what's going on. It's like a sixth sense, almost. Take last night. I could tell there was going to be trouble with those old slags before it all kicked off. I could sense it. And I knew the police wouldn't be paying attention. It's the lads they're watching out for. But I could tell. I had you covered.'

She starts walking again.

Helen hurries alongside her. 'Covered?'

'I was watching out for you,' Siân says. 'And when it kicked off, I was ready. That's what life's about. Being ready. That's what I meant when I said there's different ways of being clever. Not everyone knows that. Their heads are full of all this stuff they've learned, all these facts and figures and things you're supposed to know. They're so wrapped up in the small stuff, they don't see the bigger picture. In fact, half the time they're afraid to even look at the bigger picture. So they just keep their blinkers on and their heads down. Then one day they wake up and wonder why life has passed them by. It's because they were never ready.'

Helen thinks of how punctual she is, how she always plans ahead and pays attention to detail. These are lessons she learned from Owen, and they've served her well, haven't they? She's good at her job. She has things under control, or so she likes to think. But how prepared is she, really? How equipped was she for what had happened last night? How reliable are her instincts?

'What's up?' asks Siân.

'I was just thinking about what you said, about people going through life with their heads down.'

'And?'

Helen looks at her. 'I think I'm a bit like that.'

'I think you probably are.' Siân smiles. 'Not far to the ford now. Do you want to keep going or should we turn back?'

Helen can see the river crossing through the trees ahead, the surrounding woodland sloping steeply down to the white water. She remembers her mother warning her not to play near the river. Her mother had told her a lot of things.

'No,' she says firmly. 'Let's keep going.'

CHAPTER FOURTEEN

The daylight is fading and the temperature has dropped when the Jackal shudders and lurches to a halt. Owen reaches instinctively for his rifle. His first thought is that they've taken a hit. After this morning's mortar attack on the base, his nerves are frayed. But the reality proves to be more mundane. The transmission has packed up. Owen listens as the driver radios it in. The turnaround will be four hours. They're told to sit tight.

'Great,' snaps Jackson. 'So what do we do now?'

'We follow orders and sit tight,' Owen says. 'And since you're so keen for something to do, you can be first on stag.'

Tensions between him and Jackson have been building steadily for days now, and the situation isn't helped by the fact that the source of the tension is sitting in the truck up ahead. There are three vehicles on the patrol, carrying a total of twelve men. Owen watches as the truck in front stops and Collins jumps out and stretches. There's something about the lad that fascinates him. It's the way he carries himself, as if he's aware that he's being watched and is putting on a show – flexing his arms that little bit more than necessary, tilting his head to accentuate his jawline and the full length of his neck.

Quickly, Owen looks away.

Jackson is staring straight back at him, lip curling.

'Collins can go first.'

'You'll do as I say, Jackson,' Owen says firmly. 'Isn't that right, sarge?'

The sergeant grunts in agreement.

'Fine,' Jackson replies. 'So long as it's one of the other lads who relieves me, and not your boy there.'

Owen's face flushes. Has word got round about what happened at the gym? Have people seen him and Collins talking outside the cookhouse and jumped to their own conclusions? Surreptitiously, he glances at the faces of the other soldiers in the vehicle but their expressions give nothing away. Maybe they hadn't heard Jackson's remark. Out here in the desert, voices are carried away on the wind as easily as lives are lost.

'Collins can take over after Jackson,' the sergeant says. 'Then you, McGrath.'

Jackson frowns but doesn't voice any objections.

Owen looks up at the inky blue sky. The sun has disappeared and the moon is already rising, full and fat and as bright as a searchlight. So that's one more reason to feel unsettled. This was supposed to have been a five-hour patrol. Another hour and they'd have been heading back to base camp. Instead they're out here in the open, just a few miles from where Armstrong was killed, in what the army euphemistically refers to as 'an area of interest'. In other words, they're in a former Taliban stronghold, still considered enough of a threat to require regular surveillance. In many ways, this is what soldiers live for. Desert patrols are all about proper soldiering, living on your wits. But nobody wants to be stuck out here at night. Especially under the glare of a full moon.

The vehicles are lined up in a row, with the machine gun in the centre. Soldiers jump down onto the ground and begin busily arranging their sleeping bags close together on one side. Four hours will give them time to catch up on some sleep. When your days are filled with nerve-wracking tedium, you're grateful for any shut-eye you can get. Owen is amazed at how easily he adapts to these irregular sleeping patterns. Back home he was a creature of habit. He needed eight hours' sleep a night and a cool, darkened room. Here he survives on four or five. And tonight 'on the ground' will mean precisely that. Someone will be on stag, someone will be manning the radio and the rest of the patrol will collapse in the dirt, huddled close in their sleeping bags for extra warmth. Sleep usually comes quickly, which is the body's way of coping when it's this exhausted.

Owen arranges his sleeping bag as far away from Jackson's as he can. He closes his eyes and tries to think of Helen. She'll be at home now, curled up on the sofa with her feet tucked under her, reddish-blonde hair piled on top of her head in a clip, the way she often wears it at the end of a long day. His heart warms at the thought of her and he feels a pang of guilt. He still hasn't finished that letter. Later, when they arrive back at the base, he'll send her an email. He won't tell her about this morning's incident at the gym. She'd only worry. He'll thank her for her parcel, tell her he loves her and reassure her that everything is fine. Perhaps if he can convince her, he can convince himself too.

He turns onto his side, rests his head in the crook of his arm and pulls his sleeping bag up against the cold night air. Seconds later, he's asleep. He dreams about the last man he shot – a man who keeps falling to the ground and then standing up again, his face a blur of blackened blood. He wakes briefly, gulping for air. He gazes up at the moon, hears the snores of sleeping soldiers and drifts off again. Soon he's dreaming about his wife. He's kissing her like he hasn't kissed her in a long time, gripping the sides of her head between his hands, his tongue exploring her mouth, wanting to crawl inside her and hide forever. Owen groans, 'Helen.' He caresses her shoulders, his hands trailing across her skin to cup her soft breasts.

It's then that he realizes it isn't Helen he's kissing after all. It's Collins. He tries to speak but no words come. He feels the young soldier's mouth pressed against his own and a shiver of excitement runs through his body like an electric shock.

Suddenly he's being nudged awake. Collins is hovering over him. 'Time for you to relieve me, Corporal.'

Owen flinches. It's the term everyone uses. When someone is on stag, and you're next in line to take over, you 'relieve' them. But there's another meaning too, an in-joke among the lads. It makes light of the intimate bonds that form between them and the suspicions that arise whenever men live together in such close proximity. And there's something in the lad's face, the faint hint of a smile, that tells Owen he's being teased. How long has Collins been standing over him?

'Right,' says Owen, climbing out of his sleeping bag. Thank God he didn't wake up with an erection. Though he wouldn't be the first soldier to go on stag with more than one thing on his mind. It's one of the few occasions in the army when you have anything approaching privacy, and it's an occasion many soldiers take advantage of by enjoying a good wank. An image of Collins masturbating flashes into his head. His throat tightens as he forces the thought away.

'Alright, Corporal?' Collins asks, removing his helmet and dropping it onto the empty sleeping bag next to Owen's. 'I doubt I'll get much sleep tonight.'

Owen looks at him. There's a gleam in his eye, a look that seems to suggest he was reading Owen's thoughts. Is he flirting with him? Maybe he thinks he sees something in Owen the others can't? Well, he's wrong. Much as he likes the lad, there's nothing queer about his feelings for him. The dream was just a dream. He's definitely not that guy.

'Corporal?' Collins says, snapping him out of his reverie. 'You're on stag.'

'Get some shut-eye,' Owen answers abruptly, and leaps to his feet.

'You're the boss, Owen,' Collins replies.

There's no mistaking it this time. It's not just the familiarity of Collins calling him by his first name. There's a definite look there. The lad's eyes are practically shining.

'Correct,' Owen says. 'Now get some sleep.' He nearly adds, 'Or you'll be no use to me', but catches himself in time.

He reaches for his helmet, strides over to the vehicle and climbs up behind the top-mounted, 50-calibre machine gun. The proximity of the weapon brings a familiar feeling of comfort. Owen has seen some terrible things in the army. He's seen men blown apart, men shivering with fear and covered in shit. And he's done things too. He's killed people, including that kid in Iraq. But he's a soldier, and for him a gun still represents something noble. It means protection, and protection is what being in the army is all about. It's why he's still here, in this Godforsaken hell-hole. And for the next hour, it's his only focus.

Despite himself, his thoughts return to Collins. The lad was squeezed into this same space only minutes ago. Is it just his imagination, or can he still sense his presence? Is it the warmth of his body, the smell of his sweat, or the thought of what he might have been doing? An hour from now Owen will be lying next to him, their sleeping bags inches apart. The thought unsettles him. He swallows, closing his eyes for a split second.

A twig snaps. Owen jumps. Swivelling round, he sees Collins standing at the rear of the vehicle, a smile pulling at the corners of his mouth.

'It's okay,' the lad says. 'They're all asleep.'

'What are you doing?' Owen demands.

'I think you know,' Collins replies, and climbs up into the vehicle.

CHAPTER FIFTEEN

The Cozy Café is anything but. Helen's heart sinks as she takes in the shabby pine furniture and dirty vinyl flooring. But Siân is already through the door.

The waitress wears a faded blue apron and a bored expression.

'Menu's on the table,' she sighs. 'We close at six. I'll be back to take your order.' She turns and slopes away.

'A smile would do for starters,' Siân says, pulling out a chair. 'She's hardly rushed off her feet, is she?'

Helen looks around. The only other customer is a middle-aged man with thick-framed glasses and a long red beard, dressed in what look like traditional Arab robes, with a round white skull cap. He's seated in the far corner, reading a book and muttering under his breath. He has the look of someone who's used to drawing attention and isn't bothered in the slightest.

Siân has clocked him too. She leans across the table and raises a knowing eyebrow. 'I call him the only Muslim in the village. He was in the local paper last week, accusing the council of being Islamophobic. He wants them to build a mosque in the centre of town – just for him.'

'Who is he?' Helen whispers back.

'God knows! Lives in Blackmill. Calls himself Mohammed something or other. A year ago he was Welsh Methodist.'

'Maybe he had a religious conversion?' Helen says quietly, and immediately wishes she hadn't. She can feel the man watching her from the corner of her eye. If she only had more sense, she'd have changed the subject.

Siân laughs. 'Or maybe he's just a nutter. Anyway, let's order. I'm starving.'

It's hours since they left the house. The ford was every bit as beautiful as Siân had promised. They'd sat for a while idly chatting and watching the river slide by. Then the sky had closed in and it had started to rain, so they'd decided to head for the nearest café.

Studying the menu, Helen feels a sudden craving for the all-day breakfast. She thinks of Owen and his famous fry-ups, then forces the thought away.

'Tea and toast,' says Siân, cornering the waitress.

Helen nods in agreement. 'Me too, please.'

'We close at six,' the waitress sighs.

'Yeah, you said,' Siân replies. 'Better make it snappy then, hadn't you?'

As the waitress shuffles off, a young woman pokes her head inside the café. Her make-up is thick, her eyebrows raised in a look of permanent surprise. But what really strikes Helen is her outfit. Her jeans are orange and skin tight. Her crop top is also orange. It's hard to tell where the top ends and her heavily tanned stomach begins.

'Oh my God!' Siân says in a stage whisper. 'She's been Tangoed!'

'She doesn't look that bad.' Helen giggles nervously, conscious that the girl is staring over.

'Come off it! She looks a right state!'

'I'd kill for a tan,' Helen says, trying to take the focus off the girl, who is still hovering by the door. 'I only ever go pink in the sun. Pink, and then white again.'

'You've got lovely skin. Like an English rose.'

'Except I'm Welsh. I wish I looked more like you. You've got a great colour.'

Siân frowns. 'Are you saying I look like her?'

'Of course not!' Helen is relieved to see that the girl has gone.

'Good. Cos I've never been near a sunbed in my life. This is my natural skin colour. Proper Welsh, see. My dad always said I was a thoroughbred.'

Siân says this proudly, as if it's some kind of achievement and not an accident of birth.

The waitress arrives with a tray, and places the teas and toast on the table. 'Enjoy your meal,' she says, without a trace of enthusiasm.

Helen thinks of her own father. He'd always tried to boost her confidence, telling her she was special. Would she have turned out differently had he lived? Would she have travelled more, seen more, done more? Or was she always destined to be the person she was now? Is her lack of confidence simply part of her nature, as ingrained in her as Siân's skin tone?

'Penny for your thoughts?'

Helen smiles. 'Your dad sounds great.'

'Yeah, he was.' Siân takes a sip of her tea.

'Was?'

'He died.' Siân shrugs. 'It's okay. I don't mind talking about it. Actually I think it helps to talk about things. And it keeps him alive in a way. Gone but not forgotten.'

Helen feels a shiver of recognition go through her. She's never met anyone who lost their father before, certainly nobody as young as Siân. For all their differences, it suddenly strikes her that she and Siân have something in common that few people can relate to, a connection far deeper than mere friendship. It's almost as if they have a shared history, almost as if they're sisters.

She looks across the table and smiles sympathetically. 'What happened?'

'Hit and run. A few years ago. He was dead before they reached the hospital.'

'I'm so sorry. Did they catch whoever did it?'

'Yeah. Drunk driver. Two years, they gave him. "Diminished responsibility". Makes you sick.'

'What about your mum?'

'Oh, she fucked off years ago. Said she was never cut out to be a mother, and just upped and left. I was six. Selfish cow.'

'Do you know where she is now?'

'Nah. Don't care either. She's dead to me. Has been for years.'

At least my mother's not dead to me, Helen thinks. *She may not be perfect, but at least she's there*.

She looks at Siân and feels her heart go out to her. Losing one parent was hard enough. But losing both? It's no wonder she can come across as abrasive. Helen pictures her as a little girl, abandoned by her mother and already learning to tough it out.

'Anyway, enough about me,' Siân says. 'What are your family like?'

'It's just my mum. My dad died when I was ten. A group of lads attacked him outside our house. One of them had a knife.'

Siân's eyes widen in horror. 'Oh my God! That's awful! Did the police catch the bastards?'

'No.' Helen feels the tears come. She blinks them back.

'To absent fathers,' Siân says, raising her teacup. 'Long may they watch over us.' She sets down the cup, reaches across the table and grasps Helen's hand. 'I'm so glad I was there for you last night. I think our paths were

110

meant to cross, don't you?'

Helen nods.

'Good.' Siân pushes back her chair. 'Hold that
thought. I'm just popping to the loo.'

Statement from Lisa Johns
Aged 17
Neighbour of Richard and Mandy Thomas
NB – may know more than she's letting on

The night before he died, Mr Thomas arrived home
shortly after 7 p.m. A neighbour, Lisa Johns, spoke
to him.

'I was in my front garden when I saw Richard –
sorry, Mr Thomas – coming up the street,' said Ms
Johns. 'I waved and shouted hello. He looked at me
and sort of smiled. But he didn't seem his usual self
so I called out to him, "Are you okay?" "I'm fine,"
he said, and stopped at my gate. But he didn't look
fine.'

In what way? Ms Johns paused before
answering. 'He looked like he'd been drinking. His
eyes were glassy-looking. And he smelt funny too.
At first I thought he'd been smoking. I'd never seen
him smoke, so I thought it was strange. But then I
realised it was more of a wood-smoke smell, like
he'd been near a bonfire. You know, the way kids
smell on bonfire night?'

Ms Johns confirmed that Mr Thomas didn't
have a carrier bag with him, and that he appeared to
be in an agitated state. 'He wasn't carrying
anything,' she said. 'I remember because I reached
for his hand to try and comfort him and both his
hands were free. I told him, "You don't seem fine,

111

Richard."'

Asked if she and Mr Thomas were on first-name terms, Ms Johns hesitated before replying. 'I've known him for a couple of years now. We've often chatted about stuff, the way neighbours do. I always called him Richard and he always called me Lisa. But he was different that night. When I told him he didn't seem fine, he snapped at me. "Mind your own business," he said.'

How did she react? 'I was shocked, to tell you the truth. He'd never spoken to me like that before. Not once. I said we were neighbours, but we were more like friends really. I mean, he'd told me things – y'know, personal things. I knew him and his wife argued a lot. I'd hear her over the garden fence. "Richard, do this! Richard, do that!" She was always going on about the amount of time he spent in his shed. If you ask me, he only went in there to get away from her. I don't think he got a moment's peace. In fact, if she wasn't such an old nag, he'd probably still be alive now. It's because of her that he was out mowing the front lawn when it happened. And now he's dead.'

So Ms Johns saw Mr Thomas at the time of the attack? What else did she see? 'I didn't say that! I didn't see anything. I was inside the house when it happened, on the phone to my fiancé.'

At this point, Ms Johns broke down in tears. 'Sorry,' she said. 'It's been such a shock. That poor man. But it's not his wife I feel sorry for. It's that daughter of his. Poor little Helen. She was so close to her dad.'

***

112

When Siân returns to the table, her eyes are shining. Helen wonders if she's been crying. Behind that tough exterior is a young woman who grew up without a mother, and who only recently lost her father. Her grief is probably still raw.

'I've been thinking,' Siân says as she sits down. 'I remember reading about your dad.'

'Really? It was such a long time ago.'

'My dad kept newspaper cuttings. Local news stories, mostly. Your dad seemed really brave. The paper called him a local hero.' She smiles sympathetically. 'It must have been really tough on your mum.'

'I suppose.'

'You don't sound too convinced.'

'She didn't waste much time. She has this new bloke. Frank.'

'And you don't like him.'

'Not really. He drinks. And he thinks he knows what's best for everyone – me, my mum.' She takes a bite of toast before adding thoughtfully, 'I think he's the reason she stopped visiting my dad's grave.'

'He sounds a bit of a control freak.'

Helen smiles as she imagines Siân saying this to Frank's face. Then her smile fades at the thought of tomorrow. Her mother will be expecting her for Sunday lunch. And Frank will want to know all about her girls' night out.

'What's the matter?' Siân asks.

'Nothing. I have to see them tomorrow, that's all. Family duty.'

'Why go? If you can't stand him?'

'I'm expected.'

'And do you always do what's expected of you?'

'I suppose I do, yes.'

113

Siân stares at her for a moment. 'Can I ask you something?'

'Okay.'

'Who do you want to be?'

Helen laughs nervously. 'You mean, when I grow up?'

'I mean now. Are you happy with who you are? I mean, really happy?'

'I don't know what you mean,' Helen says. But she does. She knows exactly what Siân means. 'How happy are you, really?' It's the sort of question posed by women's magazines: 'Take Our Happiness Quiz', or 'Ten Tips To Help Make You A Happier Person'. The tips mostly seem to involve taking time to enjoy nature, cutting down on alcohol or taking up yoga or meditation. Sometimes there are case studies involving women at the end of their tether, ready to walk out on their families and never look back. Helen has often wondered about those women. Do they hate their husbands and children that much? It seems such a cruel thing to do – the kind of thing Siân's mother had done.

Still, she'd be lying if she said that she never fantasized about disappearing – not for good, but just for a day, or even a few hours, just long enough to know how it feels. She'd wonder how long it would take for Owen to realize that she was missing. She'd imagine the frantic phone calls to her mother, and the panicked response on the other end of the line. 'No, she's not here. We thought she was with you.' But then she'd picture the look of horror on her husband's face and know in her heart that she could never subject him to such an ordeal.

'Can I be honest?' Siân says, leaning across the table.

Helen flinches. 'Of course.'

'I think you're afraid. You're afraid to say no to your mother. Afraid to stand up for yourself. Afraid to ask for help. Don't get me wrong. I'm not having a go. We're all afraid of something.'

'Even you?' Helen thinks of the fearless way Siân intervened last night.

'Even me.'

'What are you afraid of?'

'Me? Oh, lots of things. Snakes. Spiders. Losing my devastatingly good looks.' Siân rolls her eyes. 'I didn't mean that last bit.'

Helen laughs. 'I can't imagine you ever being scared.'

'Of course I am. But the secret is not to let your fear hold you back. You have to face it, show it who's boss.'

Helen stares at this strange woman and wonders how someone she's only just met can know her so well. Siân is right. She is afraid. In fact, her whole life is hemmed in by fear – fear of embarrassment, fear of failure, fear that her husband might not make it home alive.

'C'mon,' says Siân, pushing her cup and saucer away and placing a crisp ten-pound note on the table. 'Let's go.'

'Where are we going?'

Her friend grins. 'To face your fear, of course.'

CHAPTER SIXTEEN

As they leave the café, Helen can feel her anxiety rising. 'What do you mean, face my fear?' she asks. Already she has visions of being pushed from a plane with a parachute strapped to her back.

Siân smiles and narrows her eyes against the early evening sun. 'The weather's cleared,' she says. 'How's your head?'

'Much better, thanks.'

'Great. If you need more painkillers, just say. I've got plenty in here.' She hoists her bag onto her shoulder. 'I'm like a travelling chemist.'

It's a big bag to be carrying around, Helen thinks. *What else has she got in there?*

'Thanks,' she says. 'So where are we going?'

Siân taps her nose. 'That's for me to know and you to find out. Come on.'

The air is soft and filled with the fresh smells of summer. Helen inhales deeply, enjoying the warmth on her face. *Relax*, she tells herself. *What's the worst that can happen?* She waits for the warning voice in her head to answer back, but no words come. She feels different, somehow. Nothing much has changed. She still hasn't heard from Owen. She still has to face her mother and Frank tomorrow. But meeting Siân has opened a window of possibility that didn't exist before. Her new friend is outspoken and a bit rough around the edges, but there are far worse crimes than speaking your mind. At least nobody could accuse Siân of only telling people what they want to hear. She may be blunt but at least she's honest.

Besides, Helen has never met anyone quite like Siân before. She's fascinated by her combination of bravado and vulnerability, flattered that someone so physically attractive and charismatic should find her interesting enough to spend time with. Nobody has paid Helen this much attention in a long time. She's determined to show Siân that she's not some feeble creature who's afraid of her own shadow and doesn't know how to enjoy herself.

They haven't walked far when Siân grabs her arm.

Helen follows her gaze. Trundling along the pavement opposite is a woman on a mobility scooter, her enormous backside mushrooming over the sides of the seat. She wears carpet slippers, leggings and a black T-shirt with white lettering that reads, 'I'm Up. I'm Dressed. What More Do You Want?' Her greasy hair is pulled back tightly from her face, which is the colour of uncooked pastry.

'See that?' says Siân. 'That's what happens when people just give up. Can you imagine letting yourself go like that? I'd rather die.'

'You don't mean that,' Helen says.

'Okay, maybe not die. But I wouldn't parade around in a T-shirt like that. It's people like her who give people on benefits a bad name.'

'Maybe she can't help it,' Helen says. 'Maybe she's disabled.'

Siân snorts. 'I bet there's nothing wrong with her that a good kick up the arse wouldn't fix.'

'It's the weekend. She might have a job for all we know.'

'Seriously?' Siân rolls her eyes. 'Does she look like a

wage slave to you? No offence.'

Helen smiles despite herself. 'None taken.'

'Trust me,' says Siân. 'I know a scrounger when I see one. Last week there was this drunk guy outside McDonald's, begging with a bloody great burger in his hand! He asked me for money to buy something to eat. I said to him, "Why? Would you like fries with that?"'

Helen laughs. 'You didn't!'

Siân frowns. 'Are you calling me a liar?'

'No,' Helen says quickly. 'It's just funny, that's all. I can never think of witty one-liners at the time. They always come to me later.'

'It's like I was saying before. It's all about being ready. Now, are you ready to face your fear?'

Helen tries to stop her voice from wavering. 'You still haven't told me where we're going.'

'Are you always this anxious?' Siân asks, linking arms with her. 'Don't look so worried. You'll be thanking me later, I promise.'

She steers her along the high street, past shops selling over-priced groceries, estate agents, hairdressers and a boutique with a window display full of wedding dresses. The sign above the window reads 'Blushing Brides'.

'I don't know why they bothered opening a bridal shop there,' Siân says. 'It must be a front for something.'

'What makes you say that?'

'Well, they can't do much business, can they? Look around. I bet there's not a single kid within a five-mile radius whose parents are married. Most of the poor bastards don't even know who their father is.'

Helen doubts this very much, but chooses not to argue. 'Have you ever thought about getting married?' she asks.

'Yeah, I've *thought* about it.' Siân laughs. 'Thought what a bloody nightmare it must be!' She looks at Helen.

'No offence. I just don't think I'm cut out to be a blushing bride.'

'But you've had boyfriends.'

'A few. But most of the blokes around here are such losers. I'd rather be on my own than with some knuckle-dragging meathead.'

'They're not all like that. There were some nice-looking lads in town last night.'

'So you noticed them, did you? And you a married woman!' Siân grins. 'The trouble with good-looking blokes is they're too into themselves. There was one at the gym the other day. Fit body. Not a bad face. Then he saw me looking at him. I swear to God he flexed his bicep, kissed it and said, "All the girls love the guns!" So I told him.'

'What did you say?'

'I said, "Yeah, and some of the boys do too!" That soon shut him up.'

'You're mad, you are,' Helen says. For a split second she sees a shadow move across Siân's face, like the tiniest of clouds scurrying across the sun. Then it's gone.

'C'mon,' says Siân. 'We'll cut through the underpass. It's quicker that way.'

The approach to the underpass is littered with cigarette butts and the discarded remains of fast food packaging. Helen's pulse quickens as she follows Siân into the half-light. She struggles not to gag at the smell of urine. Someone – possibly a local primary schoolteacher or the leader of a kids' playgroup – has attempted to brighten up the walls with paintings of trees and children's handprints. But the handprints look sinister, like something out of *The Blair Witch Project*. Next to one of the trees, someone has scrawled 'Huw is gay as fuck for BA' with a black marker pen.

As they emerge into the daylight, a group of girls are huddled together, smoking and passing around a bottle of cider. Helen hangs back nervously, but Siân marches forward and the girls quickly part to make way.

She's fearless, Helen thinks. *Totally fearless. Why can't I be more like that?*

Siân turns to her and smiles reassuringly. 'C'mon, slow coach!'

Half expecting a foot to come out or an insult to be thrown in her face, Helen takes a step forward. Memories of last night's attack come flooding back. Her skin prickles. But there's Siân, waiting a few yards ahead. Siân won't let anything bad happen to her. She walks on. The girls don't give her a second glance.

Statement from Duncan Roberts
Aged 48
Neighbour of Richard and Mandy Thomas

It's not known if Richard Thomas left his house again after returning home on the night before he died. The next confirmed sighting was the following morning, when he was seen leaving the house at around 10.40 a.m. by a Mr Duncan Roberts, who lives in the house directly opposite.

'I saw him from my front window,' Mr Roberts said. 'Even from a distance, I could see that he was a bit grey around the gills. I said to the wife, "Someone had a few too many last night!" We're regulars at The Jolly Brewer in Park Street. I've seen him in there, a bit worse for wear. But I don't remember him ever looking as rough as he did that morning. He looked like he'd been up boozing all night. He was wearing a bulky jacket, which struck me as a bit odd considering how hot it was. I'd been out to buy the paper and it was already warm. He came out of his front gate and turned left up the street. I don't know where he was heading. The shops are all in the other direction. There's just a few houses up there. And the Black Path where the kids hang out. Maybe he just needed a walk to clear his head. But he must have been sweltering in that jacket.'

Mr Roberts stated that he and Mr Thomas weren't what he would call friends. 'I can't say I ever really took to the man. Not that I'm not sorry about what happened. Nobody deserves that. And with a wife and kid, too. I hope they catch the little bastards who did it, and when they do, they should lock them up and throw away the key. But he wasn't really a man's man, if you know what I mean. He preferred the company of women. I've lived here for seven years and don't think he ever exchanged more than a few words with me. I'd seen him talking and laughing with that Lisa Johns, who lives a few doors down. They seemed very close. Oh yes, he could always find time to talk to pretty young girls.'

Asked if he was implying that Richard Thomas and Ms Johns were involved in some kind of relationship, Mr Roberts replied, 'I never said that. But it looks a bit odd when a married man starts hanging around with a younger woman. It's not for me to say if there was anything going on between them or not, but some people might jump to conclusions.'

When asked what he meant by 'some people', Mr Roberts replied, 'Mandy Thomas, for one.'

'Look!' says Siân. She grabs Helen's arm and points across the road at the local community centre.

Helen must have driven past the centre hundreds of times without paying too much attention. It's a small building with arched windows and a pitched roof, suggesting that it had once been a place of worship. Now the windows are covered with chicken wire and the walls are painted pale blue. Outside is a hand-painted sign: 'A Night of Clairvoyance. Tue. 7.30pm. £5.'

'What do you reckon?' Siân asks. 'Fancy it?'

Helen shrugs. 'I don't really believe in any of that stuff.'

'What stuff?'

'Clairvoyants. Psychics. Talking to the dead.'

'No, me neither. You must talk to your dad, though. When you visit his grave, I mean.'

'Sometimes. But that's different.'

'You must miss him.'

'I do.'

Siân links her arm through Helen's. 'What was he like? What do you remember about him?'

'Lots of things. Sometimes he'd come home really late, but he'd always read me a bedtime story. He always had more time for me than Mum did. Nothing he did ever seemed to please her.'

'Did they argue a lot?'

'A fair amount.'

'What about?'

'Silly things. She was always so uptight. Still is, in fact.'

'She sounds a bit of a cow,' Siân says.

'She's not really,' Helen replies – partly out of a sense of loyalty, and partly because her own mother's failings pale in comparison to Siân's mother abandoning her as a child. 'She's not perfect. But she did her best. Or what she thought was best.'

An image of her mother and Frank pops into her head. She's seated at the dining table. Her mother is fretting over the roast dinner, refusing her offers of help. Frank sits with his newspaper and a can of lager, sounding off about something he's just read, oblivious to the fact that nobody is interested. The air is heavy with the smell of burning fat, the windows wet with steam, the walls closing in.

'Okay?' asks Siân.

Helen nods and forces a smile. 'Never better.'

They walk in silence for a while, past school playing fields and the local sports centre where Owen sometimes works out when he's home on leave.

'That's where I go to the gym,' Siân says proudly. 'Four times a week. Weight training. Spin class. Kick boxing.' She smiles. 'I'm fighting fit. You should try it.'

'I don't think it's my thing.'

'It's okay, really. They're not all gays and meatheads.'

'I know. My husband trains there sometimes.'

Siân turns to her.

'Of course! I thought I recognized him in that photo. That'll be why.'

'But he hasn't been there in months.'

'I never forget a face. It's like I said before. I'm sharp.'

Helen pictures Owen returning from the gym – his hair still damp, his face flushed. She forces the thought away.

'Siân, about your father –'

'What about him?'

'You must miss him.'

'Of course. But it gets easier with time, doesn't it?'

Helen thinks back to the period after her father died. It had taken her months to adjust to the fact that he was gone. In some ways, she's still adjusting, even now.

'Sometimes I have conversations with my dad in my head,' she says. 'Do you ever do that?'

'Oh, I talk to my dad all the time.' Siân nods knowingly, then looks away. 'Here we are.'

Straight ahead is a large concrete building, painted in various shades of grey. Next to it is a small car park. A blue sign on the wall boasts 'Hot food, karaoke and dancing till 2am.'

'It looks nice,' Helen says cautiously.

'*Nice*?' Siân laughs. 'It looks like a communist checkpoint! There should be a sign over the door. "Abandon hope all who enter here!"'

She steps forward and holds open the door. 'Shall we?'

CHAPTER SEVENTEEN

Owen tears the page from his notebook, folds the sheet of paper and tucks it safely into the chest pouch of his body armour. The letter has taken him an hour to write, propped up on his elbows as the night winds howled and Collins lay snoring gently a few feet away.

Now, as he rolls up his sleeping bag, a feeling of unease creeps over him. His stomach clenches.

Hunger probably, he thinks. *Or guilt…*

Shaking the thoughts away, he grabs his rifle, reaches for his kit bag and hoists it onto his back. Everything will be alright. He has a wife waiting for him at home. That's where his future lies. That's who he is. He just needs to get a message to her and let her know he's safe. It'll take days for the letter to arrive. He can't leave it that long, knowing how worried she'll be. But he can't risk a phone call. What if she hears it in his voice? An email, then. Yes, if it's the last thing he does today, he'll send an email to Helen. Something short and sweet, telling her he loves her and he's safe and not to worry. The rest can wait until later.

He looks at his watch – 4.47 a.m. The sun is just starting to rise, pale streaks of pink and orange spreading slowly across the horizon. But the moon is still visible and the night winds haven't died away completely. As he steps up to the vehicle, sand swirls in small circles around his feet.

This is what life's about, he thinks. Small circles. Routine. Order.

Breakfast will be waiting for them back at the base. He pictures a steaming plate piled high with bacon and eggs, fried tomatoes and buttered toast. Comfort food. Food fit for a soldier.

But still there's that feeling of unease deep in his stomach.

The lads from combat support arrived during the night and fixed the transmission. It took longer than expected, and it was only afterwards that someone discovered that one of the radios was on the blink. Owen will need to swap vehicles so that the sergeant can be certain that radio contact is maintained with the base.

'Mount up,' the sergeant bawls. 'We're moving off in five.' He turns away to consult his map.

'I'll take the lead vehicle,' Owen says. 'Collins, you join the sergeant in the rear. Jackson, you're driving me.'

'Fuck that!' Jackson replies.

Owen eyeballs him.

'I hardly slept a wink,' Jackson says with a knowing smirk. 'Best if I take the rear, eh?' He nods towards Collins. 'Your crow here can drive.'

Owen bristles. 'Crow' stands for 'combat recruit of war' and is a term applied to a soldier fresh out of training. Prefixing it with 'your' is Jackson's way of adding further insult to an already loaded choice of words. Owen glares at him but says nothing. Now isn't the time to rise to the bait.

'Fine,' Owen says, avoiding eye contact with Collins and keeping his sights firmly on Jackson. 'Collins can drive.'

'Don't forget to buckle up,' Jackson says as Collins steps forward. 'And don't worry, McGrath. I've got your back.' He gives a vicious grin and slouches off to join the sergeant in the second vehicle.

There's flurry of activity as soldiers gather up their kit and take their positions. The Jackal's protection system is among the best in the world, with armour plating beneath the crew compartment and on the sides of the vehicle. But the top of the cabin is left open for greater visibility. As Owen jumps in, the sergeant gives the order to move off.

'Alright, Corporal?' Collins smiles, adjusting his harness.

Owen keeps his eyes fixed straight ahead. 'Just drive,' he grunts.

As the patrol pulls away, he leans forward in his seat and surveys the scene. The desert is beautiful. As the sun rises, the skies seem to go on for ever. Here and there are small settlements, clusters of pomegranate trees and purple rock faces. And far off in the distance are the poppy fields – a symbol of all that's wrong in this harsh, unforgiving place. The production of opium is officially outlawed, but there's no rule of law in most of the southern parts of Afghanistan. Even for the locals, life here is governed by fear. Fear of the warlords. Fear of the security forces. Fear of insurgents.

Owen recalls the first time he saw men pinning red paper flowers to their lapels and laying wreaths at the cenotaph back home. He was eight years old and the poppies were for men who'd died in combat before he was born. He remembers thinking then that paper flowers were a strange way to show your respect for men who'd given their lives for their country. But that was all such a long time ago. He's worn many poppies since, and laid many wreaths.

'Corporal?' says Collins.

Owen snaps out of his reverie and stares through the

A few hundred yards ahead is a small village – just a few buildings clustered together. As they approach, he reaches instinctively for his radio, forgetting for a moment that the damned thing isn't working.

He drops the radio onto the seat next to him and lifts his binoculars to his eyes. Everything is sandy brown, from the narrow paths to the mud-brick houses with their weather-beaten wooden doors and flat roofs. So far, so ordinary. Clothes dangle from branches overhead. Is someone still living here, or has the place been abandoned? Owen scours the scene for signs of life but all he sees is a rotting dog corpse, buzzing with flies. Someone's pet, perhaps? Or a guard dog with nobody and nothing left to guard?

Then his eyes are drawn to a large bank of poppies to the left of the village, the familiar pink buds turning red on long green stalks. Something isn't right. The poppy harvest is supposed to be over. His pulse quickens. The feeling of unease he felt earlier returns, more pronounced this time. Collins senses it too. His body is rigid.

Owen lowers his binoculars and scans the road ahead.

What's wrong with this picture?

Barely has the thought formed when there's a sudden blinding flash. The force of the explosion blasts his body high into the air. There's a ringing noise in his ears as his world melts away into a scorching white nothingness. He smells burning flesh and wonders if it's his own. The stench of petrol fumes fills his nostrils and catches the back of his throat. As he hits the ground, he feels the crunch of bone as his arm snaps.

Then the white turns to black. The ringing sound fades. And somewhere in the darkness he hears a distant voice shout. 'Man down! Man down!'

CHAPTER EIGHTEEN

Helen can't believe the time. Had she known that Siân intended to stay out so late, she'd have cried off hours ago. She's in no fit state for another marathon drinking session. But one hour became two and two became four and still there's no indication that Siân is ready to call it a night. Helen has tried several times to make her excuses and leave, but each time Siân came back at her with another reason to stay: 'I've just ordered us a meal.' 'The karaoke's on later.' 'Just one more drink.' 'But it's Saturday night!'

The food was awful. Helen can feel the greasy chicken and chips sitting heavily in her stomach. She has no interest in the karaoke, and no desire to repeat last night's performance and get completely plastered. But to complain now would seem ungracious. There's also the unspoken understanding that Siân had cut short her own Friday night out in order to take care of her. She hasn't said as much, but Helen can't help feeling that she owes Siân. And really, where's the harm? Siân does have a point. It is Saturday night. What would she be doing at home? Having nightmares in her empty bed or watching a late-night film and waiting for the phone to ring.

It's now close to midnight and Siân has gone to the bar for another round of drinks. 'Just a Diet Coke for me,' Helen insisted. She's been trying to pace herself, alternating between soft drinks and white wine spritzers. She wonders how much wine they put in the spritzers. She's only had a few but is feeling surprisingly light-headed. Still, it'll be time to go home soon, surely?

She looks around. She's not sure what time this place closes, but nobody appears to be leaving just yet. At the next table, a bunch of lads in tight-fitting T-shirts are downing pints like there's no tomorrow. She overhears one of them say something about a birthday party, though it isn't clear whose birthday it is, whether the party is taking place at some other venue or is already in full swing. At another table, a couple of women her mother's age are sharing a bottle of wine. The bar area is crowded with an assortment of people in jeans and sportswear. A few of the older men keep leering over at her. Others are kept in check by women with pinched expressions and plunging necklines.

Helen looks for Siân but there's still no sign of her. She checks her phone and sees that the signal is weak and the battery is low. Damn. She should have charged it before leaving the house. There's a missed call from an unknown number. Funny, she thinks. She didn't hear it ring. There's no voicemail and still no word from Owen. Telling herself not to worry, she turns up the volume on the phone and slides it back into her pocket.

A hand grabs her shoulder. 'Here we go,' says Siân.

Relieved that it isn't one of the men hitting on her, Helen smiles up, before spotting the two glasses and bottle of wine she's carrying. 'I thought you were getting me a Diet Coke?'

'I was,' Siân replies, placing the glasses on the table. 'But the queue for the bar was so long and by the time they finally served me I thought, "Fuck it, it's Saturday night!" You don't mind, do you? I can go back if you like.' She shrugs guiltily and gestures towards the bar.

'It's okay,' Helen says. 'I'm fine with wine.' She giggles as the words trip off her tongue. Those spritzers must have been stronger than she thought.

'Fine with wine.' Siân smiles and takes her seat. 'Listen to you. Very refined.' She fills the glasses. 'Who was that on the phone?'

'Missed call. Unknown number.'

'Sales, probably. Double glazing. Or life insurance. I don't know why people bother.'

I'm glad my dad bothered, Helen thinks. Or I'd never have bought the house.

'Cheers,' Siân says, handing her a glass. 'To us!'

Helen raises her glass, sloshing wine over her hand and onto the table. 'Oops!' She really ought to make this her last drink. 'I should make a move soon,' she says. 'It's getting late.'

Siân frowns. 'And miss all the fun? The karaoke's about to start.'

'I'm not a huge fan of karaoke.'

'But that's the reason I brought you here. You can't go yet.' She grins. 'Now, have a look at this and pick a song.' She hands Helen a menu. Printed on the back are dozens of song titles.

Helen shakes her head. 'I can't get up in front of all these people.'

'Of course you can. That's what the wine is for – Dutch courage.'

'But I can't sing.'

'Most of them can't sing. That's not the point.'

'So what is the point?'

Siân rolls her eyes. 'What's the worst that can happen? People laugh at you. Big fucking deal! Let them. You'll probably never see them again. And who knows? You might even enjoy it.'

Helen sips her wine. 'I doubt that very much.'

'Then do it for me. Show me I didn't back a loser.' Siân smiles, then adds quickly, 'Just teasing. Now, have a look at that list. I'm off to the loo.'

Helen watches as she weaves her way through the crowded bar, people parting to make way. Her eyes fall on the woman they saw earlier, riding the mobility scooter. She's standing at the bar. Siân has spotted her too. Turning to face Helen, she lifts her right hand above her head, makes an 'L' shape with her thumb and forefinger and mouths the word 'loser'. Then she's gone.

Helen stares at the list of song titles. Some she doesn't even recognize. Others she vaguely recalls from her childhood. She remembers her father singing along to his CDs at night, out of tune but with such enthusiasm it didn't seem to matter. Then her mother's voice echoes in her head.

'For Christ's sake, Richard! You'll wake the neighbours!'

How typical of her, Helen thinks. *Always worried about what other people might think*. She cringes.

I'm nothing like my mother, she tells herself. *I can do this*.

Her phone vibrates in her pocket. She takes a quick gulp of wine and slides it out. The number is unfamiliar but the area code is local. She's about to answer when Siân reappears.

'Who are you calling?'

'Nobody.' Helen puts the phone away. 'Are you okay?'

Siân's eyes are glistening. 'Why shouldn't I be? Have you picked a song?'

'Not yet.'

'Good. Cos I just put a request in.'

She pats Helen's shoulder as she sits down.

'Don't look so worried. We'll sing the first one together.'

'What is it?'

'Bonnie Tyler.' Siân sniffs and wipes her nose with the back of her hand. 'She used to own a club in town. Not a lot of people know that.' She reaches for her glass.

'What's the song?'

'Wait and see! We're up third. Now, get that wine down you.'

The first person to take to the stage is a young man in pale jeans and an Adidas sports top. He warbles his way through 'Angels' by Robbie Williams, fluffing a few lines and singing slightly out of key.

'Rubbish,' Siân mutters.

'Give him a big round of applause!' shouts the compere. She wears a black sequinned top and has a halo of blonde curls. She grins lasciviously at the blushing young man. 'My name's Clare, darling. But you can call me Angel any time you like!'

She turns back to the audience. 'And now it's time for our very own karaoke queen! Singing "I Will Survive", please welcome – Megan Davies!'

Helen is surprised to see the mobility scooter woman climb awkwardly onto the stage. She's changed her T-shirt. This one is also black, but the white lettering reads, 'Vodka Made Me Do It'.

'Vodka made you do what, luv?' Siân shouts, her voice loud enough for the woman to hear. 'Fiddle the social?'

Helen squirms in her seat. 'Ssh!'

'Don't shush me!' Siân snaps back. Then she flashes a

135

smile. 'It's audience participation. It's all part of the fun. Look at that sad sack! This'll be a right laugh!'

As the music begins, the 'sad sack' on stage transforms herself from a lumpy woman in black leggings and a T-shirt into a polished performer. She belts out the words with such confidence, and with such power, that Helen breaks into a grin.

She could win *The X Factor*, she thinks happily, her mind cloudy with wine. If she wore a different outfit, and talked about her mobility issues. They love a good sob story.

She turns to Siân. 'She's really good!'

'I've heard worse,' Siân replies, stony-faced. 'Anyway, we're up next. I'm off to the loo.'

'Again?'

'Stage fright.'

'You?' Helen giggles. The wine is really having an effect. 'But you're not frightened of anything!'

Siân leaps up. 'Keep an eye on my bag. I'll be back in a tick.'

Then she's gone.

Helen reaches for her glass and knocks back the last of her drink. It tastes strangely salty, but that's probably from the food she ate earlier. She places the glass back on the table and looks around. Most people have their eyes fixed firmly on the stage. Some are grinning. Others are cheering. There are even a few wolf whistles. The woman is wowing everyone.

I can't do this, Helen thinks. *I don't have that woman's voice. I don't have Siân's courage. I shouldn't be here. I should be at home. What if Owen calls? How will I even hear my phone ring with all this noise? I should go. I have to go.*

The room spins as she raises herself unsteadily to her

feet. There's a huge round of applause as the woman belts out the final chorus before shuffling off stage looking extremely pleased with herself and resuming her position at the bar.

The compere hurries back on stage.

'Wasn't she fabulous? If it's the vodka that made her do it, that's the best bloody advert for vodka I've ever seen!'

The crowd roars with laughter.

'Well done, love!' she continues, to more applause. 'Right, everyone. Settle down, please. It's time for our next contestants. Singing Bonnie Tyler's "Holding Out For A Hero"...'

Helen hears her name and her stomach churns. She looks around frantically. Siân is nowhere to be seen.

The compere leans forward, shielding her eyes with one hand and peering out into the audience. She sees Helen standing and gestures to her to come forward. 'Is that you, love? Where's your friend? Don't be shy. Come on up!'

Helen shakes her head and feels her knees begin to buckle. Her skin is clammy and she's finding it hard to breathe. Someone starts slow clapping. Others join in. A few people shout words of encouragement. Someone else boos. There's still no sign of Siân.

Helen's mind races. *Where is she? It wasn't my idea to do this. It's late. I'm drunk. I shouldn't be here. Home. I have to go home.*

She pushes her way through the crowd and stumbles out of the door. As it closes behind her, she hears another burst of laughter and wonders if the butt of the joke is her.

Outside, the night sky is black with barely a star in sight. She hurries unsteadily across the car park and along the road past the leisure centre. The cool night air rushes into her lungs and she stops to steady herself, fearing she might be sick.

Not far now, she tells herself. *Go home, drink some water and sleep it off.*

By the time she reaches the underpass, her lungs ache. She hesitates, wishing for a moment that she wasn't alone. A knot of fear tightens in her chest and lifts the hairs on the nape of her neck. She stands rigid and listens. Nothing. Then, trying not to think of who might be lurking in the darkness ahead, she takes a deep breath and steps inside. There is still the strong smell of urine, but she keeps her mind focussed on thoughts of home. Seconds later, she re-emerges, gulping for air.

She's a hundred yards from her house when she hears footsteps behind her and a woman's voice calling her name. She stops and turns. It's Siân, illuminated under a streetlight, catching her breath. Her red bag is on the ground between her feet.

'What the hell happened to you?' she demands. Her eyes are blazing, her features stiff with rage. 'Someone could have nicked my bag!'

'You disappeared. I didn't know what to do.'

'I went to the toilet! You could have waited!'

'I'm sorry,' Helen says, and bursts into tears.

Siân's stares at her for a moment, then her face softens.

'It was supposed to be a bit of fun, the karaoke. If I thought it would freak you out like that –'

'Sorry,' Helen sobs. Her face burns with embarrassment.

'It's okay.' Siân steps forward. 'C'mon, I'll walk you the rest of the way.'

She links her arm through Helen's, pulling her towards her to show there's no hard feelings.

'You had me worried,' she says. 'But it's okay now.

There's no harm done.'

Helen nods. *It's okay*, she tells herself. *Almost home now. Safe and sound.*

As they approach the house, she senses that something isn't right. Parked outside her house is a Land Rover. As they draw closer, the driver's door opens and a uniformed officer steps out. From the far side of the vehicle a woman emerges, also in uniform.

'Mrs Helen McGrath?' the male officer asks.

Helen nods, her heart racing.

The man's expression gives nothing away. 'My name is Captain John Davies. This is Captain Elaine Enfield. Can we step inside, please?'

CHAPTER NINETEEN

As the female officer helps Helen to locate her keys, Siân pushes her way forward. 'I'm coming with her.'

The male officer blocks her way. 'And you are?'

'Siân.'

'Siân who?'

'Just Siân will do for now.'

Helen is dimly aware of some kind of altercation behind her. But she isn't paying attention. She half walks, half drifts into the house. Then the door closes on Siân and it's just her and the two officers standing in the hall.

'It's about your husband,' Captain Davies says. 'Owen McGrath. He's not dead. I repeat, he's not dead. But he has been injured.'

Helen legs buckle and she finds herself supported by the female officer. What's her name again?

'Captain Enfield will help you,' the man says as they steer her towards the stairs. 'Just sit for a moment. Take slow, deep breaths.'

Helen lowers herself onto the stairs and tries to contain the panic welling up inside her.

He's not dead. But he has been injured. How bad is it?

The man continues talking but she can't hear what he's saying. She sees his lips move, but there are no words – just sounds, bubbling away, signifying nothing.

His face looms towards her and his hands rest on her shoulders. 'Are you alright, Mrs McGrath? Do you understand what I've just told you? Nod if you understand.'

Helen nods, then shakes her head.

'There's been an incident involving your husband, Owen. I repeat, he's not dead. He's on his way home. You need to come with us.'

'Where?' Helen asks, although deep down she already knows the answer. It's where all wounded soldiers are taken.

'Birmingham,' Captain Davies says. 'The military hospital.'

An image of Owen missing a limb flashes through Helen's mind. Her mouth goes dry. 'How bad?' she asks, her voice sounding very thin and small compared to the Captain's booming tones. Then, in a firmer voice, 'How bad is he?'

'That, I can't say. But we need to leave as soon as possible. What about the woman outside? Is she a friend of yours?'

'Sort of.'

'And would you like us to let her in?'

Helen hesitates. Do I want Siân to come in?

She turns to the female officer. Her face is stiff, the eyes coldly professional. Then she adjusts her gazes to the small textured glass panel in the front door. Siân's face is visible through the glass. She looks worried, like any normal person would.

Helen nods. 'Yes.'

Captain Enfield opens the door and Siân rushes in. 'What's happened?' she demands. 'Is it her husband? Is he –'

'He's not dead,' Captain Davies says. 'But he has been injured. We're taking Mrs McGrath to the hospital. In Birmingham.'

'I'm coming with her.'

Captain Davies exchanges a look with the other officer. He turns to Helen. 'Is that okay with you, Mrs McGrath?'

Helen nods numbly.

'Then you'd best pack a few things. Captain Enfield will assist you.'

'No need,' Siân says. 'I've got this covered.' She hoists her bag over her shoulder and pulls Helen to her feet. 'C'mon. It's okay, I've got you. Just tell me what you need and leave the rest to me.'

Helen's heart is beating so loudly, she can barely hear a word – just the steady thump, thump, thump in her chest. If her heart is still pumping blood, then why does her skin feel so cold?

'Up we go,' says Siân, her voice somehow distant even as Helen feels her arm snake around her waist.

She holds onto the banister and struggles to keep control of her legs. With Siân helping to support her weight, she places one foot in front of the other and slowly they make their way up the stairs. When they reach the landing with its creaking floorboard, she feels Siân's grip tighten. 'Almost there,' she says, and leads Helen into the bedroom.

Helen sinks onto the bed and buries her head in her hands. There's a sharp click as Siân closes the door. She places her bag on the chair next to the dressing table and unzips one of the many side pockets.

'Helen!' she hisses. 'Helen!'

Slowly, Helen raises her head.

From what looks like a multivitamin bottle, Siân shakes something out into the palm of her hand.

'Take this.' She hands Helen a small white pill.

'What is it?'

'Something for the shock.' Siân takes a small bottle of water from her bag. 'Here, drink this.'

Helen stares at the pill. It's lozenge shaped and has letters and numbers stamped on one side.

'C'mon,' says Siân. 'Get it down you.'

Helen places the pill on her tongue and takes a gulp of water.

'Good girl. Now, where's your overnight bag?' Siân scans the room. 'It's okay. Got it.'

She hauls the small suitcase down from on top of the wardrobe, unzips it and places it open on the bed. 'Now, what do you need?'

Helen tries to think, but her head is spinning. She doesn't feel drunk anymore. This is a different kind of dizziness – sober and more terrifying.

'Don't worry,' says Siân. 'Leave it to me.' She opens the chest of drawers and begins scooping underwear into the case. Then she moves down to the next drawer, and the next, grabbing neatly folded piles of clothes – tops, T-shirts, a pair of jeans.

Numb with shock, Helen watches as Siân methodically fills the case. She recalls the last time she used it. It was her birthday, and Owen had surprised her with a weekend away in Pembrokeshire. It rained all day Saturday and the best part of Sunday – the kind of grey, drizzly rain that reminded them they hadn't left Wales. 'The green, green grass and grey, grey skies of home,' Owen had joked. But none of that mattered. They were together. They were happy. And they were safe from harm.

'Almost there!' Siân flashes a smile before leaving the room. From across the hall, Helen hears her open the bathroom cabinet. Moments later, she returns with a toilet bag and places it in the case.

'There,' she says. 'All done.'

'Thank you.' Helen feels her eyes prickle.

'No problem.' Siân stares at her. 'You're going to be okay, y'know. Whatever happens, I'll be there for you.'

Helen blinks back tears. Only two people have ever really been there for her. One is dead and the other is lying in hospital. 'I don't know what I'd do if –'

She shudders and clasps her hand to her mouth, afraid to even say the words.

'Hey,' says Siân, perching next to her on the bed and gripping her tightly by the shoulder. 'You heard what the captain said. He's not dead. Where there's life, there's hope. That's what people say, isn't it?'

'I suppose.'

'There you go, then. Now, is there anything else you need?'

Helen shakes her head.

'Right,' says Siân. She stands and zips up the case.

Captain Davies calls from downstairs. 'Mrs McGrath? Is everything alright up there?'

Siân opens the door. 'Hold your horses, Captain!' She turns to Helen. 'Ready?'

'I just need the loo.'

In the bathroom, a strange feeling of calm washes over her as she splashes cold water on her face and studies her reflection in the mirror. She looks pale, but that's nothing new. Her eyes are a little glassy, but that's probably from the wine. Other than that, she looks remarkably composed. She half expects her features to contort with fear and her mouth to form a silent scream, but none comes. Maybe it's the shock. Or maybe it's the certainty of knowing that Owen is alive. She doesn't know how badly he's been hurt, but at least he's not dead.

Siân is waiting for her on the landing. Her bag is slung over one arm. In her other hand she holds the small suitcase. 'We need to go.'

'Right,' says Helen. It suddenly dawns on her that Siân doesn't have a change of clothes of her own. 'Sorry. I should have asked. Do you need to borrow something? Some underwear at least?' She moves towards the bedroom.

'No!' Siân steps in front of the door, her eyes glittering in the dark. She smiles and hoists her bag further up her shoulder. 'Don't worry about me,' she says, patting the bag. 'I've got everything I need right here.'

Statement from Mark Yardley
Aged 51
Relationship to the victim – none

It now appears that, apart from his wife, daughter and whoever was responsible for his murder, the last person to see Richard Thomas alive was a passer-by.

On the day in question, Mr Mark Yardley had been visiting his mother at Glanrhyd Hospital. Situated on the outskirts of Bridgend, roughly a mile from where Richard Thomas lived with his wife and daughter, the hospital provides a range of inpatient mental health facilities including respite care, rehabilitation and long-stay beds. The hospital is easily reached by car or the nearest bus stop on Tondu Road. It is also linked via the Black Path to the street where Mr Thomas lived.

Mr Yardley previously cared for his mother at home and now lives alone in Wildmill – 'the top end, not the part where all the druggies hang out'. After leaving the hospital, he was making his way home on foot.

'I usually take the bus,' he said. 'But it was such a beautiful day, I decided to walk back instead. I thought some fresh air would help clear my head.'

Mr Yardley said he left the hospital at around noon.

'Normally I stay for lunch, but I could tell that Mum didn't want me there. She has days like that. Most of the time she enjoys the company, but sometimes it's as if the sight of me is enough to set her off. So I had a quiet word with the nurses and slipped out. I went and sat by the river for a bit. It's nice there, by the old railway bridge. I'm not sure how long I sat there – fifteen, twenty minutes, maybe? Then I headed over to the Black Path.'

Mr Yardley said he had been walking along the path for 'no more than five minutes' when he heard raised voices up ahead.

'I thought it was just kids messing about at first. Then I heard an older man's voice. He was shouting, something about his wife and how people should mind their own business. And then I heard some lads yelling back. One sounded really angry. But it was hard to make out the words. They were all shouting over each other.'

It was only when Mr Yardley approached that the shouting stopped. Mr Yardley saw a man he now identifies as Mr Richard Thomas.

'There were three lads with him, aged between fifteen and seventeen. I didn't get a good look at their faces. They were wearing those hoodies, and they had their heads turned away. Mr Thomas was holding a fleece – cradling it front of him with both arms. It looked heavy, like there was something wrapped inside it. He smiled and nodded at me. His face was very red. Maybe he was hot, or feeling a bit sheepish. Perhaps it was all that shouting. I said "hello" but nobody said "hello" back. They just stood there – him smiling, the lads looking the other way. I didn't stop. I felt a bit awkward, to be honest. So I just kept walking. As soon as I'd passed by, I could hear them start up again.'

Mr Yardley explained that he couldn't hear what was said as he was now walking away from the source of the commotion.

'I just kept going. I didn't look back. Part of me wanted to, but I was worn out from seeing my mum, and it really wasn't any of my business. Of course, if I'd known then what I know now…'

Mr Yardley was approaching the end of the path when he heard hurried footsteps behind him.

'The next thing I knew, he came barging past. Mr Thomas, I mean. He almost knocked me over. He didn't stop to say sorry or anything. He just kept running. And I noticed then that he wasn't carrying that fleece. Maybe it wasn't his. Maybe it belonged to one of those lads he was with. It didn't seem important at the time. I wish I'd tried to stop him, and find out what was going on. Perhaps I could have helped. But you never know, do you?'

Asked why he hadn't come forward earlier, Mr Yardley insisted that he hadn't made the connection between the man he saw on the Black Path that day and the one he later read about in the *Gazette*.

'It was only when I saw the police appealing for witnesses on the evening news that I put two and two together.'

Mr Yardley stressed that, prior to this, he had never met Richard Thomas. And Mandy Thomas?

'Never met her either. But I remember thinking it was odd that she wasn't on the TV with the police, appealing for witnesses. They usually have the wife on there, don't they? You'd think the wife would show some concern when her husband has just been murdered.'

PART TWO

CHAPTER TWENTY

He's not the man she married. That man had been strong, vibrant, full of life. When he held her in his arms she'd felt safe, as if no harm could ever come to her. But that sense of security is little more than a memory. This man is nothing like that. It's not just the lateness of the hour or the anxiety brought on by another bout of insomnia. Something has changed.

Sitting up in bed, she watches as he lies there snoring, sleeping off the pints of lager and whisky chasers he'd been drinking all evening. She can still smell the alcohol on his breath. Frank Powell – the life and soul of the Conservative Club. He must have spent the best part of a hundred pounds at the bar tonight. Good old Frank, always first in line with the next round, always so flash with his cash – and always ready with the excuses.

'But it's a cheap bar, Amanda. I can't see what your problem is.'

Always *her* problem, never *the* problem or, God forbid, *his*. It would never occur to him that his drinking was becoming an issue, or that it triggered memories she'd tried so hard to suppress.

Frank isn't a violent drunk. Nor is a secret drinker – not like her first husband. He doesn't hide bottles of vodka in hard to reach places or lock himself away for hours on end. He doesn't lie to her or force her to lie for him. He isn't deceitful. So why does she feel such a crushing sense of disappointment?

She'd spent the evening nursing a glass of lager and lime and making small talk with his friends, Peter and Sheila. Like Frank, they enjoyed a drink and saw no shame in getting completely wasted.

Amanda had refused the offer of another lager.

'But it's Saturday night,' Sheila had said, leaning against her husband, her voice slurred after a few too many vodka and tonics. 'What else are you going to do?'

There are many things Amanda would have preferred to be doing. Watching a film at the local cinema. Or enjoying a nice meal at that restaurant in Cowbridge, the one where she and Frank used to go, back when they were first married. But those days are long gone. There are no trips to the cinema now and no fancy meals in posh restaurants – just TV dinners and nights out at the Conservative Club.

The only time Amanda feels that she has anything approaching a proper family life is when her daughter joins them for Sunday lunch. But even those occasions are fraught. Helen makes no secret of the fact that she isn't fond of Frank. This isn't entirely his fault. Helen has always worshipped her father. No man, however perfect, could ever compete with memories forged when she was Daddy's little girl, too young to know any better. Amanda has lost count of the number of times she's been forced to hold her tongue. So what if her daughter's memories aren't entirely accurate? It's bad enough that she lost her father. To rob her of her illusions would have been unnecessarily cruel.

As for Frank, he finally seems to have given up trying to win Helen over. Looking down at him, Amanda's expression softens. It can't have been easy for him, trying to be a good father to someone else's daughter and having it thrown back in his face. But where does it leave her? In the unenviable position of peacemaker, constantly trying to smooth things over while her husband and daughter take pot shots at each other.

The mattress creaks as Frank shifts, grunts and turns over in his sleep. She waits until he settles and his breathing becomes regular before quietly slipping out of bed and padding down the hallway to her daughter's old room. Hidden in the back of the bedside drawer is a blister pack of sleeping pills. Her doctor was reluctant to prescribe them at first, given her history of dependency on anti-depressants. But it's not as if she takes them every day. They're just for occasional use, for nights like tonight, when she can't sleep and her mind is plagued with nagging doubts about the life she's chosen for herself. She pops a pill out of its foil and plastic packaging, places it in her mouth and gulps it down.

For a few minutes she stands staring around the room, at the books and posters Helen left behind. She was always such an introverted child, even before she lost her father. She rarely brought friends home. For years, Amanda worried that she'd never find a husband. There was never any talk of boys. Amanda and her own mother had often talked about the kind of man she hoped to marry. But she doesn't have that kind of relationship with her own daughter. Helen doesn't confide in her. She never has. So when she announced that she and Owen were getting engaged, Amanda was as surprised as anyone – surprised and more than a little relieved. The first time they met it was clear to her that Owen was a decent man. He would take good care of her daughter. What more could a mother ask for?

Amanda sighs, switches off the light and heads back to

bed. Frank is in the same position as before, face down, with his arm spread across her side of the mattress. Gently, so as not to wake him, she lifts his arm and slides beneath the bedclothes. She lies there for what seems like hours, listening to his steady snoring and the beat of her own heart. Finally her body gives in and she slips into a cold, black tranquilizer sleep.

The Black Path, Bridgend
– Wikipedia entry

The Black Path is a footpath which runs from the top of the Wildmill estate to an unnamed road close to the McArthur Glen shopping precinct (known locally as The Pines). It's a remnant of an early nineteenth-century horse-drawn tram road, built to carry coal and iron ore from the Maesteg area to Bridgend. The path runs for about half a mile alongside the River Ogmore and is separated by a narrow field from the railway line. Roughly halfway along the path is the site of an old blast furnace. The location is easily identified by a raised mound, marked by a large tree with a bald patch where the bark has peeled away. All that remains of the furnace is some broken brickwork.

Long regarded as a local beauty spot, the Black Path is still popular with cyclists. In recent years, the area has also become a gathering place for local youths – as evidenced by the leftovers of bonfires, barbecues and broken bottles.

***

Helen opens her eyes and tries to swallow. Her mouth is dry, with the aftertaste of something vaguely metallic.

Blood thumps in her ears and her vision is blurred. She blinks several times and turns her head.

Through a veil of fog she sees Siân sitting on another bed a few feet away, watching the television with the sound turned down.

'Morning, sleepyhead,' she says brightly.

Helen stares at her, wonders why everything is taking so long to come into focus. 'What happened?'

'You fell asleep in the car. We're in Birmingham.'

Suddenly it hits her. Owen. The hospital. The uniformed officers waiting outside her house. She tries to lift her head and the room spins – beige carpet, high gloss furniture, flatscreen TV.

'This isn't the hospital. What am I doing here? I need to see Owen.'

'Relax. It's not far. They offered us a bed there but you were dead to the world and I thought a hotel would be more comfortable, so I checked us in here. And don't worry about the bill. This is on me.'

'That's really kind of you,' Helen says. 'But I can't stay here.'

'I said I'd take care of you, didn't I?'

'Yes, but –'

'So let me, okay?'

Reluctantly, Helen nods. She's too exhausted to argue. She can pay Siân back later. 'Why can't I remember checking in?'

Siân smiles. 'Like I said, you were dead to the world. Just as well I'm strong for my size, eh?'

Helen hauls herself up. She feels weak and tired, but the giddiness is receding and her vision is clear. There's a glass of water on the bedside table. She takes it and gulps, barely slaking her thirst. *That's it*, she thinks. *I'm never drinking again.*

She takes another sip and wipes her mouth, spittle sticking to her fingers. 'I need to see Owen.'

'Of course,' Siân says, slipping off the bed. 'I've spoken to the hospital. They're expecting us in an hour. I've ordered breakfast and I put your clothes away.' She slides open the door of a large mirror-fronted wardrobe to reveal the contents of Helen's case neatly arranged on wooden hangers.

'I'm not hungry.'

'But you have to eat something. We need to keep your strength up.'

What strength? Helen thinks.

'C'mon,' Siân says. 'Why don't you have a quick shower before breakfast arrives?' She opens the door to the bathroom and turns on the light, like an estate agent showing a potential buyer around a new home. 'They've got everything here – bath, shower, complimentary toiletries. The shower gel is to die for.'

She grabs a fluffy white bathrobe and tosses it to Helen. 'The towels are behind the door.'

Helen climbs out of bed and pulls on the bathrobe. Her whole body aches. She wonders if she's coming down with something.

'Are you feeling okay?' asks Siân.

What a stupid question, Helen thinks, then hates herself for being so irritable.

'I'm fine,' she says and reaches for her jeans, which are neatly folded on a chair next to the bed. She pats the pockets, looks around the room. 'Where's my phone?'

'Here,' says Siân. She slides the phone from her own pocket and hands it over. 'It fell out in the car, so I held onto it for you.'

Helen checks the screen. There are no voice messages, no missed calls and no texts. She frowns.

'What's the matter?' Siân asks.

'I was expecting a call.' Helen wonders why her mother hasn't rung. It's not like her to leave anything to chance. Arrangements are always made, confirmed, checked and double-checked with painstaking precision. 'Never mind,' she says. 'It's not important.'

'Right,' says Siân. 'Breakfast is on its way. How about that shower?'

Helen glances at the phone again, sees that the battery is low. She groans. 'I forgot my charger.'

'Good job you have me then, isn't it?' Siân unzips one of the pockets of her bag and produces the charger. 'I grabbed it as we were leaving the house. Pass me the phone and I'll charge it while you get yourself ready.'

Helen hands it back.

'Off you go,' says Siân. 'You'll feel better after a nice shower.'

I doubt that very much, Helen thinks. She turns to move and her head swims. She reaches for the chair to steady herself.

'Okay?'

'Just a bit dizzy.'

'Hangover, probably.' Siân turns her attention back to the TV.

Helen nods.

But something isn't right. It's not just the room that's strange. There's something else, something she can't quite put her finger on. Then it hits her. It's a feeling of total remoteness. It's as if all of this is happening a long way away, to someone else. Despite everything, she feels eerily calm.

Maybe this is what shock feels like, she thinks.

Shaking her head, she drifts into the bathroom and closes the door.

When Helen re-emerges from the bathroom ten minutes later, Siân is lying on the bed, still staring at the television.

'Fucking God squad,' she says. 'They get on my nerves.'

'What are you watching?' Helen asks, towelling her hair.

'Some twat in a dog collar going on about the sins of the flesh. Like he'd know anything about it. The only flesh he's ever fingered is his own. Wanker.' Siân looks up. 'You're not a Christian, are you?'

Helen thinks of all the times she prayed as a young girl, wonders if her lack of faith is tied to the fact that her father died. 'Not really.'

'That's a relief. I can't be doing with Bible bashers. Blessed are the meek and all that crap. They don't know what they're on about. The meek aren't blessed. They're fucked. Any idiot can see that.'

'Siân? Can I ask you something?'

'It's not about the Bible, is it?'

'No.'

'Then shoot away.'

'What was that pill you gave me last night?'

'Just some herbal thing I get from Holland and Barrett. It's supposed to help calm your nerves. Did it work?'

'I think so.'

Siân grins. 'There you go, then.'

She leaps up from the bed and hurries over to the door. Just inside the room is a trolley covered with a white linen cloth. She wheels it over and positions it between the two beds.

'Room service came while you were in the shower. I left it covered to keep it warm.'

She whips off the cloth like a conjurer performing

a magic trick. 'Ta-dah!'

Helen stares at the enormous amount of food spread before her. There are bowls of fruit salad and cereal, a basket of bread rolls and pastries and slices of toast in a rack. There's a pot of tea, another of coffee, a jug of milk and a selection of jams, honey and marmalade in tiny jars. And there in the middle are two stainless steel plate covers, which Siân lifts to reveal generous helpings of smoked salmon and scrambled eggs.

'I'll never eat all that,' Helen says.

Siân's face falls. 'But we need to keep your strength up.'

This time, Helen doesn't tell herself she has no strength. She has to be strong – if not for herself, then for Owen. She shakes her head. 'No,' she says firmly. 'I'm not eating all that. Just coffee and a piece of toast. And then I want to see my husband.'

'Of course,' Siân says. 'Sorry. I wasn't thinking. You get some clothes on and I'll fix your coffee. Milk and sugar?'

'Please.' Helen feels a pang of remorse and forces a smile. 'Sorry. I just don't have much of an appetite.'

'Don't be daft. You get dressed. Don't mind me.'

Turning towards the wardrobe, Helen sees Siân's reflection in the mirrored door, watches as she reaches for her bag and dips her hand into one of the many pockets. Siân catches her eye and smiles. 'My sweeteners.'

CHAPTER TWENTY-ONE

Angela opens the back door and steps out into the garden. There are only a few clouds now. Looking up at the sky it's hard to believe that less than an hour ago it was bucketing down. But the air is still damp and there are puddles next to the bins. Yesterday's washing hangs heavy on the line. She's been so busy fretting about Kath, she forgot to bring it in.

She reaches into her dressing-gown pocket for her cigarettes, lights one and takes a long, deep drag. She doesn't normally smoke this early in the day, but then this weekend has been anything but normal. She's hardly slept a wink since Friday. First there was the ambulance ride to A&E and hours spent sitting on a grey plastic chair, waiting for Kath to regain consciousness and the staff to decide if and when she was well enough to be taken home. By the time they left, it was gone five in the afternoon. The remainder of the day was spent back at Angela's, with Kath weeping and wailing and Angela trying to comfort her and failing miserably. It was just as well Kath didn't know the whole story or she'd have been a complete mess.

Angela throws back her head and blows a long plume of smoke into the air. She feels the familiar rush of nicotine and a sudden surge of anger rising in her chest. What sort of man would spike a woman's drink? If she'd had even the faintest idea who it was, Angela would have shopped him there and then. In fact, had it been up to her, the police would have gone back to that bar and searched every man in the place. But there were no police. Kath was distressed enough, without getting the law involved. The first thing she said when she came round in the hospital was, 'Don't make a big thing out of it, Ange! I don't want my mam finding out!'

So it had been left to Angela to lie to Kath's mother, inventing some story about a stomach bug and explaining that she'd crashed at her place.

'She can't come to the phone right now,' she said when Kath's mother asked to speak to her. 'She's resting. Yes, I know it's after lunch, but she was up most of the night.'

Kath was always quick to defend her mother, though from the few times they'd met Angela had seen sufficient evidence to suggest that she was a cold-hearted cow who treated Kath as little more than the unpaid help. Angela had been sorely tempted to tell her the truth, just to see how she might have reacted to the news that her daughter had spent the night in hospital.

'That's right,' she'd imagined herself saying. 'One of those date-rape drugs. She's lucky to be alive. She was having trouble breathing and there was a moment when it looked as if her heart might stop. So just be nice to her, okay? The last thing she needs now is you coming down on her like a ton of bricks. I think she's been through enough, don't you?'

But Kath's pleading eyes and pitiful expression swayed her and she'd stuck to the agreed script.

'Thanks, Ange,' Kath sobbed when the phone call was finally over, and then the tears had come thicker and faster than before. It had taken another two hours before

164

she was in any fit state to be driven back home.

Angela sucks hard on her cigarette and stares at the wet clothes on the washing line. She'll have to tumble dry them now, or they'll never be ironed in time for work tomorrow. She can't see herself staying awake much past 9 p.m. tonight. She barely managed five hours sleep last night, despite being exhausted from the night before. She could happily crawl back into bed now, she's that tired. But she has a Pilates class this afternoon and some paperwork to prepare for tomorrow morning.

She thinks of Helen. She seemed to be enjoying herself on Friday night – at least as far as Angela can remember. It was all a bit of a blur towards the end. Then Kath had collapsed on her way to the toilet and it had been left to Angela to convince the security guard that her friend wasn't simply pissed and that someone ought to call an ambulance. She'd sobered up pretty quickly then, but with all her fears over Kath, she'd forgotten all about Helen. It wasn't until they were at the hospital and Kath was in the clear that she'd remembered. She texted Helen then – twice. And she called and left her a voice message yesterday afternoon and another one last night. But she still hasn't heard anything.

She takes another drag on her cigarette. Surely Helen isn't angry with her? It wasn't as if she'd just gone swanning off somewhere. It really was a matter of life or death. She hasn't repeated this to Kath, but before they left the hospital one of the nurses had taken Angela aside and informed her that without her swift intervention, there was a strong possibility that Kath wouldn't have pulled through.

'Your friend has a lot to thank you for,' the nurse had said, smiling tightly and placing a hand on Angela's shoulder. 'We had a girl die last weekend. Respiratory failure. Now do us both a favour and make sure we don't see Kath in here again, okay?'

Angela felt quite proud of herself then. But she isn't feeling so good now. Something isn't right. It's not like Helen to have her mobile switched off, not when she's waiting for news from her husband. And it's not like her to not respond to messages. Maybe she's lost her phone? Or perhaps she's tied up with her mother? Angela remembers her saying that she tends to spend more time at her mother's when Owen is away.

The sun appears. Angela takes one last puff of her cigarette before stubbing it out. She's overreacting. Lack of sleep and the stresses and strains of the weekend are catching up with her. Kath didn't die. Helen isn't sulking. She'll see them both at work tomorrow and everything will be just fine.

Helen is in the bathroom, putting the finishing touches to her make-up. It seems silly to be worrying about her appearance when Owen is lying in a hospital bed. But she wants to look her best for him. Assuming he's conscious. Assuming he can see her. She pictures her husband with bloodied bandages over his eyes. Her throat tightens and she pushes the thought away.

She's never stayed in a hotel like this before. She wonders how much it's costing. The complementary toiletries lined up next to the sink are brands she doesn't recognize, but they look expensive – all sandalwood, lavender and sage, promising to lift the spirits and promote relaxation and rejuvenation. Helen's spirits don't feel lifted. She barely managed a slice of toast at breakfast. But thanks to the coffee she's feeling more energized than she was half an hour ago. The caffeine courses through her veins.

She brushes her teeth for the second time and rinses her mouth out with the complementary mouthwash. The metallic taste has finally gone. She applies a second coat of lipstick and smacks her lips together.

Dropping the lipstick into her handbag, she turns to find Siân watching her from the doorway and her heart jumps. 'You startled me.'

'Sorry,' says Siân. 'Reception rang. The captains are waiting downstairs.'

Helen snaps the bag closed. 'We should go.'

'It won't kill them to wait a few minutes. This is about you, not them.'

'Right,' says Helen. She follows Siân into the room. Her phone charger is plugged into the wall socket next to her bed. There's no sign of her mobile. 'Have you seen my phone?'

Siân is busy checking herself in the wardrobe mirror and seems not to hear. 'I'm not sure about that Captain Enfield,' she says, fiddling with her hair. 'I bet she's a right lezzer.'

'Why do you say that?'

'Stands to reason. Uniforms always attract that type. Same with police. And prison officers. Lesbians, the lot of them.'

Helen feels she ought to say something. But she doesn't have the energy for an argument. 'She's only TA anyway.'

Siân doesn't respond.

'Territorial army,' Helen says. 'Volunteer force. She's not a professional soldier.'

'Yeah, I knew that. They let them in the army now though, don't they? Queers, I mean. That can't be right.'

'Why not?'

'Don't get me wrong. I've met some nice queers. But I

don't think they should join the army. It's not fair on the other men, is it? I bet your husband has a few things to say about it.'

'My husband is in a hospital bed.'

'Yeah. Sorry.' A wounded look flashes across Siân's face. Then it's gone. She fishes something out of her pocket. 'Your phone. Fully charged.'

Helen takes the phone and checks the screen. Nothing.

'Ready?' asks Siân.

Helen swallows. 'As I'll ever be.'

The entrance to the Queen Elizabeth Hospital is sleek, modern and somehow unreal. Helen catches sight of her reflection in the glass doors and feels as if she's looking at someone else. Inside, the light is bright and there's the smell of floor polish and disinfectant. As Captain Davies ushers her down the corridor, closely followed by Siân and Captain Enfield, she takes a few deep, steadying breaths and feels an icy calm wash over her.

'Okay?' asks Siân.

Helen nods without looking back.

Can't talk now. Must keep moving. Must stay focussed.

A couple of nurses march briskly by, trailed by three men in military uniform. They all wear the same inscrutable expression. A sign on the wall reads 'The Best in Care' above familiar logos for the Royal Navy, Army and Royal Air Force.

'Your husband is in the trauma ward,' Captain Davies says as they make their way along the gleaming corridor. 'Normal visiting hours are two to four and six-thirty to eight-thirty.'

'She's not waiting till two o'clock,' Siân chips in. 'She needs to see him now!'

Captain Davies clears his throat. 'As I was saying to

Mrs McGrath, *normal* visiting hours are two to four and six-thirty to eight-thirty. However, every effort is made to enable family members to see patients as soon as possible.'

'I should hope so,' says Siân. 'This is her husband we're talking about!'

'I'm well aware of that, miss!' the captain says, glancing over his shoulder before turning his attention back to Helen. 'As you'll see, the hospital provides care for both service personnel and civilians. The trauma ward has special facilities for service personnel only. The creation of a military atmosphere on the ward is very important. It ensures that our people are cared for in the right environment.'

He stresses the words 'our people' as if they're a breed apart. *Maybe they are*, Helen thinks. *How many civilian's wives live in anticipation of days like this?*

They turn down another corridor. 'The ward is made of single rooms and four bed bays,' the captain continues. 'Your husband is in a single room. When we reach the ward I'll hand you over to Sue Blackwell from the Defence Medical Welfare Service. She'll talk you through the support services available and answer any questions you may have before –'

'She doesn't need bloody support services!' Siân snaps. 'She needs to see her husband!'

Captain Davies shoots her a warning look. '*Before* escorting Mrs McGrath to the bedside,' he says. 'Now, is everything clear?'

'Yes,' Helen says, though everything is far from clear. There are so many emotions bubbling up inside of her, she's finding it hard to focus. The eerie calm she felt a few moments ago has gone. She feels the panic rise up inside – a familiar sensation, never too far from the surface. Her stomach seizes.

He's avoiding telling you how bad it is. What if Owen has lost a limb? What if he'll never walk again?

'Mrs McGrath?' The captain's voice sounds far off, like someone calling from a distant room.

Ask him! What are you afraid of? Go on! Ask him!

'Mrs McGrath? Do you understand what I just said?'

'For fuck's sake!' Siân's voice chimes in. 'Of course she understands! She's not thick!'

Helen's throat tightens. *Shut up, Siân! I can't think straight. Please, just shut up*!

A woman approaches. She wears a short-sleeved white blouse with black epaulettes and a knee-length black skirt. Her honey blonde hair is tied back in a ponytail. Pinned to her chest is a name tag with a red cross.

'Mrs McGrath? I'm Sue Blackwell. Defence Medical Welfare Service. Captain Davies tells me you're staying at the Indigo Hotel.'

Helen nods.

'Very nice. Maybe it wasn't explained to you properly, but we do have accommodation for family members on site. I can show you around afterwards if you like?'

'We haven't come for the guided tour,' Siân snaps. 'How many more times? She wants to see her husband!'

The captains exchange a look.

'Right,' says Captain Davies. 'Time we were going.'

He gives a nod to Captain Enfield, who steps forward and takes Siân by the arm. 'Come along, miss.'

'Don't you "miss" me!' Siân says, pulling her arm free. 'I'm not going anywhere.'

'Well, you can't stay here,' Captain Davies says firmly. 'Family members only. I can escort you to the cafeteria, or you can sit in the waiting room. It's up to you. But you're not allowed on the ward.'

170

As they usher Siân away, Helen feels her throat relax. Finally she finds her voice. She turns to the blonde woman in the crisp white blouse. 'I'd like to see Owen now, please.'

CHAPTER TWENTY-TWO

'The consultant will explain everything to you in more detail,' Sue Blackwell says. 'But I need you to prepare yourself before we go in.'

Helen nods and feels a wave of panic rise up inside her.

'Owen has sustained several injuries,' Sue continues. 'He's going to look quite different from how you last saw him. But his injuries aren't life-threatening and he's in good hands. Is that all clear?'

Helen nods again, more vigorously this time. She has a thousand questions but can't seem to latch onto a single one.

The next wave of panic hits her the moment they're through the door. Nothing she's seen or heard, not even her darkest imaginings could have prepared her for the grim reality of the trauma ward. She tries not to stare, but as Sue ushers her on, Helen's eyes are drawn to the men who occupy the beds in the bays on either side of her. Most are asleep – or unconscious. Others are propped up on their pillows, gazing back at her with blank expressions. One man lies flat on his back, eyes closed, his left arm folded above his head. What remains of his right arm rests on top of the covers. She averts her eyes but can't help imagining what further horrors lie hidden beneath the sheets.

Please God, let him be in one piece!

'This way.' Sue leads Helen on past a man sitting upright in bed, a pair of crutches propped against the wall beside him. He catches her eye as she passes. She forces a smile.

'Alright, gorgeous?' he calls and winks at her.

A voice shouts, 'Man down!' Startled, she looks around. A lad no older than twenty is thrashing around in his bed, the sheets tangled, his eyes tightly closed.

'It's okay,' Sue whispers. 'He's not in pain.'

'How do you know?'

'Morphine. It controls the pain and reduces the chances of a patient developing post-traumatic stress disorder. But it can't help with everything. Some of the men still have hallucinations.'

'What kind of hallucinations?'

'Bad dreams. Flashbacks. I've seen men sit up in bed and load imaginary rifles.' Sue gives a tired smile, then continues briskly, 'It's one reason why we try to keep military personnel and civilians apart. And the men do better when they're in a military environment. It's easier for them to adjust. You can be sure your husband will receive the best care available. Here we are.'

They've reached a closed door at the far end of the trauma ward. Sue pauses and wipes her hands with antibacterial lotion from a dispenser on the wall. Helen follows suit.

'Are you ready, Mrs McGrath?'

Helen nods. They go in.

The first thing she notices is the sunlight. It comes streaming in from the window, creating a haze around the only bed in the room. It takes a few moments for her eyes to adjust, a few more for her brain to tell her that what she's registering is in fact real. And then it hits her.

'No,' she whispers, moving towards the bed on legs that feel as if they might give way at any moment. 'Please, no.'

She barely recognizes him. His face is puffed up, the skin bruised and pitted with small shrapnel wounds, his hairline caked in blood and dirt.

'Owen?'

No reaction. His eyes are closed. The area around his right eye socket is swollen. His top lip is thick and split like a boxer's. There's a gauze dressing over his left cheek and another on his right shoulder. IV drips dangle from his right arm. The left arm is in plaster.

'Owen? It's Helen.' She reaches for his right hand and sees that her own hand is trembling. As the tips of her fingers brush against his, she flinches and draws back. His skin is cold.

Slowly, she lowers herself into the chair beside the bed. Tears prick her eyes and begin to roll down her cheeks. She lets them come – knowing, somehow, that she has to let the tears out before she'll have the strength to continue. Then she takes a tissue from her bag. She wipes her eyes, takes a deep breath and reaches once more for his hand. This time she doesn't flinch. She holds it in hers, sees the dirt under his nails, feels the roughness of the skin. Then she places her other hand on top and gently rubs the tips of his fingers between hers until, finally, she feels a little warmth.

'Mrs McGrath?' Sue touches her shoulder. 'Mr Croft is here to see you.'

Helen looks up to see a man standing in the doorway, dressed in a surgical gown and carrying a clipboard. She rises to her feet as he strides over to the bed.

'Is he going to be alright?' she asks, holding back more tears.

The surgeon studies his notes before replying gently, 'Your husband sustained a head injury, which is why he's in a coma. We're controlling the pain with morphine and monitoring his blood pressure. Apart from that, he has a broken arm and some minor cuts and bruises. Those marks on his face should heal fairly quickly. The bones will take a little longer.'

'Bones?' Helen repeats. She stares down at the bedclothes. Are his legs broken too?

'His arm, Mrs McGrath. It's broken in two places – the humerus and the radius. That's the upper arm and the forearm. The cast will have to stay on for six weeks. After that, he'll need physiotherapy to help restore strength and flexibility.' He smiles at her. 'But the breaks are clean. There shouldn't be any lasting damage.'

She feels some of the tension leave her body. 'What happened?'

'There was an explosion. That's really all I can tell you. What you need to focus on is the fact that he's doing remarkably well. He's breathing unaided. He coughs, yawns, blinks and shows rapid eye movement. Which means the lower brain stem is working.'

'Is that good?'

'Yes, it's good. All we can do now is wait for him to wake up.'

'What if he doesn't wake up?'

The doctor's face is impassive. 'As I say, we'll just have to wait. Now, if you'll excuse me, I'm needed in surgery.' He moves towards the door.

'Will it help if I talk to him?' Helen asks.

The doctor turns back and smiles. 'It certainly won't do any harm. Just don't expect him to start talking back to you. Not yet anyway.'

And then he's gone.

Sue Blackwell gives a small nod. 'I'll leave you two alone,' she says, and follows the doctor out.

A cyclist is in a critical condition after it is believed he was attacked by two men and stabbed in the stomach.

The 41-year-old man was found in an area of Bridgend known as the Black Path at around 10 p.m. last night.

He is being treated at the Princess of Wales Hospital for a serious puncture wound to his stomach.

One man has been arrested in connection with the incident and is being held at Bridgend Police Station, while police continue the search for a second male suspect.

It is believed the attack happened between 9.30 p.m. and 10 p.m.

Both suspects are said to be white and in their late teens or early 20s, with local accents.

Police are appealing for any witnesses to come forward.

Behind her, Helen hears the door click as she edges her chair closer to the bed. She folds her hands restlessly in her lap. Her stomach tightens. He looks so different, it's hard to believe that this is the man she knows so well and loves so much. Even the intimacy of being alone with him fails to deliver the feeling of familiarity she's craved for so long. His face is strange to her – the sounds of the machines stranger still.

The last time she and Owen were alone together, the atmosphere had been tense. It was the morning he left for Afghanistan, before he walked out of the door and into the vehicle that would drive him to the base and the military plane. When he went to kiss her goodbye, she'd turned her head slightly, so his kiss grazed her cheek rather than met her lips. He tried to lighten the mood by joking about coming home and making babies and she humoured him the way she often did. 'Of course we will. But one thing at a time. Just keep your mind on the job. I want you back home in one piece.'

How those words haunt her now. Her head swims. There's too much to take in. Already she's struggling to recall what the doctor said. What use is she, if she can't even remember that? She feels alienated and out of her depth, intimidated by the busy medical staff and gleaming paraphernalia of the hospital. Everyone else has a role to play, each piece of equipment a function to serve. Right now it feels as if her only role is simply to hold herself together and remember to breathe. She wonders how she'll even manage that.

Her stomach rumbles, reminding her of how little she's eaten in the past twenty-four hours. She should have listened to Siân when she had the chance. A little more gratitude wouldn't have gone amiss either. It's hardly Siân's fault that she's a nervous wreck or that Owen is in hospital or that everything is such a mess. All she's done is find them a nice hotel, encourage her to eat something and try to make a shitty situation more bearable.

Nice work, Helen. The first friend you've made in years and she's probably sitting somewhere on her own, miles away from home, asking herself why she even bothers. No wonder you've always been such a loner. It's a wonder anyone bothers with you at all.

She breathes deeply and the nagging voice recedes, bringing her back into the room, back into the moment, back to the man she loves. She presses her fingers to her temples and tries to gather her thoughts. She should talk to him, say something. Who knows? It might even help. She might even make herself useful after all.

'Owen,' she begins, and then her mind goes blank. What's wrong with her? She's waited a long time for an opportunity to talk to him. All those lists she made. All the calls that never came. All the conversations they never had. She must have something to talk about, surely? But now the moment has finally arrived, the words won't come.

She looks at his face for reassurance, but the swelling and the bruises and the split lip make her heart ache and her throat tighten. She reaches for his hand again. His skin feels warmer than before, and for a split second she imagines him opening his eyes and turning to her. 'Come on, babes,' he'd say with a grin. 'Get on with it. I'm bored senseless here.' But there are no words of encouragement, no signs of life apart from the sound of his breathing and the steady rise and fall of his chest.

She sits listening to the bleeps of the machines for what seems like an eternity. Her eyes travel from the tubes in his arm to the marks on his face to the dirt in his hair. Then she leans forward and kisses him gently on the cheek. His stubble feels like sandpaper against her lips.

'Owen,' she says softly. 'It's me, Helen. I don't know if you can hear me, but the doctor says you're doing okay. You're in the hospital now, but I'll soon be taking you home.' She thinks of the morning he'd left for Afghanistan, the distance between them. 'I've been thinking,' she says. 'Maybe it's time we started a family.–' Her voice cracks and she swallows hard, blinking back tears.

What are you saying? What if he can hear you? Is that really the best you can come up with? Making promises you won't keep?

She lifts her head and gazes around the room, struggling for something else to say. She thinks of work – but Owen has no interest in office gossip and has often complained about the long hours she puts in. She pictures her mother and Frank – but the last time they visited, Owen had shared a beer and a joke with Frank, and they'd ended up arguing in the car on the way home. Then her thoughts return to Siân. There's no history there, no emotional baggage. Siân is a safe subject.

'I'm here with a friend,' she says in a brighter voice. 'You don't know her. We only met a couple of days ago. I went out with the girls from work on Friday and –'

She pictures herself back home, falling over drunk, surrounded by women spoiling for a fight, unable to fend for herself.

Good idea! Tell him the state you were in. That'll really help!

'Her name's Siân,' she continues. 'I think you'd like her, Owen. She's really –'

She wants to say 'fearless' but stops herself. A word like that will need some explaining.

'She lost her dad, too,' she says, remembering how she'd first opened up to Owen about her father dying, how sympathetic he'd been. 'It was only a few years ago. A hit and run. Not like the way I lost my dad. But there's definitely a connection there. I can feel it.'

She pauses before continuing. 'Do you remember that time you wrote to me saying how important it was to have friends you can trust, people who'll watch your back? It was when you were in Iraq. Well, I was reading some of your old letters the other night. I know you were talking about soldiers watching out for each other, and that's a bit different. But you were right. I honestly don't know what I'd have done without Siân these past couple of days. She's really been there for me. Y'know, the way friends are supposed to be there for each other.'

She trails off. 'Sorry, I'm rambling. My head feels a bit foggy. I think I might be coming down with something. But please don't worry about me. Like I said, I've got plenty of support. You just concentrate on getting better. Then I can take you home.'

She feels her throat tighten again, and wonders what to say next.

There's a movement in her peripheral vision. Sue Blackwell appears in the doorway. 'I think that's probably enough for now,' she says gently. 'Let's go and find your friend.'

CHAPTER TWENTY-THREE

Siân isn't in the waiting room. She's not in the cafeteria either.

'Maybe she just popped to the loo?' Sue Blackwell says brightly. 'Since we're here, why don't you take a seat and I'll bring us both a cup of coffee? Or maybe you'd prefer tea? Mrs McGrath?'

Helen blinks. 'Sorry?'

'Are you alright?'

'Yes, I'm fine. A bit of a headache coming on.'

The officer smiles sympathetically. 'Lack of sleep, I expect.'

It sounds more like a statement than a question, so Helen doesn't bother with a reply. She doesn't know what to say, anyway. Her head is all over the place. She's lost for words, out of control, like a driver behind the wheel of a car whose brakes have failed. She keeps trying to picture Owen the way he looked before – the soft brown eyes, the dimple in his cheek. But all she sees is the way he looks now – almost unrecognizable, his face all swollen, with those red marks and that dirt in his hair. Why haven't they bothered to wash his hair? Is there something they're not telling her?

'You can talk to me,' the officer continues. 'I'm here to help.'

'Thank you, Ms Blackwell.'

'Please, call me Sue.' She gives another of her smiles. Practised. Polite. Professional.

Helen tries to smile back. 'You're very kind. I'll be fine, really. I just need to find my friend.'

'Of course. And we will find her, just as soon as we've had a little rest.' She turns to the nearest table and gestures to Helen to take a seat. 'What can I get you? Tea? Coffee?'

'Coffee, please. Milk and sugar.'

'Right,' says Sue. 'Two coffees coming up.'

Helen heaves a sigh of relief as she sits down. Her head is pounding. She turns and stares at the officer standing at the counter. Is she married? Sue Blackwell has glossy blonde hair and a sporty confidence that reminds Helen of some of the girls she used to know at school. They were the kind of girls who always wore freshly pressed cotton blouses and were destined to go to university before marrying the captain of the rugby team. Their husbands would arrive home from work every night at 6 p.m., except on Fridays when they'd finish early and take their wives out for dinner at one of the smart restaurants along the coast. They would produce beautiful children who would make them proud and bring them even closer together. Their husbands would never risk their lives in the line of duty, and would live long enough to see their offspring happily married with children of their own. Nothing bad would ever happen to these people.

Helen presses her fingers to her temples. She tries to imagine herself in one of those women's shoes, curled up on the sofa at home with Owen's arm around her. He's watching the television. There's a game on, a rugby match he really wants to see. But he's turned the sound down to give her his full attention. 'I'm so happy,' he says.

'You're going to be the best mum ever.' She glows with pride, secure in the knowledge that she's giving him the one thing he's always wanted. He places his hand on her swollen belly and swears to her that he can feel the baby kicking. 'He's going to play for Wales,' he says. 'Just you wait and see.'

But when she places her own hand on her stomach, it doesn't feel right. There's no movement, no sign of life. Something is wrong. She turns to Owen for help. One side of his face is frozen, his eyes staring straight ahead. He opens his mouth and makes a dreadful moaning sound. Then she's phoning an ambulance, crying out in pain, screaming down the phone. The ambulance arrives, siren wailing, lights flashing. She runs outside. But there's no ambulance. There's no car parked outside her house. There's no street. She looks around and sees that she's back in the garden of the house where she grew up. She's ten years old again, standing by the rabbit hutch her father built for her, staring in horror at a lifeless lump of tiny bodies squashed together under the straw.

A buzzing sound brings her back to the strip-lit misery of the cafeteria with its calming pastel walls and huddles of anxious-looking people. Her phone is vibrating in her handbag.

She fumbles around for a few moments and the buzzing stops. Finally she fishes the phone out of the bag and stares at the screen. There's a missed call from her mother. Should she call her back? And say what exactly? The last thing she wants is her mother and Frank turning up. What good would it do? She has enough to cope with already, without the added complication of family tensions.

Sue appears with a plastic tray, two cups of coffee and a saucer with sachets of sugar and sweetener. She sets them down on the table and smiles. 'Okay?'

'Not really,' Helen replies. She pauses, wonders how much she's willing to confide. 'I don't know what to do,' she says. 'I just feel so helpless.'

Sue nods as if she's heard this a million times before. *Maybe she has*, Helen thinks. She puts the phone back in her bag and reaches for her coffee.

'She's still not answering,' Amanda says, placing the handset back in its cradle. 'That's it. The lunch will be ruined.'

Frank is seated at the kitchen table, poring over his newspaper. 'Calm down, love,' he says gently. 'Have you tried calling the house?'

'Of course I've tried calling the house!' Amanda snaps. 'I don't need you to tell me that. She's not at home and she's not answering her mobile. Do you have any other bright ideas?'

Frank shrugs. 'She's probably on her way. You know she never likes to answer the phone when she's driving.'

'Well, it wouldn't hurt her to call first. How am I supposed to time the lunch if I don't know when she's coming? I'm not a mind reader.'

'She knows lunch is at one.' Frank says gently. 'Lunch is always at one. It's been at one for as long as any of us can remember. And it'll be at one when we're both old and grey and can barely remember our own names or what we had for breakfast.'

Amanda narrows her eyes. 'That's right. Mock me.'

'I'm not mocking you. I'm just trying to raise a smile.'

He lifts his eyebrows and looks at her expectantly, but to no avail.

'I called her last night from the club,' Amanda says. 'Not that you'd remember. You were too busy drinking with your cronies.'

Frank sighs. 'Do we really have to go through this again? For once, can't we just enjoy our lunch?'

'That's easy for you to say. You're not the one doing all the cooking.'

'I offered to peel the potatoes, but you weren't having it. I offered to make the gravy, but you always have to do it your way. Tell me what to do and I'll gladly do it. But don't complain about me not helping when you won't let me.'

Amanda catches his eye for a moment, then looks away. 'This is typical of Helen,' she sniffs, moving towards the cooker and opening the oven door to check on the roast. 'No thought for other people.' She reaches for an oven glove and inspects the roasting pan, poking at the meat with a carving knife. 'The beef will be dry at this rate.'

'No, it won't,' Frank says. 'We'll take it out and wrap some foil around it. You're supposed to let the meat rest anyway.'

'Thank you, Gordon Ramsay,' Amanda replies. 'I think I know how to roast a joint of beef.' She slams the oven door shut and reaches into a cupboard for a large serving plate.

'I know you do,' Frank says.

His tone is soothing but it only seems to needle her all the more. She grabs a tea towel and begins wiping the plate. 'Don't humour me, Frank.'

Her husband rises from the table and moves towards her. 'I'm not,' he says, extending his arms towards her. 'You're a wonderful cook. Have you ever heard me complain about your cooking?' He puts one arm around her shoulders. 'All I'm saying is that maybe you should calm down a bit.'

'I'm perfectly calm!' Amanda snaps, shrugging him off.

Frank smiles. 'Really? Then why are you rubbing the pattern off that plate? C'mon, love. Just try and relax a bit, eh? It's a family meal, not an endurance test.'

She places the plate on the kitchen counter and glares at him. 'And what's that supposed to mean?'

'You know what it means. Whenever Helen comes here, you get yourself so worked up it's impossible for anyone to relax.' He walks over to the fridge and takes out a can of lager.

Amanda bristles as he cracks open the can. 'And you're perfect, I suppose?'

Frank's smile tightens. 'Hardly. I'm a few stone overweight. My wife thinks I drink too much. And my stepdaughter still hasn't forgiven me for not being her father.'

'Don't you dare bring Richard into this!' Amanda's voice is suddenly shrill.

'You're right,' Frank says. 'I'm sorry. Forget I even mentioned it.'

'Don't play games with me, Frank.'

'I'm not. I've said I'm sorry. Let's just leave it.'

But she can't. He can tell by the look on her face that he's touched a nerve. He waits, knowing she won't let it go, that it's not in her nature.

'I don't know why you insist on talking about Richard,' she says.

Frank sighs. 'Let's not do this now.'

'Why not?' Amanda says. 'If there's something on your mind, let's hear it.'

'It's not a question of what's on my mind,' Frank replies. 'It's what's on yours.'

He sees her hackles rise, knows there's no going back

now. She won't be happy until they're tearing chunks out of each other.

'It's not easy,' he says, as calmly as he can. 'It's not easy living in another man's shadow. I'm not him, Amanda. I'm nothing like him.'

'I never said you were.'

'No, you didn't. But you don't have to. I see it in your eyes. Every time we go to the club. Every time I so much as glance at another woman. I see the way you look at me.'

'You sound paranoid, Frank. Anyone would think you had something to hide.'

'Now you're being ridiculous,' Frank says. 'I'm not the one hiding things around here.'

'Meaning?'

'Meaning if you hadn't been so intent on hiding the truth from Helen, it's quite possible that she and I might have had some sort of relationship. Instead she looks at me like I'm a constant disappointment to her. And who can blame her? I can't compete with a dead man, especially when you've allowed her to grow up thinking he was some sort of saint.'

Amanda snorts. 'I've done nothing of the sort!' She reaches for the plate and begins wiping it again furiously with the tea towel.

'You have,' says Frank. 'We both know you have. And I'm sure you had your reasons. But it's not fair, love. It's not fair on me and it's not fair on her. She's a grown woman, for Christ's sake. I think she's old enough to cope with the truth.'

Amanda slams the serving plate down on the counter. 'I'll decide what's best for Helen!' she snaps. 'She's my daughter!'

Frank's face clouds. 'Thanks for that,' he says.

'Thanks for reminding me of my place around here.'

'That's not what I meant –' she begins.

'Forget it!' He snatches the newspaper from the table and storms out of the room.

'Feeling any better?' Sue Blackwell asks.

'A little,' Helen lies. Panic keeps washing over her in waves. Despite Sue's assurances, she can't escape the feeling that things are far worse than she's been told. She's heard about doctors giving families false hope, of worried wives and girlfriends being shielded from the truth. What if Owen doesn't make a full recovery? What if there's brain damage? The rush of caffeine seems to have sharpened her senses. The nagging voice in her head is screaming louder than ever.

She pushes the half-empty coffee cup away and attempts a smile. 'Sorry. I can't seem to shift this headache.'

Sue nods. 'Why don't I go and get you some –' she begins, then stops and turns her head as something catches her eye. 'Isn't that your friend?'

Helen follows her line of vision. A young man in army fatigues stands at the entrance to the cafeteria, his back to her. There's something vaguely familiar about him, but it's probably just the uniform. Standing next to him, close enough for their bodies to almost touch, is Siân. One hand toys with her hair. The other paws playfully at his chest. The soldier seems to be enjoying the attention. Reaching for Siân's waist, he pulls her towards him. She smiles and tosses her hair before catching sight of Helen. She whispers something in the soldier's ear, pulls herself away and comes running over.

'I've been waiting for ages,' she says.

Helen sees that she's wearing lipstick – bright red, to

match her shoulder bag. She doesn't recall her wearing it earlier, but then what business is it of hers?

'Who's that?' Helen asks, staring past her to where the soldier was standing moments earlier. But he's already disappeared.

Siân shrugs. 'Just some bloke.' She pulls up a chair and reaches for Helen's hand, clasping it in hers. 'So how is he? Have they let you see him yet?'

'Mrs McGrath has seen her husband,' Sue replies. 'He's resting now, but I've told her she can come back later.'

Siân ignores the officer and stares deep into Helen's eyes. 'Well? How is he?'

Helen struggles to find an answer. Voicing her fears will make them more real, and she's conscious of Sue's watchful presence.

'Never mind,' says Siân. 'We can talk later. Somewhere more private.'

'I think Mrs McGrath could do with a rest,' Sue says. She turns to Helen. 'Shall I fetch you something for that headache?'

'No need.' Siân smiles and pats her bag. 'I've got plenty of painkillers.'

'I see. Well, perhaps we can find a quiet place for Mrs McGrath to have a lie down?'

'I'll take her back to the hotel,' Siân replies, rising to her feet.

'I was thinking of somewhere a bit closer. As I mentioned earlier, we do have accommodation –'

'The hotel is nicer,' Siân says firmly. 'And it's better that she's with someone she knows.' She takes hold of Helen's arm and pulls her up.

Sue stands and takes something from her pocket. She presses a business card into Helen's hand. 'Here's my number. Call me if you need anything.'

Siân slides a protective arm around Helen's shoulders. 'Thanks,' she says. 'But I can take it from here.'

CHAPTER TWENTY-FOUR

Angela's abdominals ache as she leaves the sports centre. She pauses for breath on the steps outside and feels the afternoon sun on her hot, flushed face. Her hair is still damp from the shower and her clothes, though clean, feel horribly constricting. She tears off her zip top and tucks it into her holdall, together with her sweaty gym kit. Fuck it, she thinks. One more thing for the wash.

Today's Pilates class had been hard going. The instructor, Mel, had commented on the fact that she was looking a little off-colour.

'Heavy night?' she'd asked.

'Something like that,' Angela had replied. There was no need for Mel to know that she'd spent the best part of Friday night in hospital, or that she was so worried about Kath, she'd barely slept a wink since. It's no wonder she's looking off-colour. It's a wonder she's still functioning at all.

'You'll feel better afterwards,' Mel had said cheerily, and she was right. She may not have performed all of the exercises to the best of her ability. But there was satisfaction in knowing that she hadn't skipped the class completely, or wimped out halfway through like some of the women did. Angela prides herself on her resolve. Once she sets her mind on something, she's determined to see it through.

She takes out her mobile. There are no missed calls or text messages. The time is ten past two. She slips the phone back into her pocket and thinks of all the things she still had to do today. First stop, the newsagent. Then home to tackle the mountain of ironing left over from yesterday and prepare some paperwork for tomorrow's meeting with Natalie.

The newsagent is almost out of papers. There's no sign of the *Sunday Times*, and she can't bring herself to buy the *Mail on Sunday*.

'Alright, love?' the newsagent calls from behind the counter.

Angela has been going to the same newsagent for the best part of five years. The fact that Mr Jones calls her 'love' is no reflection of the level of affection he feels for her. He calls all his female customers 'love'. Angela wonders how he greets those customers who aren't female and decides that terms of endearment probably aren't necessary. Where men are concerned, a simple 'alright' would do.

'I was looking for the *Sunday Times*,' she says.

'Sorry, love,' Mr Jones replies. 'I sold the last one ten minutes ago. You'll never guess who I just had in. That so-called Muslim chap. Y'know, the one who lives over in Blackmill?'

Angela nods. She's seen the man the newsagent is referring to – middle-aged, white and recently taken to wandering around town in traditional Arab dress. A bit of a nutter, probably, but he seems harmless enough.

'Funny bugger, he is,' Mr Jones says. 'He was going on about that story in the *Gazette*. I don't know if you've seen it?'

Angela shakes her head. 'I don't really bother with the local paper.'

'It's front page. Big piece on that drug baron they locked up a few years back. Dennis Bevan. Nasty piece of work. He's the reason half them kids in Wildmill are hooked on heroin. Anyway, he's got a parole hearing coming up and our Muslim friend reckons he's paying them all with blood money. The police. The prison service. Even the judge. It's all a big conspiracy, apparently.'

'Right,' says Angela, not wishing to be drawn into a lengthy discussion on the subject.

But the newsagent isn't done yet. 'You should have heard him, ranting and raving. I know he likes to tell everyone he's off the booze since his religious conversion, but I swear I could smell whisky on his breath.'

Angela smiles politely. 'It takes all sorts.'

Mr Jones gives her a look that says this isn't quite the response he's looking for. 'Right, then,' he says crisply. 'What can I get you?'

'I'll take the *Observer*, please,' Angela replies.

The newsagent frowns.

'And the *Gazette*,' she adds quickly, reaching into her pocket and counting out her change. As she turns to leave the shop, an older woman shuffles up to the counter carrying a large bottle of Coke.

'And the *Mail*, please,' Angela hears the woman say, which immediately draws a sharp intake of breath from the newsagent.

'You'll never guess who I've just had in here,' he begins. 'That Muslim.'

'Hang on,' says Siân. 'I need the loo.'

Up ahead, Helen can see the glass sliding doors of the hospital and a cluster of people gathered outside smoking.

She wonders what possesses people to smoke, knowing what the risks are. Then she pictures Natalie and Simon at work, enjoying a cigarette break while the rest of the staff are hunched over their keyboards.

Damn, she thinks. I'd better call the office and tell them I won't be in.

She remembers Simon saying he needed a word and wonders if her days on the job are numbered. Well, there's no point in worrying about it now.

'Helen?'

'Hmm?'

'I said I need the loo. Just wait here, okay? I'll be two ticks.'

Helen nods. 'I'll watch your bag.'

'It's alright,' Siân says, hoisting the bag higher on her shoulder. 'I think I'll freshen up a bit. Don't go anywhere. I won't be long.'

Helen watches as she disappears down the corridor. Suddenly she feels terribly alone. She takes a deep breath and feels it shudder through her body. Her head pounds – a dull, nagging pain that grips the back of her skull and tightens around her temples. But the headache is the least of her worries. There's an image in her head now. She keeps trying to block it out, but it won't go away. She sees herself standing next to Owen's bed. Weeks have passed and he's still unconscious. In fact, his condition has deteriorated. The marks on his face have turned into festering sores. He's no longer breathing unaided but has a ventilation tube in the side of his mouth.

'I'm sorry, Mrs McGrath,' the doctor says. 'It's bad news, I'm afraid.'

Tears roll down her cheeks.

The doctor shakes his head sadly. 'The brain damage

is worse than we thought. There's not much else we can do.'

No!

She closes her eyes and presses her hand to her forehead.

Stop torturing yourself! You heard what the doctor said. He's going to get better.

But he didn't really say that, did he? He said his arm would heal. He didn't say anything about his brain.

In her mind's eye, she sees the doctor gravely shake his head and a nurse pull up a sheet like a shroud over her husband's face.

Stop it! What would Owen think if he could see you now? If you can't be strong for yourself, at least be strong for him.

She's brought back to reality by a sudden cry. She opens her eyes, wonders for a split second if the sound came from her. Then she sees her. At the end of the corridor, no more than twenty feet from where she's now standing, someone has left a door open. Framed in the doorway, seemingly oblivious to the fact that she can be seen, is a well-dressed woman in her late forties. Even from this distance, Helen can see that she's distraught. Her face is white and her eyes are red. She's being comforted by a man with neat, greying hair and a thin moustache. He wraps his arms around her and she buries her face in his chest, her shoulders heaving.

It all goes quiet for a moment. The man appears to be whispering words of comfort in the woman's ear as he strokes her hair. Then the woman's whole body begins to shake and she lets out a sound like nothing Helen has heard before. It's halfway between a howl and a wail, a sound an animal in pain might make. It barely sounds human at all. The man continues holding her as the woman claws at his chest, whimpering and wailing and gulping for air. Finally she goes limp. He cradles her head on his shoulder and turns his face towards Helen. The look in his eyes sends a chill through her.

This is what grief looks like, she thinks.

The man pushes the door shut and a voice – her mother's voice – echoes in her ears. 'Helen! Haven't I told you it's rude to stare?'

It was the day of her father's funeral. Her mother had insisted that a funeral was no place for a child, so she'd spent the afternoon with Mr and Mrs Roberts from across the road. Her mother had come to collect her with her friend Jackie. They were standing on the doorstep, both dressed in black. Jackie's bleached blonde hair was tucked under a small pillbox hat and it was clear from her face that she'd been crying. Her mother's face was impassive. She looked more irritated than upset, as if burying her husband was little more than an inconvenience.

'Come along, Helen,' she said briskly. 'We haven't got all day.'

She sounded as if she was simply hurrying her along to school.

As soon as they were home, her mother sent her upstairs to her room. Helen lay with her ear pressed to the floor, listening to the adults talking in hushed tones in the room below. Finally they said their goodbyes and she heard her mother's footsteps on the stairs. She turned off the bedroom light and climbed under the covers, pretending to be asleep as the door cracked open and her mother whispered goodnight.

'There you are,' a voice says, snapping her back to the bright light of the hospital corridor. Siân is staring at her with an intensity she finds unsettling. 'Are you okay?' she asks.

'Yes,' Helen replies. Her voice shakes. Her eyes blur with tears.

Siân's face softens. 'C'mon,' she says. 'Let's find a cab.'

Martin Collins isn't given to excessive displays of emotion. He has the stiff bearing of a man who's spent a lot of time in the military and is proud of it. A former army staff sergeant, recently retired, his greying hair is still worn in the same severely cropped style. His thin lips and clipped moustache rarely twitch or widen into a smile.

As he leaves the hospital with his grieving wife by his side, he keeps his eyes locked firmly ahead. Heading towards his car, he sees the young woman who caught his eye earlier in the hospital corridor. She's being bundled into a taxi by another woman with black hair and a red shoulder bag. Watching her now, she looks every bit as shaken as his wife. He wonders for a moment if she, too, has been asked to identify the body of someone she loved – her brother perhaps, or her husband.

Martin's son wasn't married. There's no wife to grieve for him, and no children to worry about. That's a blessing, at least. For years, Martin has been learning to count his blessings. He sighs to himself and fumbles in his pocket for his car keys. Jamie hadn't turned out the way he'd hoped. He hadn't excelled at school. There were no girlfriends, no prospect of grandchildren. But he had followed in his father's footsteps and joined the army. Even now, there's comfort in knowing that he'd devoted his life to serving his country. His son died a hero. That's what people will say. That's how Martin will remember him.

As he jerks open the car door he hears a wailing sound and turns to see his wife standing several feet away. Her face is a mess of emotions – all the feelings he's keeping locked up written large across her features. Her mouth gapes. Her eyes are wild. Tears course down her cheeks.

'Barbara?' he says, walking towards her.

She backs away, hands raised in front of her face like she's fending off an attacker.

'Barbara?' he says again, and reaches for her shoulder.

'Don't!' she says, shrugging his hand away. 'Don't touch me!'

Martin looks around to see if anyone is watching. The taxi containing the two young women is pulling past. He averts his eyes and looks at his wife. 'Come along, Barbara,' he says. 'We have to be strong.'

'Strong?' She gives a dry, manic laugh, totally devoid of humour. 'Is that the best you can do? My son is dead. My beautiful boy is dead. And you're telling me to be strong?'

Martin swallows hard before responding. 'He was my son too.'

'Was he? Was he really? Then tell me about him, Martin. Tell me what kind of man he was!'

Martin glances around the car park. 'Barbara, please. This is hardly the time or the place.'

'I don't see why not. He's dead. What better time to remember him?'

'Of course I remember him. Do you honestly think I'd forget my own son?'

'You didn't even know him, Martin. You didn't want to know.'

'Barbara, please. Let's go home. We can talk then.'

He takes a step forward but she backs away again, arms folded across her chest. 'Come on, Martin. I'm waiting.'

He sighs and shakes his head. 'I don't know what you're talking about.'

'I'm talking about my son, Martin. Your son. The one you drove away. The one who'd be alive now if it wasn't for –'

She starts sobbing again and reaches into her handbag. Her expects her to take out a tissue but instead she clutches a handful of blue envelopes. She waves them at him.

'Do you know what they did to him, Martin? Do you know what they did to our son in your precious army?'

He shakes his head again, more out of desperation than anger.

'Of course you don't. How could you? You never asked. You never listened. So I'll tell you, shall I? They bullied him. They called him queer and they bullied him. One time, they got him drunk and strapped him to his bed while he was asleep, so that he woke up soaked in his own urine.'

Martin looks away. 'That's just horseplay, Barbara. It happened when I was in the army and I'm sure it happens now. It doesn't mean anything.'

'Did it happen to you?'

He flinches. 'What?'

'Did they tie you to your bed? Did they call you queer and spit in your food?'

'Of course not!'

'Then don't you dare tell me it's just horseplay. Don't you dare insult the memory of my boy by making light of what he went through. You haven't the faintest idea what it was like for him. How many friends did you make in the army, Martin? A dozen? A hundred?'

He bristles. 'I knew a lot of good men, Barbara. A lot

of brave men. But I don't see what that has to do with anything.'

'Our son made one friend, Martin. Just one. A man called Owen. If it hadn't been for that man, he'd have been totally alone. But then you'd know that if you'd bothered to read his letters.' She stuffs the blue envelopes back into her handbag and snaps it shut. 'Shame it's too late now,' she adds icily.

'I did my best, Barbara.'

'Best?' She snorts and turns her head away. When she looks back again, her eyes are challenging him to say something.

'He loved the army,' he says gently. 'You know that.'

'He joined the army to please you. What were you thinking, Martin? That it would help straighten him out? That it would make a man of him?' Angrily, she brushes the tears from her cheeks. 'He didn't need straightening out. What he needed was a father who loved him.'

'I did love him,' Martin says. 'I loved him just as much as you did.'

'Of course you did,' his wife sneers. 'You loved him so much you sent him away to die.'

'For heaven's sake, Barbara! He died serving his country. You can't hold me responsible for that.'

His wife stares at him coldly. 'He died serving you, Martin. And don't you ever forget that.'

For the first time in years, Martin Collins feels his temper rise. He takes a deep breath and squares his shoulders.

'I'll wait for you in the car,' he says, and marches briskly on.

CHAPTER TWENTY-FIVE

Angela has been home for the best part of an hour – enough time to fix herself a sandwich and flick through the *Gazette*. Most local news stories don't hold much interest for her, but she's read all about Dennis Bevan and his upcoming parole hearing. According to the paper, Bevan was sent down several years ago for a series of drug offences including the possession and supply of heroin on what the paper described as 'a massive scale'. An earlier trial had fallen apart amid allegations of police corruption. Bevan had friends everywhere, apparently – including two senior police officers and a local magistrate. It was only when a former associate was persuaded to testify against him that the prosecution finally had enough evidence to secure a conviction and send Bevan down for life.

Angela is well aware that Bridgend has a drug problem. It wasn't that long ago that the town earned the dubious distinction of being named the heroin capital of Europe. But she hadn't realized that such a large part of the problem could be traced back to one man.

Flicking through the rest of the paper, she feels her heart sink. There's little to inspire a sense of civic pride. If anything, the tensions in the town appear to be getting worse. A cyclist who was stabbed at the Black Path is out of hospital and giving evidence to the police. A local doctor's son has been jailed for ten years over a series of assaults, including a particularly vicious attack on his pregnant girlfriend, whom he'd punched twice in the stomach. A man is in a critical condition after being attacked outside a pub the previous Saturday night. Meanwhile, the local council has just unveiled its latest plans to turn the town centre into 'a continental-style café area'.

Which continent? Angela wonders. It's more like a war zone.

Her thoughts turn to Helen. She still hasn't heard from her. She reaches into her pocket for her mobile. Helen's is the last number she called. She hits redial and presses the phone to her ear, expecting the call to go straight to voicemail like all the others. Instead, the phone is answered on the second ring.

'Yes?' an unfamiliar voice says.

Angela's first thought is that she somehow dialled the wrong number. But that's impossible. A quick glance at the screen confirms it. 'Sorry,' she says. 'Is that Helen?'

'Do I sound like Helen?' the female voice asks.

She doesn't. There's an edge to her voice, a hardness that Helen doesn't possess.

'Is Helen there?' Angela asks.

'She can't come to the phone now. She's sleeping.'

Angela checks her watch. 'But it's the middle of the afternoon. Is she okay?' She thinks of Kath and the spiked drink that landed her in hospital. 'She's not ill, is she?'

'Who is this?'

'My name's Angela. I'm a friend of Helen's from work.'

'Oh, I know who you are,' the voice sneers. 'You're the one who got her so drunk on Friday night she could barely stand up. Then you fucked off and left her to fend for herself. It was lucky for her I came along when I did.'

'What happened?' Angela asks. 'Was she hurt?'

'Not seriously,' comes the reply. 'No thanks to you.'

A mixture of remorse and indignation rises up in Angela's throat. 'Can I speak to Helen, please? It's important.'

'I just told you. She's sleeping. I can't wake her up now. Not with everything she's been through.'

'I thought you said she was okay.' Guiltily, Angela pictures Helen as she last saw her – drunk, vulnerable, out of control. What the hell happened to her?

There's a pause and the burble of voices in the background, like someone switching channels or turning up the sound on the TV. Then the woman is back. 'She'll be fine,' she says coolly. 'But she won't be coming into work for a few days, so be a good girl and pass the message on. Do you think you can manage that?'

Angela can picture her smirking as she speaks. 'Who am I speaking to?' she demands. 'Are you a friend of the family?'

'Something like that,' the woman replies. 'I'll tell Helen you called.'

Then the line goes dead.

Helen wakes with a dry mouth, a thumping headache and no sense of her surroundings. It takes a few moments for her eyes to adjust to the fading light and unfamiliar shadows of the room. Slowly, it comes back to her. She's in a hotel in Birmingham, with Siân. The next realization makes her stomach tighten. Owen is in the military hospital, in a coma. The thought of him makes her call out.

'Siân?'

There's no reply.

'Siân? Are you there?'

Still nothing. The display on the digital clock next to the bed reads '17.04'. She's been asleep for hours. The painkillers Siân gave her earlier must have worn off. With an effort, Helen heaves herself out of bed. She feels a sudden rush of blood to the head and takes a few seconds to steady herself before padding into the bathroom. Turning on the light, she sees that the bathroom mirror is steamed up and beads of water are still clinging to the glass shower door. The wash basin is wet too. There's a smudge of foundation on the rim and, next to the basin, a paper tissue with a blot of red lipstick. A damp towel hangs limply behind the door.

She wipes the mirror with one hand and studies her reflection, wonders if it's true that traumatic events can prematurely age a person. She's heard of people whose hair turned white after a tragedy, but never of someone whose skin turned to chalk. Her face is a blur.

She fills a glass of water from the tap and gulps it down, before refilling the glass and returning to the room. The sheets on Siân's bed are still folded down. Her red bag is lying on the floor next to the bed. She can't have gone far. She probably just slipped out for some fresh air or a bite to eat.

Helen hasn't eaten in hours. She isn't hungry. The headache is so strong, the thought of food makes her nauseous. She stares at Siân's bag, remembers her placing the bottle of painkillers back in one of the outer pockets. She kneels down and opens a pocket. Sure enough, there's a bottle marked paracetamol. The seal is already broken, so she unscrews the lid and tips two blue and white plastic capsules into the palm of her hand. Her skull tightens. She pops the pills into her mouth and swallows them down with some water.

As she returns the bottle to the bag, her fingers brush against something cold and metallic. It's a coin. But not just any coin. It's an old penny, the kind no longer in circulation – the kind her father used to collect. It's just like the ones she keeps in the box under her bed at home. The coin is dated 1970, the year they stopped minting those old pennies. Just like the one she held in her hand a week ago.

She turns on the bedside light and inspects the coin more closely.

It can't be the same one, can it?

It looks so familiar. But then she remembers her mother telling her how common those old coins were and how little they're worth. It's probably just a coincidence. She makes a mental note to ask Siân about it later.

A wave of tiredness washes over her and she climbs back into bed. She places the coin next to the clock on the bedside table. The time is now 17.12. Soon it'll be time to get dressed and return to the hospital. But first she'll wait for the headache to pass and for Siân to reappear. Within seconds, she slips into a deep sleep.

The voices are barely audible at first – whispers in the dark, impossible to make out. There's no moon to light her way, but she knows where she is – the Black Path. The tangled trees are as familiar to her as the dark soil underfoot. The air is damp, and the smell of smoke hangs in the air. Somewhere in the distance, she hears the crackle of a bonfire.

She walks slowly, carefully placing one foot in front of the other, afraid of what lies ahead. Gradually the voices become louder. There are boys laughing, and then a man's voice shouting. She can't decipher the words but she recognizes the voice.

'Daddy?' she calls out. 'Is that you?'

There's a movement behind the trees and then a figure emerges. As he steps forward she sees that it's her father. But he looks different from the man of her childhood. His skin is grey, his eyes red and hollow. When he opens his mouth, his teeth are as black as the soil.

'Helen,' he says. 'Come with me. There's something I have to show you.'

She reaches for his hand but he turns away and walks quickly ahead. She tries to follow, but the light is so dim and her legs are so heavy she can barely keep up. With a growing sense of panic, she watches him disappear into the gloom.

'Daddy!' she cries out. 'Wait for me!'

Then she sees it – a white gravestone rising up out of the black earth. She falls to her knees, sees her husband's name etched into the stone. Something brushes against her hand. She looks down and sees a wreath made of paper poppies. The flowers are heavily weathered, the colour faded from deep red to the palest purple. He's been dead a long time.

Frantically, she starts clawing at the soil, pulling up chunks of earth with her fingers, tears pouring down her face as her nails break and bleed.

'Helen?'

The voice seems to come from another place. Is this a dream, or has she woken up?

'Helen!' The voice is closer this time. 'What's wrong?'

'He's dead!'

'Your father?'

'My husband. Owen.'

'Where are you?'

'The Black Path.'

'Who else is there?'

'Nobody. I can't see anybody.'

Strong hands grip her shoulders. A light explodes into her face and she opens her eyes, gasping for air.

Siân's face looms over her. 'It's okay. You were having a bad dream.'

A rush of air fills Helen's lungs as the nightmare fades and the room comes into focus. She rubs her eyes.

'What time is it?'

'Half eight.'

'I overslept.' She throws back the covers and hauls her body up into a sitting position.

'What do you think you're doing?' asks Siân.

'Why didn't you wake me? I have to go back to the hospital.'

Helen tries to swing her legs out from under the covers, but they feel like lead.

'You need to rest,' Siân says.

'I need to see Owen,' Helen snaps. 'I can't believe you didn't wake me.' Angry, she summons all her strength and struggles to her feet. Her head spins, tiny stars exploding in the blackness.

'Are you okay?' Siân asks.

Obviously not, Helen thinks and reaches for the wall to steady herself. 'I feel a bit dizzy.'

'I'm not surprised,' Siân says. 'You've had a terrible shock. You've hardly eaten. Now do you see why I thought it was best to let you sleep?'

Helen feels her anger subside, nods and lowers herself back onto the bed.

Siân smiles down at her. 'You'll be fine,' she says. 'You just need to take better care of yourself. Drinks lots of fluids. Get plenty of rest. And try not to worry about Owen. He's in good hands. I was at the hospital earlier.

There's no point in you going there now. You can see him again in the morning.'

Still smiling, she places a restraining hand on Helen's shoulder and tucks her back in bed, like an over-efficient nurse dealing with a difficult patient.

'There,' she says. 'Now try and get some more sleep.'

Helen sees that her eyes are glazed. There's alcohol on her breath, coupled with the smell of – what, aftershave? She wonders where Siân has been all this time, why she didn't leave a note. She wonders how she's managed to sleep so long when her nerves are so shredded.

Siân frowns. 'What's the matter?'

Helen tries to gather her thoughts. There's something else she was meaning to ask. What was it? She glances at the bedside table. There's no coin there.

CHAPTER TWENTY-SIX

'Why are you looking at me like that?' asks Siân.

'Like what?'

'Like I've done something wrong.'

Helen forces a smile. 'I'm not.' But try as she might, she can't escape the feeling that something isn't right. The memory of the coin seems so vivid. She can still recall the feel of it in her hand, the way the light from the bedside lamp glinted on the metal.

'Are you pissed off because I left you on your own for a couple of hours?' Siân says. 'Because this isn't easy for me either, y'know. And I thought we'd agreed that you need to rest.'

Helen watches as she saunters over to the mirror and inspects her face, wiping the remains of her lipstick from her mouth. There's a purple mark on her neck that looks suspiciously like a love bite.

She looks back over her shoulder. 'Well?'

It's clear from the way Siân walks and the tone of her voice that she's had a fair amount to drink. Now probably isn't the best time to challenge her.

But Helen can't help herself. 'There was a coin –'

Siân cuts her off. 'Oh, that!'

Helen doesn't know whether to feel relieved or more agitated. She hadn't imagined the coin. But what was it doing in Siân's bag?

'You were talking about it in your sleep,' Siân says.

'Was I?' Helen props herself up in bed, struggling to remember.

'Yeah. Something about a coin and the Black Path. You seemed okay at first. But then you started tossing and turning. I figured you were having a nightmare so I woke you up.'

Siân turns away from the mirror, sits on the edge of the other bed and starts smoothing the bedspread with one hand. 'I don't suppose there's anything worth watching on the TV,' she says, and reaches for the remote.

Is she deliberately avoiding eye contact, Helen wonders. 'How long have you been back?' she asks.

Siân shrugs, flicking channels. 'Dunno. About half an hour. I was trying not to disturb you. If I'd known you were having a bad dream I'd have woken you earlier.'

She seems to feel Helen watching her and turns to meet her eyes. 'So what's the significance of the coin? I remember you telling me about the Black Path. But where does the coin come in?' She frowns. 'You're not worried about money, are you? Cos I told you I've got this covered. However long it takes. It's not a problem.'

'My dad used to collect old coins,' Helen says. 'I have some at home. They're in a box under the bed.'

Siân smiles. 'That's so sweet. Are they worth anything?'

'I don't think so.'

'Well, they obviously mean a lot to you. That's the main thing.'

Neither of them speaks for a moment.

'I know what you're thinking,' Siân says.

Helen's scalp prickles. 'Do you?'

'Of course. The hospital. It's bringing it all back – what happened to your father.'

Helen feels her throat tighten and her eyes fill with

212

tears. She blinks and wipes her face with the back of her hand. Siân is right. Her head's a mess. She mustn't let her emotions get the better of her. She mustn't give in to dark thoughts and paranoid fantasies. She'll go mad.

'Hey,' says Siân. She comes over and places a comforting hand on Helen's shoulder. 'We have to stay strong for Owen, remember? Hang on. I'll fetch you a glass of water.'

She disappears into the bathroom. Helen hears the tap running and her voice calling, 'Won't be a sec. Just waiting for the water to run cold.'

Moments later, she's back. 'Drink up,' she says, handing Helen the glass and perching on the edge of the bed. 'It's probably shock, you know. You've been through a lot these past few days. It's no wonder you're having nightmares.'

Helen takes a sip of water. Her head feels foggy. Her mouth is still dry. She takes another mouthful of water before placing the glass on the bedside table. 'Thanks,' she says. 'Those painkillers really knocked me out.'

'What painkillers?'

'The ones in your bag.'

Siân's face stiffens. 'I don't like people going through my things.'

'Sorry. I didn't think you'd mind.'

'It's alright.' Siân eyes her for a moment, then tilts her head sympathetically. 'You poor thing. You're really not yourself, are you?'

Helen chokes back tears, swallowing them with heavy breaths. She's not sure she even knows who she is anymore. A sudden thought lodges itself in her brain. 'I should call work. Tell them I won't be in.'

'No need,' Siân says. 'Angela called while you were sleeping. I answered the phone so it wouldn't disturb you.

I hope that's okay.'

'Of course. What did she say?'

'She said she'd cover for you. She seemed to think she was doing you a big favour. If you ask me, it's the least she can do after the way she abandoned you on Friday.'

'Maybe she was calling to apologize?'

Siân snorts. 'She didn't sound very apologetic. Anyway, forget about work. It's all sorted.'

'I should call my mum too,' Helen says, though the thought of it makes her chest tighten.

'Do you really think that's a good idea?' asks Siân. 'I mean, from what you've told me, I don't think she'll be much help. The last thing you need is someone else stressing you out.'

Helen pictures her mother's anxious face, wonders how she'll cope with her and Frank at a time like this. 'I know, but she's still my mum. She'll be wondering where I am.'

'Do you want me to call her? I don't mind.'

'But what would you say?'

'Whatever you want me to say. But if I tell her the truth, she'll be here like a shot. Her and that stepfather of yours. Is that really what you want?'

Helen thinks, imagining the combination of her mother's nervous energy and Frank's know-it-all remarks. 'Not really.'

'I didn't think so,' Siân says. 'Why don't you wait a few days? Give yourself time to adjust. Now, let's put the kettle on.' She leaps to her feet and goes over to the hospitality tray. 'They've got some herbal teas here. Camomile will help you relax. Or there's peppermint?'

'Either is fine.'

Siân turns on the kettle and picks up the room service menu. 'We should order you something to eat. What do you fancy? The club sandwich sounds good. Or there's a burger.'

'I'm not hungry.'

'But you should try to eat something. You haven't had anything since breakfast, and you hardly ate then. We can't have you wasting away.'

Helen wonders if it's a measure of how stressed she is that such an innocent remark can conjure up images of death and disease.

'I'm fine, really,' she says. 'So what happened at the hospital?'

Siân shrugs and drops two teabags into a couple of mugs. 'Sue wasn't too friendly, to tell you the truth.'

'What do you mean?'

'She's a bit self-important, don't you think? But I managed to grab a moment in her busy schedule.'

'What did she say?'

'That I should let you sleep. And that you can see Owen again in the morning.'

Siân pours boiling water from the kettle into the mugs. Helen can see the purple mark on the side of her neck, the deep bruise surrounded by smaller red dots. It's definitely a love bite. 'You've been gone a long time.'

Siân glances over her shoulder and smiles coyly. 'I bumped into that soldier. Remember? The one I met earlier?'

'I remember.'

'Don't be like that,' Siân says, bringing the mugs over and placing them on the bedside table. 'And before you accuse me of anything, I didn't forget about you. In fact, it's you I was thinking of.'

'What do you mean?'

'I thought he might be able to tell me something about what happened.'

'And did he?'

'He was a bit cagey at first, but I have ways of making men tell me things.' Siân smirks and lies back on her bed, piling pillows behind her shoulders and unbuttoning the top of her jeans. 'I took him to the nearest pub and plied him with alcohol. You know how soldiers like a drink.'

'Owen's not really a drinker.'

'Well, this guy certainly is. He knocked back three pints in under an hour. You know how some men can drink really heavily and you wouldn't even know they were drunk?'

Helen thinks of Frank and nods.

'He's one of those types. But then I got him onto the whisky. That soon loosened his tongue.'

'Well? What did he say?'

'They were out on patrol and there was some sort of explosion, one of those improvised devices. Owen was thrown clear of the vehicle. One of the other lads wasn't so lucky.'

'I don't think "lucky" is the word you're looking for,' Helen says. 'My husband is in a coma.'

'Yeah, but he's alive.'

'Oh. I see.'

Siân nods. 'Blown to bits, apparently. And he was only nineteen. His parents came to identify the body.' She reaches for her mug of tea and blows gently on the surface of the steaming liquid to cool it. 'That can't have been easy for them.'

Helen remembers the man she saw consoling the grieving woman at the hospital. Were they the dead boy's parents? What must they have thought of her, staring at them like they were some sort of sideshow?

'Nineteen,' she repeats softly. 'Those poor people.'

'I know,' Siân says. 'It doesn't bear thinking about, does it?'

'No,' says Helen, but she can't help herself from doing exactly that.

At least Owen's alive, she thinks. At least he wasn't blown to bits.

She wonders what strange twist of fate meant that one man died while another was expected to make a full recovery. What were the circumstances surrounding the explosion? She might never know.

'Did he say anything else?' she asks, reaching for her mug. 'Your soldier friend?'

There's no response. Looking up, Helen sees that the expression on Siân's face has changed. Her eyes are wide and there's a sadness around her mouth that wasn't there a moment ago.

'Siân?' Helen says. 'What's wrong?'

Siân smiles tightly and looks away. When she does finally answer, her voice is different – smaller and less confident, almost the voice of a child. 'There's something I haven't told you.'

'What is it?'

'My brother joined the army.'

'I didn't know you had a brother. What regiment is he in?'

'He's not. Not anymore. He died.'

Helen gasps. 'What happened?'

'I'd rather not go into it. But he was a hero. And he was my big brother, so he was always my hero. I had to go with my dad to identify the body. Mum was long gone by then. The bitch didn't even bother coming to the funeral. Can you believe that? Her own son, and she couldn't even pay her respects to him when he was dead.'

Siân's eyes are dark pools of hurt.

'Sorry,' she mumbles, wiping away a tear. 'I shouldn't be telling you all this now. You've got enough to worry about. It's just that hearing about that poor boy has brought it all back. He was about the same age as my brother.'

'Oh, Siân,' Helen says. 'I'm so sorry.'

Her friend shrugs. 'What have you got to be sorry for? It's not as if you had anything to do with it.'

'Shall I put the kettle on?' Martin asks. 'Or would you prefer something stronger?'

They're back home now, in their large, detached house in Bristol. Detached is exactly how he and Barbara would appear to anyone peering in at them through the tall, Georgian-style windows. Her – remote, withdrawn, perched on the edge of the sofa. Him – seemingly calm, collected, slowly pacing the front room.

He walks over to the windows and draws the curtains on the well-lit street and the windows opposite. He's had more than his fill of prying eyes today.

His wife still hasn't answered his question. She hasn't said a single word to him since they left Birmingham. He tried several times to initiate some kind of conversation but each time his efforts were met with a stony silence. Looking at her now, there's no reason to suppose that her reaction will be any different.

'Right,' he says. 'Well, I think I'll have a brandy.' He moves over to the drinks cabinet. 'Barbara? Are you sure I can't fix you something?'

His words fall on deaf ears. Opening the brandy and pouring himself a glass, Martin thinks of the last time he and his son were alone in this room. It was the Christmas before last. The brandy had been open then, too – not for drinking, but for the brandy sauce his wife always insisted on making from scratch.

'I should go and give Mum a hand in the kitchen,' Jamie had said. That was so typical of him. It wasn't just that he was always so attentive to his mother. It was also that he would do anything to avoid spending time alone with his father.

'Hang on a minute, son,' Martin had said. 'There's something I need to say'.

And then he'd closed the door and told Jamie something he'd never told anyone, not even his wife. It was something that had happened a long time ago, when he was Jamie's age. It was something he still found difficult to talk about, but something he wanted the boy to know.

'So you see, son,' he said afterwards. 'I'm not quite as narrow-minded as some people think.'

'I never said you were, Dad,' Jamie replied, blushing heavily before hurrying off to help his mother. Thinking back, Martin couldn't recall much of that Christmas. But he remembered those few minutes alone with Jamie in this room. It was the last conversation he had with his son.

'I'm going to sleep in the spare room,' Barbara announces, rising from the sofa.

Martin stares into his brandy glass. The spare room is where Jamie sleeps, he thinks, then corrects himself. It's where Jamie *slept*. 'I'll see you in the morning,' he says.

Tomorrow he'll have to start making the necessary arrangements. His wife isn't up to that. He listens as she climbs the stairs, waiting for the footsteps on the landing and the click of the bathroom door.

He sighs and takes a sip of his brandy. His hand trembles. Then the tears come.

CHAPTER TWENTY-SEVEN

There's no change in Owen's condition the next day. Helen spends every hour she can by his bedside, occasionally nodding off in her chair and then jerking awake, lost for a few seconds before it all comes crashing back and the anxiety kicks in.

She tries to glean as much information as she can about her husband's condition, but when she finally manages to corner Mr Croft after his morning rounds, he simply repeats what he told her yesterday. Her husband is in a coma. His condition is stable. He'll wake up when he's ready.

'But what if he doesn't?'

'We have no reason for concern. He's breathing unaided. His vital signs are good. We just have to wait.'

Helen finds herself mildly irritated by this response. Waiting is something she knows all about. It's something every soldier's wife or girlfriend knows about. They wait for letters, for phone calls, for news. Life is like a long series of waiting rooms, one opening into the other. She doesn't need a man in a white lab coat to tell her how to wait.

'That's doctors for you,' Siân says when they meet in the cafeteria for lunch. 'Arrogant sons of bitches.' Her voice is loud enough for everyone in the room to hear, including the two women in nurses' uniform who've just walked in.

'Please, Siân!'

'I'm just saying. I've known my share of doctors. Cocky buggers, most of them.'

Helen sighs. 'That's not really helping.'

It's not really true, either. Frustrating as it is, Helen knows that Mr Croft is just doing his job. It isn't a job she envies. In the short time it's taken her to become more familiar with the day-to-day running of the trauma ward, one thing Helen has noticed is that the staff are run off their feet.

'Is it always this busy?' she asks Sue Blackwell later that afternoon. She's sitting by Owen's bedside. Siân has gone off in search of a decent cup of coffee when Sue pops her head around the door.

'Not always,' Sue replies. 'But often.'

Helen is about to ask about the weeping woman she saw yesterday, but stops herself. It isn't any of her business, and she already feels as if she's intruded on another woman's grief. Then she remembers Siân's conversation with the soldier. If he knows about the explosion, then maybe Sue will too.

'I'm afraid I can't say,' is Sue's response.

'What does that mean?' Helen hears herself snap. 'You can't say? Or you won't say?'

Sue blinks several times before answering. 'I don't have that information,' she begins. Then she changes tack. 'Mrs McGrath? I hope you don't think I'm prying, but I wanted to ask you something. It's about your friend –'

Someone coughs – a dry, throaty sound. It takes Helen a few seconds to realize that it's coming from Owen.

There's another cough, louder this time, and both women turn their attention to the man in the bed.

'Is he alright?' Helen asks.

'He does this a lot,' Sue says. 'It's nothing to worry about.'

'Is he waking up?'

The coughing stops. The only sounds now are Owen's gentle snoring and the beeps of the machines.

Sue smiles. 'I don't think so. Not yet. But it's a good sign.'

'Is it?'

'It is. Now we just have to –'

'Don't tell me,' Helen snaps. Normally she'd let it pass. But things aren't normal anymore. 'Wait,' she says bitterly, repeating the word she's heard so many times. 'We just have to wait.'

Western Echo –
Former soldier found dead at the Black Path

A 26-year-old man was found hanging from a tree in the early hours of Monday morning at the Black Path in Bridgend. A cyclist spotted the body and alerted the emergency services. They arrived within fifteen minutes, but were unable to resuscitate the man, who was pronounced dead at the scene.

Identified as Alex Watkins of Brackla, the deceased is believed to have taken his own life. Mr Watkins left the army three years ago, after serving in Afghanistan, where he was severely injured by an improvised explosive device and lost the lower half of his left leg. He is said to have suffered from depression following the breakdown of his marriage. According to neighbours, he was unable to find a job and developed a dependency on drugs and alcohol. Police are not treating the death as suspicious.

The funeral will be held on Saturday at Bridgend Cemetery. Mr Watkins' parents, who separated when he was in his teens, have specified that there will be no flowers but have asked that donations be made to the charity Help for Heroes, formed to assist those wounded in Britain's current conflicts.

'Do you think he can hear us?'

Helen is half asleep in the chair. Several hours have passed since her conversation with Sue Blackwell. Now the nurses are gone and the light outside the window is starting to fade.

The voice belongs to Siân. She's crouched down next to the chair. 'Well?'

'I'm not sure,' Helen murmurs. 'The doctor said talking to him might help.'

'That's good news. They must think he can hear something or there'd be no point.' She turns and stares at Owen. 'He looks peaceful, doesn't he? Like he's just taking a nap.'

No, he doesn't, Helen thinks. *He looks like he's been through hell and back. God knows what's going on inside his head.*

'I passed Sue in the corridor earlier,' Siân says. 'Any news?'

'Not really. He'll wake up, but she can't say when. Until then, I just have to wait.'

'*We'll* wait,' Siân says, patting Helen's hand. 'I'm your friend, remember? We're in this together.' She gives a reassuring smile before standing and walking over to the bedside. 'They'll be pumping him full of barbiturates,' she says, staring down at Owen with all the authority of a trained medical professional. 'That's to reduce pressure on the brain. And to stop him from lashing about like those blokes out there, and tearing out his drips. I swear one of them pointed an imaginary rifle at me earlier. Poor bugger. Probably thinks he's still at war.' She looks across at Helen. 'He hasn't done anything like that, has he?'

'Of course not!'

'That's okay then. But the more you talk to him, the better. C'mon, don't be shy!'

Helen coughs. She thinks the cough might turn into a sob, but it doesn't. 'I think I've run out of things to say.'

Siân smiles. 'Let me have a go.' She sits on the edge of the bed. 'He's a good looker, your fella.'

He's looked better, Helen thinks. She stares at the marks on his swollen face and the paraphernalia of medical care surrounding the bed. His eyes are closed and his breathing is faint, as if he's in a deep sleep. His right hand rests on top of the bedclothes, the fingers raw and blistered. A drip feeds into a vein above the wrist, held in place with white surgical tape. He looks so alien to her – even more so with Siân sitting so close him.

'Hello, soldier,' Siân says. Helen notices a small movement of Owen's fingers. It's only a fragile gesture, but it's enough to convince her that he's aware of Siân's presence, as if he somehow recognizes her voice.

'See that?' Siân beams. 'He knows we're here.'

Helen nods. *He knows you're here. But what about me?*

Siân takes Owen's hand and cradled it between her palms. 'There, there,' she says, gently stroking his fingers. 'I know you can hear me, Owen. You're going to be okay. The worst is over now. You're safe. I'm here with Helen. I'm taking good care of her, so there's no need for you to worry. We're waiting for you to wake up, then we're going to take you home. Everything will be fine. You'll see.'

She looks at Helen. 'You'd think they'd have cleaned him up a bit, wouldn't you?' She lets go of Owen's hand and reaches into her pocket, taking out a paper tissue. She dampens it with her tongue and begins gently dabbing at the dirt around his hairline.

'There,' she says, leaning back and appraising her work. 'That's better.' She turns to Helen. 'What do you think?'

Helen doesn't know what to think. She's all emotions. Feelings wash over her in waves – fear, frustration, jealousy. She isn't proud of it, but what she really wants is for Owen to pull his hand away and for Siân to make her excuses and leave.

How mean you are, she thinks. *Here's your friend trying to make the best of things and all you can think about is your own petty jealousy!*

She watches as Siân tucks the tissue back in her pocket.

'We've been having quite a few adventures, your wife and me,' she says. 'We went to the social club and Helen sang karaoke. You should have heard her, Owen. She was brilliant.'

No I wasn't, Helen thinks. *I didn't even sing. I bottled it and ran away.*

'And we went for a long walk and fed the horses,' Siân says. 'At the farm up behind your house. Helen was a bit nervous at first, but she soon got over it. I reckon we'll make a horsewoman of her yet.'

I never said anything about riding horses, Helen thinks.

Siân smiles at her before continuing. 'We ran into that Muslim too,' she says, a note of contempt creeping into her voice. 'You know the one I mean. If he's that keen, why doesn't he just fuck off to Afghanistan? It wouldn't surprise me to see a picture of him in the paper, setting fire to poppies.'

Owen's hand twitches again, more vigorously this time.

'I think that's enough now,' Helen says quickly.

'What's wrong?'

'You're upsetting him. I saw his hand move.'

Siân frowns. 'But that's a good thing. It shows he's listening.'

'All the same. I think we should let him rest now.'

Siân promptly lets go of Owen's hand and stands up. 'Whatever,' she says, thrusting her hands deep into the front pockets of her jeans. 'You're the boss.'

'Sorry –' Helen begins. Then she stops herself. 'Those things you were saying. They weren't really true.'

Siân smiles. 'I know that. I was just trying to help. Surely it's better for him to hear that you're doing okay? The last thing you want is him worrying about you. I'm sure he has enough on his mind already.'

'I suppose so.'

'I think it's time we got you back to the hotel,' Siân says. 'You look knackered.'

'I am.'

'Let's go. I gave the nurse my number. She said she'll call if there's any change.'

Helen is too tired to protest. She hauls herself to her feet and kisses Owen on the cheek before turning towards the door.

'See you tomorrow, Owen,' Siân pipes up as they leave the room. 'Sweet dreams.'

It isn't until they've left the trauma ward and are halfway along the corridor that Helen has a realization. In all the time that Siân had been talking to Owen, she hadn't introduced herself. She hadn't given her name. Not once. It was if she somehow expected him to know who she was. It was if they'd already met.

'Siân?' Helen begins.

She's interrupted by someone calling her name. 'Mrs McGrath!'

Turning, she sees Sue Blackwell pursuing her along the corridor. 'Mrs McGrath, come quickly!'

Helen feels her stomach lurch. 'What is it? Has something happened?'

'It's your husband. I think he's waking up.'

'See!' Siân smiles triumphantly. 'I told you talking to him would help!'

Helen doesn't respond. They rush back to the ward. Mister Croft is already there. A nurse is checking the readings on the monitors. As she moves away, Owen sits bolt upright in bed – his eyes wild, his face contorted with panic. He screams. 'Man down! Man down!'

'Owen!' Helen cries. 'You're awake!'

She steps towards the bed but the nurse blocks her way. 'Give him room, please!'

Owen stares at the man in the lab coat. 'It wasn't me! It wasn't me!'

'What does he mean?' Helen asks.

'He's in shock,' the nurse replies. 'Stand aside, please.'

Helen does as she is told.

The doctor's voice is firm. 'Owen, listen to me. You're safe. You're in the military hospital in Birmingham. Your left arm is broken, but apart from that you're fine –'

'And the others?'

'I can't say, I'm afraid.'

'The boy?'

'He means Collins,' Siân says.

Collins, thinks Helen. *Who the hell is Collins?*

She wonders if it's the lad killed in the explosion, wonders why Siân didn't mention his name before.

'Yes, Collins,' Owen says. 'Where's Collins?'

Mister Croft turns to the nurse and gives a nod. 'We're going to give you a sedative, Owen. Nothing too strong. Just something to help you to relax.'

The nurse busies herself with one of the drips.

'What are you doing?' Helen asks.

'It's just a mild barbiturate,' the doctor replies. 'It's nothing to worry about.' He turns his attention back to Owen. 'You'll feel better in a few minutes. Get some rest and we can talk again in the morning.'

This seems to satisfy him for the moment. He lies back on the pillow and stares up at the ceiling.

As the nurse moves away, Helen walks over to the bed. 'Owen, thank God you're okay!' She reaches out to touch his hand.

He flinches and turns to look at her. His eyes wide and are blank. A frown forms on his face. 'Do I know you?'

CHAPTER TWENTY-EIGHT

'He didn't even know who I was,' Helen sobs. 'How could he not recognize me?'

'Ssh!' Siân slips a comforting arm around her shoulders. 'You heard what the doctor said. He's in shock.'

It's almost eight-thirty and they're in the back seat of a taxi, heading towards the hotel. Helen's first instinct was to spend the night at the hospital in case there was any change in Owen's condition, but Siân managed to convince her that what she really needed was a good night's sleep. 'You look exhausted,' she said as they left the hospital. Then, with a cheeky grin, 'It's no wonder he didn't recognize you!'

'But I'm his wife,' Helen says now. 'Supposing he doesn't remember we're married?'

'Of course he will.'

'What if he doesn't love me anymore? You hear about that, don't you? People waking up from a coma and falling in love with someone else.'

'That only happens in soap operas,' Siân says.

'No, it doesn't. It happens in real life, too. I don't know what I'd do if he stopped loving me.'

'Now you're being ridiculous. That's not going to happen.'

'How would you know? You don't know what it's

like. You've never been married. You said you'd never had a serious relationship.'

Siân removes her arm and smiles tightly. 'Things will look better in the morning. They always do.'

'Do they? Or is that just something people say to console themselves?'

Siân doesn't answer. Miserably, Helen turns her head and stares out of the window. The lights from oncoming cars flash past the glass, illuminating the inside of the cab and making her fears seem more real somehow.

'What if he never remembers me?'

'He will.'

'How can you be sure?'

'Trust me.'

'So you're a doctor now, are you?'

'You need to calm down a bit,' Siân says. 'Working yourself up like this isn't helping anyone.' She arches an eyebrow. 'You don't want me to slap you, do you? Cos I will if I have to. A good slap works wonders with hysterical women.'

Helen meets her gaze, then realizes she's joking. 'Sorry. I shouldn't be taking this out on you.'

'Forget it. No harm done. Just remember to breathe, okay?'

They drive on in silence, through a series of underpasses and past building works and The Bullring shopping centre. Buses clog the city streets, which are filled with late-night shoppers.

'Remind me I need to go to The Bullring,' Siân says. 'I could do with some new clothes. We could get something for you, too. Cheer you up a bit.'

Helen holds her tongue. She doesn't need cheering up. She needs to know that Owen is going to make a full recovery. Nothing else matters. Gazing out of the window, she spots a couple dining outside a busy restaurant. They look so happy together. Will she and Owen ever experience that feeling again? She knows how fragile life can be. Happiness can be snatched away in an instant. A life can be snuffed out.

She turns to Siân. 'Who's Collins?'

'Was,' Siân replies. 'Past tense. He's dead, remember?'

'Yes, but who was he?'

'Some young private. He served with Owen. They were quite friendly, apparently. But what does it matter?'

It matters to Owen, Helen thinks. *He woke up asking for him.*

'Try not to think about it,' Siân says. 'You'll only make it harder on yourself.'

'But Owen never mentioned anyone called Collins. In his letters, I mean. Not once.'

The corners of Siân's mouth twitch impatiently. 'Do you honestly think that he always tells you everything?'

'Of course. Why wouldn't he? He's my husband.'

'Men don't always tell their wives everything, do they? Especially when they're away from home.'

'I'm not talking about some men,' Helen says. 'I'm talking about Owen. I think I know my own husband.'

But does she? She thinks of all the weeks and months that she and Owen had spent apart. He'd always been so attentive, even when he was thousands of miles away. Barely a day went by when he didn't contact her. There were letters, emails, phone calls. Until recently. Had something happened to him in Afghanistan? What hadn't he told her?

'All men keep secrets,' Siân says. 'And Owen's a soldier, is he? They're trained to keep their mouths shut.'

'What's that supposed to mean?'

233

'It's a dirty job. Do you really want to hear all the gory details? I know I wouldn't.'

Helen casts her mind back to the time after Owen returned from Iraq, the nights he'd spent tossing and turning in his sleep, the sudden cries in the dark, the sheets soaked with sweat. She'd known then that something was bothering him, that he was reliving some unspeakable horror in his dreams. She'd pushed him a couple of times, but he refused to talk about it. 'What's the point?' he'd say. 'What difference will it make?'

It would have made a lot of difference to her at the time, knowing that he trusted her enough to share his nightmares, the way she'd shared hers. In the days that followed what should have been a happy reunion, his silence settled between them like a dark cloud. It wasn't until he finally broke down and told her about the dead boy that she saw any hope for the future. The bitter irony wasn't lost on her. Her husband had killed someone, but at least he wasn't pushing her away.

'Are you okay?' asks Siân.

'I'm fine,' Helen lies.

'You're not still thinking about that Collins guy, are you?'

I am now, Helen thinks. Why has Owen never mentioned him? Is it because they'd witnessed some horror of war together – something so terrible, he couldn't bring himself to share it with her? Is it worse than what happened in Iraq? How much worse could it be?

Siân leans over and pats her hand. 'Try not to think about it. The important thing is that Owen's alive and he's making progress. He'll remember you soon enough, you'll see. You just focus on staying strong. And get plenty of rest. You look like you could use it.'

She unzips one of the pockets of her red bag, reaches

234

in and takes out a packet of cigarettes and a lighter.

'I didn't know you smoked,' Helen says.

'I don't. Not really. Just every now and then.'

The cab driver glances back over his shoulder. 'No smoking in the car.'

Alright, Osama,' Siân snaps. 'Keep your hair on.'

Helen squirms. The driver is Asian, no older than thirty, with kind eyes and a neat little goatee beard. He bears no resemblance to Osama bin Laden.

'I thought you were dead, mate,' Siân says. She smiles at Helen and rolls her eyes. 'Just goes to show, you can't trust everything you see in the news.'

The driver sighs. 'My name is not Osama.'

'Where are you from?'

'I'm from Edgbaston.'

'Yeah, but where are your family from?'

'Edgbaston.'

'We've got a right comedian here.' Siân nudges Helen with her elbow.

Embarrassed, Helen edges further over in the seat, until her face is practically pressed against the window.

Please stop it, she thinks.

'I need a cashpoint,' Siân announces loudly. 'They have cashpoints round here, don't they Osama?'

The driver takes a deep breath before answering. 'Yes, we have cashpoints.'

'Then take me to the nearest one. I'm sure you know where it is. Since you're from Edgbaston.'

The taxi comes to a sudden stop at a set of traffic lights. Helen lurches forward, nearly falling off her seat.

'Careful, Osama!' Siân snaps. She turns to Helen. 'I told you to put your seatbelt on.

Obediently, Helen buckles up. The lights change and the taxi moves forward. They've barely gone a hundred yards when the driver pulls over. 'The cash machine is there,' he says, without looking at Siân. 'Your friend can wait in the car.'

'What's the matter? Afraid we'll do a runner?'

'It's okay,' Helen says quickly. 'I'd rather wait anyway.'

'Suit yourself.' Siân leaps out and leans through the driver's open window. 'No funny business now, Osama. She's a married woman!'

Helen's face burns with embarrassment. She wants to say something but she's afraid it will only make matters worse. An awkward silence settles in the car. Nervously, she coughs. The driver catches her eye in the rear-view mirror. He has such a kind face that she feels a sudden urge to apologize on Siân's behalf.

'I'm sorry about my friend. I don't know what gets into her sometimes.'

Before the driver can respond, there's a knock on the passenger window and Siân is back.

'That was quick,' Helen says.

'I didn't want to hang about.' Siân climbs into the car and slams the door. 'There's all sorts out there.'

She smiles conspiratorially, ensuring that her choice of words doesn't go unnoticed.

Don't include me in this, Helen thinks. *I don't share your views*.

But she doesn't say anything, and her failure to speak up fills her with shame.

They haven't gone far when Siân leans forward in her seat and taps the driver on the shoulder. 'See that pub just ahead on the left? Pull in over there.'

The pub is large, sandwiched between two office buildings. There's a small forecourt with a few parked cars and a huddle of people out front smoking.

'Why are we stopping?' Helen asks.

'Why do you think?' Siân grins as she takes out a crisp twenty-pound note and hands it to the driver. 'I fancy a drink. And the bar at the hotel is full of creepy old businessmen.'

Helen unfastens her seatbelt.

'What do you think you're doing?' asks Siân.

'I thought we were going for a drink?'

'*I'm* going for a drink. You'll only cramp my style. Go back to the hotel and get some beauty sleep. You look like you could use it.'

Helen flinches. 'Thanks!'

'Thank me when you wake up tomorrow looking five years younger. Don't wait up. I'll see you in the morning.'

Siân turns back to the driver. 'That's twenty quid I gave you, and it's only eight quid on the meter. Just make sure she gets back safe and sound.' She winks. 'That's precious cargo you're carrying.'

And then she's off.

Helen watches her hurry across the forecourt and disappear into the pub. She doesn't look back once.

'Your friend is very rude,' the driver says.

'I'm sorry.'

He turns around in his seat. 'Are you sure you want me to keep driving?'

She thinks for a moment. 'No,' she says firmly. 'I'm getting out here.'

The driver nods and begins counting out her change.

'No,' Helen says. 'Keep it. Please.'

Gingerly, she steps out of the car.

CHAPTER TWENTY-NINE

As she watches the taxi pull away, Helen begins to doubt the wisdom of her decision. Siân couldn't have made it any clearer that she wants to be left alone. So what is she doing, running after her like some annoying kid sister, poking her nose in where it's not wanted? The poor woman has probably had enough of her emotional demands for one day and needs some time to unwind. She's entitled to that much, surely?

Perhaps, but Siân's behaviour was strange, to say the least. Why all those coded words and knowing looks in the back of the cab? The way she spoke to the driver was unbearable, and she seemed to know more about this lad Collins than she was letting on.

But what bothers Helen most is that her friend would choose to abandon her at a time like this. Yes, she was a little hysterical – but given the circumstances, surely that's only to be expected? And yes, she probably could do with an early night. But she really doesn't want to be alone right now. She wants company, and since Siân is the only person she really knows in this strange city, she isn't left with a lot of options.

Right, she tells herself, smoothing down her top and adjusting her handbag on her shoulder. *Let's not make a big deal about this. Just go into the pub, find Siân and smooth things over. We'll have a few drinks and later we'll go back to the hotel together.*

As she passes the smokers and approaches the pub's scuffed front door, Helen feels her resolve weaken.

I can't do this, she thinks. *What if she tells me to fuck off?*

Then her husband's voice sounds inside her head. *Of course she won't, babes. You told me yourself what great friends you are.*

She takes a deep breath and pushes open the door.

The first thing that strikes her is just how big the place was – and how busy. Everywhere she turns there are people – groups of men standing at the bar, gaggles of women deep in conversation or casting lingering looks at the men, a few couples sitting quietly together in a row of American diner-style booths along one wall. There's no sign of Siân.

Helen pushes her way through the throngs of people towards the bar. Laughter explodes from a far corner of the room. A group of women to her left giggle as she squeezes by. Are they laughing at her? Siân kept telling her she looked exhausted. Is she really that rough? She stops in her tracks and looks around for the ladies.

There's a commotion ahead. A man raises his pint glass, spilling beer down the front of his shirt. A woman squeals as the crowd parts to reveal a large black dog.

Helen stops in her tracks. Large dogs make her nervous. Once, when she was small, her father had taken her for a walk in the field next to the river. As they passed the entrance to the Black Path, a Labrador had come tearing towards them, jumping up at her, barking excitedly. She remembers the flash of teeth, the drool dripping from its jaws and the panic that quickly reduced her to tears. Her father said the dog was just being friendly, but when they arrived home her mother hit the roof. What was her father thinking? Anything could have happened to her. At the very least she'd need a tetanus injection. It was lucky for him the dog hadn't caused any serious damage. It could have ripped her face open. Didn't he read the newspapers?

This dog is more powerful than a Labrador. Is it a Rottweiler? She isn't sure. But it looks dangerous, like the dogs some of the local youths back home lead around on chains to let everyone know how hard they are. Only this dog isn't on a chain.

She braces herself as it comes towards her – head raised, mouth open, black lips stretched over bright white teeth. It slavers at her feet and begins sniffing – first her ankle, then her knees, then up her thighs. She tenses as it reaches her crotch, turns her body to one side, shielding herself with her handbag. The dog licks her hand and she flinches.

'Zoltan!' A burly middle-aged man with a ruddy face pushes his way towards her. 'Zoltan! Leave the young lady alone!'

He grabs the dog by the collar. 'Sorry, luv. He looks a lot tougher than he is. But he helps ward off trouble.' He smiles and pulls the dog away. 'I'm the landlord. John McCauley. But everyone calls me Mack. Now, what can I get you? On the house.'

'There's no need, really.'

'Please. I insist.'

'An orange juice, please. But I need to use the ladies'.' She can feel the dog's saliva on her hand and can't wait to wash it off.

'Past the bar, first on the right. I'll have your drink on the bar for you when you get back. Now, are you sure I can't get you something stronger?'

Helen shakes her head. Alcohol is the last thing she

wants. The thought of it makes her nauseous. She's been feeling out of sorts for days – tired, spaced out, as if she's permanently hungover or coming down with something. Finally it feels as if the fog is lifting.

The floor of the ladies' is damp. There's a tampon vending machine hanging off the wall and two sinks, wet with hair and used tissues. She washes her hands and a strand of hair catches on her wedding ring. She shudders and rinses it off.

Standing inspecting her face in the mirror, she hears a woman cursing under her breath in one of the two cubicles. There's a groan, followed by a shuffling sound and then a loud sniff.

Helen takes a brush from her handbag and tugs it through her hair. The harsh strip lighting wasn't designed to flatter anyone. It gives her hair a brassy glow and hollows out her eye sockets. But she isn't looking nearly as bad as she'd feared. A little tired and drawn maybe, but that's hardly surprising.

There's another sniff from the cubicle, louder than before. Is the woman crying? Helen taps gently on the door. 'Are you okay in there?'

Silence.

She hesitates.

There's still no response. Flustered, she slips the hairbrush back into her bag and leaves.

As promised, a glass of orange juice is waiting for her at the bar.

'There you go,' the landlord says. 'One vodka and orange. Easy on the vodka.' He winks and continues wiping the bar. 'Just pulling your leg.'

She thanks him and takes a small sip, half expecting to detect the taste of alcohol. All she tastes is orange juice. Relieved, she takes another sip and surveys the room.

There's still no sign of Siân.

'Is there a beer garden?' Helen asks.

The landlord shakes his head. 'Sorry. If you want to smoke you have to go out the front.'

She scans the booths. Most appear to be full. The one furthest from her is occupied by a man. The partitions between the booths are high, and there's a pillar separating the front of the booth from the one next to it. Helen can only see the back of the man's head with its tightly cropped hair. But he seems agitated. He keeps scratching the back of his neck and nodding his head as if in time to music. The only sound in the bar is the buzz of conversation.

She wonders where Siân could have got to. Did she slip into the toilet while her back was turned? Helen positions herself at the end of the bar and waits. People come and go. Finally she sees Siân emerge from the ladies. She waves to catch her attention but Siân doesn't see her. She's deep in conversation with another woman, both walking and talking animatedly. They stop next to a pinball machine and shake hands. Siân whispers something in the woman's ear before turning and making her way over to the booth where the nodding man is sitting. He budges up and she sidles in beside him.

Is this the soldier Siân met at the hospital? Helen hadn't seen his face then and she can't see it now. She can't even tell if he's wearing uniform. But the cut of his hair and the cosy way he and Siân are sitting together suggest that it's the same man. Why didn't Siân say she was meeting him? Why all the secrecy?

The couple in the next booth drain their glasses and stand up to leave. Helen watches as the man pulls on his denim jacket and drapes the woman's pink cardigan over her shoulders. The man reminds her of Owen. He was always so attentive, back in the days when going out wasn't such a rare occurrence. 'You're my wife,' he'd say. 'I have to take care of you.' What would he think if he could see her now? What is she even doing here? But she's come this far. Did she really follow Siân into the pub just to leave meekly? As the couple pass by, she grabs her drink and hurries over to the vacant booth, staying close to the wall so she can't be seen.

Ducking into the booth, she places her glass on the table in front of her and positions herself carefully, pressing her head back against the pillar. Then she listens. The first thing she hears is the chink of glasses followed by Siân saying, 'Cheers!'

'Cheers,' the soldier replies. 'You took your time.'

His voice is muffled and he's slurring slightly.

'Hold your horses,' says Siân. 'There'll be plenty of time for that later. Now, where were we?'

'Pink mist,' the soldier says.

'Pink mist?'

'It's what we say when someone's blown to bits. Only in his case it couldn't be more fitting. There were bits of him everywhere. Skin, bones, chunks of flesh. They found one of his ears hanging from a tree.'

Helen feels a chill run through her. There's no feeling in the man's voice. He could just as easily be describing a dead dog or cat. She knows that soldiers are trained to deal with life-threatening situations, that their reactions are more hardened than most. But Owen would never talk about a fellow soldier so callously.

'That's disgusting!' says Siân.

'Could have been worse,' the soldier says. 'At least it was only the queer. Right little smart arse he was, too. Thought he was really clever. Not looking so clever now though, is he?' He laughs.

There's a pause before Siân speaks. 'Collins wasn't popular then.'

Helen strains to hear their conversation.

'His sort never are,' the soldier replies.

'At least the other guy's okay.'

The laughter stops. 'You reckon?' Helen can hear the sneer in the soldier's voice.

'What's that supposed to mean?'

'McGrath and Collins. They were very close, if you catch my drift.'

Helen's pulse quickens.

Siân giggles. 'No way!'

'Oh, yeah. Very close, those two.'

'But he's married. I've met his wife.'

'Yeah? And what do you make of her?'

Silence.

The soldier sniggers. 'Exactly. Anyway, I know what I saw.'

Helen digs her fingernails into the palm of her hand. *Who are you?* she thinks. *And why are you saying these things?*

'Tell me more,' Siân says. 'I'm all ears.'

'And I'm ready for a whisky chaser.'

'I thought you were more interested in chasing women.'

'One woman. And she's sitting right here.'

'Not now, she's not. She's off to the bar to buy you a large one.'

The soldier laughs. 'Are you made of money, or what?'

'What can I say? We have to take care of our boys.'

'I'll take care of you later.'

'I'll hold you to that. Back in a tick.'

Helen leans back in the booth and watches as Siân

snakes her way through the crowd towards the bar, arms aloft, an empty pint glass in each hand, looking for all the world as if she owns the place. The landlord smiles as he sees her approaching. She hands him the empty glasses before turning to blow the soldier a kiss. Helen turns her face away, prays she hasn't been seen.

When she looks back again, Siân has disappeared. Helen cranes her neck and peers around the edge of the pillar.

The soldier has shifted position and is staring intently in the direction of the bar. He looks like he's on watch. He has a strong profile – strong and menacing. His teeth are clenched so tightly, Helen can see the muscle in his jaw twitch. A vein on his temple throbs as if it's about to pop.

He must sense her staring because his eyes flicker in her direction, not fully focussing but affording her a quick glimpse of his face. Her skin crawls. She's seen that face before. The last time was just over a year ago, at a military funeral. He was accompanied by his wife, who arrived wearing enormous black sunglasses, despite the fact that it was raining. Later, Helen bumped into her in the ladies toilet, reapplying make-up to an eye circled with purple bruises. Shocked, she'd been about to say something, but the wife had shot her a warning look before shielding her eyes once more behind her sunglasses and marching past with her shoulders back and her head held high.

Helen didn't say anything to Owen. The timing wasn't right, and she knew it would upset him, given his own family history. But she hadn't forgotten. Months later, Owen had recounted a story involving a group of soldiers from his regiment who'd gone on a training exercise and ended up in a brothel. 'Poor Leanne,' he said. 'If she only knew what kind of man she's married to.'

Helen knows exactly what kind of man Leanne is married to. It's the same man Siân is fawning over now – Jackson.

CHAPTER THIRTY

Helen's heart races as she ducks deeper inside the booth. A hot flush creeps up her neck. Jackson is here. The wife beater. The soldier who was nearly thrown out of the army for breaking a man's jaw. He's the one Siân has been seeing. What the hell is she doing consorting with a man like that – buying him drinks, listening to his insinuations, laughing at his jokes?

Part of her wants to corner Siân immediately and demand some answers. But now isn't the best time. Not here. Not when she has Jackson for company. Far better to wait until they're alone, back at the hotel. Then she'll see what Siân has to say for herself.

Helen feels a mixture of anger and humiliation wash over her, wonders how she could have misjudged Siân so badly. All that talk about looking out for her. All those declarations of friendship. And then to sit there gossiping about her and Owen with a thug like Jackson. What a fool she's been to be taken in by her. What a stupid fool.

Her mind races. She needs to get away. But how can she sneak out of the pub without being seen? How will she get back to the hotel? She looks in her purse and sees that she doesn't have a lot of options. A few pound coins and some small change won't get her very far in a cab, and she isn't carrying any bank cards. Did she leave them at the hotel? She can't remember. She hasn't used them since Friday – before this whole nightmare began. Maybe she should call Sue Blackwell? She rummages in her handbag for the card with Sue's number but it isn't there. Strange. She could have sworn she had it earlier.

There's still no sign of Siân at the bar. A barmaid is busy serving a group of women who look as if they've come straight from the office. She lines up three shot glasses and fills them with what looks like tequila. Further along the bar, the landlord is pulling pints. He has a kind face, Helen thinks. Maybe if she asks nicely, he'll loan her the money for a cab. If she explains the situation, tells him her husband is in hospital, perhaps he'll take pity on her. She looks in her bag, checks again for the card with Sue's number.

'Helen?'

Her scalp prickles. She looks up.

Siân smiles down at her. Her lipstick is smudged and her eyes look a little pink, despite the heavy black eyeliner. 'Lost something?'

Helen says the first thing that comes into her head. 'I can't find my room key.' She lowers her eyes and pokes around inside her handbag, covers the plastic key card with her hand. 'No, it's not here.'

'Budge up,' Siân says, squeezing in beside her. 'What are you doing here? I thought you were going straight back to the hotel.'

'I was,' Helen lies. 'But then I realized I'd forgotten my key.'

Siân eyes her suspiciously. 'But they know you at the hotel. Someone would have let you into the room.'

'Of course!' Helen blinks. 'I hadn't thought of that. I wasn't thinking straight.'

'You weren't spying on me, were you?'

'Of course not.'

'Really?'

Helen clears her throat, plays for time, plasters a smile to her face. 'Actually, I wanted to talk to you. I wanted to say sorry. For the way I was before, in the taxi. Getting hysterical like that. You must think I'm a right pain.'

'It could have waited.'

'I know. But I didn't know how late you'd be, and I didn't want to leave it until the morning. You've been so good to me. I'd hate you to think I didn't appreciate it.'

'I see,' says Siân. 'Apology accepted. But that still doesn't explain why you're sitting here on your own.'

Helen snaps her handbag shut and places it on her lap. 'I couldn't find you. Then, seeing as I was here, I thought I might as well stay and have a few drinks.' She gestures at the glass of orange juice on the table in front of her.

'Right,' says Siân. 'And how were you planning to pay for them?'

'What?'

'You only have a few coins in your purse and you left your cards at the hotel.'

And how the hell do you know? Helen thinks. 'Did I?'

Siân looks at her as if she can't decide whether she's incredibly stupid or far cleverer than she's given her credit for. 'They're in the safe,' she says. 'Poor Helen. You'd forget your head if it wasn't screwed on. So how did you pay for your drink?'

'I didn't. The landlord gave it to me. On the house.'

'Really? Strange men buying you drinks. What would your husband say?'

Helen tenses. 'It's just an orange juice. I don't think he'd mind.'

'Don't look so worried. I won't tell him if you don't.'

'I'm not worried. There's nothing to tell.'

'Ssh!' Siân winks and nudges her shoulder. 'It'll

be our little secret.'

Sure, Helen thinks. *Yours, mine and Jackson's.*

She glances into the next booth. Jackson has gone. She wonders if he and Siân were aware of her presence all along, wonders how much of their conversation was for her benefit. She thinks for a moment, decides to push back a little.

'What happened to your friend?' she asks, as casually as she can.

'What friend?'

'I thought you said you were meeting someone. That soldier from the hospital.'

Siân frowns. 'I never said that. You must be hearing things. I'm quite capable of going out for a drink on my own. We don't all need a man to take care of us.'

'I just thought –'

'Never mind what you thought. Your head's all over the place.' Siân reaches for her bag. 'I've got some more of those tablets here. Take a couple before bed. They'll help calm you down.'

She stands and hoists the bag onto her shoulder. 'C'mon, let's go.'

Helen looks up at her, sees the way her eyes flit around the room, the anxious way she chews her lip. For someone who'd been so eager to stop off at the pub in the first place, she suddenly seems desperately keen to leave. Is she worried in case Jackson reappears and exposes her for the liar she is? Helen has no real desire to stay either. She wants to put as much distance between herself and Jackson as possible. But she can't resist testing Siân's nerve, just to see how she'll respond.

'What's the rush?' Helen says. 'Let's stay and have another drink.'

'Nah, it's best if we get you back to the hotel. You

look knackered. Shall I call us a cab? Or did Osama offer you a free ride?'

'What?'

Siân smirks. 'The cab driver. Since you're cadging free drinks, I thought maybe you'd come to some arrangement.'

'No.'

'Good. Cos there's no such thing as a free ride with some people.' She grabs Helen's arm and hauls her to her feet. 'C'mon, then. Let's go.'

As they turn to leave, Helen replays Siân's conversation with Jackson over in her head, wonders if there's even the slightest possibility that she misheard or misinterpreted what was said. She thinks how much easier it would be to put this all down to a misunderstanding or pretend that it never happened. But she can't. She knows what she heard, knows she's only grasping at straws.

Progress towards the door is slow. The pub is even busier now than when Helen arrived. Voices are raised. Snippets of conversation sound in her ears. 'I don't know why people are so stuck up about Edgbaston –'; 'She's a right misery guts but so is he, so they're well suited –'; 'Dave would kill me if he found out –'

'Get out of the way!' Siân snaps, digging an elbow into a startled-looking man in glasses. 'Mind my fucking foot!'

A woman's face appears, smiling broadly. It's the same woman Helen saw coming out of the ladies with Siân earlier. But as she comes forward and opens her mouth to say something, Siân scowls at her. 'Not now!'

The woman looks confused. 'But –'

'Are you deaf?' Siân hisses. 'I said not now!'

It's not a huge scene. The room doesn't fall silent. Most people seem oblivious to the fact that the exchange has even taken place. But as the woman melts away into the crowd, Helen realizes she's holding her breath.

'Wait,' she says, stopping dead in her tracks.

Siân turns to her, clinging to her wrist. 'What's the matter?'

'There's no point in us both going. It's still early. You should stay and enjoy yourself. I can make my own way. I just need to borrow some money for a taxi.'

'What do you think I am? A cash dispenser?' Siân raises her eyebrows. 'I can't let you go back on your own, not after the day you've had.' She tightens her grip on Helen's wrist and pulls her towards the door. 'C'mon. I'll call us a cab.'

Outside, the air is cool and a group of women are huddled together in a haze of cigarette smoke. One has bare arms. The others wear lightweight jackets or cardigans.

'You're shivering,' Siân says.

'I'm fine,' Helen lies.

'Hang on.'

Siân stops and rummages in her bag before taking out a large cotton scarf and wrapping it around Helen's shoulders.

'We can't have you walking around like that. You'll catch your death.'

Helen flinches.

'See?' says Siân. 'I knew you were cold.'

It's not the cold, Helen thinks. *It's you*.

She wants to scream, Get your hands off me, you two-faced bitch! Instead she forces a smile. 'Thanks.'

'All part of the service.' Siân takes out her phone, dials and presses it to her ear. 'I need a cab from The Admiral Tavern. Quick as you can. Yeah, well, there are other cab firms, y'know. Right. Okay. We'll be waiting outside.'

She slides the phone back into her pocket. 'They'll be here in a few minutes.' She smiles and rolls her eyes. 'As if I'd leave you here on your own! The state you're in, anything could happen.'

'But I only had an orange juice.'

'I didn't say you were drunk. I meant the way you are generally. People pick up on it, y'know. Men especially. They can tell when a woman's vulnerable. They can smell it on you.'

Helen glares at her, but refrains from arguing. Even in the fading light of the forecourt, it's clear that Siân is far from sober. And it's not just the alcohol talking. Her pupils are dilated. There's spittle in the corners of her mouth. She looks like someone on drugs. Is that what she was doing in the ladies earlier, with the woman she just turned on?

'Imagine if you'd ended up in one those unlicensed taxis,' Siân says. 'You know what happens to women who climb into cars with strange men, don't you? How do you think I'd feel if something like that happened to you? How would I explain it to Owen? I promised him I'd take care of you. Now, where's that fucking cab?'

As Siân turns and scans the road, the door to the pub swings open and a man emerges. It's Jackson. A cigarette dangles from the corner of his mouth. He fumbles in his trouser pocket and takes out a lighter.

Helen watches as he cups his hands and lights his cigarette. It's then that his eyes meet hers. There's a moment's hesitation, then a knowing smirk spreads across his face and he saunters towards her.

'Helen McGrath! As I live and breathe!'

Helen's eyes flick to Siân and back to Jackson. His choice of words isn't lost on her. Nor is his tone. He has a way of being flirtatious without being remotely friendly.

'Jackson,' she replies. 'What are you doing here?'

'I'm on leave. You?'

Helen frowns. 'Owen. He was –'

'Oh, yeah!' Jackson nods and sucks on his cigarette. 'Sorry about that. Bummer.'

'So why aren't you at home?' Helen asks, ignoring the hint of a smile on his lips. 'Leanne must be missing you.'

Siân continues to scan the road for the taxi. To Helen's surprise, she hasn't even acknowledged Jackson's presence, nor he hers. Anyone would think they were sworn enemies or total strangers without the slightest interest in one another.

'Don't you worry about Leanne.' There's a glint in Jackson's eye. 'She knows what comes with being married to a soldier.'

'You haven't forgotten you're married, then?' Helen says coolly.

Jackson's face darkens. There's still no reaction from Siân.

'I'm sorry,' Helen says. 'This is my friend Siân. I thought you two knew each other. Didn't you meet at the hospital?'

Siân glances at Jackson and shakes her head. 'No.'

Jackson smirks. 'You've got your wires crossed, Helen. Maybe it's the stress.' He pinches the cigarette between his forefinger and thumb, takes one last drag and tosses the stub away. 'Don't forget to say hi to Owen for me. Tell him I'll be seeing him soon.'

A horn sounds as the cab pulls up. Siân rushes forward and flings open the passenger door.

'C'mon, Helen,' she calls. 'Get in the car!'

Jackson winks. 'Run along, Helen! Do as your friend says. I'll catch you later.'

CHAPTER THIRTY-ONE

The short drive to Helen's house takes longer than expected. The roads are choked with traffic. As he turns off the main road and into the street where she lives, Frank sees a group of teenage lads playing football on the patch of grass in front of her house. He glances at the clock. It's past nine – time these boys were in school, surely? He slams his foot on the brake as one lad runs into the road in front of the car, chasing after the ball. Frank hits his horn. The boy flips him the finger before grabbing the ball and running back to join the others.

Where are the parents? Frank wonders. Do they even care what their kids get up to? His own father would have clipped him around the ear if he'd shown that much disrespect to an adult. And he'd have hit the roof if Frank had skipped school, or come home with grass stains on his shirt. Not that his father was ever a bully. 'Firm but fair' was his motto. But there were times when Frank was afraid of him. Long before he became a parent himself, he'd already decided that he would never raise a hand to his own child.

Helen's car is parked outside the house. Maybe she's home after all, Frank thinks. Maybe she has the same stomach bug Amanda suffered from a few weeks ago. But as he drives closer he spots the milk on the doorstep. She'd have to be really sick not to take the milk in.

Something isn't right.

He parks the car and peers in through the front window. The curtains are open but there are no lights on and no sign of anyone inside. Through the frosted glass panel of the front door, he sees a pile of post on the mat. He fishes in his pocket for the spare key. Helen doesn't know he has it. It was Owen who'd taken him aside one Sunday afternoon and pressed it into his hand, shortly before he left for Afghanistan. 'Y'know,' he'd said. 'Just in case of an emergency.'

Frank pauses. Is this an emergency? He doesn't know. Still there's a strong sense that something isn't right, coupled with the equally powerful sense that Helen wouldn't be too pleased to find him letting himself into her house. He presses the doorbell and listens for a response. When none comes he knocks hard on the door. Then he kneels down and peers through the letterbox. 'Helen?' he calls. 'Helen! Are you in there?'

Someone coughs. Frank looks up to see a man his own age, with sallow skin and thin greying hair tied back in a ponytail. In one hand he holds the remains of a roll-up.

'There's no point knocking,' he says. 'There's nobody in.'

Frank climbs to his feet. 'And you are?'

The other man doesn't offer his hand. 'Rob. I live next door.'

'Do you know where Helen is?'

'Who's asking?' Rob grins at him.

'Frank. I'm –' He hesitates. 'I'm Helen's stepfather. So do you know where she is?'

'Couldn't say. Someone came and took her away, early hours of Sunday morning. I heard them talking outside.'

'What do you mean, "took her away"? Who was it?'

Rob takes a drag on his roll-up. 'Someone from the army, by the looks of it. They went in the house, then she came out with a bag and they drove off.'

'I see,' Frank says. So it is an emergency after all. Owen has been injured – or worse. No wonder Helen hasn't called. The poor girl must be in bits.

'Was she alone?' Frank asks. He hates the thought of her being all alone at a time like this.

'There was a girl with her,' Rob replies. 'Black hair. Big mouth on her. I didn't catch her name.'

Frank racks his brains. This doesn't sound like any of the women Helen works with, and he isn't aware of her having any other friends.

'Did you see anything else?' he asks.

Rob shrugs. 'No. But the other girl left a wrap of coke on my doorstep.' He grins, exposing large yellow teeth. 'No coke in it though, more's the pity.'

'Right,' says Frank. 'Well, thanks for your help.'

'Aren't you going to look inside the house?'

'No. I think I'd better be on my way.' Frank returns the key to his trouser pocket and begins walking towards his car.

'What about the milk?' Rob calls after him.

Frank replies without looking back. 'You have it.'

By the time he's buckled up, switched on the ignition and pulled away from the kerb, the milk has disappeared and so has Rob. The boys who were playing football a few minutes earlier have drifted off somewhere. The street is deserted.

So there's nobody to witness the stocky man who emerges from a white transit van parked at the far end of the road. He's dressed in jeans and a T-shirt. Shading his eyes with one hand, he surveys the street before leaning back into the van and taking a bulky manilla envelope off the dashboard. He walks up the street, stopping at the door where Frank stood just a few moments earlier. Then, after glancing quickly in both directions, he forces the envelope through the letterbox.

Glamorgan Tribune
– Woman Raped at the Black Path

A 23-year-old woman was drugged and raped by three men in what police have described as 'a brutal and premeditated attack.'

The woman was lured to the Black Path in Bridgend by a man she met at The Jolly Brewer pub. Two other men were lying in wait for her there. She was drugged, sexually assaulted and left unconscious near the site of the old blast furnace, where a cyclist found her in the early hours of Sunday morning. The woman is being treated at the Princess of Wales Hospital.

Police believe the attack took place between 10.30 p.m. and 11.30 p.m. on Saturday night. All three suspects are said to be in their late 20s. The first is described as white, with fair hair, blue eyes and a Cardiff accent. The other two suspects wore balaclavas. One has an eagle tattoo on his right forearm. Police are appealing for witnesses who may have seen the woman leaving The Jolly Brewer with the first man between 10 p.m. and 10.30 p.m. All information will be treated as confidential.

The front door opens before Frank has time to insert his key.

'Where've you been?' Amanda asks. 'I've been trying

to reach you all day. I was worried sick!'

She looks flustered, Frank thinks. But that's nothing new. His wife looks flustered most days. And today she has every reason to be. She just doesn't know it yet.

Several hours have passed since Frank spoke to Helen's neighbour – hours he has put to good use, making calls and gathering every piece of information he could find.

'Can I at least come inside first?' he asks. 'Or would you rather have the whole street knowing our business?'

She steps aside to let him pass. 'Angela's here,' she says. 'From Helen's work.'

Frank removes his jacket and hangs it at the bottom of the stairs. 'I know who Angela is.'

'Do you? I don't see how.'

Frank frowns. 'Helen's mentioned her often enough.' Not for the first time, he wonders when his wife simply stopped listening to things that don't really interest her.

'She's in the kitchen,' Amanda says, hovering at his side. 'She says Helen hasn't been at work all week.'

'I know,' Frank replies. 'And I know why. It's bad news, I'm afraid.'

His wife's face whitens. 'What's happened? Is she hurt?'

'It's Owen.'

Amanda's hand rises to her mouth.

'He's not dead,' Frank says firmly. He reaches for his wife's arm but she pulls away from him and stands with both arms held in front of her chest, elbows tucked at her sides, hands clutched tightly together. She looks as if she's bracing herself for something. 'He's in hospital,' Frank continues. 'Helen is with him.'

As quickly as he can, he tells his wife everything he knows. After driving to Helen's house this morning and talking to her neighbour, he called up one of his drinking buddies at the TA and was eventually put through to someone who confirmed that Owen had been injured. Next, he contacted the military hospital in Birmingham, telling them he was Helen's stepfather. Finally, after trying and failing to locate a liaison officer named Sue Blackwell, he'd spoken at length to one of the nurses.

'She says Helen is bearing up well. And she's not on her own. She has someone with her. A pushy young woman called Siân.'

'Siân?' Amanda thinks for a moment. 'Helen's never mentioned any Siân.'

'I didn't think so,' says Frank. 'And from what the nurse said, I'm not sure I like the sound of her.'

They walk into the kitchen. Angela is sitting at the table, cradling a mug of tea. She lifts her head as Frank and Amanda enter the room. 'Is something the matter?'

'It's my son-in-law, Owen,' Frank says, and quickly repeats what he'd just told his wife.

Angela eyes widen. She shifts in her seat. 'Oh my God,' she says. 'I was just saying to Mrs Powell that Helen hasn't been at work all week. Of course I covered for her. I told the boss she was off sick. If I'd known things were this bad –'

'When did you last see her?' Frank asks.

'Last Friday.'

'You went out after work, didn't you?'

'Yes.'

'And you haven't heard from her since?'

Angela colours slightly. 'No.'

'What's the matter?' Frank asks. 'Did you two fall out or something?'

'Of course not! We were just out having a laugh. Helen was pretty drunk. We all were. But then our friend

Kath collapsed, and by the time the ambulance came I couldn't see Helen anywhere.'

Amanda clears her throat. 'So what you're saying is, you just left her there. A young woman, drunk, on her own.'

'I didn't know where she was. She just disappeared. And I had to take Kath to the hospital.'

'I see,' Amanda sniffs. 'Well, so long as Kath's alright.'

'She could have died,' Angela says, welling up. 'Someone spiked her drink.'

'Go easy on the girl, Amanda,' Frank says. 'Can't you see she's upset enough already?' He turns to Angela. 'So let me get this straight. The last time you spoke to Helen was on Friday night?'

Angela nods. 'It's not that I haven't tried. I have.'

'Not hard enough, obviously,' Amanda chips in.

Frank glares at her. 'Please, Amanda! You're not helping!' He smiles reassuringly at Angela. 'Is there anything else you can tell us? What about a woman called Siân? Have you heard of her?'

Angela shakes her head. 'No. Who's she?'

'She's with Helen now,' Frank says. 'At the hospital in Birmingham.'

Angela thinks for a moment. 'I don't know her,' she says. 'But I think I might have spoken to her on the phone. I tried to call Helen. I really did. But she never answered. I left messages and sent texts, but she never replied. Then I called again and some woman answered Helen's phone.'

'When was this?' Amanda asks.

'Sunday. Sunday afternoon. She told me Helen was sleeping and she wouldn't be coming into work.'

'And you've left it until now to tell us? I've been

cursing my daughter for not returning my calls and now you're telling me that some woman we've never even heard of has her phone?'

'Stop it, Amanda!' Frank says. 'Go on, Angela. What else did she say?'

'Not a lot. It was more the way she spoke to me. She was rude and ... strange.'

'Strange? In what way?'

'Like she was Helen's only friend in the world. Like she was in control. And she refused to give her name. When I asked who she was, she cut me off.'

'Right,' says Frank, checking his watch. 'I need to make a few calls. Amanda, can you pack us a suitcase, please? First thing tomorrow we're driving up to Birmingham.'

CHAPTER THIRTY-TWO

'Good morning, Mrs McGrath.' Sue Blackwell's tone is even more cheery than usual, as if she's been wrong-footed or feels she has some making up to do. 'Sorry I didn't see you yesterday. It was my day off. How are you feeling?'

Slumped on a grey plastic chair next to the nurses' station, Helen barely glances up at her. 'I'm okay,' she says, her voice sounding every bit as weary as she feels. Her back aches. Her eyes are sore from lack of sleep.

'Are you sure?'

Helen raises her head to offer a smile and sees the red welt on Sue's cheek. She speaks without thinking. 'What happened to your face?'

Sue puts her hand to her cheek and smiles ruefully. 'It was your husband, Mrs McGrath.'

'What? Owen would never hit a woman.'

'No, of course not. It's not what you think. I checked on him earlier and, well, he lashed out at me. Involuntarily. It's quite common in trauma cases.'

'He's awake?'

'No. He's still unconscious. But believe it or not, this is a good sign.'

Another smile.

Helen sighs and lowers her head. The doctor had told her that it might take a few days for Owen to come round fully. The phrase 'quite common in trauma cases' is becoming a bit of a mantra. Not that this makes it any more comforting.

Sue takes a seat beside her. 'Your friend not with you today?'

'No, she's gone into town for a few things.'

The truth is, Helen no longer trusts Siân. How can she, after the other night? No harsh words have been exchanged. She didn't challenge Siân about Jackson when they got back to the hotel. She lost her nerve. She isn't proud of herself but, really, what good would it have done? Siân was clearly in an altered state. Things could have escalated pretty quickly. Rightly or wrongly, Helen decided that it wasn't worth the risk.

But of course she's wary. She's been avoiding Siân as much as possible. Yesterday she was up and out of the hotel bright and early and didn't return until after dark. Had she seen Sue yesterday, Helen would have asked her about alternative sleeping arrangements at the hospital. She's about to broach the subject when Sue speaks.

'I had a phone call earlier,' she says brightly. 'It was your father, Frank.'

'Frank's not my father.'

'Oh. Perhaps I misunderstood. He said you were his daughter.'

'Stepdaughter,' Helen corrects her. 'What did he want?'

Sue looks confused. 'He wanted to know how you are. He and your mother are worried about you. He said they'd left messages but they've not heard anything.'

Helen frowns. 'I haven't had any messages.'

'Are you sure?'

'Of course I'm sure. I may be tired and emotional but I'm not stupid.' Helen checks herself and flushes with embarrassment. 'Sorry. I didn't mean to snap at you.'

Sue tilts her head, offers another of her professional smiles.

'That's okay. He said something else. Your friend Angela? From work? She's also been calling you and sending texts.'

Helen reaches into her pocket for her phone. There are no texts or missed calls.

'Does anyone else have access to your phone?' Sue asks.

'Not really.'

'Only apparently Angela called and someone answered your phone. A woman.' Sue pauses. 'We think it was your friend, Siân.'

Helen's mind races. Not only has Siân been sneaking around with Jackson. She's also been intercepting phone calls and, perhaps, deleting voice mails and text messages. Why would she do that?

'There's one more thing,' Sue says. 'It's a little delicate.'

'Go on.'

'When I arrived today and got the message saying your stepfather had called and that he and your mother were worried about you – well, to be honest, I was a bit surprised.'

'Why?'

'Because your friend told me that both your parents were dead.' Sue pauses. 'I hope you don't mind me asking, but how well do you know this Siân person?'

Better than you think, Helen thinks. She shrugs. 'Not that well.' She makes a mental note to keep her phone with her at all times.

'Frank and your mum are driving up today,' Sue says in a brighter voice. 'They should be here this soon. They know all about Owen.'

Helen blinks. 'They're coming here?'

Sue looks puzzled.

'Shouldn't they be? They're your –'

She sounds as if she's about to say 'parents' but stops herself. 'They're your family.'

Helen's phone rings. The screen says the number is withheld.

'Aren't you going to answer that?' asks Sue. 'It might be them. Maybe they're stuck in traffic.'

Helen knows exactly who it is. But she answers anyway.

'Helen!' Siân says. 'I'm in Selfridges, at The Bullring. I've found the most perfect dress for you. You have to come and try it on.'

'I'm at the hospital,' Helen replies, as evenly as she can.

'But you'll want to look nice for Owen when he wakes up, won't you? There's a woman here doing free makeovers. We'll be back at the hospital in no time. A couple of hours tops.'

Helen looks at Sue and silently mouths the words, *It's her!*

Sue knits her eyebrows and makes a circling motion with her hand, urging her to wind up the call.

Helen turns her head away.

'Okay,' she says. 'I'll call a cab.'

She's vaguely aware of Sue rising from her chair.

'Who are you with?' Siân asks.

'No-one. I'm in the cafeteria.'

'I knew you'd be hungry. That's what you get for skipping breakfast. If I didn't know better I'd say you were avoiding me.'

'Don't be daft. I just wasn't hungry, that's all.' As she

speaks, Helen feels her stomach rumble.

'Right, well I'll wait for you here then.'

'Great,' Helen says. 'I'll see you there.'

She has no intention of going to meet Siân – but there's no need for her to know that.

'Are you sure you're alright, Mrs McGrath?'

Helen looks up to see Sue standing over her again, a concerned look on her face.

She has a way of talking that makes Helen feel ever so slightly patronized. But Sue isn't her enemy here. 'I'm fine,' she says.

'You're not really going to meet her, are you?'

'Of course not.'

Sue looks relieved. 'Good. Well, it sounds to me as if you might be hungry. Shall we get you something to eat?'

'What about Owen?'

'They'll call me if there's any change.'

At the cafeteria, Helen finds an empty table while Sue joins the queue.

'They've stopped serving breakfast,' she says when she returns. 'But I've got you some sandwiches to keep you going.'

'It's busy in here today,' Helen says, taking a bite of a cheese and tomato sandwich.

Sue lowers her voice. 'They brought more men in last night. I expect these are the families.'

Helen eats her sandwich, quietly contemplating how many soldiers have been injured and what state they're in. She pictures the man in the trauma ward with a bloody stump for an arm. She hasn't seen him for a few days and wonders if he's gone home.

'Have you thought any more about staying here at the hospital?' Sue asks. 'We can make a bed up in Owen's room if you like. I'm sure you'll want to be with him when he comes round.'

Helen smiles. 'That would be great.' The prospect of another night at the hotel with Siân isn't one she relishes. 'But what about my things?'

'We can pop over together and fetch them, while she's out shopping.'

'Thank you.'

Sue rises from the table. 'I'll just go and make a few quick calls. I won't be long.'

Five minutes pass, then ten. More people arrive. Helen gazes around the canteen at the wives, girlfriends, mothers and fathers who've come to see their loved ones. They all shared the same stricken look. Maybe that's why they avoid making eye contact with one another.

She thinks back to the days immediately after her father died, how her mother refused to look at her. Had she been too quick to judge her mother? Possibly. But her behaviour in the months that followed was harder to forgive. Her mother had visited her father's grave half a dozen times at most – and that was before she betrayed his memory by shacking up with Frank.

They'll be here soon. Helen pictures Frank at the wheel, and her mother's anxious state as they drive to Birmingham – arguing over directions, navigating the tricky road system, fretting over potential traffic jams. Usually the prospect of seeing them fills her with dread. But faced with the choice between them and Siân, she knows which she prefers. Better the devil you know.

'Helen!'

She looks up. Sue is standing in the canteen doorway, her face flushed.

'It's Owen,' she says. 'He's awake.'

As they approach the door to Owen's room, the first thing Helen hears is his laughter. He sounds happy, like his old self.

Then she hears another voice. It's a woman – a nurse perhaps, or an orderly. Then Sue opens the door and Helen sees immediately that the woman she heard isn't a member of hospital staff.

She's seated on the far side of the bed. Owen's head is turned towards her, away from the door. Her head is tilted to one side, so low that it's practically resting on the pillow beside him. But what really disturbs Helen is the way she's holding her husband's hand. It's not the gentle touch of a concerned friend or relative. Her fingers are locked in his, their palms pressed tightly together like a couple in love, too absorbed in each other to even acknowledge the fact that other people have entered the room.

Helen's first instinct is to rush to Owen's side. But her path is blocked by a stainless steel nurses' trolley. She sees that the top drawer is open, as if whoever wheeled it in had left in a hurry.

Siân looks up as Helen approaches, but makes no attempt to loosen her grip.

'Isn't it great?' she says. 'He's awake!' She gives Owen's hand a squeeze and he tilts his head towards her. He still hasn't looked at Helen.

'What are you doing here?' Helen asks. 'I thought you were out shopping?'

'I was,' Siân says. 'Then it dawned on me that one of us should be here in case Owen woke up.' She flashes her teeth. 'Turns out I was right.' The smile fades. 'I tried calling you, but I couldn't get a signal.'

Helen is dimly aware of soft conversations outside the room, and the squeak of shoes on the linoleum floor.

Her pulse quickens.

'What about you?' Siân asks. 'I thought you'd be on your way to the shopping centre.'

Of course you did, Helen thinks.

'I was waiting for a taxi,' she lies. 'Then a nurse called Sue with the news.'

'Where is the nurse?' Sue demands. She shuts the drawer on the trolley and moves it out of the way.

Siân shrugs, turning her attention back to Owen. 'We're doing okay, aren't we? You and me?'

Helen bristles. Part of her wants to launch herself at Siân and tear her hand away. But for some reason Owen seems to find her presence comforting. The last thing Helen wants is to upset him. She takes a deep breath and tries to contain the anger.

Footsteps approach. A nurse enters the room, closely followed by Mr Croft.

'How's the patient?' he asks in a brisk voice.

For the first time, Owen turns his head towards the door. He stares at Helen blankly for a few seconds, then a faint smile of recognition forms on his face.

She feels a surge of love for him, so strong she thinks she might break down and cry. He looks so frail and bewildered – a shadow of the man she'd waved goodbye to all those months ago.

'Owen,' she says softly. 'Thank God you're okay.'

His eyes flicker and he stares past her to the doctor, the nurse and Sue Blackwell. His smile gives way to a look of pure panic.

'Get away from me!' he yells – eyes wild, arms flailing. 'Get away!'

'You're perfectly safe, Owen,' the doctor says calmly. 'You're in hospital. We're here to help.'

'What's wrong with him?' Helen asks.

Sue lowers her voice. 'He's confused. He thinks we're the enemy.'

'But I'm his wife.'

'It's not personal. He's disorientated. But don't worry. He's in safe hands.'

Helen's eyes are immediately drawn to Siân's hands as they flutter around her husband's flailing arms, stroking and soothing until they rest once more on the bedclothes.

'Naughty boy!' she chides. 'Now look what you've done! You'll pulled out your drip!'

Helen watches as the nurse rushes forward to reattach the drip. Owen whimpers and turns to face Siân, reaching for her hand. Of all the people in the room, she's the one he turns to – a woman he barely knows, a woman who was gossiping about him just a few nights ago. Helen's stomach tightens.

'We can't have you all in here,' Mr Croft says. 'He needs room. So if you wouldn't mind leaving, miss?'

Siân doesn't move.

'This man has just woken from a coma,' the doctor adds firmly. 'I really must insist.'

Siân looks at Owen and squeezes his hand. 'You don't want me to go, do you?'

His voice is a rasp. 'What's your name again?'

'I'm Siân. Remember?'

He frowns. 'Siân,' he repeats. 'Siân.'

Helen feels a rush of anger.

Sue must sense it because she steps forward. 'Come along, miss. Time for you to leave.'

'I'm not going anywhere.'

'Yes, you are,' Sue says firmly. 'You heard what the doctor said. Now come away, please.'

'Can't you see?' Siân says, lifting Owen's hand. Their fingers are still curled together. 'He wants me here.'

'He *needs* his wife,' Sue replies. 'Now are you going to come quietly or do I have to call security?'

Siân dips her chin and looks up through wounded eyes. 'I was only trying to help.'

'Of course you were,' Helen replies evenly. 'But I'd like to be alone with my husband now.'

'Well, if you put it like that,' Siân says. She turns to Owen. 'Sorry, soldier, but they've given me my marching orders.' She rises to her feet and turns to Helen. 'I'll see you back at the hotel.'

'Mrs McGrath won't be going back to the hotel,' Sue says. 'She'll be staying here, with her husband. I'll send someone along to collect her things.'

'No need. I can bring them later when I come to visit.'

'Owen has had enough visitors for now,' Sue says firmly. 'And Mrs McGrath's family will be arriving shortly. She'll have all the support she needs.'

Siân looks from Sue to Helen and back again. She lowers her eyes. 'I see. Well I'd hate to be in anyone's way.' She moves towards the door.

She looks so small and dejected that Helen can't help but feel a pang of pity. 'I'm sure we'll see each other again,' she says. 'Back home.'

Siân glances back over her shoulder, her eyes glittering and dark. 'Just try and stop me.'

PART THREE

PART THREE

CHAPTER THIRTY-THREE

Return of a hero
by *Gazette* reporter

A local man who served in Iraq and survived a bomb blast in Afghanistan has returned home a hero. Lance Corporal Owen McGrath survived an explosion which killed one fellow soldier and injured two others. The incident occurred during a desert patrol in Helmand province, when the armoured vehicle carrying Corporal McGrath and three others hit an IED. The driver of the vehicle was killed instantly. Corporal McGrath escaped with head injuries and a broken arm and is recuperating at home. Colleagues paid tribute to his extraordinary courage and devotion to duty. His family were unavailable for comment.

***

Helen takes the newspaper cutting she's retrieved from the bin under the sink and spreads it out on the kitchen table. The edges of the paper are torn and damp and there's a stain that might be ketchup or juice from the tomatoes she was chopping a few minutes ago. The headline is barely a week old. Beneath it is a large photograph of Owen in uniform and a smaller inset photo captioned, 'Private James Collins, 19.'

He's a handsome lad, Helen thinks, then corrects herself – was *a handsome lad*.

She wonders how his parents are coping, wonders how they'd feel knowing that their son's death has been relegated to a photo caption. She looks at the photo again, sees what kind eyes he had, what full lips. He reminds her of one of those pretty boy actors. It's hard to imagine him engaged in mortal combat, harder still to believe he's dead.

Tears prick her eyes. She wonders who they're for. Her nerves are as tattered as the paper. The last time she saw it, it was folded neatly on the bookcase in the living room. Owen must have thrown it away. She's not sure how much more of this she can take.

'Just be thankful,' her mother said when she phoned yesterday for one of her daily updates. 'At least he's on the mend.'

Helen knows she has a lot to be thankful for. During the last few days at the hospital, she'd seen the looks on the faces of the other wives and girlfriends – fretful, fearful, preparing themselves for the worst. At least her husband is expected to make a full recovery. In fact, the doctors were so pleased with his progress, they discharged him the day after he woke up.

'He should be fine,' Mr Croft assured her. 'He'll need to take things slowly at first. He may have trouble sleeping, but I've prescribed some sleeping pills in case. It'll take him a little while to adjust.'

She remembers him pausing at that point, wonders if this was the speech he gave everybody or if he was choosing his words more carefully. 'There may be certain behavioural changes,' he'd added. 'If you're concerned, speak to your local doctor. He'll need to see someone on an outpatient basis in two weeks, just to check on his progress. That sling will need to stay on his arm for another three weeks. But after that he should be as right as rain.'

On the long drive home, while Owen dozed in the back seat, his head resting on Helen's shoulder, her mother had made some comment about the hospital obviously needing the beds, but was quickly silenced by Frank.

'For heaven's sake, Amanda! They wouldn't be sending the lad home if he wasn't good and ready.'

Helen had so wanted to believe him. Frank was no medical expert. Normally she paid scant attention to what he said. But she was surprised at how pleased she'd been when he and her mother turned up at the hospital, and grateful to him for settling the hotel bill with Siân before they left Birmingham.

'Let's keep this between ourselves,' Frank had said, and for once Helen was happy to conspire with him. When her mother enquired about 'this strange woman' they'd been hearing about, Helen quickly changed the subject. She was grateful for all the effort Siân had gone to on her behalf, but relieved to be away from her and her strange, controlling behaviour.

There's been no mention of Siân since, and no word from her either. Helen is thankful for that, at least. For the first few days after arriving home she'd dreaded answering the phone, fearing it might be Siân calling to invite herself over. She'd even rehearsed what she might say. 'Owen isn't up to receiving visitors right now. The doctor said he needs complete rest. Yes, of course I'll tell him you're asking after him. Thanks for calling. Bye.'

But now that she and Owen have been home for over a week, Helen has more important things to worry about. Something isn't right. It began with the newspaper article.

She thought he'd be pleased – proud even. Instead he'd read the front page story with a look of mounting irritation before tossing the paper aside.

'What's the matter?' she asked.

'Have you seen what they've written? It's bullshit!'

'It says you're a hero!'

He laughed bitterly. 'What for? Making it out in one piece? Some hero!'

'Why are you being like this?'

He didn't reply, but pushed the remains of his breakfast aside and stormed out of the room. She kept the paper anyway, half expecting him to come back and apologize for his outburst. Instead she heard the front door slam. She ran after him, only to find him crouched on the pavement outside, staring at oncoming traffic.

'What are you doing?' she asked.

'Keeping watch,' he replied – his voice low, a faraway look in his eyes.

'Come along, Owen,' she said, taking his arm and leading him back indoors.

That was the first sign that her husband's recovery might take a little longer than expected. It wasn't the only one.

The old Owen always took such pride in his appearance, but he hasn't shaved or changed his T shirt in days. He blames it on his broken arm, but when she offers to help he rebuffs her. 'I'm not an invalid!'

Then there are the cards. Since the newspaper article was published, there's been a daily delivery of cards from well-wishers. He'd opened the first one, rolled his eyes and refused to open the rest. They lay on the kitchen table, together with the utility bills she'd opened shortly after they arrived home and the large manilla envelope she'd found lying on the doormat. There was no stamp on the front and no postmark. It was addressed to Owen, in handwriting she didn't recognise. Another well-wisher, perhaps? Or something more official?

'Leave it alone,' he snapped when she asked if he was going to open it. Then, seeing her wounded expression, 'Leave it, babes. Whatever it is, it can wait.'

He smiled as he took the envelope from her. She hasn't seen it since.

This morning, she woke to find his side of the bed empty, the sheets cold. She panicked, picturing him walking the streets in his nightclothes.

Come on, Helen, she told herself. *Pull yourself together.*

Padding downstairs, she found him sitting alone in the darkened living room, staring at the silent TV screen. The room smelt faintly sweet – a mixture of empty lager cans and clothes that were crying out for a wash.

'What are you doing?' she asked.

'Thinking,' he replied, flicking channels with the remote. He hadn't even looked at her.

Later she noticed that the framed photo of him in uniform was no longer hanging in the hallway.

'What happened?'

He shrugged. 'It fell. It's not important.'

It's not important. He's on the mend. He'll be as right as rain.

She wishes she could believe it, but she can't. This afternoon, she even considered calling his doctor. But going behind his back might make matters worse, and his next appointment is only a week away. She'll just have to wait. Waiting is something she's good at. She's had plenty of practice.

She smooths the newspaper cutting before folding it in half and hiding it in a kitchen drawer where he's less likely to find it. Then she returns to the job in hand, putting the water on to boil and chopping onions for his favourite dinner of bangers and mash. The potatoes are simmering when she hears the phone ring.

'I'll get it,' she calls, but he's already halfway down the stairs.

'Of course,' she hears him say. 'Collins was a good man. Absolutely. It would be an honour.'

She's draining the potatoes when he appears in the doorway. His face is ashen.

'When is it?' she asks, putting the pan aside.

'Tomorrow afternoon.'

'Do you have to go?'

He frowns. 'It's not a question of having to go, Helen. It's a mark of respect. The family asked if I'll be one of the pall bearers.'

'Are you sure you're up to it?'

His voice stiffens. 'Of course. It's the least I can do.'

'Did you know him well?' she asks.

'Well enough.'

'Tell me about him.'

'He's dead. What else do you need to know?'

In the back of her mind, Helen remembers Siân sniggering at Jackson's insinuations. 'They were close, if you catch my drift. Very close, those two.' She knows she shouldn't take any notice of what Jackson says. He's a trouble maker. And she knows her husband. But still there's a nagging doubt.

'Talk to me,' she says. 'Why won't you talk to me?'

He rubs his forehead, narrows his eyes. 'There's nothing to say. He was a good soldier. Now he's dead. End of discussion.'

'Don't be like this, Owen.'

'I'm not being like anything.' He strides over to the

fridge and cracks open a can of lager with one hand.

'That's your third this evening,' she says, and immediately wishes she hadn't. She sounds just like her mother.

He frowns at her. 'So what? Worried I might end up like …?' He trails off.

'Frank?' she says. 'Of course not!'

Owen looks at her strangely. 'Yeah, Frank.' He pauses. 'The thing is, Helen, people aren't always who you think they are.'

'What's that supposed to mean?'

He takes a sip of lager and licks his lips. 'People lie. Stretch the truth. Take your friend Siân, for instance.'

Helen's scalp prickles. It's the first time Owen has mentioned Siân by name. The morning he was discharged from hospital he'd woken up asking for the dark-haired woman. Helen had lied and said she was an orderly who'd come to make his bed and was no longer on duty. She'd figured it was easier that way – easier than having to explain who Siân was and how they'd met. Of course there'd been an element of jealousy too. Why was he asking for a woman he didn't even know?

'Well?' he asks now. 'What happened to her?'

'She left,' Helen replies lamely.

'So she wasn't just a figment of my imagination. Is that what you thought? That I'd be too confused to remember?' There's a scathing tone to his voice she hasn't heard before. 'Well? Is that it?'

'It wasn't like that,' she replies.

'Wasn't it? Poor pathetic man, doesn't know his own mind. Tell him anything you want. He'll never know the difference.'

'Owen, you're scaring me.'

There's a look of confusion on his face, then his eyes

soften. 'I didn't mean to.'

'Then can we just forget about it, please? Forget about Siân. Just focus on us?'

He blinks, frowns, then slams his lager can down hard on the kitchen table. 'Us? But that's precisely my point. This is about us. You lied to me, Helen!'

She flinches as the froth bubbles up and runs down the side of the can, forming a small puddle of amber liquid on the tabletop.

The old Owen would have wiped it up immediately. Instead he just stares at her. 'Well?'

Her throat tightens. 'Sorry?'

'You told me she was an orderly. Why would you say that? Why would you lie to me?'

'I didn't lie. Not exactly. She's just a woman I met. She's not important.'

'Then why not tell the truth? Is there anything else you're not telling me, Helen? Anyone else I should know about? Any more secrets you're hiding?'

She blinks at him, astonished. He's never spoken to her like this before, barely even raised his voice.

'Of course not!' she splutters. 'I can't believe you're asking me that.'

'It's like I said. People aren't always who you think they are.'

Her eyes well up. 'And you're not the man I married. I don't know you anymore!'

As soon as the words are out of her mouth, she realizes how true they are. There's a stranger in her house, eating at her table, sleeping in her bed.

They haven't had sex. He hasn't shown any interest, and the last thing she wants is to put any added pressure on him. He's clearly in no fit state – physically or mentally.

Still she yearns for some kind of intimacy, some reassurance that he still desires her.

It's so different from the way he was before, in the early days of their marriage. Back then he couldn't keep his hands off her. It didn't matter what time of day or night it was.

'Time for bed,' he'd say, stretching his arms and yawning dramatically.

She'd smile and remind him that it was still the middle of the afternoon.

'Who said anything about sleeping?' he'd say, before chasing her up the stairs with that soppy grin of his and a lascivious look in his eyes.

What she'd give to see that look now.

There's been no bedtime banter this past week. The playful, loving man she used to know has gone. In his place is a cold, distant figure who seems to view her with a mixture of bewilderment and suspicion. The closest they've come to physical intimacy was in the car, driving back from Birmingham. She remembers the weight of his head on her shoulder, how comforting and familiar it had felt. She remembers hoping then that it was a sign of things to come. How wrong she had been.

After dinner, which they eat in silence, he disappears into the living room to watch television, leaving her to do the dishes alone. The old Owen would have insisted on helping, or apologized for the fact that he wasn't much use in the kitchen with one arm in a sling. Instead he just slopes off with another can of lager, saying nothing.

She washes and dries the dishes and stands at the sink, listening to the burble of the television in the other room. There's a burst of hollow, canned laughter and for a split second she pictures her husband smiling and joking before reality kicks in.

He'll be thinking about the funeral now, she thinks. That's why he's so distant. That's why he's drinking and watching crap TV. He's trying to blot it out, at least until tomorrow. She feels sad for him, and guilty for feeling so needy at a time like this.

Stop it! she thinks. *Stop being so bloody selfish*!

But she can't help herself. She knows he isn't well. She knows he has other things on his mind. But she needs to know that he still wants her, that his feelings for her haven't changed. She shudders at the thought of Siân at the hospital, holding his hand, talking to him in that intimate, conspiratorial tone. What had she said to him? Why did he seem so attached to her?

Later in bed, she lies staring up at the ceiling while he snores gently beside her. She pictures them both in happier times – their first date, the day he proposed, their wedding day. Finally she dozes off. At some point during the night she's awakened by the sound of him whimpering in his sleep. 'Owen?' she whispers, and puts a comforting hand on his chest.

He groans and pushes her hand away.

CHAPTER THIRTY-FOUR

The funeral of Private James Collins is scheduled to take place at Greenbank Cemetery in Bristol at 2 p.m. Owen hasn't been very forthcoming with the details, but Helen has a pretty good idea of what to expect. Soldiers from the regiment will arrive in coaches from the barracks. These men are what's known as the 'rear party' and it's their job to host the funeral, carry the coffin, fire the salute and act as ushers during the service. They'll leave after an hour or two – before they have time to get well and truly plastered. Military funerals are known for their pomp and circumstance. One circumstance the army is keen to avoid at all costs is someone getting completely hammered and bringing shame on the regiment.

This isn't the first military funeral Helen has been invited to attend. On three previous occasions Owen had been part of the rear party and she'd gone along to show support and pay her respects. But this funeral will be different. Her husband didn't only serve with this soldier. He very nearly died with him. She struggles to imagine how he must be feeling.

She spent most of the night listening to Owen tossing and turning in his sleep, wondering what – or who – he was dreaming about. It was only when he began murmuring the words 'man down' that she realized he was reliving the moment when Collins was killed. She half expected him to wake up screaming or sit bolt upright in bed and start loading an imaginary rifle, like the men at the military hospital. But he was either too exhausted, or knocked out by the sleeping pill he'd washed down with the remains of a can of lager before coming to bed. He tossed and turned but didn't wake up.

Now, as they sit across the kitchen table from one another silently eating breakfast, she wonders if her husband is really up to the demands today's funeral will place on him. Every instinct tells her he's not. 'I don't see why you have to go,' she says, watching him push his food around his plate. Normally he has such a healthy appetite. This is another change in his behaviour she's noticed these past few days, another indication that things aren't right.

'It's protocol,' he replies. 'I'm expected to be there, same as everyone else. You know that.'

'But you're still recovering.'

'It's only a broken arm, Helen. It's no big deal.'

If only that were true, she thinks. If only that were all it is.

Another thought strikes her. 'Will Jackson be there?'

Owen looks at her suspiciously. 'Is that what you're so worried about? Bumping into Jackson?'

'Of course not,' she says, only partly lying. She doesn't relish the thought of seeing Jackson again – far from it – but right now he's the least of her worries.

'So you haven't seen Leanne lately?'

'Leanne? Why would I see Leanne?'

'I don't know. Maybe you were driving by the wives' estate. Maybe you were on your way somewhere.'

'What?' She shakes her head. 'Why would you even think that?'

'No reason,' he says and pushes his plate away. 'Right.

I suppose we should start getting ready.'

'You don't have to go,' Helen says. 'I can call and explain. People will understand. Nobody will hold it against you.'

'I will,' he replies. 'I'll hold it against me.'

She reaches across the table for his hand. 'I'm worried about you, Owen.'

'There's nothing wrong with me,' he says, pulling his hand away and rising to his feet. 'You don't know what you're on about. You don't understand.'

'Then talk to me,' she pleads. 'Help me understand.'

'We can talk on the way,' he says. 'I'm off to get changed.'

They don't talk on the way. While she drives, he stares blankly out of the passenger window. Several times she tries to engage him in conversation, and each time he bats her back with monosyllabic answers or meets her questions with a stony silence. Finally, she gives up, overwhelmed by a feeling of powerlessness. She settles back in her seat, finding comfort in the familiar feeling of being behind the wheel of her car. At least now she's the one in the driving seat. She keeps her eye on the road and tries not to think too much about what lies ahead.

'I feel like a guest at my own son's funeral,' Barbara says, observing the men in full military dress.

'Come, now,' her husband replies, steering her gently towards the church door. 'We both know it's the send-off he'd have wanted.'

'I never wanted him to have a send-off,' Barbara says. 'I wanted him home with me, safe.'

It's a bright, sunny day. She'd have preferred rain. A leaden sky and drizzle would have matched her mood. Instead it feels as if the weather is mocking her. She refuses to wear sunglasses. There's no shame in feeling the way she does today. Any attempt to hide her grief would be a betrayal. She wants people to see the pain she's in.

Martin displays no emotion, but that's nothing new. As they file into the church she feels his hand in the small of her back and wonders if today, finally, she might see some tears. She steals a sideways glance, hoping for a glimmer of something to assure her that she isn't alone in feeling such a devastating sense of loss. But no. His jaw is firm, his eyes dry.

A flag is draped over the coffin – the red, white and blue signifying patriotism and a devotion to duty that should have filled her heart with pride, but leaves her feeling strangely cold. Deep down, she knows that her husband is right, that this is the funeral their son would have wanted. Still she resents the military for having such a claim on him, even when he's dead.

Dead. The word sounds alien to her. Part of her still expects another letter to arrive, or for someone to call and say that it's all been a terrible mistake. He hadn't died after all. It was another soldier's body, someone else's son. He'll be coming home soon. She stares at the mahogany box outlined beneath the Union flag and knows that it isn't true. She pictures his body inside – broken, bloodied, barely recognizable – and a cold shiver runs over her skin. She remembers that awful moment when she and Martin were allowed to view his body, the certainty of knowing that nothing would compare to the horror of what she saw in that cold white room. She remembers telling herself that the healing process would begin as soon as they left the hospital. But she was wrong. There would be no escaping this feeling, no ritual that would help alleviate the pain. This is who she is now – a mother who has lost her son.

She listens as the minister welcomes everyone to the service and offers a prayer for the family. It barely registers that he's referring to her and Martin. Then the hymns begin and her husband helps her to her feet.

She doesn't know the words. It's a long time since she's been inside a church and right now, words of faith mean less to her than ever. She knows she's supposed to find comfort in them, but she can't. What kind of god would allow this to happen? Mothers are not supposed to bury their children.

Blinking back tears, she turns her head and surveys the room. The church is full. There are rows of men in uniform and their wives and girlfriends dressed in black. She wonders what's going through the women's minds. Is this their first military funeral? Will it be their last? Are they looking at their men now, wondering how long it will be before it's their turn?

Her eyes fall on a familiar face a few rows from the front. She's only seen him once before, at the hospital, but he has one of those faces that stands out in a crowd. There's a thuggish quality about him, a hard look in his eye that certain types of women find attractive. Barbara recalls the black-haired woman pressed against him in the hospital corridor. It was such a vulgar display, and so inappropriate. She'd noted his wedding ring and somehow known that this woman wasn't his wife. Her suspicions were confirmed when she overheard him boasting about the number of 'ragheads' he'd taken out. Men rarely spoke like that to women who knew them well. Such macho posturing was usually reserved for those they were still trying to impress.

It suddenly strikes Barbara that this man was probably there when her son died. She knows it's wrong to wish harm on others, least of all those willing to risk their lives for their country. But she can't help herself. Why couldn't it have been him who'd died, instead of her brave, beautiful son?

The man's eyes flicker towards her. His face is impassive, but she's certain she detects the hint of an amused smile. A flush of anger washes over her and she turns her face away.

Across the aisle, six uniformed men stand in the front row. It's these six soldier who carried her son's coffin into the church, and who will carry it to its final resting place. She doesn't know them. She's barely been introduced. But there's one man whose presence here means everything to her. There's a reason why she'd asked for him to be a pall bearer, even with his broken arm. It's the same reason he'd agreed, despite his injuries. Next to her and Martin, he's the person most affected by Jamie's death. He was her son's friend, and possibly more.

Her husband still hasn't read Jamie's letters. Had he read them, he would know that this man had held a special place in her son's affections. Jamie had written about him many times. He'd described the secret spot where they sunbathed together, and the camaraderie which developed into a close friendship. Reading between the lines, Barbara wondered if that was all it was. It seemed pretty clear to her that her son had feelings for this man. Several times he'd described him as his hero. But what was also clear was that this man wasn't gay. As Jamie had mentioned in one of his letters, Lance Corporal Owen McGrath had a wife.

Barbara is pretty certain she saw the wife earlier, standing quietly outside. A pretty, pale thing, she'd looked lost and rather lonely, the way soldiers' wives and girlfriends often looked at military gatherings. Barbara remembers seeing her tired, anxious face once before at the hospital. Her husband had been in a coma. Things hadn't been easy for her either, poor thing. But at least the man she loved hadn't died.

Gazing over at him now, Barbara wonders if Owen McGrath is feeling a fraction of what she's feeling. Men are always so much harder to read than women. Apart from his broken arm, there's little to distinguish him from any of the other soldiers who've come to pay their respects. His face gives nothing away. He hasn't cried once during the entire funeral service. Considering what he and her son had gone through together, he seems remarkably composed.

'Let us pray,' says the minister.

The soldier obeys, his head bowed, silently mouthing the words to the Lord's Prayer. Do the words hold any meaning for him, Barbara wonders, or is he simply going through the motions? Did he have feelings for her son, or is he simply here out of duty?

It's only later, at the graveside, as they sound the salute and the coffin is lowered into the earth, that she sees the stricken look on the soldier's face. Then the tears pour down his cheeks and Barbara finally has the answer she needs. Her son's feelings for this man had been reciprocated.

CHAPTER THIRTY-FIVE

Martin is determined to be strong for his wife's sake – today of all days. But maintaining his composure at his son's funeral is one of the hardest things he's ever done. Sitting in the church with Barbara sobbing by his side, listening as the tributes were paid to his dead son, he'd very nearly broken down. But what use would he have been to her then? One of them had to hold it together and it seemed only right that the responsibility should fall to him. James had always been his mother's son. It was her he asked for whenever he phoned, her he confided in. It didn't mean that he loved his son any less. But her loss was greater. Her needs came first.

As they follow the coffin out of the church and make their way through the cemetery towards the graveside, Martin feels his chest tighten and tears prick his eyes. He falls back for a moment and, sensing his wife watching him, raises his head and stares up at the heavens. There isn't a cloud in the sky.

'It's a bit late for prayers, Martin,' Barbara says.

If she only knew! His own faith has been tested every bit as much as hers these past few weeks. He swallows hard, takes a deep breath and walks on.

Ahead of them, the pall bearer with the broken arm is struggling slightly, pausing to rest the coffin on his good shoulder and steadying it with the same hand. But Martin can see by the set of his shoulders that the lad will manage somehow. He knows all about Lance Corporal Owen McGrath and the friendship he'd shared with his son. He's read the letters. The night they returned from the hospital, when his wife had finally drifted off to sleep, he'd taken the letters to his study and read each of them over and over, trying to make sense of his loss. The story they told was a familiar one. Martin knows from personal experience that men serving together often form deep emotional attachments to one another. He also knows that, however much the army has changed, human nature hasn't. There'll always be someone who takes a dim view of such friendships, especially when one of the men involved was openly gay.

It was clear from the letters that his son had been bullied. Several times he'd said that McGrath had defended him, or that he was looking out for him. Who did he need protecting from? It hadn't taken Martin long to find out. A few phone calls to friends in high places and he knew all about the man who'd targeted his son. He knew that he'd narrowly escaped a dishonourable discharge for breaking a civilian's jaw, and that many of his superiors considered him a liability. In an ideal world, there would be no place in the army for a thug like Jackson. But the current situation is far from ideal. The forces are stretched to breaking point, fighting on too many fronts. The demand for experienced soldiers is too great.

Martin hadn't been surprised to see Jackson at the funeral. He was on leave and from the same regiment. Protocol demanded that he be there to pay his respects. What surprised Martin was that the man made little attempt to hide his true feelings. He'd seen the smug look on his face during the service.

Now, standing at the graveside, as the six riflemen sound the salute and his son's coffin is lowered into the ground, Martin watches as Owen McGrath breaks down and weeps. Their eyes meet for a moment, then the younger man averts his gaze, his attention caught by something behind Martin's left shoulder.

Turning his head, Martin is just in time to see Jackson blowing the grieving soldier a kiss.

As the mourners begin to make their way back to the car park, Helen hovers at a discreet distance from the graveside, waiting for Owen. He shows no sign of moving but stands stiffly, like a soldier on sentry duty.

The dead man's parents have their backs to her. The mother's shoulders shake slightly, the father's hand resting lightly on the small of her back. Owen stands alone on the far side of the grave, his eyes fixed firmly on the ground. His face is wet with tears.

Helen has never seen him cry like this. It pains her to see him so distressed – and it unsettles her too. She hadn't cried like this when her father died, and she was only a child then. Her father meant the world to her. Who was this soldier whose death has affected her husband so deeply? Owen never referred to him in his letters. He never talked about him on the phone. If they were such good friends, how come he never even mentioned him? She pushes away thoughts of the conversation between Siân and Jackson in the pub. There's no truth in what Jackson had said. There can't be. It's just vicious gossip, no better than she'd expect from a thug like him.

A low groan comes from the graveside. Looking up, she sees her husband shudder and clasp his hand to his mouth. Her first instinct is to rush over and comfort him, but she holds back, reluctant to draw further attention to her husband and away from the grieving parents. They'd caught her staring at them that day at the hospital. The last thing she wants is to interrupt their final moments with their son. She knows the pain of losing a parent. She can't begin to imagine the pain of a parent losing a child.

She watches as the mother makes her way towards Owen and touches his arm. He places his hand over hers and lowers his head, avoiding eye contact. She leans in to say something and he nods gently, his eyes staring down at the grave. Then he lifts his head and begins to speak.

Helen can't hear the words. She's too far away and their voices are too low. But she can tell from the body language that this is no ordinary conversation. And it *is* a conversation. Their heads are locked together for what seems like an inordinately long time. What are they talking about, Helen wonders. She wishes he'd confide in her instead. In just a few minutes he's said more to this woman than he's said to her in a month.

A voice hisses in her ear. 'How's your sex life, Helen?'

She flinches and turns her head.

Jackson steps out from behind her, a familiar smirk spreading across his face. 'Hubby not giving you the attention you deserve?'

She glares at him. 'Leave him alone, Jackson.'

'What's the matter? Touched a nerve?' His smirk becomes a leer. 'You look like you need a good seeing to. If Owen isn't up to the job I'm always happy to offer my services.'

She feels her cheeks go red and struggles for something to say.

'You're blushing!' Jackson says. 'I bet you were a blushing bride too. How was your wedding night? Did he manage to get it up? You can tell me.'

Don't rise to it, Helen tells herself. *Don't give him the satisfaction.*

'He was queer, y'know,' Jackson says. 'Collins. In case you're wondering.'

'I don't think that's any of my business.'

Jackson grins. 'Oh, I think you'll find it is. Ask Owen. Ask him about his little bum boy.'

'You're disgusting,' Helen says, stepping away.

'Me?' Jackson laughs. 'I wasn't the one shoving my cock up another man's shitter.'

'That's enough!' a man's voice booms.

The father of the dead boy is marching briskly towards them. It's hard to tell if he heard what Jackson said, but the look on his face suggests that he's in no mood to be messed with. His mouth is a thin line, his eyes pained and angry.

He waves his arm as he approaches. 'Leave her alone!'

'We were just talking,' Jackson says, spreading his hands.

'And now you've finished. So clear off!'

The soldier bristles. 'Or what?'

The older man's voice is calm but full of menace. 'Don't mess with me, Jackson. Yes, I know who you are. I know all about you. You're a disgrace to your regiment. Now I suggest you leave before I do something I might regret.'

Jackson's lip curls. 'We were done here anyway. Catch you later, Helen. You know where I am if you need me.' He winks and slouches off in the direction of the car park.

'Martin Collins,' the man says, offering Helen his hand. 'I hope that thug didn't upset you.'

'I'm fine, thank you.' She doesn't know what to say next. What's the right thing to say to a man who's just buried his son? 'Sorry for your loss' seems so inadequate.

She blinks, struggling to come up with something better.

'I'm so sorry for your loss.'

His eyes glisten. 'Thank you. I'm bearing up. How about you?'

'Me?'

'That's your husband over there, isn't it? He was at the hospital where … where they brought my son?'

'Yes, that's right.'

'How's he doing?'

Part of her is desperate to talk to someone. But she doesn't know this man. It doesn't seem right to confide in a stranger, least of all a grieving father.

'It's okay,' Martin says. 'You don't have to say anything. But there are people you can talk to, if you need to.'

Helen nods, grateful for his kindness.

'It's not always easy when men come back from war,' he continues. 'The doctors do what they can. They can fix a broken arm. But some things take longer to heal.'

He turns to watch as Jackson boards the coach. Then, satisfied that he's gone, he looks back at Helen.

'I knew a man once,' he says. 'A lot like your husband. We served in Bosnia together. He was wounded in action, in a coma for weeks. When he came round, well, he wasn't the same. He kept asking for his shoes, so he could get back to work. This went on for days. Finally a captain came and spoke to him. He told him his fight in Bosnia was over. He was fighting for his loved ones now. That seemed to do the trick.'

'How is he now?'

'Happily married, with two kids.'

'Are you close?'

Martin pauses. 'We were, once.' He looks as if he's about to divulge more, then thinks better of it. 'We haven't seen each other in a while, but we exchange Christmas cards and talk on the phone occasionally. He's his old self again.'

Helen gazes across at Owen. Will he ever be his old self again? Does he need help? How is she supposed to help him if he won't even talk to her?

The older man must have read her thoughts. 'He'll get there,' he says. 'He's a fighter.'

She turns and studies his face. 'What makes you say that?'

'He's here today, isn't he? I know a brave man when I see one.'

Helen thinks for a moment. 'Can I ask you something?' she says. 'About your son?'

'He was a brave man too.'

'And was he –'

'Gay?' Martin smiles tightly. 'Yes, he was. And I was very proud of him.'

His voice cracks. He looks away and clears his throat.

'Barbara?' he calls, his voice firm again. 'It's time we were leaving.'

CHAPTER THIRTY-SIX

'You never told me he was gay,' Helen says.

It's the morning after the funeral. Owen is seated at the kitchen table while she stands at the counter, preparing breakfast. There can't be more than a few feet between them, but it feels like miles.

He speaks without raising his head. 'Who told you that? Jackson, I suppose. What else did he say?'

She has no intention of repeating what Jackson said. Just the thought of it makes her skin crawl. She plays for time by measuring the coffee into the pot and filling it with boiling water. 'It wasn't Jackson. It was his father, Martin. He seemed like a nice man.'

'I wouldn't know.'

'You spoke to his wife.'

'So?'

'How was she?'

'How do you think? It was her son's funeral. She wasn't exactly jumping for joy.'

'Of course not. I just wondered what you talked about.'

His voice is cold. 'I don't remember.'

She stares at him but still he refuses to look at her. She takes two breakfast bowls from the cupboard above the sink and places them on the table directly in front of him. He doesn't react.

'His father told me he was proud of him,' she says, determined to get some response.

'Why wouldn't he be? He was a good soldier.'

'They both knew he was gay. His parents. It wasn't a secret.'

'So?'

'So how come you never said anything?'

He looks up at her with red, hollow eyes. For a moment Helen thinks he might cry. Then he brushes his hand across his face and turns to stare out of the window.

He can't have had more than a few hours' sleep last night. She heard him moving around downstairs in the early hours of the morning, but resisted the urge to check on him. Driving home from the funeral yesterday, he'd made it perfectly clear that he was in no mood to talk. They barely said a word before going to bed, where he stayed on his side of the mattress and she lay awake for hours listening to him toss and turn before exhaustion got the better of her and she sank into a dreamless sleep. She was up, showered and dressed when she found him crashed out on the sofa, surrounded by empty lager cans.

The cans are stacked by the bin, rinsed and ready for recycling. Another job she's suddenly responsible for, another sign that things aren't right.

'Owen?'

'What?'

'Why won't you look at me?'

He glares at her. 'There. I'm looking. Happy now?'

The expression on his face makes her breath catch in her throat. His eyes are cold, his mouth a hard line. There's no love there at all.

She lowers her voice. 'Not really, no.'

He shrugs. 'Yeah, well, that makes two of us.'

'I'm worried about you, Owen.'

'Really? It sounds to me as if all you're worried about is whether someone you never even met was gay or not.'

'That's not true.'

'I never had you down as a bigot, Helen.'

He says this with such contempt, it takes her a moment to respond.

'I'm not.'

'Then why go on about it? He was gay. Now he's dead. What difference does it make?'

'None. I just thought you might have mentioned it, that's all.'

'What do you want me to say, Helen?'

There are so many things she wants him to say. She wants him to tell her that he still loves her. She wants him to assure her that there's no truth in what Jackson had said, that it's all just a vicious lie. But she can't tell him that. Things are bad enough already. The man she loves seems further from her now than when he was stationed thousands of miles away. She doesn't know what to expect or who he is anymore. The thought terrifies her.

'Well?' he says. There's an edge to his voice, a goading tone that sounds almost menacing.

'Please, Owen,' she says. 'I'm scared.'

'And we can't have that, can we?'

'What?'

'A man's dead. A mother has lost her son. And you're scared.' His eyes flash. 'What have you got to be scared of?'

She feels her voice crack. 'You,' she says. 'I'm scared of you.'

His eyes soften. For a moment, it looks as if she's finally getting through to him. Then his face darkens.

'I don't need this right now,' he says, shoving aside the breakfast bowl and rising quickly from his chair. 'I really don't need this.'

'But what about your breakfast?'

'I'm not hungry.'

He storms out of the room and up the stairs. She hears the floorboard on the landing creak and the sound of a door slam. There's movement in the bedroom above. Maybe he's going back to bed. Maybe that isn't such a bad idea. Then heavy footsteps thunder down the stairs and he reappears, dressed in jogging trousers and the T-shirt he'd slept in. In his hand is the army beret he'd worn at the funeral.

She follows him into the hall. 'Where are you going?'

He opens the front door without looking at her. 'Out.'

'Out where?'

He turns to her, eyes blazing. 'Just out. This is doing my head in. What's with all the questions today? I need peace and quiet. Is that too much to ask?'

'Owen,' she pleads. 'We need to talk.'

'I'm sick of talking. I need to do something.'

'Do what?'

'I don't know! Clear my head. Walk it off. Whatever.'

'Owen!' she cries.

'For Christ's sake, Helen! Just leave me alone!'

He pulls the door closed behind him. Somehow it's worse than if he'd slammed it.

She sinks onto the foot of the stairs and buries her head in her hands. Her mind races.

Where has he gone? What's he running away from? Why won't he talk to me?

She thinks back to the funeral, to the hospital, to that night in the pub in Birmingham. She knows Jackson is a bigot and a bully, knows he'd say anything to stir up trouble. Still the doubts creep in. Is it possible to live with someone for years and not really know them? What was it Owen said to her the other day? 'People aren't always who you think they are.' Was he trying to tell her something?

Footsteps approach the front door. She looks up expectantly, sees a shadowy figure through the frosted glass panel. But it's just the postman. A handful of envelopes flop onto the mat. She thinks of Owen's letters, wonders if there's something she missed. He'd never mentioned Collins, not as far as she can recall. But maybe there's something in one of the letters from Afghanistan, some clue to his state of mind that will help her make sense of things.

She runs upstairs to the bedroom and pulls the shoebox out from under the bed. *Strange*. It feels lighter than before. Her stomach sinks as she lifts the lid. The box is empty. Owen's letters, her father's photos, cards, newspaper clippings and old coins – all gone. Frantically, she searches under the bed – nothing.

Her pulse quickens. Someone has been through her things. Owen wouldn't do this to her, would he? He may have been acting strangely lately, but he knows how precious those keepsakes are. Then it hits her. Siân was in this room. She brought her home drunk the night they first met. She packed a case for her the night they went to Birmingham. The coin she found in Siân's bag at the hotel – she hadn't imagined it after all. It *was* one of her father's.

Dismay turns to anger, much of it directed at herself. If only she hadn't been so drunk. If only she hadn't been so trusting. But still there's an element of disbelief. She shakes her head, climbs to her feet and begins rummaging through the chest of drawers. It's all a big mistake, surely? She's been so confused lately, out of her mind with worry, head all over the place. Maybe she'll find what she's looking for hidden at the back of a drawer, with no recollection of how it got there. But all she finds are clothes.

The bottom drawer is where Owen keeps his gym things – a few pairs of shorts and T-shirts folded in neat piles. Only now it's crammed full. A gym bag and a pair of army desert fatigues are bundled together on top. The bag is empty. In one of the trouser pockets she finds a Swiss army knife, in another a military sewing-repair kit. What are they doing here? Normally he's so meticulous about things. The trousers aren't even clean. There's an oil stain on one leg and, when she empties out the pockets, a fine layer of sand trickles onto the clothes below.

Then she sees it. Buried beneath the trousers, wrapped in one of her husband's T-shirts is a large manilla envelope – the same envelope he'd snatched from her hands a few days ago. It's been opened. She reaches inside and takes out a sheaf of double-spaced, typed, A4 pages, held together with a large paper clip. The paper is crisp and yellowed at the edges. Printed in block capitals at the top of the first page is her father's name –

RICHARD THOMAS

Next to it, someone has scrawled in blue ballpoint pen, 'I think this answers your questions.'

Who is the note addressed to? The envelope is addressed to Owen, but the handwriting on the note is different, the ink faded with age.

She begins reading.

'People aren't always who you think they are.'

She frowns. That's the phrase Owen had used. Why

would he say that? And why would he hide this from her? She continues reading.

This was the view expressed by Jane Morgan, a barmaid at The Jolly Brewer pub in Park Street. Mr Thomas, who died two weeks ago, has been described by one local newspaper as a hero who lost his life defending his family. But this reporter has uncovered a very different story. Far from being a devoted husband and father, Richard Thomas was an alcoholic who cheated on his wife with a girl barely half his age.

Helen's blood runs cold. Who is this reporter? It doesn't say. There's no name or signature next to the handwritten note. It doesn't even say which newspaper they're writing for.

Halfway down the first page, a whole paragraph has been blacked out with a heavy marker pen. She holds the paper up to the light but is unable to decipher the missing words.

More lines of text have been blacked out on the next page. Names have been circled in blue ink or underlined with a yellow highlighter pen: Lisa Johns, who used to live a few doors down but moved away shortly after her father died; Mr Roberts, who lived across the road; Jackie Evans, a friend of her mother's, better known to her as Auntie Jackie.

Lines jump out at her: 'I think he felt trapped in that marriage'; 'he looked like he'd been up boozing all night'; 'I think it looks a bit odd when a married man starts hanging around with a younger woman'; 'poor little Helen'; 'she was so close to her dad'.

Who were these people talking about? Her father

wasn't a drunk. He would never have cheated on her mother. Why would people say these things?

She turns to the last page. Someone called Mark Yardley claimed to have seen her father at the Black Path hours before he died.

Mr Yardley said he had been walking along the path for 'no more than five minutes' when he heard raised voices up ahead. 'I thought it was just kids messing about at first. Then I heard a man's voice. He was shouting, something about his wife and how people should mind their own business. And then I heard some lads yelling back. One sounded really angry. But it was hard to make out the words. They were all shouting over each other.'

It was only when Mr Yardley approached that the shouting stopped. Mr Yardley saw a man he now identifies as Mr Richard Thomas. 'And there were three lads with him, aged between fifteen and seventeen.'

Who the hell is Mark Yardley? She's never even heard of him. And what would her father be doing at the Black Path? None of this makes any sense.

It's impossible to read what comes next. Two whole paragraphs have been blacked out. Then, at the bottom of the page, one sentence is clearly visible.

'You'd think the wife would show some concern when her husband has just been murdered.'

***

Helen's heart pounds as she gathers up the sheets of paper from the floor and stuffs them back into the envelope. She wants to dismiss everything she's read as a pack of lies. It's just words on paper, written by some anonymous reporter. There's no proof that any of it is true.

But already there are doubts forming, questions she can't answer. Why did Lisa Johns move away so suddenly? Helen can picture her now, leaning over the front gate, all smiles and eyelashes and perky little breasts.

She scrambles to her feet and grabs her phone, which is charging on the bedside table.

Her mother answers on the second ring. 'Hello?'

'It's me.'

'Helen? You sound strange. Are you alright?'

'Not really.' She feels her throat tighten. 'Mum, I need to talk to you about something.'

'What's wrong? Is Owen okay?'

'Not really.' Tears prick her eyes. 'We had a row.'

'Oh'. Her mother pauses. 'Well, it hasn't been easy for either of you. I'm sure you'll sort it out.'

'But I'm not calling about him. I need to see you.'

'Right. Why don't you both come round for your tea tomorrow?'

'No. This can't wait. I'll drive over.'

'But Frank's on his way home to pick me up. He's taking me to Tesco's.'

'I'll be there in fifteen minutes.'

She slides the phone into the front pocket of her jeans, pulls on a pair of trainers and tucks the envelope in her handbag. As she reaches the top of the landing an image pops into her head – her father, swaying at the bottom of the stairs, gripping the bannister with both hands and mumbling to her mother, 'Don't let Helen see me like this!'

Hurrying downstairs, she grabs her car keys from the

dresser in the hall and steps outside. Her first thought on seeing the car is that kids have smeared mud down the passenger's side.

But it hasn't rained in days.

Then, as she draws nearer, she sees that it's far worse than that. It isn't mud. It's black spray paint.

A sudden cry makes her jump. But it's just the jeering laugh of a crow flapping overhead. The streets are deserted.

Slowly, she begins walking around the car. All four tyres have been slashed. The right tail light is broken. There's a deep scratch on the driver's side, starting above the tail light and ending at the driver's door. Written on the door in large ugly black letters is a single word – 'Cunt'.

Helen clasps her hand to her mouth and fumbles in her pocket for her phone.

First she calls her mother. Then she calls the police.

CHAPTER THIRTY-SEVEN

It's over an hour before the police car finally pulls up. She's peering through the front window, afraid to wait outside in case she draws attention to the graffiti on her car and one of the neighbours starts asking questions. She watches as two uniformed officers step out and inspect the car. She wonders what's taking them so long.

Eventually there's a knock on the door.

'Sorry we're late,' the older of the two men says. 'There's been a fire over in Blackmill.'

'Come in,' she replies, and leads them through to the kitchen.

'I'm Officer Garrett,' the older officer says. 'And this is Officer Hughes.' He takes out his notebook. 'When did you last use your car?'

'Yesterday. We went to a funeral.'

'I'm sorry to hear that. And when did you notice the damage?'

'This morning. It must have happened during the night.'

'Do you have any idea who might be responsible?'

'No,' she replies, though she's spent the past hour asking herself the very same question and keeps returning to the same answer – Jackson. She'd angered him yesterday and a man who beats his own wife is capable of anything.

'You're sure?' Garrett asks.

She nods. 'Quite sure.'

Tempting as it is to point the finger at Jackson, she has no proof, not even a clear motive. It would be her word against his. Besides, the thought of him scares her. What he might do. What he might say. The last thing she wants is a man like that trampling all over her personal life.

'It's so warm in here,' she says, walking over to open a window. The heat has been building for days, much like the tensions in the house. And this visit from the police isn't helping matters. She's beginning to regret calling them. She knows it's the right thing to do. It's what Owen would have done. But Owen isn't here. Where is he?

'Mrs McGrath?'

She turns. 'Sorry?'

The younger officer can't be much older than her. His face looks vaguely familiar but she can't quite place him.

'Is there anyone you've argued with?' he asks. 'A neighbour perhaps?'

'No.'

'Any debts? Anyone you've fallen out with?'

'Of course not.'

He raises an eyebrow. 'Is there something more personal you'd like to share with us?'

'What do you mean, *personal*?' She recognizes him now. His name is Michael Hughes. He was in the year above her at school and had always been pretty full of himself. Joining the local constabulary has done little to deflate his preening sense of self-importance.

'People don't always tell us everything,' Garrett says. 'Especially if there's something they'd rather keep quiet about. I take it you're married, Mrs McGrath?'

'Yes.'

Hughes smirks. 'And there's nobody else?'

314

Helen glares at him. 'I'm not cheating on my husband!'

'I didn't say you were. But sometimes people don't give us the full facts.'

Garrett raises a calming hand. 'What my colleague is trying to say is that it's usually someone you know.'

He has a kind face and seems genuinely concerned for her welfare. Helen wants to trust him. She wants to place her faith in someone, anyone, who can help her through this nightmare.

'Is there anyone you can think of?' he asks. 'Anyone at all?'

She hesitates before answering. 'No.'

'What about your husband?'

'He's a soldier. He's just come back from Afghanistan. He was injured.'

The men exchange a look.

'Could we have a word with him?' Garrett asks.

'He went out for some fresh air.'

'How long ago?'

She glances at the kitchen clock. 'A couple of hours.'

'And you've not heard from him since?'

'No.'

The radio on Garrett's chest crackles into life. He pulls it up to his ear and turns away for a moment. When he turns back, the expression on his face has changed. His voice is harder too. 'How is your husband, Mrs McGrath?'

'What do you mean?'

'How would you describe his state of mind? Has he been acting strangely at all?'

'No,' she lies. She feels herself flushing, wonders if it shows.

'Does your husband have a problem with Muslims?' Hughes asks.

'What makes you say that?'

'You said he was injured in Afghanistan. He wouldn't be the first soldier to harbour a grudge. An experience like that can affect people in all sorts of ways.'

She scowls at him. 'My husband is a professional soldier. What's all this got to do with my car?'

'I think you'd better sit down,' Garrett says.

'I'm fine standing, thank you.'

'The fire in Blackmill,' he continues. 'We think it may have been started deliberately. The house belongs to a man who recently converted to Islam. He's a bit of a local celebrity by all accounts. Red-haired chap. Maybe you've seen him around?'

Helen pictures the man from the café, that afternoon with Siân. 'I think I may have seen him once. Is he okay?'

'I think we ought to speak to your husband.'

'My husband doesn't have anything to do with any fire! Now what about my car?'

Garrett shrugs. 'We'll have a word with your neighbours, see if any of them saw anyone hanging around your car. But I'll be honest with you. This sort of thing happens a lot around here. Unless someone saw something or you have an idea of who might be responsible, we don't have an awful lot to go on.'

'So whoever did this just gets away with it?'

'We'll do our best, Mrs McGrath. But like I said, we don't have much to go on.'

She can tell when she's being fobbed off. It's obvious from the hurried way they draw the conversation to a close that the police aren't really interested in finding the person responsible for damaging her car. They have bigger fish to fry. Someone set fire to a man's house, and thanks to her unguarded comment they now think that

316

Owen might be responsible. It's him they really want to speak to. Everything else is just procedure.

Helen watches anxiously from the window as they go through the motions of knocking on a few doors. Nobody answers, though this doesn't mean that nobody is home. People around here are wary of authority. The police are viewed with suspicion at best, contempt at worst. Usually she finds such attitudes small-minded. But for once she's grateful. The officers had told her they'd make enquiries about her car, but who's to say that they won't be asking questions about her husband?

As the squad car pulls out of the road, she heaves a sigh of relief. At least she's in the clear for now. But the feeling is short-lived. The police suspect that Owen is guilty of arson. And the worst part is, she can't say for certain that they're wrong. She glances at her watch. Where the hell is he?

Time passes. She drifts from room to room, unable to settle. She boils the kettle and sits coiled on the sofa, nursing a cup of tea until it goes cold in her hands. Head cocked, she listens for the door, wonders if she should go out looking for him. And start where exactly? He could be anywhere by now. She wonders if the police are watching the house.

Now you're being paranoid, she thinks. But is it any wonder?

Anxiously, she wanders back into the kitchen. The unused breakfast things are still on the table. Returning the empty bowls to the cupboard, it suddenly strikes her that she should eat something. But the thought of food makes her nauseous.

The phone rings in the hallway. *Please let that be him!* She isn't quick enough. It rings off just as she grabs the handset. She dials 1471 and presses the receiver to her ear. The caller withheld their number.

Upstairs, another phone rings. It takes her a moment to recognize the ringtone. It's Owen's iPhone. She runs up to the bedroom. The phone is flashing on his bedside drawer but rings off before she reaches it.

She pauses. Should she really be answering her husband's phone? Is this what she's reduced to? Spying on him?

It's not spying. He's your husband. You're worried about him.

Besides, she knows the passcode. If Owen didn't want her using his phone, he'd never have told her the passcode. She slides a finger across the screen and enters the four-digit code – the day and month they were married. The display shudders and buzzes angrily. Strange. She tries again. Nothing. She tries entering the day and month of her birthday. Nothing. Then she tries his. Still nothing.

She sighs and sinks onto the edge of the bed, glances down at the chest of drawers. The bottom drawer is still open. Why did Owen hide the envelope there? Where did it come from? Why was it addressed to him and not her? It's not like him to hide things from her. But then why change the passcode on his phone? What else is he hiding? The stresses and strains of the past few weeks bubble up inside her. Her head feels like it's about to explode.

People aren't always who you think they are.

A car pulls up outside. She goes to the window, thinking it might be the police. A familiar red hatchback is parked opposite her house. She watches as Frank steps out and walks around to the passenger door. Her mother is the kind of woman who likes men to open doors for her. But it isn't her mother who emerges from the car. It's her husband. She runs downstairs and opens the door.

'Owen! Where the hell have you been?'

He's standing on the doorstep, his eyes staring down at the pavement. She reaches for his hand but he pulls away.

'Frank? What's wrong with him?'

'Let's get him inside,' Frank says, looking around. 'We can talk there.'

She steps aside as he steers Owen into the house. His head is still bowed, the look on his face one of bewilderment mixed with fear.

'Owen? Please say something!'

Finally, he looks at her. His eyes are red and pained.

'I think it's best if we get him to bed,' Frank says gently. 'I'll take him up. Did the doctors give you anything for him? Something to help him sleep?'

'There are some pills in the bathroom cabinet.' She frowns. 'But shouldn't I try talking to him first?'

Frank shoots her a warning look. 'I'll just take him up. Then we can have a chat.'

She hesitates, torn between a feeling of possessiveness and the understanding that Frank is better equipped to deal with this situation than she is. It doesn't look as if Owen can make it up the stairs unaided. He's barely able to stand.

She steps aside.

It's only as he brushes past her that she notices the smell on his clothes. Smoke.

She's in the kitchen when Frank reappears. 'What's going on?' she asks, and bursts into tears.

'Why don't we sit down?' He steers her to a chair and sits next to her. 'Try not to worry, Helen. I'm sure

319

everything's going to be alright. My guess is he's suffering from post-traumatic stress disorder. It's quite common. His doctor will know what to do.'

'But he's been gone for hours. Where has he been?'

'I don't know. I was on my way over to see you and got stuck in traffic. I think there's been some sort of accident somewhere. Anyway, I was just starting to move again when I saw him standing at the bus stop.'

'Where was he going?'

'Search me. The bus came but he didn't get on.'

'Did he say anything?'

'Not a word. He recognized me, but that was about it.' Frank tilts his head. 'Your mother told me about your car.'

'And did she tell you we had a row?'

He nods. 'Yes, she did. But you're going to have to make some allowances for him, Helen. The poor lad's not himself.'

You don't know the half of it, she thinks, but says nothing.

'But he'll come through this,' Frank says. 'You both will.' He pauses. 'So what did the police say? About the car?'

'Not much. They didn't sound very confident that they'll find whoever did it'.

'You haven't fallen out with any of the neighbours?'

She shakes her head.

Frank thinks for a moment. 'It could be kids, I suppose. Some people's parenting skills leave a lot to be desired.'

Helen's eyes fill with tears.

'Well, it's probably best if you put it to the back of your mind for now,' Frank adds quickly. 'Leave it with me. I'll have one of the lads come and take the car to the workshop. We'll get it back on the road for you in no time.'

She nods. 'Thanks.'

'You look tired. Have you been sleeping?'

'Not a lot. I've been worried sick.'

'I can stay if you like. Keep an eye on him while you get some rest?'

'No, it's alright. You go. Mum will be wondering where you are. I'll be fine.'

'Are you sure? I'm happy to stay. Or I can call her. Maybe you'd rather be with your mum?'

She smiles tightly. 'Not really.'

Frank gives her a knowing look. 'She loves you, you know. We both do.'

Embarrassed, Helen begins to rise from her chair.

But her stepfather is already on his feet. 'You stay there,' he says, placing a hand on her shoulder. 'I'll show myself out.'

She watches as he heads towards the door, then stops and turns to her. 'Car keys?'

'On the dresser in the hall.'

'Right.' He hesitates. 'Well, call us if you need anything.'

'I will. And Frank?'

'What?'

'Thanks. Y'know – for bringing him home.'

He shrugs and smiles. 'Glad I could help.'

Several hours have passed since Frank left. One of the neighbours has arrived home from work and is listening to dance music. The bass vibrates through the thin party wall. On the green in front of the house, a group of kids have gathered to play football. Helen heard the catcalls when they spotted the graffiti on her car. The laughter suggested that they were amused by it, but weren't the ones responsible. There was as much surprise in their voices as delight.

There's still no sound from upstairs. Part of her wishes that Owen would wake up so they could talk. Then she remembers the way he looked when Frank brought him home. He's not up to answering her questions. Tomorrow she'll try to persuade him to see the doctor. But for now she'll let him sleep.

She drifts into the kitchen. The daylight is starting to fade. She still hasn't eaten. There isn't much in the fridge, so she puts two slices of bread in the toaster and nibbles the hot buttered toast standing at the counter.

Where did he go?

The phone rings. She runs to answer it, hoping the sound won't disturb Owen. It's probably just her mother, ringing to see how she is.

'Hello?' she says quietly.

There's a short pause, then a familiar voice. 'Is Owen there?'

'Siân?'

'There's no fooling you, is there?'

Helen pictures the smirk on her face. Her temper rises. 'How did you get this number? What do you want?'

'Are you deaf? I want to speak to Owen.'

'You can't. He's sleeping.'

'Poor thing. He must be worn out.'

'Siân, I don't know what this is about, but I don't want you calling us.'

'I'm not calling you. I'm calling Owen.'

'What for?'

'He knows what it's about. Ask him. And tell him to call me. Bye for now.'

The line goes dead. Helen's hand shakes as

she replaces the receiver.

That bloody woman!

She wonders how Siân got the number and what she could possibly want with Owen. Then her eyes focus on the answerphone. The green light is blinking, indicating a missed call. Strange. She didn't hear it ring. It must have been earlier, when she was talking to the police or inspecting the damage to her car.

She's about to press the playback button when her ears prick at the sound of the bed creaking upstairs. Either Owen is turning over in his sleep or those pills the doctor gave him aren't as strong as she thought. She waits with her finger poised. Then, when there's no further sign of movement, she hits play.

There's no voice message, just background noise and the sound of someone breathing. She leans closer and turns up the volume. The breathing grows louder and more laboured, as if the caller has been running. The background noise is the rumble of traffic. Maybe it's a crank call. Or maybe someone pocket dialled her number by mistake. Then she hears it – faint at first, but growing louder. It's the sound of an approaching fire engine.

CHAPTER THIRTY-EIGHT

A shaft of light falls through a gap in the living room curtains and creeps slowly across the back of the sofa. Helen hears a car door slam outside. She tenses. Have the police come to arrest Owen? Then an engine starts and she realizes that it's just one of her neighbours setting off for work.

She's been awake for hours, huddled over her laptop in her night dress, gathering all the information she can find on post-traumatic stress disorder. One report says that more than one in ten soldiers returning from active service are affected. Many of the symptoms sound familiar. Sufferers tend to avoid any discussion of the event that triggered the condition, but relive the trauma in sudden flashbacks and nightmares. Many experience 'survivor's guilt' at living when others have died. Alcohol and drug abuse are common.

Helen thinks of Owen crying uncontrollably at the funeral, collapsed on the sofa with his empty lager cans, whimpering in his sleep. She almost feels relieved. Behaviour she'd thought so odd is well documented. But there's another feeling too – a sense that there's something else hovering just out of reach, like an image floating in and out of her peripheral vision, something she's glimpsed but can't quite see. Maybe it'll come to her later.

She's made a mental note of other symptoms –

difficulty falling or staying asleep, irritability, angry outbursts and a condition known as 'hyper-vigilance' where the person affected is in a state of high alert, anticipating danger where none is present.

She remembers him crouched outside the house, staring at the horizon as if it wasn't the familiar rooftops of South Wales he was seeing but the skies of southern Afghanistan.

These are all things she should be discussing with his doctor. She'll phone the surgery later. If she can talk the receptionist into making an appointment, maybe she can use her powers of persuasion on Owen too.

She clicks the website closed and searches for a local news site. It doesn't take her long to find what she's looking for. 'Fire in Blackmill', the headline reads, 'Police suspect arson.'

Next to the headline is a photograph of the man she saw at the café that day with Siân. He's standing outside a small terraced house. There are no flames, but two firefighters in high-visibility jackets can be seen in the background. Black smoke billows from one of the upstairs windows. The man doesn't appear to be injured. He stares directly into the camera with a look of righteous indignation.

'Mr Ibrahim-Morris converted to Islam in 2013,' the caption reads. 'Police are treating the fire as suspicious.'

And now they have a suspect, Helen thinks.

Owen is still sleeping soundly upstairs. The pills must have really knocked him out. It's the first decent night's sleep he's had since he came home.

It scares her even to consider the possibility that he's been anywhere near that fire. But she knows she can't rule it out. She doesn't know where he was yesterday. She doesn't know what's going on inside his head. And she can't forget the smell on his clothes when Frank brought him home.

She hears the bed creak and her husband's voice call out. 'Helen?'

She closes the website and clears the search engine's history.

'Helen?' he calls again, louder this time.

She jumps to her feet, heads up the stairs. 'I'm coming, Owen.'

He's sitting up in bed, a faint smile on his lips.

'It's okay,' she says soothingly, perching on the edge of the bed and touching his cheek. 'I'm here.'

He doesn't flinch. That's something. By now she's used to him recoiling from her touch.

'How are you feeling?' she asks.

'Tired.' He yawns and stretches. 'I saw Frank.'

'I know,' she says. 'He brought you home.'

He nods. 'I remember.'

She reaches behind him to plump up his pillow. 'What else do you remember?'

'Not much.'

'But you were gone for hours. Where did you go?'

'For a walk.'

'Where?'

'Nowhere special. Up by the river. I needed to clear my head.'

She rises from the bed and walks over to the window. 'You didn't go to Blackmill?'

'No. Why?'

'Frank said he saw you at the bus stop. We thought maybe you'd taken a bus somewhere.'

He shakes his head. 'No. I was on foot.'

She peers through the curtains, turns and looks back at him.

'Your clothes smelled of smoke. Were you near a fire?'

'It was some kids by the river. I told them bonfire night wasn't for months yet. But they didn't mean any harm. I helped them put it out. I was the same at their age – always building bonfires.'

'What about Siân?' she blurts.

He looks surprised. 'Siân?'

'The woman from the hospital.'

'I know who Siân is. What about her?'

'Have you heard from her? She seemed quite fond of you.'

He smiles. 'Is that what all this is about? Some woman taking a shine to me?'

If only, Helen thinks. *If only that was all.*

'Listen,' he says. 'I know I haven't been myself lately. But things will be better now, I promise.'

'You haven't been well, love.' She moves towards him, sits on the bed and reaches for his hand. 'I've been so worried about you.'

He smiles sadly. 'I know. I'm sorry. My head's been all over the place. But I'm feeling much better now.'

She studies his face. The haunted look has gone. The light in his eyes has returned. 'You do seem better,' she says carefully. 'But I still think you should see the doctor, just to be sure. I can call and book an appointment if you like.'

He nods. 'That might not be such a bad idea.'

The relief is so strong she thinks she might cry. 'Oh, Owen,' she says, hugging him. 'That's wonderful.'

He winces. 'Mind my arm.'

'Sorry.'

But he's still smiling. That's another good sign.

'I'll make the appointment,' she says. 'When's best?'

'Whenever. It's not as if I have anything better to do.' He frowns. 'Shouldn't you be back at work?'

'They said I could take all the time I need.'

'I don't need babysitting.'

'Don't you?'

'No. Seriously. I'm feeling a lot better.'

She gets to her feet, thinks for a moment. 'I have a few things to do this morning,' she says. 'I thought I'd get something nice for dinner and I need to see Mum.'

'Any particular reason?'

She hesitates. 'Frank said she wanted help with some form or other. I shouldn't be long. An hour or so tops.'

'Okay,' he yawns. 'Give her my love.'

'You're sure you'll be alright on your own?'

'Of course. I'll probably doze off again in a minute. I won't even notice you're gone.' He raises his eyebrows. 'Just do one thing for me.'

'What?'

'Put some clothes on. I don't want any wife of mine wandering the streets in her nightie. What will the neighbours think?'

She laughs, surprised at the sound coming out of her mouth. She's forgotten what laughter sounds like.

The cab driver is a cocky young lad who knows the roads and seems to want to know everything about her, but she sinks back in the seat and pretends to check her phone, answering in monosyllables until he gets the message. Her handbag is on her lap. Inside is the envelope. Soon she'll have plenty to say for herself.

Her mother opens the front door before Helen has finished paying for the taxi.

She must have been watching from the window, Helen thinks.

She looks tense. Her smile seems forced. Her eyes are wary.

'How's Owen?' she asks as she ushers her daughter inside.

'Better than he was,' Helen says, brushing past her.

'Frank told me about yesterday,' her mother says, closing the front door and following her up the hall. You've just missed him. He's gone to see about your car.'

'Right,' says Helen. She doesn't mean to sound so ungracious. She's grateful to Frank. But she needs to remain focussed.

They go through to the kitchen, where her mother offers her a cup of tea and Helen refuses.

'It's about Dad,' she says, reaching into her bag. She opens the envelope, takes out the sheaf of papers and spreads them on the kitchen table.

Her mother stares at the first page for a moment, her eyes scanning the neatly spaced, typewritten words, the colour slowly draining from her face. 'I don't understand,' she says. 'What exactly am I looking at? Where did you get this?'

'Someone posted it through my door. Wasn't that thoughtful of them? Well, aren't you going to read it?'

Amanda lowers herself onto the nearest chair and folds her hands in her lap. 'I'd rather not.'

'What's that supposed to mean?'

'I don't need to read it.'

'But I think you should.' Helen takes another sheet of paper and thrusts it in her mother's face. 'Remember Lisa Johns? You must remember Lisa. She used to babysit when I was little.'

Her mother clears her throat. Her eyes dart from the paper to Helen and back again, before settling on the phone in the far corner of the room. She looks as if she's willing it to ring.

'Then there's Auntie Jackie and Mr Roberts,' Helen continues. 'They're all here. All the friends and neighbours. All saying what a great man my father was.' She laughs bitterly. 'Well? Aren't you going to say something?'

'Sit down, Helen!' Amanda's voice is steely – a tone Helen hasn't heard in a long time.

Suddenly she's ten years old. Her mother is gripping her by both shoulders, telling her to come inside. Helen's breath comes in short gulps. She's panicked, gasping for air. Somewhere in the distance, a siren wails. She feels the warm sun on her face, sees something unspeakable from the corner of her eye.

'Helen! I said sit down!'

She meets her mother's gaze, pulls out a chair and lowers herself onto it.

Silence.

'Your father loved you very much,' her mother says, her voice softer now. 'I want you to remember that.'

'I know.'

'But he wasn't a saint. He was a good father. But he wasn't such a good husband.'

'What's that supposed to mean?'

'I think you know what it means. It wasn't a happy marriage, Helen. Not by a long way.'

Helen allows the words to sink in, feels the full weight of them settle in her belly. She thinks she might be sick.

'I don't know who wrote this,' her mother says, pushing the sheets of paper away. 'But whoever it was, they certainly seem to have been well informed.' She offers a weak smile, then a frown forms on her forehead. 'There was this one reporter. He kept calling at the house. I refused to talk to him, but he kept coming back. I had to threaten him with the police in the end. No decency, some people. Harassing a grieving widow.'

Helen can't help herself. 'Why were you grieving? If Dad was such a bad husband?'

'Of course I was grieving. I loved your father. I can't say I always liked him very much. But you don't suddenly stop loving someone, even when they betray you. He was still my husband.'

'You got over him pretty quickly.'

Her mother looks as if she's been slapped across the face. 'How can you say that?'

'You weren't alone for very long. You had Frank.'

'Yes, I did. And I'm not ashamed of that. Frank was a good friend.'

'Friend?' Helen sneers.

'Yes, friend. There was nothing going on between me and Frank, not at the beginning. He was a tower of strength to me, and that was all. I don't know what I'd have done without him.' Amanda pauses. 'I didn't think I'd ever trust a man again. Not after the humiliations your father put me through. Not after what he did.'

'So it's all true, then? About his drinking? And his affairs?'

Her mother nods. 'Lisa was the last. She wasn't the first. And it wasn't just my heart he broke. That young girl was engaged. Her fiancé moved away shortly afterwards. I'd have probably done the same if I didn't have you to think about.'

Helen rises quickly from the table and walks over to the kitchen window. Heavy clouds hang over the lime trees behind the house. The sky is the colour of slate. She pictures Lisa with her father, his hands around her narrow waist, his face nuzzled against her neck. Had she seen them together? Or is it just her imagination playing tricks?

She turns to her mother. 'Why didn't you say something before?'

'What was I supposed to say? That your father was an alcoholic? That he was unfaithful? What good would it have done?'

'You could have said something.'

'And have you grow up hating him? That wouldn't have been fair, Helen. Your father meant the world to you. You were devastated when he died. You didn't sleep. You wouldn't eat. You locked yourself in your room for weeks.'

'Did I?' Helen asks. This isn't how she remembers it.

Her mother nods. 'I was worried sick about you. I didn't know what to do for the best. Frank said I should have taken you with me to the funeral. Maybe I should have. But the doctor didn't think you'd cope. Then when that reporter came knocking on the door, wanting to talk to you – well, I told him where to go. I know you're angry with me now, but I only did what I thought was best. I was trying to protect you.'

Helen frowns. 'The reporter wanted to talk to me? What about?'

'About that afternoon.'

'But why me?'

Her mother looks confused, then her face colours.

'What?' Helen says. 'What is it?'

'Don't you remember? You were there when it happened.'

The realization hits her so hard, she feels as if she's been winded. She's standing in the driveway. Her father is by the front gate, arguing with some boys. He's been drinking. She can always tell when he's been drinking. His face is red and his voice is raised. It's like

333

he's a different person.

The shouting grows louder as the boys crowd around him. They appear to be about eighteen. The two fair-haired boys look like brothers. The third has black hair. He's shorter than the others, but wiry and more muscular. She watches as he shoves her father, nearly knocking him off his feet. Her father pushes back. The boy staggers, pulling something from his pocket. It glints in the sunlight. He grins.

Her father holds up his hands. 'Please. There's no need for this.'

'Leave it,' one of the blond boys says. 'This is stupid.' But there's a look of excitement on his face, a look that says he's enjoying this however much he protests otherwise.

The black-haired boy scowls and waves the weapon. The handle is red, the blade no longer than three inches. It looks like a toy in the boy's hand, Helen thinks. It looks as if he's just playing.

'Listen to your friend,' her father says. 'Put the knife down.'

The boy tilts his head. His eyes narrow. Then his arm shoots forward and Helen sees the flash of the blade before it plunges into her father's stomach.

There's a look of surprise on her father's face and a rush of air from his mouth. Then the knife comes out and goes in again – over and over in slow motion, turning his shirt red.

'Twist it,' one of the other boys shouts. 'For fuck's sake, Dean! Finish it!'

Dean. The boy's name is Dean.

He turns to look at her, his eyes shining. Then he grins and twists the knife.

The look on her father's face turns to one of panic. As

the knife comes out, he clasps his hands to his stomach and blood pours through his fingers.

The other boys are backing away.

'C'mon, Dean! Let's go!'

The black-haired boy looks as if he's about to say something. His eyes lock on hers, glittering and dark. Then his friend grabs his arm and they turn and flee on waves of nervous laughter and brightly coloured trainers.

Helen watches helplessly as her father drops to his knees. Then his body folds to the ground, his head hitting the concrete with a dull thud.

She tries to scream but no sound comes out.

'Helen!'

She hears her mother's voice calling from far away.

She sees the boy's face – and the blood spreading slowly around her father's body, as dark as death.

She remembers everything. The alcohol on her father's breath. The look in the boy's eyes. And the silence – that strange silence that engulfed her the day her father died.

People aren't always who you think they are.

She runs to the sink and retches. Nothing. She gulps and takes a deep, steadying breath, screws her eyes tight shut. Immediately the image of her father comes into her head – his blackening blood, his gaping mouth, his bulging eyes. She heaves, throat burning as vomit spews from her mouth and through her fingers. Her stomach spasms and up it comes again – everything she's been bottling up for weeks, months, years splashing into the sink.

Finally it stops. She's been gripping the draining board so hard, her knuckles are white. Her fingers tremble as she runs the cold tap and washes the filthy mess away. Tearing off some kitchen towel, she wipes her mouth and hands, stares out of the window at the sullen sky.

'Helen?'

She flinches at her mother's touch, then turns and falls sobbing against her shoulder. How long has it been since her mother last held her like this?

'There,' Amanda says, stroking her hair. 'Just let it all out.'

Tears burn down Helen's cheeks. She swallows. 'Why wasn't I questioned by the police?'

'You were just a child. I didn't want to put you through all that.'

She pulls away. 'But maybe I could have helped.'

Her mother smiles sadly. 'I tried talking to you afterwards, but you just clammed up. I didn't know how much you knew, or what good it would achieve. Your father had just died. Nothing anyone said was going to bring him back.'

'What about the journalist? Do you know his name?'

'He told me his name was Gavin Edwards. He said he worked for the *Gazette*. But when I rang them to complain, they said they'd never heard of him.'

'What did he look like?'

'I don't know. It was such a long time ago. A bit flash, I suppose. I remember thinking his suit looked expensive.'

'And you didn't tell him anything?'

'No. Nothing.'

'Then how did he know I was there?'

Her mother frowns. 'Maybe he didn't. Maybe he was just snooping around.'

'Maybe.' Helen pictures the boy, remembers the way he looked at her, his black eyes shining with – what? Adrenalin? Drugs? Alcohol? What would possess him to do a thing like that?

Her mind jumps. 'Does Owen know?' she asks. 'About my father?'

'I never told him. Is that what you two argued about?'

'Someone hand-delivered that envelope to our house. Owen hid it from me.'

'I'm sure he was just trying to protect you.'

'I wish he hadn't. I wish people would stop trying to protect me.'

'You don't mean that.'

Helen stares her mother straight in the eye. 'Don't I?'

She feels her phone vibrate in her pocket. She wants to ignore it. She needs time to think. It buzzes again, louder this time. She fishes it out and hits the button. 'Yes?'

'It's me. Don't hang up! I'm with Owen.'

She stiffens.

Who is it? her mother mouths.

Helen raises her hand and shakes her head. 'Don't play games, Siân.'

'I'm not. Honestly. He needs your help.'

'Why? What's happened to him?'

'I think he's drunk or on drugs. He keeps going on about a fire. You don't think he had anything to do with that fire in Blackmill, do you?'

Helen feels her stomach lurch again. 'Let me talk to him.'

'He's not making any sense. I didn't know whether to call you or the police.'

'I'll come and get him. Where are you?'

'The Black Path. Come quickly. I think he's about to freak out on me.'

'Stay there. I'm on my way.'

CHAPTER THIRTY-NINE

'Where are you going?'

She hears her mother calling after her as she grabs her jacket and bag and heads for the front door. Barely turning, she shouts back over her shoulder. 'The Black Path.'

'Why? At least wait for Frank! You're not thinking straight!'

Maybe she isn't. But what choice does she have? She left Owen alone for five minutes and now, somehow, he's with Siân. And it's all her fault for not keeping an eye on him.

'Sorry, Mum, I've got to go.'

Outside, she walks briskly, turning right at the front gate and heading up the main road.

The sky is overcast. Heavy clouds threaten rain. As she hurries under the old railway bridge she hears a low rumbling overhead. At first she thinks it's the roar of a passing freight train. Then she realizes it's the sound of thunder. She looks in her bag, remembers she left her umbrella at home, continues on.

A bus is turning into Cemetery Road. Her father is buried there.

Don't think about that now!

But she can't help herself. Since his death, she's visited the cemetery countless times. Among the buried are generations of local soldiers who died in two world wars, the Falklands, the Gulf, Bosnia, Iraq, Afghanistan. Growing up, she'd often consoled herself with the thought that her father was in good company – a hero among heroes.

Some hero he turned out to be.

A car horn blares as she steps into the road. A red Toyota swerves to avoid her.

'Stupid cow!' The driver waves an angry fist through the open window, his voice barely audible over a thumping bass line. 'Look where you're bloody going!'

Shaken, she stops and stares after the car as the driver takes off, ignoring a sign to 'Reduce Speed Now'. She recalls a car journey from a long time ago. She couldn't have been more than seven or eight. Her father was driving. Her mother was telling him to slow down. 'It's not just your own life you're risking, Richard!'

Had he been drinking? She already knows the answer.

There are more rumbles of thunder as she follows the road through the Wildmill estate. Normally the streets would be filled with people. Today they seem ominously empty. Hurrying into the underpass, she feels the change in the air. The humidity is unbearable. A storm is on the way. She should have waited for Frank. Too late to turn back now.

By the time she crosses the junction into The Saints estate, her heart is racing. She pauses to catch her breath and the strange familiarity of the place washes over her in waves. It's years since she's been within walking distance of her old address. Still these streets are as familiar to her as the back of her hand. She turns a corner and there it is – the house where she spent the first eleven years of her life.

It looks smaller than she remembers. The front lawn has been paved over. A few shrubs stand in pots next to the door. A straggly pink clematis clings to a trellis by the window. The driveway is empty. She wonders who lives here now, whether they even know that this was once a crime scene. An image of her father begins to force its way into her mind. She pushes the thought away and runs on, cutting through the quiet back streets until her lungs ache and the road doesn't go any further.

She's reached the end of the cul-de-sac. On her left is the River Ogmore – the same river she was forbidden to play near as a child. Straight ahead is the entrance to the Black Path. She stops. The sun is now partially obscured by heavy clouds, casting long shadows that seem to converge where the road ends and the path begins.

Pull yourself together! Owen needs you!

Steeling herself, she steps off the pavement and onto the Black Path.

She's walked here many times in her dreams, but never before in the cold light of day. The wooded slopes seems strangely unthreatening. Dappled sunlight filters through the leaves. In the distance, she hears the babble of the river. Above her, a bird sings. This is nothing like her nightmares. She can even see the beauty of it.

But as the ground dips and she moves deeper into the woodland, her skin starts to prickle. This is more like it – the path she walks at night, the one that's always waiting for her. The earth beneath her feet is as black as coal. Huge trees line the narrow track, their ancient trunks twisted and split or choked with moss and ivy. Branches lean in to block her view or huddle together overhead, forming a dense canopy. The undergrowth is thick and teeming with possibilities. Even in the half light, it's easy to imagine a threat behind every tree.

A woman was raped here.

She reaches into her handbag for her phone, shoves it

into the front pocket of her jeans. Glancing over her shoulder, she pulls her jacket tightly around her waist and walks on. A familiar fear grips her as the track begins to twist. The shadows deepen and the edges of the path blur into the undergrowth. There won't be any sightseers here today, nobody out enjoying an innocent stroll, nobody to hear her scream. They'll all be safely tucked up at home, waiting for the approaching storm to pass. It's just her, Siân, Owen and whoever else is lurking out there in the darkness. She stops, listens, strains to see the path in front of her. Nothing but trees and shadows and eerie silence. A sudden gust of wind makes the leaves whisper. It's as if they're conspiring against her.

'Helen!'

Is that Owen calling? Blindly, she runs into the trees, towards the source of the sound. Branches slash her cheeks. Her foot catches on an exposed root and she plunges to her knees, brambles grazing her forearms as the ground comes up to meet her, hands disappearing into the dense, dank undergrowth. Hauling herself up, she feels something cold and wet clinging to her fingers. She looks and lets out a cry of disgust. It's a used condom. She flicks it away, rubs her hand furiously against her jeans, listens to the steady thud of her heart.

There's a crack of thunder, followed by the patter of rain on the canopy high above her head. She huddles for cover in the gloom beneath the trees and calls out into the darkness.

'Owen?'

Then, when there's no answer, 'Siân?'

Still nothing.

She fumbles in her pocket for her phone. There's no signal. She's in a blind spot. The phone is useless, a dead weight in her hand. Panic swells inside her like a balloon.

Somewhere in the distance, she hears a woman laugh.

'Siân?'

Silence. The rain stops. She slides the phone back into her pocket and continues walking.

Soon the path twists and turns before opening into a small clearing. At the far side, a large tree grows out of a raised mound of earth. The trunk is split in two and the roots are exposed, white like bones against the dark soil. Next to the tree is an old arm chair with the stuffing hanging out. A wooden window frame with part of the glass missing lies propped against it. Littered around the edges of the clearing are empty beer cans and the discarded remains of fast-food packaging.

In the centre of the clearing, someone has been busy building a bonfire. It is big. Chunks of timber form a rough teepee shape, about six feet across. Laid on top are fallen branches, broken scaffolding planks and what looks like the remains of an old Welsh dresser. At one side is a stained single mattress, piled high with binliners spilling with rubbish. Large logs lie at intervals around the base, forming a rough fire ring. Wedged between the larger pieces of timber are smaller bits of wood, balls of newspaper, shreds of cardboard.

Whoever's responsible for the bonfire hasn't been gone long. A few curls of smoke rise from one of the binliners. There's the faint smell of burning plastic.

A twig snaps and she spins round, her heart pounding.

'Hello, Helen. What took you so long?'

She's standing a few feet away, arms folded tightly across her chest, red bag slung over one shoulder. Even in the half light, Helen can see that her eyes are huge, the pupils dilated.

'Where's Owen?' she demands. She sounds far braver than she feels.

Siân frowns. 'That's not very polite, is it? How about, "Hello Siân, how nice to see you again?"'

'Don't play games, Siân. You told me you were with Owen. Where is he? What have you done with him?'

'I haven't done anything with him. It's not me you should be worried about. I'm not his type.' Siân steps forward. 'He's a bit of a dark horse, your husband. But you must be used to that by now. The men in your life are just full of surprises.'

'Just tell me where he is!'

'First things first.' She takes something from her pocket and holds it between her forefinger and thumb. 'Recognize this?'

'Where did you get that?' Helen tries to grab it but Siân pulls her hand away.

'You know damn well where I got it,' she says, sliding the old penny back into her pocket. 'It was in that shoebox under your bed. I read your letters too. And that newspaper cutting about your father. What a load of crap that was. It just goes to show, you shouldn't believe what you read in the press.'

Furious, Helen stares at her. 'You had no right going through my things.'

'You didn't seem too bothered at the time. Mind you, you were too drugged up to the eyeballs to notice.' Siân smirks. 'Christ, you're thick! All those glasses of water I fetched for you. All those drinks when we were out together. All those teas and coffees.'

'What was in them?'

'What wasn't in them? Tramadol. Valium. Rohypnol. Plus a few things you won't find at your friendly local pharmacy. There's not a lot I can't lay my hands on.'

Helen remembers the pounding headaches and heavy limbs, the feeling of being permanently hungover or coming down with something.

'You could have killed me.'

'Where's the fun in that? It was far better to fuck with your mind.'

'But I trusted you!'

Siân laughs. 'You know what your problem is, Helen? You're too trusting. Not like your husband. He likes his secrets, doesn't he? A bit like your father.'

'Just tell me where Owen is. Or I'll call the police.'

'I wouldn't do that. Not if you want to leave here alive.'

Helen blinks at her, wonders if she heard correctly, instinctively knows that to show fear now will only make things worse. She lifts her chin. 'I'm not afraid of you.'

More laughter. 'Of course you are. You're afraid of everything. But you know what scares you the most? The truth. Cos the truth hurts, doesn't it?'

'I've had enough of this,' Helen says. She reaches instinctively for her phone, remembers there's no signal.

Siân leaps towards her. 'No, you don't!'

One hand locks around Helen's forearm, fingers digging deep into the flesh. The other grabs her jaw, twisting her head to one side, sending a shooting pain down her neck.

'You stupid bitch!' Siân hisses, her face contorted with rage. 'You don't decide when this is over. I decide! Got it?'

Helen freezes, motionless except for the heart pounding in her chest and the breath quickening in her throat. 'You're hurting me,' she says. 'Let me see Owen. Please.'

Siân thinks for a moment, then pushes her away. 'Okay.' She looks over Helen's shoulder and signals with her hand. 'You can bring him out now.'

There's a movement in the trees, then a figure slowly emerges from the shadows.

'Owen!'

He looks at her with barely a flicker of recognition. His eyes are glazed, his movements sluggish. Another man comes into view. It's Jackson, steering him forward with one arm held firmly behind his back.

'Owen!' Helen cries again.

Jackson releases his grip and Owen stumbles forward, his knees buckling beneath him.

'Look at the state of him,' Jackson sneers. 'He can't even stand up straight.' He grins and rubs his hands together, clenching and unclenching his fists.

Helen takes a step forward, but Jackson shoots her a warning look. He whips out a hunting knife and runs his thumb along the blade. 'Any closer and I'll slit his throat.'

This can't be happening, Helen thinks. She stares at Jackson. 'You can't be serious.' But she doesn't doubt for a second that he's capable of carrying out his threat.

Siân's smirk confirms her fears. 'I wouldn't push it. He's got nothing to lose.'

CHAPTER FORTY

'Haven't you heard?' Siân says. 'They've kicked Jackson out of the army.'

Helen glances at him.

He glowers back at her and spits out of the corner of his mouth.

'That little queer's parents made a complaint,' Siân adds. 'And your husband backed them up. Said that Jackson bullied his little bum chum. Owen's not exactly Jackson's favourite person right now.'

She gives Jackson a nod. 'Put him in that chair. This may take a while.'

Jackson slides the knife into his boot and manhandles Owen onto the armchair. His head lolls forward, arms hanging limply by his sides.

'What have you done to him?' Helen demands.

Siân shrugs. 'Nothing. I didn't have to. Ask Jackson.'

Jackson grins.

'He was gagging for it,' Siân says. 'Ketamine. GHB. Not smack, though. He prefers his gay-boy drugs, your Owen. Maybe he's trying to tell you something.'

Helen struggles to contain the panic rising up inside her. 'Please,' she says. 'Let me go to him.'

Siân considers this for a moment. 'Okay. But don't expect too much in the way of conversation. He's not exactly the sharpest tool in the box right now.'

Helen rushes over to her husband, crouching beside the armchair and lifting his head. Owen's eyes roll back and his mouth falls open. She feels for his pulse. It's faint. She looks up. 'Something's wrong. He's not breathing properly.'

'"Something's wrong,"' Siân mimics. 'No shit, Sherlock. Don't look at me. I warned him not to mix his drugs, but he wouldn't listen. Maybe you should take him to see a drugs counsellor. What do you reckon, Jackson?' She sniggers.

'Owen!' Helen shakes his shoulders.

He doesn't react.

She pulls her phone from her pocket, but before she can check for a signal Jackson is on top of her. He snatches the phone from her hand and throws it deep into the trees.

'What are you doing?' she screams. 'What if he dies?'

'Then him and lover boy will be together again.' Jackson hacks up a lump of phlegm and spits on her husband's bowed head. 'Fucking queers!'

Helen huddles protectively around Owen, pulls a tissue from her pocket, wipes the mess from his forehead.

She looks up at Siân. 'Please! I thought you liked Owen. Help him!'

Siân smiles icily. 'Sorry, but I'm a bit busy at the moment.' Reaching into her bag, she takes out a handful of blue envelopes. Helen recognizes them immediately.

'Quite the romantic, our Owen,' Siân says, fanning the envelopes like a hand of cards. 'Now which one shall we choose? One where he tells you how much he's missing you? Or one where he talks about making babies?' She makes a gagging gesture. 'You didn't you tell him you were on the pill, did you?'

Helen feels the colour rush to her cheeks. She glances

at Owen. His eyes are shut.

'There's nothing I don't know about you, Helen,' Siân continues. 'Why did you lie to him? Don't you want kids? Or were you worried that he might be queer?'

'Of course not!'

'Did you know about him and Collins? Is that why he stopped writing to you when he was in Afghanistan?'

Siân opens one of the envelopes and begins reading. 'No, no mention of him here. I wonder why that is?'

Helen tries to get to her feet, but Jackson grabs her by the shoulder and pushes her roughly to the ground. He smirks and boots Owen in the leg. 'Fall in, soldier!'

There's still no reaction.

'Not much use, is he?' Jackson says. 'Now, if you were *my* wife –'

'I'd probably be sporting a black eye.' Helen glares at him. 'I know what kind of man you are.'

Jackson glowers. 'Watch your mouth.'

'Or what? You'll break my jaw?'

'That's enough, you two!' Siân snaps. She crushes the letter in her hand and tosses it onto the smouldering pile. The paper blackens and bursts into flames. Smiling, she throws in the remaining letters.

'Get this fire going, Jackson.'

'Why me?'

'You're the expert. Don't they teach you this stuff in the army?'

Jackson steps forward, rips open one of the bin bags and tips out its contents, scattering disposal nappies and other household waste. Black smoke billows as the flames die down.

'It's going out, idiot!' Siân shouts. 'Don't you know anything?' She looks around. Then a smile spreads across her face. 'Helen, bring us that window frame.'

'Get it yourself.'

'Not very cooperative, are you?'

Helen holds her ground as Siân comes towards her, knows she has to stay strong, knows somehow that her husband's life depends on it. He doesn't look at all well. There's still no movement and what little colour there was in his face has drained away. He needs medical attention, and quickly. She looks around for an escape route, wonders how far she'd get before Jackson caught up with her, what vile punishment he'd mete out. Her skin crawls.

Siân drags the window frame over to the bonfire and heaves it on top. She turns to Jackson. 'Where's the petrol?'

He frowns.

'Don't tell me you left it in the car.'

'For fuck's sake, Siân! I did all the dirty work getting him here.' He gestures towards Owen. 'I've only got one pair of hands.'

'And half a brain.' Siân reaches into her bag and takes out a clear plastic bottle with a red warning label on the side. 'Just as well one of us knows what they're doing.' She unscrews the top and shakes the bottle over the fire. There's a whooshing sound as the flames catch. 'There. That should do it.'

Soon the fire is roaring, the flames climbing higher as the wood crackles and hisses. Helen feels the heat on her face. She looks at Owen. He's sweating heavily, beads of moisture dripping off his nose onto his chest, blossoming into a wet patch on his T-shirt.

'Pay attention!'

Helen looks up, sees Siân brandishing her framed wedding photo. It's been ripped off the wall at home. The picture wire is still hanging from the back.

'Your marriage is a sham,' Siân says. 'Just like your

mother's.' She holds the photo over the flames.

'Don't!' Helen pleads.

'Too late.' Siân tosses the photo onto the fire. 'Your father couldn't keep it in his trousers. Neither can your husband.'

Helen wipes a lock of damp hair from her eyes. 'What has my father got to do with this?'

'Everything. If it wasn't for him, we wouldn't be here now.' Siân's face softens. 'I'm not to blame for this, y'know. I'm just evening up the score. If you want someone to blame, blame him.'

'But what did my father ever do to you?'

'Not me. My brother.'

Helen's pulse quickens.

'He used to bring me here when I was little,' Siân says, her voice distant and childlike. 'We'd build bonfires and he'd tell me stories. But then he started seeing her and everything changed. She didn't like me hanging around. I'd hide in the woods and watch them sometimes. Then one day I followed her home from school and that's when I saw them together. They were right here where we are now – her and your father.'

Helen's heart is in her mouth. She swallows. 'You mean Lisa?'

'That cunt!' Siân's face is a mask of hatred. 'I always said she was a slag. But Dean couldn't see it.'

Dean. Helen pictures the black-haired boy with the dark, glittering eyes, twisting the knife in her father's stomach.

'So I told him,' Siân continues. 'I told him what I'd seen. I thought that would be the end of it. Him and Lisa – over. Then things would go back to the way they were before.' She gives a bitter laugh. 'More fool me.'

Jackson steps forward, a look of bored malevolence on

his face. 'Get on with it, Siân.'

She scowls at him. 'Don't tell me what to do! I give the orders around here. Not you.'

'Your brother killed my father,' Helen says. Her words hang heavy in the air, as noxious as the choking smoke and suffocating heat of the fire.

Siân shrugs. 'He deserved it. Okay. Story time over.' She points at Helen's bag. 'What have you got in there?'

'Nothing. Just my purse.'

'Give it here.'

Helen hugs her bag to her chest.

Jackson brandishes the knife. 'Just do it!'

Helen watches as Siân rifles though the contents of her bag, taking out the purse and stuffing it into her pocket. 'I reckon that's the least you owe me.' She tosses the bag onto the fire.

'Owen was never meant to be part of the plan,' she says, staring deep into the flames. 'It was just meant to be the two of us – you and me.' She turns. 'I've had my eye on you for a while.'

'Why are you doing this?' Helen asks. 'What have I ever done to you?' Tentatively, she begins to stretch her legs.

The light from the fire flickers in Siân's eyes. 'You were there that day. You saw everything. Dean told me. Then Dad sent one of his mates round to check if there were any other witnesses, see what the chances were of someone talking to the police.'

'The reporter,' Helen says.

'Someone who owed him a favour. He did a thorough job, too. Really went to town on it. I think he thought he'd sell the story, win some local press award or something. As if Dad would've allowed that! But he wasn't taking any risks, so he sent Dean away. He was supposed to come back when it had all blown over. But one night he got into a fight and that was it – dead before he was twenty.'

'You told me your brother joined the army.'

'I lied. We all do it. Me. You. Jackson. Your father. Owen. We're not very different, really.' Siân smirks. 'People aren't always who you think they are, Helen. Sound familiar?'

'This is all very interesting,' Jackson says. 'But I need a piss.' Grinning, he stands over Owen and begins unbuttoning his flies.

Helen throws her arms protectively around her husband. 'What do you think you're doing?'

'Don't you know what happens to queers in the army? We piss on them.'

'Not here!' Siân snaps. 'There are ladies present.'

'She's no lady. She's a stuck-up cunt.'

'I didn't mean her. I meant me.'

Jackson shrugs and rearranges himself. 'In that case, I'm off for a slash in the woods.' He slopes off into the shadows.

Helen studies Owen's face. His breathing is shallow, his lips pale. Spittle foams from the corners of his mouth. What if he dies now, right in front of her? She's been here once before. She can't let it happen again.

'He needs an ambulance,' she says. 'You can't just let him die.'

Siân tilts her head. 'Can't I? People die from overdoses all the time. More British soldiers commit suicide than are killed in battle. I read that somewhere. And when people find out that he tried to burn down that Muslim's house ...' She smiles and kicks at an ember at the edge of the bonfire.

'Owen didn't start that fire,' Helen says. 'You did.'

'Prove it.' Siân empties the remains of the bottle over the flames, grinning with delight as they leap higher. 'I've got something else of yours here,' she says, tossing the bottle away and reaching into her bag. 'Look! A birthday card from your father. What were you? Ten? It must have been the last thing he gave you before he died.'

She holds it in the direction of the blaze.

'Don't!' Helen says. 'Don't you dare!'

'Or what? Your husband can't help you now.'

'Don't!' Helen says again, louder this time.

'Who's going to stop me?'

'Me.'

'Yeah? You and whose army?'

A knot of anger tightens in Helen's stomach. She looks around. There's still no sign of Jackson. Stiffly, she climbs to her feet.

Siân tuts and rolls her eyes, gives an amused grin. 'Think you're a match for me? Don't make me laugh. I'll rip your fucking face off.'

'Give me the card,' Helen says. She takes a step forward.

'Make me!' Siân hoists her bag onto her back and moves closer to the fire, waving the card in front of her. 'Well, what are you waiting for?'

Helen lunges.

'You'll have to do better than that!' Siân laughs, dancing backwards, arms above her head. 'Come on. Let's see how brave you really are!' Her eyes shine wildly as she hops onto one of the logs at the edge of the fire, gestures with one hand for Helen to follow her.

'Stop it, Siân! This isn't a game.'

'What's the matter? Afraid you'll lose?' Siân holds out the card.

Helen lunges again, missing by inches.

'Loser!' Siân steps off the log and onto the corner of the window frame. 'Well, do you want your precious card or not?'

She takes another step, her body weight pressing the far end of the frame deep into the centre of the fire. Something spits and makes a loud popping sound, sending a shower of sparks into the air.

Helen shrinks back. 'Be careful!'

More laughter. 'I'm not like you, Helen. I'm tough, me. Bulletproof. Fireproof.'

Arms out to her sides, Siân edges along the narrow frame like a tightrope walker. Small tongues of orange and yellow flicker along the charred wood, the paint blistering inches from her feet. Another amused grin. 'See?'

A loud crackle wipes the smile from her face as the fire shifts and falls in on itself. The wood beneath her feet buckles, shooting up another shower of sparks. A white-hot ember hits her ankle. She flinches. 'Fuck!' And then another.

She looks as if she's about to jump to safety, but then a sudden gust of wind makes the flames change direction, creating a wall of fire and sending her staggering sideways onto the blackened glass. There's a crack like a gunshot as the glass gives way and her right foot falls through the jagged hole. She screams, struggling to free herself, unable to find a firm footing.

Again, the fire shifts, producing more sparks. Something hisses inside her bag and the flames begin to lick her back. Frantically, she tries to release the bag from her shoulder while still straining to free her foot. She begins to lose her balance, arms flailing as her eyes widen in panic. 'Shit!'

One arm raised to shield her face, Helen edges closer

to the blaze. The heat prickles her skin as she reaches out.
'Grab my hand!'

Siân's fingers lock around hers. Their eyes meet.
There's a brief struggle as Helen tries to pull Siân free
from the fire and Siân seems to pull her towards it, a look
of grim determination on her face – eyes crazed, even the
hint of a smile.

Helen panics. *The crazy bitch wants us both to die*!

She pulls her hand free and watches in horror as Siân
claws at the air and falls backwards into the blaze, landing
with a crash on the burning window frame. There's a dull
thud as her skull makes contact with the wood and her
eyes roll back in her head. Helen wonders if she's been
knocked unconscious. Then Siân's hair catches fire and
she cries out in agony. There's another loud hiss and then
her bag seems to explode, turning the flames blue and
producing clouds of black smoke that billow around her
twisting, turning body.

Helen coughs as the smoke catches in her throat,
making her lungs burn and her eyes stream. Transfixed
with horror, she watches as the flames rise and Siân sinks
deeper into the heart of the blaze. Her blistering hands
grasp at the edges of the burning frame in a desperate
attempt to pull herself free. But her bag is caught on
something, the smouldering strap pulled tight across her
shoulder, searing into the flesh, holding her down.

The fire roars, drowning out the sound of Siân's cries.
Her head jerks from side to side. There's another loud
crack as the pane beneath her head shatters and a shard of
blackened glass slices through her exposed neck. Blood
spurts out in a crimson arc, hissing where it hits the
burning wood.

Helen clamps her hand to her mouth, stifling a scream.

It seems to take forever for Siân's body to stop

moving. Her eyes are open but lifeless. As the flames tear through her clothes, the air is filled with the sickly sweet smell of burning flesh. Helen gags, dropping to her knees on the black earth. There's a rumble of thunder and a sudden downpour of rain. The flames die back, hissing and spitting.

'Helen?' Owen moans.

With a start, she turns to face him.

Jackson emerges from trees. But he's not alone.

'Frank!' Helen cries. 'Oh, Frank! Thank God you're here!'

EPILOGUE

'Aren't you getting dressed?' Owen says.

Helen looks up from the kitchen table. She's still in her bathrobe, cradling a second cup of coffee.

Her husband is standing in the doorway, dressed in a pale blue shirt and a pair of chinos. His arm is no longer in a sling. The marks on his face have healed.

He raises a quizzical eyebrow. 'What?'

'Nothing,' she says. 'It's just good to see you looking so well.'

What a difference a few weeks of counselling have made. He's like his old self again – before he left for Afghanistan, before Siân and the hospital and everything that followed.

No, she reminds herself – *almost* like his old self. His wounds have healed. He's stopped drinking. He's even sleeping normally. But something has changed. There's no point in pretending otherwise.

'Well?' he says. 'Are we going or not?'

She drains her coffee and stands up. 'Just give me a few minutes.'

A week earlier, arriving home from one of his counselling sessions, Owen had seemed preoccupied and restless. He'd been unable to settle down to watch the DVD he'd chosen.

'What's wrong?' she asked.

He shifted uncomfortably on the sofa. 'Nothing.'

'Owen?'

Silence.

Finally he turned to her. 'There's something I need to tell you, Helen. You're not going to like it.'

She set her glass of wine down on the floor. 'Well?'

'It's about Collins.'

'It wasn't your fault he died,' she said. 'You know that, don't you? The doctor explained all that. It was part of your illness.'

'It's not that.' He lowered his eyes and took a deep breath. 'I don't know where to begin.'

'Then don't,' she said, placing a hand on his arm. 'We don't have to talk about this now.'

'Yes,' he insisted. 'Yes, we do.' He struggled for a moment, rising from the sofa and pacing the room before coming back to face her. 'Do you know what courage is, Helen?'

'Of course,' she said, soothingly. 'It's what you do. Fight for your country. Risk your life.'

'No, it's not any of that stuff. It's being true to yourself. That's what Collins was. He was true to himself. He was a good man. A brave man. He annoyed the hell out of me too. But I admired him.'

'But that's good, isn't it? It's good that you remember him like that.'

'Yes. But that's not all. There's more to it.'

She felt a knot form in her stomach.

'I wrote you a letter,' he said. 'The morning before it happened. I never sent it.' From the back pocket of his jeans, he took out a crumpled piece of paper. 'Read it. Please.' He unfolded it and handed it to her.

Later, Helen would reflect bitterly on the fact that the

one letter Siân hadn't destroyed in the fire was the one with the potential to destroy her marriage. Part of her wished that Owen had never written it, or that it had burned along with all the others. What purpose did it serve, other than to burden her with information she had no desire to know? But her immediate reaction was one of confusion mixed with disbelief.

'So all those lies Jackson was spreading –'

'They weren't lies.'

'Oh.' She looked away, trying to convince herself that she wasn't really hearing this, that it was all some huge misunderstanding. But when she looked back her husband still had the same contrite expression on his face.

'I had feelings for him,' he said. 'Feelings I've never had for a man before. It wasn't dirty, not the way Jackson described it. But there was –' He paused. 'There was intimacy.'

She felt her cheeks flush. 'I see.'

'No,' he said. 'I don't think you do. Things happen in the army. Men do things they wouldn't normally dream of doing. We kill people. Innocent people, sometimes. And we have to live with that.' Tears pricked his eyes. 'And sometimes we develop feelings for people we wouldn't normally have. And we have to live with that, too.'

It had taken her a while to reply.

'You said "we", Owen. I don't know if I can live with that. I don't know who you are anymore.'

'Of course you do. I'm the same man you married.'

She laughed angrily. 'How can you say that? After what happened?'

'I'm still the same man, Helen.'

'So you're telling me you're not gay?'

'No. I'm someone who made a mistake.'

'So if Coll –' She couldn't bring herself to say his

name anymore. 'If he hadn't died?'

'Nothing else would have happened. Ever. I swear to you.'

She wasn't proud of what she'd said next, but she couldn't help herself.

'Well I guess there's no way of knowing now, is there?'

They hadn't spoken about it since, though for the past week it was all she could think about – her husband and that young soldier. The words had been said. There was no going back now. But maybe there was a way of going forward? She trawled various websites and found interviews with women whose husbands had told them they were gay. Many had been married for years without the slightest suspicion. Some felt as if the man they thought they'd known had suddenly become a stranger. Others compared it to a bereavement. 'It was as if he'd died.'

But Owen hadn't died. He could so easily have been killed, but he'd survived. And he hadn't told her he was gay. On the contrary, he'd insisted that he wasn't. It was a mistake, he said. A moment of madness, never to be repeated. Was he in denial? Was he lying to himself – and to her? She'd asked herself these questions a thousand times and couldn't come up with a satisfactory answer. All she knew for certain was that he'd had feelings for someone other than her – feelings which raised huge doubts about their future together.

Her own feelings were all over the place. She felt hurt, angry, betrayed. Was it the infidelity that bothered her the most, or the fear that he was still hiding something? She wanted to trust him. She wanted to believe that he confessed everything because that's the kind of man he was – honest, decent, determined to do the right thing.

Then the nagging doubts would creep in. She tried not to picture them together, but every so often her mind would throw up an image and her stomach would tighten. Her husband with another man. Just the thought of it and she felt her whole world slipping away.

Upstairs in the bedroom, Helen opens her underwear drawer and a shiver runs over her skin. Try as she might, she still can't shake off the thought of Siân in the bedroom, rummaging through her personal belongings.

Weeks have passed since that dreadful day at the Black Path. Both she and Owen were taken to hospital and interviewed at length by the police. Helen described how she'd tried to pull Siân from the fire. The burn marks on her hand and wrist were examined and deemed consistent with her story. It didn't take much to convince the investigating officers that Siân's death had been accidental. They were already familiar with her and her family. Her brother wasn't the only relation she'd lied about. Siân's father hadn't died in a hit and run accident. He was alive and well and serving time for the supply of heroin.

Partly thanks to the press interest in Siân's father's criminal activities, the story was reported in the local newspaper, where Jackson's name was also mentioned. Frank had also given a police statement and seen to it that Jackson was held responsible for his part in Owen's abduction. True to form, Jackson protested his innocence, insisting that it was Siân who'd lured Owen out of the house and that he had no idea what her intentions were. But it was obvious to everyone that Siân couldn't have been acting alone. She may have been the brains behind the operation, but Jackson was definitely the brawn. With Owen's help, the police quickly established that it was

Siân who'd supplied the drugs – and Jackson who'd administered them. He was charged with reckless endangerment and was currently on bail, awaiting trial.

Siân's funeral was a quiet affair. Her father was allowed out on day release from prison to pay his respects. There were no other mourners. Helen hadn't attended the funeral but couldn't resist reading about it afterwards. Despite everything, she felt more pity for Siân than hatred. According to the newspaper, her father had been in and out of prison for most of his adult life. His wife had stood by him the first time he was sent down, but left when Siân was eight. It couldn't have been easy growing up with no mother to guide her and a career criminal for a father. Compared to Siân, she'd had it easy.

'Helen?' Owen calls. 'Is everything alright?'

'Yes,' she shouts back. 'I'm just coming.'

She reaches into the wardrobe for a lightweight jacket. The weather has turned. The leaves on the trees outside the window are changing colour. She's changed too. She isn't the person she was a few months ago.

Shortly after Siân's funeral, an eyewitness came forward, placing Siân and Jackson at the scene of the fire in Blackmill. Helen had felt such relief on hearing the news. At least Owen hadn't lied to her about that.

She pulls on the jacket and runs downstairs.

He's waiting for her at the door, the car keys in his hand. 'You're sure you're ready for this?'

'Yes,' she says.

They step out into the street. Her car is parked in the usual place, fully repaired with the bodywork gleaming like new. Frank's team had done a good job.

'I'll drive,' she says, holding out her hand for the keys.

'Are you sure?' Owen flexes his arm and winks.

'I'm fully operational now.'

'Keys!' She clicks her fingers.

He smiles and hands them over. 'Okay. You're the boss!'

It's been months since she last visited the cemetery. After the revelations about her father's alcoholism, she'd felt let down. The knowledge of his affair with Lisa disgusted her. Arriving at the cemetery gates, the feelings rise up again.

'It's okay,' Owen says, sensing her apprehension. 'We can come back another day.'

'No,' she replies. 'We're here now.'

She parks the car and they walk together to the grave. The headstone is smothered in green lichen. As she reads the wording, her stomach turns – 'Loving Husband and Father.'

Loving to whom? Father to how many?

'You need to forgive him,' Owen says, reading her thoughts. 'You know that, don't you?'

'Do I?'

'He was your father. He loved you. He wasn't perfect. But he was still your dad.'

She kneels beside the grave. A rotting bunch of flowers reminds her of her last visit. She hasn't come bearing fresh flowers today. There are no symbolic tokens to show how much she misses him. Just being here is hard enough.

Owen squats beside her. 'How are you feeling?'

She shrugs. 'Confused. He can't have been happy, can he? In his marriage, I mean?'

'Why do you say that?'

'Happily married men don't have affairs, do they?'

Owen colours.

'It's as if his whole life was a lie,' Helen says, conscious that it isn't only her father she's talking about. 'That's the part I hate the most – the lies.'

There's a long silence.

'I can't change what happened,' Owen says finally. 'But what I did is in the past. It'll never happen again. And I can live with it. The question is, can you?'

Helen stares down at her father's grave. Somewhere beneath her is the man she has idolized all her life. He wasn't the hero she'd grown up worshipping but an ordinary man who lacked the courage even to be honest. She stands and gazes out across the cemetery, across the rows of graves where soldiers far less fortunate than her husband lie buried. She thinks of all the widowed wives and grieving girlfriends, the fatherless children, the mothers who've lost their sons. Mothers like Barbara Collins. Her son is no threat to anyone now.

She turns to face her husband. 'Do you love me, Owen?'

'Yes,' he says. 'More than anything. And you? Do you think you'll ever be able to trust me again?'

'That's a lot to ask of me right now.'

'But maybe in time?'

'Maybe.'

'I've been thinking. What if I leave the army? Frank said he'd help me find a job closer to home.'

She gives a brittle laugh. 'Out of harm's way?' It isn't really harm she means, but temptation.

He looks wounded. 'Please, Helen. I don't want to be away from you ever again. I want us to be a proper family. You, me, maybe a couple of kids.'

She shakes her head. 'It's too soon to be talking about kids.' She pauses. 'I've been offered a promotion at work.'

'You never said.'

'I only found out myself a few days ago. Natalie's leaving.'

His shoulders droop. 'I see.'

'It'll mean longer hours and more responsibility. But I think I'm ready for a challenge.'

'It sounds as if your mind is already made up.'

'It is.'

He looks at her strangely for a moment. 'I know,' he says. 'About the contraceptive pills.'

She feels the blood rush to her face.

'It's okay,' he says. 'I understand. You were afraid, weren't you? In case something happened to me? How you'd cope?'

She nods. 'Something like that.'

'So what do you say? How about we make a fresh start, from today? No more secrets?'

'It won't be like before, Owen.'

'I know it won't. I still have to win back your trust. But are you at least willing to let me try?'

She looks at him and feels a rush of love so strong it takes her by surprise. She sees the pain in his face, the promise in his eyes, knows somehow that he'll be true to his word.

'We'll see,' she says. 'Now let's go home.'

ACKNOWLEDGEMENTS

This book could not have been written without the encouragement and support of a great many people:

Paulo Kadow helped in so many ways, I can't begin to thank him enough.

D.J. Connell and V.G. Lee provided constructive criticism, fresh insights and fortifying wine.

James Wharton shared his experience of gay life in the British army and helped enormously with the scenes set in Afghanistan. Any mistakes are mine alone.

James Niven shared his own experience of military life and Tracy Williams advised on the realities of being married to a serving soldier.

Rhiannon Fletcher and Lisa Garrett took me on a Bridgend girls' night out which didn't end anything like the one described in these pages – thank god.

Matt Bates gave me a boost just when I needed it most. Thanks, Matt. You're a star.

And finally, my agent Sophie Hicks, editor Rebecca Lloyd and all at Accent Press. The path was long but the destination couldn't feel more right.